SUFISM
THE HEART OF ISLAM

SUFISM
THE HEART OF ISLAM

Sadia Dehlvi

HarperCollins Publishers India

a joint venture with

New Delhi

First published in India in 2009 by
HarperCollins *Publishers* India
a joint venture with
The India Today Group

Copyright © Sadia Dehlvi 2009

1 3 5 7 9 8 6 4 2

ISBN: 978-81-7223-797-4

HarperCollins (*Publishers*)
A - 53, Sector 57, Noida 201301, India
77-85 Fulham Palace Road, London W6 8JB, United Kingdom
Hazelton Lanes, 55 Avenue Road, Suite 2900, Toronto
Ontario M5R 3L2 and 1995 Markham Road, Scarborough, Ontario M1B 5M8, Canada
25 Ryde Road, Pymble, Sydney, NSW 2073, Australia
31 View Road, Glenfield, Auckland 10, New Zealand
10 East 53rd Street, New York NY 10022, USA

Computerised calligraphic images by Quyamuddin Nizami
Cover calligraphy: 'There is no god but Allah Muhammad is the Messenger of Allah.'

Typeset in Adobe Thai 13/14.5
Jojy Philip New Delhi - 15

Printed and bound at
Thomson Press (India) Ltd.

To

The memory of Shah Muhammad Farooq Rahmani Qadri Chisthi Sabri for accepting me as a disciple on the Sufi path.

&

My mother Zeenat Kauser at whose feet I seek paradise.

&

To all seekers of the Truth.

Allah

CONTENTS

FOREWORD

بسم الله الرحمن الرحيم

Sufi *dargahs* all over India draw more worshippers than mosques. The mosques are for congregational prayers, with larger attendances at set times on Friday and religious days such as Eid ul Fitr, Eid ul Azha and Eid e Milad un Nabi, than on other days.

Sufi *dargahs* have worshippers coming round the clock and besides Muslims, draw Hindus and Sikhs in large numbers. Indeed, in Indian Punjab and Himachal Pradesh, besides the Muslim caretakers (*mujawirs*) appointed by the Waqf Board, worshippers are almost entirely non-Muslims. I believe this strange anomaly is due to the fact that people go to mosques to offer *namaz* (prayers) as prescribed by the tradition set by the holy Prophet (*sunnah*). They visit Sufi *dargahs* to beg for favours: the sick come to be healed, women to beg for happy married lives and to be able to bear children, while some even come to beg for success in cases pending before law courts.

Clear evidence of this phenomenon is offerings of ornate coverings (*chadar*) to drape the grave, and the red strings tied on the marble trellis around tombs as wishes (*mannat*) with promises of giving in charity—the most popular being provisions for the community kitchen (*langar*) where the hungry are fed free of charge.

One has only to visit the *dargah* of Khwaja Moinuddin Chishti, Gharib Nawaz (Patron of the Poor) and see the huge cauldrons in which rice and lentils are cooked to feed thousands who come to be fed. As mosques are most frequented on Fridays, *dargahs* draw larger crowds on Thursday afternoons and evenings where there are *qawaalis*, at times spontaneous dancing and people passing out in a trance (*hal*).

Orthodox Muslims of the Wahabi or Deoband beliefs disapprove of *qabar parasti* (worshippers of tombs) as un-Islamic. You will see that all *dargahs* are built around the graves of Sufi saints. It is their names that are invoked by seekers of favours.

Reverence of the Sufi saints continues even after their life. Most Muslims like to be buried close to where their patron saint rests. In Delhi the two largest graveyards are around the tombs of Hazrat Nizamuddin Auliya and Khwaja Qutubuddin Bakhtiar Kaki. Muslims believe that on the Day of Judgement their Pir (spiritual mentor) will intercede on their behalf with Allah.

An aspect of Sufism in India must always be kept in mind. It was not Muslim invaders who converted millions of Indians to Islam by the sword, as many historians tell us, but the gentle preachings of Sufi saints who opened their hospices and welcomed men and women of all castes and creeds to join their brotherhood. And they did so in large numbers, of their own free will. Of the dozen or so Sufi *silsilas* (orders) the most prominent was the Chishtiya to which most of the saints mentioned in Sadia Dehlvi's compilation belonged.

Another important aspect of Sufi teachings was its impact on the saints of the indigenous Bhakti movement in northern India. It included saints like Kabir, Namdev, Tukaram, Nanak and the Sikh gurus. No better evidence is to be found of the phenomenon than the inclusion of their hymns in the Sikh holy scripture Granth Sahib, compiled by the fifth Sikh Guru Arjun Dev. This was installed in the Harmandir Sahib (Golden Temple) in Amritsar whose foundation stone was laid by the Sufi Mian Mir of the Qadriya *silsila*.

There are 134 hymns by Baba Farid Shakarganj (1173–1265 AD).
I quote one of the most popular among Sikhs:

Bole Shaykh Farid …

If I knew that I would die
Never to return again
I would not follow the false ways of the world
Nor let my life be spent in vain.

In your speech be true, in your actions be right,
And spread no falsehood.
O Farid, tread the path the Guru shows.
What takes six months to quicken with life
Dies an instant death.

It is swift as the flight of swans in the spring
And the stampede of beasts in a forest of fire.
It is a flash of lightning amid the rains
And transitory as the winter hours
When maidens are in love's embrace
All that is must cease: on this ponder.

Farid, the earth questioned the sky:
'Where are the mighty captains gone?'
'In their graves they rot,' was the reply
'And are rebuked for tasks not done.'

(Asa)

KHUSHWANT SINGH

ACKNOWLEDGEMENTS

Prophet Muhammad ﷺ stated, 'Whoever has not thanked people has not thanked God.'

I thank Haji Ghulam Qutubuddin of Jais, a *khalifa* from our Rahmani Chishti Order for all his prayers and for giving me the *ijaza*, traditional permission required to write this book. I thank my parents, brothers Vaseem and Faheem, my sister-in-law Himani, Khushwant Singh, Mushirul Hasan, Raza Rumi, Rakshanda Jalil, Parveen Talha, Mayank Austen Soofi, Perwaiz Waris and all my other friends for their encouragement and support. I thank my son Arman Ali Reza for his unconditional love and belief in the importance of this book, forgiving me of the neglect often caused to him while working on it.

Special thanks to Sufi brother Syed Salman Chishti, a young *khadim* at the Ajmer Sharif Dargah for providing me with resource manuals and his prayers. I thank Maulana Ahmad Ashraf, my Arabic and Persian teacher for helping with translations of Urdu and Persian manuscripts. I have never met Shaykh Hamza Yusuf, Dr Nuh Keller, Dr Abdal Hakim Murad (Tim Winter) or Dr Tahir ul Qadri but shall remain eternally grateful to them for helping me understand the rightful traditions of Islam through their lectures that I have been following on the internet.

I thank the eminent scholars Carl W. Ernst, Coleman Barks, Kabir

Helminski, Shaykh Hamza, Tim Winters, Andrew Harvey, Nasrollah Pourjavady and William C. Chittick for their enlightening books on Sufism and for giving me the permission to use some of their translations of Sufi poems.

May God bless the soul of Annemarie Schimmel whose work I have quoted liberally in this book. The great German scholar of Indo-Islamic culture continues to inspire many writers, including myself, to work on Sufism and its impact on the subcontinent.

I thank Jojy Philip for designing the pages, Majid Ahmady of the Iran Culture House, New Delhi for giving me most of the calligraphic images from their library and Quyamuddin Nizami for tirelessly working on the calligraphies used in this book.

Finally, immense gratitude to V. K. Karthika and Sheema Mookherjee at HarperCollins *Publishers* India for their helpful comments at various stages of the manuscript.

Allah
Muhammad ﷺ
Ali
Fatima
Hasan
Hussain

PREFACE
MY TRYST WITH SUFIS

Our Lord! Condemn us not if we forget or fall into error; our
Lord! Lay not on us a burden Like that which Thou didst lay
on those before us; Our Lord! Lay not on us a burden greater
than we have strength to bear. Blot out our sins, and grant us
forgiveness. Have mercy on us. Thou art our Protector; Help
us against those who stand against faith.
The Quran: Chapter of the Heifer (2:286)

The most common response on hearing the title of my book has been: 'But what has Sufism got to do with Islam?' I realize that Islam is perceived as a faith with harsh laws, whereas Sufism represents wonderful poetry, dance, art and an appealing form of universal love. It is difficult for some Muslims and most non-Muslims to accept that Sufism is the spiritual current that flows through Islam. Sufi Masters are called *ahl e dil*, 'people of the heart'. They teach that religion has no meaning unless warmed by emotions of love, and interpret Sufism as being the heart of Islam.

However, I do understand that Sufism has come to mean something quite different in the language of the New Age. Disillusioned with religion and the problems associated with it in secular democratic societies, people tend to mix and match elements from various religious traditions that personally appeal to them. In the following narrative I have attempted to explain how Islam and Sufism are inseparable. The Quran informs us that Islam is not something that began with Prophet Muhammad ﷺ some 1400 years ago, but with the creation of the universe in which Adam was the first Prophet. Sufism is the timeless art of awakening the higher consciousness through submission to the Divine Will. The Sufi doctrine goes far beyond history and is rooted in the primordial covenant all unborn souls made with their Creator.

Many friends view my visits to *dargahs*, Sufi tombs, as senseless medieval superstition. Some orthodox Muslims even insist that Sufism is an innovation in Islam—a sinful practice that our ancestors picked up from Hindu idol-worshipping traditions. They reason that since most of our ancestors were Hindus, some of us are still using pagan methods like singing to please the gods.

It is true that like most Muslims in the subcontinent, my ancestors professed the Hindu faith. I have a family tree that goes right up to someone called Om Prakash Arora. My forefathers settled in Delhi during the mid-seventeenth century when it was under Mughal rule. We belonged to a Saraiki-speaking community from the district of Bhaira, close to the city of Multan. According to family legend, a group from the community was travelling to Hardwar for a dip in the holy Ganges. On the way they met the Sufi Shamsuddin Tabriz (not to be confused with Rumi's master) who asked them if they would accept Islam if he brought the Ganges right before their eyes. The miracle took place and each one of them converted to the Sufi's faith.

Delhi was chosen as the city to migrate, and many families still use the Sufi's name Shamsi for a surname. Despite entering the fold of Islam at the hands of a Sufi, the majority of the community hold extreme Wahabi beliefs and dismiss those of us seeking intercession to God through Sufis, as heretical 'grave worshipping' people.

My grandfather, whom we called Abba, added Dehlvi (one belonging to Delhi) to his name, which became the family title. Abba was a successful man who began life in a modest way. He published *Shama* magazine, which grew to become the country's leading film and literary publication. Eight more magazines followed, which established our family as one of the leading publishing houses of the time. Despite the riches and glory that followed, Abba remained humble and attributed his life's success to the blessing of God and the Sufis. He was a *hafiz*, memorizer of the Quran, and each dawn the house resounded with his recital of its verses. Ever since I can remember, he visited the *dargah* of Hazrat Nizamuddin Auliya every Sunday, and the *dargah* of Hazrat Shah Farhad every Thursday. He had huge cauldrons of food distributed at these places. Even during the last days of his life when he was bedridden, he requested to be taken to both these *dargahs* on a wheelchair. I accompanied Abba on his last trip and saw him weep like a child at the threshold of the Sufis.

My grandmother, Amma, did not accompany him on these visits to the *dargahs* and did not believe in Sufi intercession. Amma and Abba lived in matrimonial harmony, never letting their varied beliefs hamper their love and respect for each other. As children we were taught the basic Islamic values but were largely left to discover our own path. The pattern continued with my parents except that my mother went the Sufi way, while my father along with his siblings, followed their mother's beliefs. In a way, my family represents the fundamental difference of *aqeeda*, creed, between Muslim communities.

Throughout his life, Abba remained steadfast in prayer and charity. During his life, we knew no trouble. Following his demise, the family landscape changed where everything began to collapse. Family relationships deteriorated and one by one the magazines closed down. Two decades later all our fortunes vanished and the huge ancestral house in which we lived had to be sold. My father who sometimes visited Sufi *dargahs*, discontinued the tradition and could no longer afford carrying on the extravagant charitable activities of his father. The troubles increased and it felt like all of us had lost our protective cover. I began to read something awful into the way our lives were turning. I believed we had forgotten the path Abba had consistently walked on.

When we sold our house in Diplomatic Enclave, Delhi, I wanted to live near the *dargah* of Hazrat Nizamuddin Auliya and considered myself lucky on finding a flat there. Each Thursday I light a candle for my beloved grandfather and seek the blessings of Delhi's patron Sufi.

I would also like to share the miracle of my son's birth. The best of infertility specialists had categorically told me that due to various complications it appeared virtually impossible for me to have a child. I was 32 years old, with the biological clock ticking away. I wanted a child desperately, but the doctors were not hopeful. My mother reprimanded me for giving up hope and despairing upon God's graces. She advised me to go the *dargah* of Khwaja Moinuddin Chishti popularly called Gharib Nawaz, Patron of the Poor. I travelled to Ajmer and pleaded for his blessings, vowing to come back for thanksgiving if the prayers were granted. In Delhi, I regularly visited the *dargah* of Hazrat Shah Farhad and lit candles for the grant of a child. I had seen dozens of childless couples being blessed with babies through the many years that I had been going there.

My prayers were answered and a few months later there was an embryo kicking away in my womb, causing boundless joy. My son Arman Ali was born in Karachi through a Caesarean section and while being wheeled away after the operation I faintly heard the doctor comment on the miracle birth. According to the Islamic calendar, Arman is born on the sixth of Rajab, a date that marks the annual *Urs*, death anniversary, of Khwaja Gharib Nawaz. The sixteen-year-old lad is a musically talented child, a gift that I believe is from the Sufi Master.

Each year we both make an annual pilgrimage to Ajmer for the *Urs* and bow our heads in gratitude to Khwaja. Along with thousands of other *aashiqs*, lovers, I queue for long hours to touch the threshold. After offering a *chadar*, sheet, on the tomb, I pour my heart out to Khwaja. Sitting in the Begum Dalan, the pillared marble porch constructed by Jehanara, the eldest daughter of the Mughal Emperor Shahjehan, I listen to *qawaalis* and try absorbing the *nur*, radiance, flowing from the *gumbad*, dome. Every sunrise and sunset, thousands of little birds miraculously arrive from all directions on the tree adjacent to the tomb in time for the prayers and then fly off again, never shedding their droppings on Khwaja's white dome. I envy their ability to fly across the desert hills each day to sing praises of *Khwaja e Khwajgaan*, the Master of all Masters.

Sufism essentially consists of a path that teaches how to free oneself from the ego and rise to higher spiritual levels. The road is endless and how far one wishes to travel is largely a matter of personal choice. The Sufi way contains a method of guidance and transformation that is not an easy route. I must admit that writing this book has changed me completely. I began working on the manuscript at the lowest ebb in my life. A time when one was battling with feelings of guilt, betrayal, grief, and desperately low levels of self-esteem. Witnessing the collapse of family fortunes and relationships, life had fallen like a pack of cards around me. Amongst the rubble I searched for the lost values of respect, love, trust, honesty, and loyalty, and sought the strength of my family with whom I had grown up. The only life I knew was over and I couldn't find the courage to make a new one.

For years I cried in my sleep, haunted by ghosts that made me feel sad and bitter. While researching the biographies and discourses of the Sufi Masters, I slowly began to understand traumatic experiences as both nourishing and necessary for those who truly seek to purify and liberate the mind, body and soul. A particular passage from the Chishti Master Baba Farid's life impacted me deeply. The Sufi blessed his disciples with the prayer, 'May God endow you with pain.'

Although I had been initiated in the Chishti Sufi order more than two decades ago, my levels of faith often fluctuated with my mood swings. At times I did not wish to believe in anything anymore. Flashes of a turbulent life forced me into self-reflection. Slowly, I managed to unravel the mysteries of pain and how it confronts you with your own arrogance. From a 'why me' attitude, my emotions changed to, 'why not me'. I discovered that spiritual endeavours leading to states of ecstasy were usually rooted in grief. God, by His own admission to Moses, revealed that He lived in broken hearts. All Sufis believe that both affliction and bounties are the blessings of God. Something stirred my soul and I began to see myself as blessed rather than cursed by God. It changed my relationship with Him from one of animosity to one of friendship and love.

I made a conscious, sustained effort to apply some basic principles of Sufism to my shattered life. I vowed to develop *rida,* resignation to the will of Allah; *tawakkul,* trust in Him; *sabr,* patience; and *mohabba,* love. I found that it soon provided me the strength of a lioness and the flight of a falcon. I no more fear life or death, for I see life as an endurance of God's will, and death as something that unifies us with the Creator.

Regarding more mundane matters, I do not particularly agree with the usage of the word 'fundamentalists' and its interpretation by society at large and by the media in particular. Nevertheless, if we go by its definition of being anti-modern, Christianity, Hindusim, Judaism and Buddhism all have almost 20 per cent of followers who could be called fundamentalists. Similarly, Muslim orthodoxy flowing from the Wahabi, Salafi and Ahle Hadith ideologies that remain opposed to Sufi intercession, exceed no more than 20 per cent in the world. Their voices are louder and therefore we do not get to hear enough from the silent majority of Sufi followers.

Regretfully, the non-Muslim and particularly Western perceptions of Islam barely acknowledge its spiritual aspects. Hostility to the Muslims peaked in the twelfth century when horrific villainous pictures of the Messenger as a crafty politician were propagated. Some objective studies were done in England and France during the Renaissance period, but even these writings carried medieval biases that continued to caricature Prophet Muhammad ﷺ as the spirit of darkness and a wicked impostor. In such an environment the Prophet's spiritual brilliance, mystic experiences and humanistic ideals were completely ignored. The prejudices of over a thousand years have blinkered people's vision, and those uninitiated on the Sufi path are often startled to hear that the Messenger of Islam remains the primary source for Sufism.

Many authors continue writing derogatorily of the Prophet with an arrogant indifference. Some are even honoured by state governments for their warped creativity. Such writers present dramatic examples of the extremes to which an image can be destroyed, corrupted and then popularized globally. It makes sincere efforts of interfaith dialogue and mutual respect practically impossible.

Negative writings on Islam have resulted in a lack of appreciation of its history and culture—particularly in the understanding of the passion and veneration Muslims have for their Prophet. Devout Muslims will never utter the name of Prophet Muhammad ﷺ without following it with a *durood, sallallahu alayhi wa sallam,* 'May peace be upon him'. In print the blessing is usually abbreviated after the mention of his name, or calligraphed as in this book. The tradition is based upon a Prophetic saying, 'Whoever utters a blessing for me is blessed by the angels as often as he recites the blessing, be it often or rarely.'

I have been deeply concerned about the extreme voices within the Muslim community. Islam increasingly seems to have been hijacked by the discourse of anger and the rhetoric of rage. In attempts to enquire of the crisis, I began the journey of trying to understand Islam and read the Quran with scholarly guidance. I turned to the traditional Islamic teachings of Imam Junayd of Baghdad, Imam Ghazalli, Imam Nawawi, Imam Mawlud and other recognized classical scholars. Through the internet I heard lectures of the American Islamic scholars Shaykh Hamza Yusuf, Shaykh Nuh

Keller, the British scholar Tim Winter (Abdal Hakim Murad) and Dr
Tahir ul Qadri of Pakistan.

I learnt that Islam was clearly about moderation and reflection,
and how Prophet Muhammad ﷺ had warned us of extremism.
What I love about the Quran is that it constantly urges us to reflect
and reassures us that Humanity is the best of creation. It reminds us
that Mercy and Compassion are the foremost of Allah's attributes.
The answers to many issues facing Muslim communities can be
found in revisiting the scholarship of the Sufis. These Masters have
established traditions of knowledge transmission that go back all the
way to Prophet Muhammad ﷺ who said, 'Pass on knowledge from
me even if it is only one verse.'

In a world where the debate on 'clash of civilizations' threatens to
rage on, it is essential to dismantle the old myths and propaganda
about Islam. I have written this book so that readers may have some
understanding of Islamic traditions. I have used verses from the
Quran not to establish Sufi linkages with Islam, but because Sufism
cannot be understood without references to the holy book. I would
have preferred to use modern translations of the Quran but chose
Abdullah Yusuf Ali's version for it remains the most widely accepted
translation in the world, first published in 1938 simultaneously in
Lahore, Cairo and Riyadh.

I have presented the book in traditional styles used both orally
and in textual Muslim discourses. It begins with a verse from the
Quran, *Hamd,* a poem in praise of Allah, followed by *Naat,* verses
honouring Prophet Muhammad ﷺ. All chapters begin with the
calligraphy of the words '*Bismillah hir Rahman nir Rahim*'—In
the name of Allah, Most Gracious, Most Merciful. I have used the
internationally accepted spellings for Arabic words, for example *dhikr*
for what is usally pronounced *zikr* in the subcontinent, *mohabba* for
mohabbat, *rida* for *reza,* *tareeqa* for *tareeqat,* *haqeeqa* for *haqeeqat,*
Sharia for *Shariat* and *marifa* for *marfiat.* Since this book aims at a

wide readership, I have refrained from using diacritical marks and hyphenations in the proper names.

My Sufi Master Shah Muhammad Farooq Rahmani was the principal *Khalifa* of Shah Inam ur Rahman Qudoosi of the Qadri, Chishti, Nizami and Sabri Orders. He emphasized that Sufis are torch-bearers to the path of righteousness. He believed that for those unable to seek the *sohbat*, company of Sufis, reading and being aware about their life and teachings are blessings. The mystic began each discourse with the words, 'Those who are true in their intent, those who have complete faith and those who seek the Truth are the ones who successfully achieve their goal.' He lamented that the biographers of the Sufis focussed more on their miracles than on their inner struggle, character and teachings.

Prophet Muhammad ﷺ said, 'I swear by the God who controls my life, He loves those who awaken the love of Him amongst the people.' Another Prophetic tradition affirms, 'The ink of the scholar is more sacred than the blood of the martyr.' These words sustained my efforts through the four years that it has taken to complete the manuscript.

I am not a scholar and since this is my first book, it probably has many shortcomings. All the weaknesses in the book are mine; all praise is His. I hope readers find it beneficial and that some of the contents ignite their hearts with the love of the Lord. I seek the blessings of the Blessed, those whose life and teachings are recorded here. I pray that the Lord grant me guidance, providence and may He bless us all.

New Delhi   SADIA DEHLVI
March 2009

The Quran: Chapter Heifer (2: 137)
He is the All-Hearing, the All-Knowing.

BOOK I

The Quran: Chapter Read (96:4)
He who taught (the use of) the pen.

READ!

بِسْمِ اللهِ الرَّحْمَنِ الرَّحِيْمِ

In the name of Allah, Most Gracious, Most Merciful.

Read in the name of thy Lord and Cherisher,
Who created man, out of a clot of congealed blood:
Proclaim! And thy Lord is Most Bountiful,
He Who taught the use of the pen
Taught man that which he knew not.

The Quran: Chapter Read (96:1–5)

The Quran means 'The Recital' and is the last link in a chain of revelations going back to the very origin of man. It addresses nations, communities, families, individuals and humanity as a whole, teaching the path to inner and outer perfection. All over the world Muslims read the same holy book. Only one Quran exists as preserved through the past 1,400 years, from the time of its revelation to Prophet Muhammad ﷺ. The Messenger of Allah was an *Ummi*, unlettered, unable to read and write. Whenever the Prophet received a revelation, he memorized the verses. He then instructed his companions to memorize it and the scribes to note the revelations. Scholars have documented the history of the compilation and preservation of the Quran.

بسم الله الرحمن الرحيم

In the name of Allah, Most Gracious, Most Merciful.

The language of the Quran is classical Arabic based on mathematical principles, the language spoken by the Quraysh, the tribe in which Prophet Muhammad ﷺ was born. The Quraysh were the traditional guardians of Kaaba, the House of Allah in the city of Makkah.

The first five lines in the Chapter Read are amongst my favourite verses of the Quran. These were the first words that Allah spoke to the Prophet through the intermediary of Archangel Gabriel. The revelations began at the cave of Hira where Muhammad ﷺ was meditating during the month of Ramzan in the year 610 AD. The first word to be revealed was *iqra* which translates as 'read'. *Iqra* is the basis of human knowledge and the spirit of Islam lies in nurturing the intellect to seek knowledge of the Creator.

The verse demonstrates the importance of knowledge, the written word, and the pen as an instrument of inscription. In the chapter *Al Qalam*, The Pen, Allah begins with swearing by the pen, reaffirming its sanctity. 'Nun. By the Pen and the Record which men write.' (68:1) *Nun*, an alphabet in the Arabic language is amongst the mysterious letters, which many of the Quran chapters begin with. The letter *Ha Mim* are understood as *Habibi Muhammad* ﷺ, My Beloved Muhammad ﷺ while others such as *Ta Ha, Ya Sin* are believed to be mystic names that address and glorify the Messenger. Allah and the Prophet both have 99 names defining their attributes.

As a writer I respect the pen, paper and computers for they are instruments in the pursuit of knowledge. My son used to throw pens around the house till one day I explained that God had sworn by the pen. Our love for Him must be demonstrated by respecting animate and inanimate creations that are dear to Him. 'Whoever goes out in search of Knowledge is on the path of Allah until he returns', is a well-known saying of Prophet Muhammad ﷺ.[1]

Haqq—one of the 99 names of Allah.
The Quran: The Opening Chapter (1:2)
Praise be to God, the Cherisher and Sustainer of the Worlds.

SURAH FATIHAH
THE OPENING CHAPTER

In the name of God, Most Gracious, Most Merciful.

Praise be to God, the Cherisher and Sustainer of the worlds;
Most Gracious, Most Merciful;
Master of the Day of Judgement.
Thee do we worship, and Thine aid we seek.
Show us the straight way,
The way of those on whom Thou hast bestowed Thy Grace,
those whose (portion) is not wrath, and who go not astray.

The Quran: The Opening Chapter (1:7)

IN PRAISE OF THE LORD

Lord,
 whose face is this
  reflected in spirit's mirror?
   Such beauty painted
    on the inner screen—
     who is he?
Each atom
 in all space
  is filled...
    Who transcends the galaxies,
     shows himself in every molecule—
      who is he?

Calligraphy: Allah Hu Akbar: Allah is the Greatest.

Sun
 in the costume
  of various specks of dust
   sparks forth various rays
    of light at every moment—
     who is he?
Outwardly
 you appear in the meat
  of our existence
   but he who is hidden
    in soul's marrow—
     who is he?
In soul's fete
 every now and again he sings
  a new song, melodies of peace
   touching the veils
    of the people of the heart—
     who is he?
He who manifests himself
 upon himself
  makes love to himself
   in the name
    of lovers—
     who is he?
How many times, Mo'in
 will you drag yourself and me
  between us?
   He, the goal of I and Thou,
    is there—right there!
     Who is he?

Khwaja Moinuddin Chishti
Translation: Peter Lamborn Wilson and Nasrollah Pourjavady

FRAGRANCES PERCEIVED
UPON THE PROPHET'S BIRTHDAY

The crown of all the kings is he,
with joyful heart declare!
The lord of all the Prophets he,
his acts beyond compare!
How would he be the Leader of the Poor,
if the slightest of desires had stained his heart?
Poor he remained, because that man's a Boor,
whose wedding gifts his bride from him do part.
Because he had nothing, he sat on the sand;
Because he was hungry he tied stones to his waist.
Absolute poverty's proof was in him,
Absolute wealth was his secret within.
The trusted of Prophets,
the proof of the Way;
The king with no seal,

Calligraphy: Muhammad ﷺ in mirror image.

no crown for his sway.
What more can I say?
For thy Qualities' Array
Past ken of mind and soul,
O'er a hundred worlds hold sway.
If the poet's reward is the dust on your road,
he receives in each mote a new sun.
He has praised with his soul the dust of your road,
Let him Join it, magnanimous one!
All Prophecy lacked the estate of one Brick,
A gap of greatest sanctity!
Our Prophet said: 'That precious Gap,
I close for all eternity.'
During his Ascent, heaven's veil was rent
Because he was God's intimate for ever.
The very Firmament wished to offer him a Gift,
So God adorned the night with Stars forever.
Paradise is but a single Draught
Sipped from his crystal glass.
From the two M-Letters of his Name
Two worlds have come to pass.
When his religion gave light to the world,
The other rites halted and stayed, as God knows;
For what may become of the myriad Stars
When over the world a new Sunrise glows?
His miracles Astounding cannot rightly be described.
His essence cannot rightly be explained.

Fariduddin Attar
Translation: Abdal Hakim Murad

Muhammad is the Messenger of Allah. ﷺ

A CELEBRATORY TRIBUTE TO PROPHET MUHAMMAD ﷺ

بِسْمِ اللَّهِ الرَّحْمَنِ الرَّحِيمِ

*On the steed of love, God's prophet rose, through the blazing
     heavens,*
*The messengers of God rose to salute him, noble-browed,
     he blessed them all,*
Gabriel himself, holding the reins, flew with Muhammad ﷺ,
*Like two stars, outshining all other stars, through the dark of
     the trackless void,*
Then that emissary sublime called to Muhammad ﷺ
*Go alone, thy eye alone may witness where my sight would
     flinch and fail*
Since his eye gazed unfaltering, he was called 'the witness'
*Collyrium, from 'Have We not dilated', made his vision clear
     and true*
All the stations of Allah's servant by that eye were witnessed
*Gone was the veil of self and dissipation, he saw which souls
     were high and base*
Hence his intercession is sought, for he is Muhammad ﷺ
*A falcon knows all the land that lies beneath him; thus the
     Prophet discerns souls.*

Mevlana Muhammad Jalaluddin Rumi
Translation: Abdal Hakim Murad

QASIDAH AL BURDAH
THE POEM OF THE CLOAK

Muhammad ﷺ, leader of the two worlds
and of Man and the jinn,
Leader also of the Arabs and non-Arabs and their kin.
Our Prophet, Commander of right,
prohibits evil's way,
Yet no one's speech more gentle could be
than his nay or yea.
Beloved by Allah is he upon
whose pleading we depend
From terrors of the Day of Judgement,
which on us descend.
He summoned people unto Allah,
they to him did adhere,
And clung fast to the rope that none
could ever rent or tear.
In morals and features

he, all prophets did exceed,
None could approach his knowledge,
or his bounty e'er precede.
And thus from Allah's Apostle
they acquired and did gain,
A handful of the vast sea
or a sip of gen'rous rain.
So other prophets in their rightful place
before him stand,
Regarding knowledge and the wisdom
that they understand.
He perfect is in traits concealed,
and features bright and clear,
And Man's Creator chose him
as His most beloved and dear.
Too far above all men is he
to have a partner who
Has equal qualities, because
the essence of virtue
That in him lies is indivisible,
and wholly true.

Imam Sharfuddin ibn Said al Busiri
Translation: Shaykh Hamza Yusuf

THE POEM OF THE CLOAK

بسم الله الرحمن الرحيم

The *Qasidah al Burdah* is among the invocations believed to be accepted in the *durbar*, *the* court of God and His Beloved Prophet. Although originally written in Arabic, translated versions in regional languages are recited and sung in Muslim cultures all over the world. A melodious Arabic version rendered by Egyptian singers is among my treasured music. The poem honours Muhammad ﷺ, the Seal of Prophecy as a spiritual guide and the intercessor on Doomsday.

The 'Poem of the Cloak' is usually the first literary text that most Muslim children memorize after the Quran. It remains the most influential and popular poem in the history of any language. There is no significant traditional Muslim culture that has not welcomed the poem treating it as an honoured guest in calligraphies, weddings, talismans, Sufi gatherings and other festivities.

Imam Sharfuddin Muhammad ibn Said al Busiri of Egypt (d. 1298 AD) penned the poem after a successful career of praising rulers. He had been suffering from a paralytic stroke for 15 years when he wrote these 166 verses praising Prophet Muhammad ﷺ. One night, Imam Busiri dreamt of the Prophet asking him to recite the poem. Pleased with the verses, the Prophet presented his *burdah*, cloak, to the ailing poet who on waking up found himself free of disease. He wished to keep this vision secret but as he walked through the streets of Cairo, a dervish called out asking him to recite the poem that the Prophet had so appreciated. The *Qasidah al Burdah* soon acquired fame in the Muslim world as a blessed poem. It is recited in times of trouble and used in amulets for protection against all kinds of danger. It decorates the walls of mosques, palaces of kings and the homes of ordinary Muslims.

The popularity of the *Qasidah al Burdah* stems from the fact that it responds so directly to the core emotion of the Muslim faith which is the love for Prophet Muhammad ﷺ, 'Allah and His angels send blessings on the Prophet: O ye that believe! Send ye blessings on him, and salute him with all respect.' (33:56) These salutations are the sole action that the devout share with God and the winged creations of the other worlds. Veneration and love of the Messenger form the axis of Islam for Allah's beloved leads us to Him.

SOME CLASSIC DEFINITIONS
OF SUFISM

Muhammad ibn Ali al Qassab (d. 888 AD): 'Sufism consists of a noble behaviour that is made manifest at a noble time of a noble person in the presence of a noble people.'

Junayd of Baghdad (d. 910 AD): 'Sufism is not achieved by prayer and fasting but it is the security of the heart and the generosity of the soul.'

Dhun Nun Misri (d. 859 AD): 'Sufis are people who prefer God to everything and God prefers them to everything else.'

Sahl Tustari: (d. 896 AD): 'The Sufi is one who sees everything from God and knows that God's loving kindness embraces all creation.'

Uthman Hujwiri (d. 1077 AD): 'Sufism is the heart being pure from the pollution of discord. Love is concord, and the lover has but one duty in the world, namely to keep the commandment of the beloved, and if the object of desire is one, how can discord arise.'

Amr ibn Makki (d. 909 AD): 'Sufism is that at each moment the servant should be in accord with what is most appropriate at that moment.'

Samnun (d. 909 AD): 'Sufism is that you should possess nothing and nothing should possess you.'

Ruwaym ibn Ahmad (d. 915 AD): 'Sufism consists of abandoning oneself to God in accordance with what He wills.'

Abu Muhammad al Jariri (d. 932 AD): 'Sufism consists of entering every exalted quality and leaving behind every despicable quality.'

Ali ibn Abd al Rahim al Qannad (d. 922 AD): 'Sufism consists of extending a spiritual station and being in constant union with the Divine.'

Abu Said ibn Khair (d. 1061 AD): 'Sufism is glory in wretchedness and richness in poverty and lordship in servitude and satiety in hunger and clothedness in nakedness and freedom in slavery and life in death and sweetness in bitterness...'

Allah

1

THE FOUNDATIONS OF SUFISM

بِسْمِ اللهِ الرَّحْمٰنِ الرَّحِيمِ

Surely in the breasts of humanity is a lump of flesh, if sound then the whole body is sound, and if corrupt then the whole body is corrupt. Is it not the heart?

Prophet Muhammad ﷺ

Sufism, the accepted name for Islamic mystic traditions, is often thought to have no connection, or at the most a remote one, with the faith. The general perception of Sufis is one of free-style mystics outside the boundaries of religion. Socially I come across people who refer to themselves as Sufis, often signifying nothing more than a fashionable attitude. Many others add that they are 'spiritual' but not 'religious'. These statements make good party conversation and one does not encourage a discussion on the subject because the Quran advises us not to engage with ignorance. Frankly, such words sound hollow, for spirituality simply cannot exist without religious foundations.

One has to pass through some kind of religious discipline in order to transcend its ritualistic form and unite with God. In an increasingly stressful and spiritually bankrupt world, those with a sense of the sacred, attempt purchasing spirituality in supermarkets. New Age spiritual gurus sell package deals offering Zen without Buddhism,

Vedanta without Hinduism—and now we have a Sufism without Islam. All the major religions of the world are based on Universal Truths. Worthy of veneration and sanctity, they should not be treated as fashion cults. Today we see an increasing number of Sufi aspirants seeking instant gratification instead of true mystic experiences.

Sufism developed from within Islamic traditions, drawing on the pre-Muslim mystical practices of the ascetic Christian monks. Sufis are called *Auliya Allah*, Allah's friends. *Auliya* is the plural for the Arabic word *wali*, literally meaning friend.

Sufi Masters of the tenth and eleventh centuries wrote, 'Sufism was a reality without a name and now Sufism is a name without a reality.'[1] They argued that Sufism had already been corrupted during the pinnacle of the Islamic civilization. I often wonder what these mystics would have thought of Sufism being sold as a high-end product in twenty-first century markets. Although, verses of Rumi, Amir Khusrau and other mystic poets, set to music with lilting voices, offer temporary meditative moments, their spiritual philosophies are often lost. Mystics are people from religious traditions who are on a serious and intimate quest for communion with the Ultimate Reality. Any meaningful definition of religion contains a spiritual element. The experience of merging with the Divine force lies at the foundation of religion, an aspect that motivates those travelling along the mystic path.

The point I am trying to reiterate is that although Sufism, similar to other mystic traditions, offers universal ethics and meditation practices, its internal spiritual current cannot be alienated from its outward Islamic dimensions. One cannot aspire to become a Zen Master without being a Buddhist, just as one cannot become a Sufi Master without adhering to the fundamentals of Islam.

ALL OF MANKIND BELONGS TO GOD'S FAMILY

The universality of Sufi ethics is based on the popular Prophetic saying, 'All of Mankind belongs to God's family.'[2] Rumi (d. 1273 AD) explains:

We are all children of God and His infants
As the Prophet had said, All belong to his family
From Mosquito to elephant,
All are in His family
And for them He is the best Provider
There is only one God, the God of all people and all religions.
All of mankind belongs to God's family.[3]

Shaykh Sadi of Persia (d.1291 AD) writes:

All of Adam's race are members of one frame;
Since all, at first, from the same essence came,
When by hard fortune one limb is oppressed,
The other members lose their wonted rest:
If thou feelst not for others' misery,
A son of Adam is no name for thee.[4]

ISLAM: AN UNDERSTANDING

An understanding of Sufism requires a substantial knowledge of the Quran, which forms the backbone of all Islamic traditions. The Quran, *Sunnah* and Hadith are the three authoritative sources of religious, spiritual and ethical guidance for the Muslims. They believe, the Quran comprises the immediate words of God that have been preserved in its original form. It consists of 114 *Surah*, chapters, revealed to Prophet Muhammad ﷺ through Archangel Gabriel. The revelations began in the year 610 AD and were completed over a period of 23 years. 'A Book which We have revealed unto thee, in order that thou mightest lead mankind out of the depths of darkness into light—by the leave of their Lord—to the Way of (Him) the Exalted in power, worthy of all praise!' (14:1)

The Quran declares Prophet Muhammad ﷺ the *Khatam al Ambiya*, Seal of Prophecy. 'Behold! Allah took the covenant of the prophets, saying: "I give you a Book and Wisdom; then comes to you an apostle, confirming what is with you; do ye believe in him and render him help." Allah said: "Do ye agree, and take this my Covenant as binding on you?" They said: "We agree." He said: "Then bear witness, and I am with you among the witnesses.'" (3:81)

All previous prophets pledged allegiance to Muhammad ﷺ for he is *awwal* and *aakhir*, the first and the last. Rumi honours the unique position of Prophet Muhammad ﷺ, also called Ahmad, whose way of life became the valid rule of conduct for Muslims till the end of Time.

> *Jesus is the companion of Moses, Jonah that of Joseph*
> *Ahmad ﷺ sits alone, which means, 'I am distinguished'.*
> *Love is the ocean of inner meaning, everyone is in it like fish;*
> *Ahmad ﷺ is the pearl in the ocean—look, that is what I show.*[5]

Islam, the last of the three Semitic monotheistic religions incorporates all the prophets from the lineage of Ibrahim (Abraham) and Isa (Jesus). 'Nothing is said to thee that was not said to the apostles before thee.' (41:43) There are more references to Mariam (Virgin Mary) in the Quran than in the New Testament. Both Jesus and Mary have significant roles in Sufi thought, finding frequent mention in mystic verse. Virgin Mary was a woman unconcerned with the world whom God graced with His favours. She received the gift of a pure son, *Ruh Allah*, His Spirit, who brought the Message of the *Injeel*, Bible.

Rumi writes:

> *The hermitage of Jesus*
> *Is the Sufi's table spread:*
> *Take heed, O sick one,*
> *Never forsake this doorway.*[6]

Fariduddin Attar praises the Spirit of God:

> *When God shadowed grace on the breath of Jesus*
> *The world was filled with passion.*[7]

Although the Quran mentions about 28 prophets and exalts Abraham, Moses, Jesus and Noah, prophetic sayings relate that around 124,000 *Ambiya*, prophets (plural of *Nabi*) have been sent to the earth. Of these, 314 were *Rasuls*, Messengers. According to the Quran there has never been a time when God did not send Messengers who did not speak the language of the people. 'To every people (was sent) an apostle: when their apostle comes (before them), the matter will be judged between them with justice, and they will not be wronged.' (10:47) It is for this reason that many Sufis and Islamic scholars have claimed through the ages that the Vedas, ancient Indian scriptures, were in all probability a revealed Message from Allah.

Along with the Quran, Muslims refer to the *Sunnah*, actions of Muhammad ﷺ and the Hadith, a body of literature comprising the Prophet's sayings, as reported by those who are called the *Sahaaba*, his trustworthy companions. Prophet Muhammad ﷺ said that the best among his community were his *Sahaaba*, followed by the *Tabeen*, the companions of his companions, and the *Taba e Tabeen*, companions of those companions. Muslims venerate the ranks of these three generations as the best examples of the faithful.[8]

The Hadith includes expositions on prophetic behaviour from simple advice to doctrines of perfecting faith. The chain of transmitters is called *isnad*; every generation added new members until long lines of traditionalists developed, each link connected to the previous one in an established relationship. Hadith literature came to be compiled during the third Islamic century (ninth century of the Christian era). The examination of these traditions that have spiritually nourished the Muslim community has been an outstanding area of Muslim scholarship.

The central pillar of Islam is *shahadah*, the testimony of faith: 'There is no god but Allah Muhammad is the Messenger of Allah' (*La illaha ill Allah Muhammad ur Rasul Allah*).

The Testimony of Islam.
There is no god but Allah Muhammad is the Messenger of Allah.

Sufism believes that the act of witnessing Allah is none other than the knowledge of Him.

SUFISM EMANATES FROM THE SHARIA

I find that the word *Sharia* seems to scare most non-Muslims for they associate it with medieval laws. Most media debates that involve the *Sharia* engage in a confrontationist attitude questioning the rationale of age-old beliefs. Television news channels looking for controversial sound bytes often pick up the worst representatives of Muslim opinion and then wonder why moderate voices are not heard. Non-issues are usually turned into *Sharia* debates in which the channels and Muslim radicals share a mutually beneficial relationship. Little wonder that most people simply do not relate the rigidity of the *Sharia* with Sufism, which is perceived as a compassionate ideology.

Sufis strictly follow the *Sharia,* Islamic laws based on the Quran, Hadith and *Ijma*, consensus of the Muslim community. *Sharia* is the outward conduct that prepares the mystic for the spiritual path. Sufis go through rigorous ascetic disciplines but do not enforce rigidity on their followers through *fatwa,* decrees.

The Sufi philosophy is classified into three stages: *Sharia*, the outward law, *Tareeqa*, the Way and *Haqeeqa*, the Truth. Prophet Muhammad ﷺ said, 'The *Sharia* law is my word, *Tareeqa* my actions and *Haqeeqa* my inner state.' Throughout Islamic history, Sufis developed ways suited to the times, evolving methods for guiding people on the path of righteousness. Sufism represents the vibrancy of Islam in adapting to local customs and tradition. It reaffirms unity of faith and the diversity of devotional expression in the Muslim world.

THE HIDDEN KNOWLEDGE

The Sufis originated from a group of about 45 companions of Prophet Muhammad ﷺ called the *Ashab e Suffa*, People of the

Bench. Having renounced the world, these people sat in front of the Prophet's mosque practising incessant prayer and fasting. They made the mosque their home and were looked after by the Prophet and his family. The area of the Bench is still visible and forms the outer part of the Prophet's chamber in Madinah.

Salman Farsi, Bilal and Abu Huraira were among the People of the Bench. Abu Dhar al Gjifari (d. 653 AD) was reputed for his outspoken ideology and criticism of luxury and laziness. Uwaymar bin Zaid said, 'One hour of reflection is better than 40 nights of prayer, and that one act of righteousness with godliness and faith is preferable to unlimited ritual observance.'

The Quran affirms their state, 'Send not away those who call on their Lord morning and evening, seeking His face. In naught art thou accountable for them, and in naught are they accountable for thee, that thou shouldst turn them away, and thus be (one) of the unjust.' (6:52)

Although the word Sufi did not exist in the time of the Prophet, the foundations of *Tasawwuf,* Sufism, were laid during the early days of Islam. The Messenger said, 'He who hears the voice of the *ahl e tasawwuf,* people of spirituality, and does not say *Ameen* to their prayers is inscribed before God among those with *ghafla,* heedlessness.'[9]

Sufis believe that Prophet Muhammad ﷺ was the recipient of a two-fold knowledge: *Ilm e Safina,* outer knowledge, and *Ilm e Sina* or *Ilm e Ladduni,* knowledge of the heart, as mentioned in the Quran. The Prophet entrusted his inner knowledge to some companions, bestowing upon Ali ibn Talib, his cousin and son-in-law, the title of 'Imam of the Walis' and positioning him as the fountainhead of mystic knowledge. Love and respect for *Ahl e Bait,* People of the House of Prophet Muhammad ﷺ, remains a central theme with those on the Sufi path.

The Quran narrates the tale of Khidr, the immortal guide and friend of Allah, graced with 'knowledge of the heart'. Through the story of Moses and his search for Khidr, the Quran affirms the tradition of prophets seeking Allah's friends with mystic illumination. Along with his attendant, Moses looked for, 'the meeting place of the two oceans', a miraculous source known as the Fountain of Life. Moses realized the place had been reached when the fish they had cooked sprang back to life and swam away. Here, Moses met Khidr whom Allah describes: 'So they found one of Our servants, on whom We had bestowed Mercy from Ourselves and whom We had taught knowledge from Our own Presence.' (18:65)

Moses wished to accompany Khidr on his journey but was initially refused on the grounds that he would not be able to comprehend the mystic's behaviour. He was confronted with someone whose knowledge was different from his own. Eventually Khidr led him through a series of strange actions, from damaging a boat to killing a youth and repairing a small wall of a house in a town of hostile people. When Moses enquired about the irrationality of these acts, Khidr explained that he had accomplished three hidden purposes. The boat owner had been saved from a tyrant ruler who planned on confiscating all undamaged boats, the pious parents were saved from the trauma of a son who would have grown to become a monster, and the repaired wall had saved the buried inheritance of two orphans from being discovered by the town's untrustworthy people. The great law-giving Prophet Moses was unaware of Khidr's mystic knowledge as one who was not a prophet but simply a friend of Allah.

The story of Khidr makes Sufis aware of the possibilities of inner illumination and the importance of subordinating rational thought to unconditional love of God. Moses and his search for Khidr is inscribed in the eighteenth chapter of the Quran, *Surah Kahf*, Companions of the Cave. Prophet Muhammad ﷺ recommended that devout Muslims read the chapter in its entirety every Friday.

The Quran: Chapter Light (24:35)
Light upon Light! Allah doth guide whom He will to His Light.

MUHAMMAD ﷺ—THE QUINTESSENTIAL SUFI MASTER

The books of Sahih Muslim and Sahih Bukhari, acknowledged sources of authentic reportage of Prophet Muhammad's ﷺ sayings and traditions, report on the authority of Hasan of Basra, (d. 728 AD) that Muhammad ﷺ questioned God on *Ilm e Laddunni* through Archangel Gabriel. God explained it as secret knowledge between Him and His friends. The Prophet clarified that while prophets received revelations through Archangel Gabriel, Allah bestowed inner knowledge directly to the hearts of His *Auliya*, friends.

Surah Fatihah, the Opening Chapter of the Quran, says: 'Show us the straight way, The way of those on whom, Thou hast bestowed Thy Grace, those whose (portion) is not wrath, and who go not astray.' (1:6–7) Recitation of this verse is part of the mandatory prayers Muslims offer five times a day. Interestingly, this important verse does not stress on the five essential rituals of Islam but is in the form of a prayer reaffirming Allah's sovereignty and asking Him to keep believers on the path of those graced by Him. Traditional Islam accepts that *Auliya Allah* are those upon whom Allah bestows grace.

Mystic knowledge enabled Prophet Muhammad ﷺ to know everything in the world. The books of Hadith report on the authority of his companion Hudhaifia, that the Prophet once arose speaking of everything that would happen on the Day of Judgement. The Messenger's companions accepted that his knowledge surpassed the limits of human acquisition. Numerous verses in the Quran relate to the mystic quest, the famous Light verse indicates, 'Light upon Light! Allah doth guide whom He will to His Light'. (24:35)

The most distinctive theme of the Quran used by the Sufis to understand the meaning of human existence on earth is *Misaq*, the pre-eternal covenant that Allah made with unborn human souls prior to their creation. 'When thy Lord drew forth from the Children of Adam—from their loins—their descendants, and made them testify concerning themselves, (saying): "Am I not your Lord (who cherishes and sustains you)?"—they said: "Yes! We do testify!" (This), lest ye should say on the Day of Judgement: "Of this we were never mindful." ' (7:172)

The day of the covenant when nothing but Allah existed is called *Yaum e Alastu*, when the fate of all souls was sealed by Divine predestination. The foundation of Allah's love was laid; the souls that responded instantly with a passionate yearning became His chosen friends. The friends experienced union with the Beloved understanding that moment as the most precious one. Sufism teaches that man's duty on earth is to know God and fulfil this primordial covenant with Him.

Sufis trace their spiritual enlightenment through a chain of transmissions going back to Prophet Muhammad 卐. The relationship between a Sufi Master and disciple is modelled on the oath of allegiance taken by Muhammad's 卐 companions at his hands, for Allah declared that they were in fact swearing allegiance to Him. 'Verily those who plight their fealty to thee do no less than plight their fealty to Allah. The Hand of Allah is over their hands: then any one who violates his oath, does so to the harm of his own soul, and any one who fulfils what he has covenanted with Allah—Allah will soon grant him a great Reward.' (48:10)

The Prophet initiated the first mystics from among some of his companions with the rite of *ba'ya*, oath of allegiance who in turn initiated other mystics. These unbroken chains of initiation represented in various Sufi orders are called *silsila*, the Arabic word for chain.

POVERTY IS MY PRIDE

The word Sufi began to be used during the tenth century to define Muslim mystics. Some believe the word is derived from the Arabic verb *safa* meaning purity. Others think Sufi comes from *safe awwal* meaning the first rank, reinforcing the belief that Sufis will stand in the first row of men on the Day of Judgement. However, the most accepted theory is that Sufi comes from the word *suf*, the Arabic word for wool. Prophet Muhammad ﷺ, his companions and the early mystics all wore *muraqqa*, a patched woolen garment. Hasan of Basra (d. 728 AD), the early mystic confirmed witnessing 70 comrades of the Prophet who fought at the battle of Badr wearing patched woolen frocks.[10] Muhammad ﷺ warned, 'Do not wear the woolen mantle of total devotion until your heart is pure and if you wear it while your knowledge is deficient, then Allah will tear it off your back.'

The patched woolen garment is viewed as a legacy of the prophets and the ascetics. Following the tradition, later mystics wore a simple woolen garment and came to be known as Sufis. Muslim mystics added the word *faqir*, one who is poor, to their name. Prophet Muhammad ﷺ stated, '*Al fakhru fakhri*' meaning 'Poverty is my pride.' He said that Allah loves those who are poor and lonely, defining their state, 'They are the ones who have nobody and nothing but their religion.' Once when someone declared love for Muhammad ﷺ, he said, 'Be ready for Poverty'. Poverty began to be understood not just as destitution but also as a spiritual state consisting of man's lowliness and poverty before Allah. Rumi glorifies the prophetic words:

> 'Poverty is my pride' is neither illusion nor exaggeration
> For a hundred thousand glories are concealed within its
> eloquence.[11]

THE DIVINE LIGHT

Prophet Muhammad ﷺ said, 'Beware of the true believer for he sees through the Light of God.' Abu Huraira, a companion of Muhammad ﷺ recorded him as saying, 'There will be some Divine bondsmen other than prophets, who will be envied by the prophets and martyrs.' When the companions asked the Messenger to identify them, Muhammad ﷺ replied, 'They are the ones whose hearts will be filled with Divine light. As a result they hold each other dear in spite of being neither kindred of a common lineage. Their faces will be radiant and they will be seated on the throne of Divine light. They will be without fear or grief.' The Prophet described their state as found in the Quran ' Behold! Verily on the friends of Allah—there is no fear, nor shall they grieve.' (10:62)

Muhammad's ﷺ sayings are classified into two kinds, Hadith and Hadith Qudsi. The latter are Allah's words spoken by the Prophet other than the verses of the Quran. In a Hadith Qudsi Allah says, 'He who is hostile to a friend of Mine I declare war against him. Nothing is more pleasing to Me, as a means for My servant to draw near to Me with added voluntary devotions until I love him: and when I love him I become the hearing with which he hears, and the eye with which he sees, and the hand with which he grasps, and the foot with which he walks.'[12]

Rumi explains:

> *He said to him: I am your tongue, your eye*
> *I am your senses, your contentment and your anger.*
> *Go, be detached! That one who hears through Me*
> *And sees through Me is you.*
> *Not only are you the possessor of the secret,*
> *But you are the secret too.*[13]

The ecstatic utterances of numerous Sufi Masters can be understood in the light of the above Hadith. The Chishti Sufi Master of the thirteenth century, Baba Masud Farid is said to have once exclaimed, 'For 40 years Masud has done what Allah asked him to do and now Allah does what Masud asks him to do.'

A Sufi tries to achieve the spiritual rank where his actions become a manifestation of God's actions. He is like a droplet of water which merges with the ocean. According to Divine promise, the world shall not be without a *wali*, friend of God, until the end of time. Muhammad ﷺ endorses this conviction, 'A group among my community will never cease to support the Truth until the day of

Resurrection. They are God's *khalifas*, vicegerents on the earth and His elect creatures; it is they who will guide people to His religion.'

Encouraging traditions of learning, Muhammad ﷺ said, 'The search for knowledge is incumbent upon every Muslim, male and female.' Muslim scholars devoted their lives to understanding the Quran and Prophetic traditions. Those who pursued the study of *Sharia* laws came to be known as jurists. The scholars who devoted themselves to the development of virtuous inner qualities came to be known as Sufis.

There has never been a time in Islamic history where Sufism has not been taught as an important Islamic discipline. Over 75 per cent of Islamic philosophy and literature contains the work of Sufi scholars. The Sufis made an immense contribution to the magnificent Islamic arts and architecture. Kufic, the oldest style of calligraphy is attributed to the Prophet's cousin and son-in-law, Imam Ali of Kufa (d. 661 AD), who used enchanting styles for inscribing verses of the Quran. Calligraphy remains a favourite art of the Sufis for they encourage glorifying places of worship. Through the centuries, Sufism came to be associated with thousands of teachers, numerous institutions and a vast literature. The method adopted by Sufi Masters came to be called *Tasawwuf*, Islamic mysticism. Similar to the study of *tafsir*, Quran exegesis and Hadith, Sufism preserves the spiritual aspect of Islam.

SUFISM IN TODAY'S WORLD

In recent times, Sufi poetry has gained immense popularity in the West where Mevlana Rumi is the most popular poet. However, I notice that most published selections of Mevlana's poetry are devoid of his religious discourse. Muhammad Jalaluddin Rumi is usually presented merely as Rumi, a mystic without the Muhammad, and without the Islam. Rumi's verses express his deep love for Prophet Muhammad ﷺ while explaining mysteries of Divine love. Jami (1414–92 AD) the Persian mystic poet called the Mevlana's Mathnawi 'the Quran in Persian'. Rumi's monumental works weave numerous prophetic traditions in poetic verse. The Whirling Dervishes, who meditate in the tradition of their Sufi Master Rumi, begin their dance with a *naat sharif*, poetry in honour of Allah's Messenger:

> *Ya habib Allah rasul Allah ki akta tui*
> *O God's beloved, O Messenger of God—unique are you!*
> *You chosen by the Lord of Majesty—so pure are you!*[14]

Rumi's Master, Shamsuddin Tabrez did not negate the disciple's knowledge of Islamic theology but inspired him to travel beyond the laws to discover the spiritual horizons. In expunging the Islamic element from popular Muslim mystic poets, the West loses out on the opportunity to engage in dialogue with Islam.

There are, of course, historical reasons that led to misconceptions that Sufism is a sect outside the fold of Islam. European writings on Sufism began in the late thirteenth century with the story of Rabia Basri, the famous seventh-century female mystic of Basra. Her story was transported to Europe by Joinville, the chancellor of Louis IX, and used in a French treatise explaining Divine love.[15] The next round of writing took place in the sixteenth and seventeenth centuries by travellers to the Far and Middle East. They wrote of the whirling dervishes, howling ascetics, music and other that took place in Sufi circles and presumed that these activities had little to do with Islam. Unfortunately, historical sources and translations of Sufi texts were unavailable to Western scholars until the late nineteenth century. However, some modern writers continue distancing Sufism from Islam. Some even compare Sufis and their disciples to a brotherhood similar to Freemasons. In the introduction of the book *The Sufis* by Idries Shah, Robert Graves writes, 'The Sufis are an ancient spiritual freemasonry whose origins have never been traced or dated; nor do they themselves take interest in such researches, being content to point out the occurrence of their own way of thought in different regions and periods.' Although Idries Shah's books contributed to generating an interest on Sufism in the West, they are not serious studies on the subject.

At the time of the Christian crusades, Islam came to be viewed as a militant religion of the Arabian Desert devoid of any spiritual content. Islam has been the target of prejudice for centuries and objective translations of Islamic literature are a recent phenomenon in the Western world. A vast number of Western intellectuals continue propagating Islam as intolerant, medieval and barbaric. However, there are now innumerable Muslim and non-Muslim scholars who are unbiased in understanding the faith. For example, Annemarie Schimmel and Karen Armstrong, two non-Muslim scholars of global repute, have attempted to understand and analyze Islam from 'within'.

I learnt that following the tragedy of 9/11, the Quran became one of the best-selling books in America. It seemed the world could no longer afford to remain ignorant of Islam. The Quran literally means 'The Reading' or 'Recital' and was revealed in the spiritual tradition of the Torah and the Bible.

As Thomas Cleary points out: 'For non-Muslims the reading of the Quran provides an authentic point of reference from which to examine the biased stereotypes of Islam to which Westerners are habitually exposed. This exercise may also enable the thinking individual to understand the inherently defective nature of prejudice itself, and thus be more generally receptive to all information and knowledge of possible use to humankind.'[16]

Surprisingly, conversions to Islam have quadrupled after 9/11, a period where 'the war on terror' is viewed by many as a war on Islam. The global average of people embracing Islam is placed close to 500 a day. In the US alone, the Muslim population is estimated between seven and eight million people, a quarter of which are new converts. The numbers continue to grow at around 20,000 new conversions a year, with women four times more than men. I obtained these figures from news reports of the American television news channels

Allah

CNN and NBC via clips that are posted on the Internet. CNN interviewed some American families of the 9/11 victims who began with studying Islam to understand the violence it seemed to have caused and eventually became Muslims. It would not be off the mark to state that Sufis are largely responsible for this wave of conversion that includes celebrities, priests, rabbis and academics in different parts of the world. Although Sufi orders do not function as missionaries, they enable those participating in their activities to transcend Muslim stereotypes.

Sufi orders flourish in countless countries including China, Morocco, Bosnia, Somalia, Indonesia, Russia and other areas of Asia, Africa, Europe and America. Recently, some Western Sufi Orders have sprung up where the disciples need not participate in Islamic religious duties. One such example is The Sufi Order International founded by the mystic musician Hazrat Inayat Khan (1882–1927 AD) who travelled to the US in the early twentieth-century and established the first Sufi order in the West at a popular level. Although a Muslim mystic and initiated in the traditional Chishti Sufi Order, Inayat Khan disconnected his teachings from Islamic laws. Kept alive by members of his family, the order continues to assert that Sufism can exist independent of the essential tenets of Islam. In recent years, many such semi-Islamic and non-Islamic Sufi organizations have arisen in the West.

بلغ العُلى بکمالِه
کشف الدُّجى بجمالِه
حَسُنَت جميعُ خِصالِه
صَلُّوا عَلیهِ وآلِه

Balaghal ula be kamaaelhi
Kashafat duja be jamaalehi
Hasanat jamio khasaalehi
Sallu alaihe wa aalehi

He (Muhammad ﷺ) attained the supreme position for his excellence,
He illuminated the darkness with his radiance,
He is the possessor of the highest ideals,
Send peace and blessings on him and his progeny.

Shaykh Sadi

2

THE ESSENCE OF THE SUFI EXPERIENCE

بِسْمِ اللَّهِ الرَّحْمَنِ الرَّحِيمِ

Your name is beautiful,
You yourself are beautiful, Muhammad 🪷!
Your words are accepted near God, The Lord
Your name is beautiful,
You yourself are beautiful Muhammad 🪷!

Yunus Emre

To describe the essence and depth of the Sufi experience in words is almost an impossible task. We have seen throughout history that Muslims do not react to attacks on God but will never allow any disregard for Prophet Muhammad 🪷. They deeply love, trust and venerate their Prophet who forms the exemplary model for each believing Muslim. The central figure in Islam, therefore, forms the axis of the Sufi doctrine. A knowledge of Sufism requires not just an understanding of Islamic essentials, but a look into the life and role of Muhammad 🪷.

For mystics, Prophet Muhammad 🪷 mirrors Allah's attributes. During my Sufi initiation, I was taught that loving and following the Prophet was to love God. He remains the perfect vehicle to inner enlightenment, for even in slumber, he remained connected to Allah.

As Rumi glorifies:

> *The Prophet said, 'My eyes sleep,'*
> *But my heart is not asleep to the Lord of Creation*
> *While your eyes are closed and your heart slumbers,*
> *My eyes are closed and my heart open in the contemplation of*
> *   the Divine*
> *Do not judge me with your own inadequacy;*
> *What is night for you is bright day for me,*
> *What for you is a prison is for me an open garden.*
> *In the very midst of worldly engagement I am detached.*
> *It is not myself that sits beside you; it is my shadow;*
> *My reality is beyond the realm of thoughts,*
> *For I have passed beyond all thought,*
> *Racing ahead, far past that realm.*[1]

Sufis strive to wet their lips with the waters of *Kausar*, the Fountain of Abundance in paradise gifted to Muhammad ﷺ by Allah. 'To thee have We granted the Fount (of Abundance)'. (108:1) The spiritual path established by the Messenger fuels the Sufi quest for deeper meanings of why humanity was created. He inspires with the words, 'I have come to perfect noble character.' Ayesha, the Prophet's wife once commented, 'His character was the Quran.' Muslim piety accepts the Prophet as *Habib Allah*, the beloved of God who revealed hidden mysteries of the universe laying emphasis on the heart. In established traditions, Muhammad ﷺ said 'When in doubt ask your heart for a decision for virtue is when the heart and soul are at peace. The best Islam is feeding the hungry and spreading peace amongst those you know and those you do not know.'

Muhammad's ﷺ kindness extended to all beings particularly towards children and animals. On seeing the Prophet kissing his grandchildren, a companion remarked that he had ten children but had never kissed any of them. Muhammad ﷺ commented, 'He who does not show mercy will not receive mercy.' He promised Paradise to a sinful woman who fetched water for a dog and saved him from dying of thirst. On another occasion when a cat slept on the Prophet's garment, he cut the sleeve to leave the cat undisturbed while he got up to offer prayers. Once, while heading for an armed conflict, the Messenger noticed a bitch delivering her litter and asked his followers to change tracks, so that the animal did not get trampled. Muhammad ﷺ preached that women should be respected, allowing them an active role in social affairs. He accorded a high status to mothers declaring, 'Paradise lies beneath the feet of the Mothers.'

Most scholars agree that the Sufi philosophy is both generated and illustrated by Prophet Muhammad's ﷺ own mysticism. The Quran confirms his role as both *basher*, the harbinger of glad tidings, and *nadhir*, one who warns. 'O Prophet! Truly We have sent thee as a Witness, a Bearer of Glad Tidings, and Warner.' (33:45) He is then called *siraj un munir*, a lamp of Divine radiance. 'And as one who invites to Allah's (grace) by His leave, and as a lamp spreading light.' (33:46)

Ana Ahmad bila Mim, 'I am Ahmad (Muhammad ﷺ), without the 'm' that is *Ahad*' is a Hadith Qudsi. *Ahad* is 'One' in Arabic, the word Allah uses to assert His Oneness in the Quran. Poets through the ages, including Mirza Ghalib of Delhi, have dwelt on the tradition of defining the letter 'm' in a variety of images. Sufis interpret the 'm' as a human cloak God draped when He created the Prophet in His exemplary image. Mevlana Rumi writes that Ahmad was the veil with which he hoped to reach *Ahad*. In the lyrical treatise *Ushturnama*, Fariddudin Attar writes:

> *The radiance of the light of manifestation became evident,*
> *the M of Ahmad became invisible.*[2]

Muhammad's ﷺ unique position stems from many of his sayings such as, 'The first thing that Allah created was my Light, which originated from His Light and derived from the Majesty of His greatness' and 'Truly, Allah made me the seal of prophets when Adam was between water and clay.' The essence of Sufism stems from the belief that the universe was created from *Nur e Mohammadi,* Light of Prophet Muhammad 壽, and from this Pre-existent Light, Allah took a handful to build His Universe.

Mevlana Rumi asks, 'How could we commit error? For we are in the light of Ahmad 壽!' Prophet Muhammad's 壽 words reveal his closeness to God, 'Whoever has seen me has seen God.'[3]

Rumi elaborates:

> *If you have seen me, you have seen God*
> *And circled the Kaaba of sincerity.*[4]

The Turkish mystic Khaqani (d. 1190 AD) writes:

> *God (Haqq) loved this light and said:*
> *My Beloved friend (habibi)!*
> *And became enamoured (ashiq) of this light.*[5]

Yunus Emre (d. 1320 AD), another Turkish poet explains the Sufi *aqeeda,* creed, that God created the two worlds for His Beloved:

> *I created him from My own light*
> *And I love him yesterday and today!*
> *What would I do with the worlds without him*
> *My Muhammad 壽, My Ahmad 壽, My Light.*[6]

The Prophet said: 'Outwardly, we are the last but inwardly we preceded everyone.'[7] Rumi illustrates the Hadith:[8]

> *If for fruit the gardener*
> *Felt no desire or hope*
> *Why then would He have planted*
> *The root of the tree*
>
> *Inwardly then, that tree arose*
> *From the fruit*

Though outwardly the fruit
From the tree arose.

That is why the Prophet declared:
Adam and all the prophets
Are my descendants
Under one banner.

And this too is why Muhammad ﷺ
The master of all arts, declared:
Outwardly, we are the last of all,
But inwardly we preceded everyone.[8]

Sanai (d. 1131 AD) the Persian poet from Ghazna who began the tradition of *naatiya*, eulogies in the Persian language, wrote *The Walled Garden of Truth*. Commenting on the seal of Prophecy he sang:

I addressed the wind 'Why do you serve Solomon?'
He said, 'Because Muhammad's ﷺ name was engraved on his seal.'[9]

The Quran tells the story of Iblis (Satan), who was once an angel of high standing devoted to God. 'Behold, thy Lord said to the angels: "I am about to create man from clay: When I have fashioned him (in due proportion) and breathed into him of My spirit, fall ye down in obeisance unto him." So the angels prostrated themselves, all of them together: Not so Iblis: he was haughty, and became one of those who reject Faith. (Allah) said: "O Iblis! What prevents thee from prostrating thyself to one whom I have created with my hands? Art thou haughty? Or art thou one of the high (and mighty) ones?" (Iblis) said: "I am better than he: thou createdst me from fire, and him thou createdst from clay." (Allah) said: "Then get thee out from here: for thou art rejected, accursed. And My curse shall be on thee till the Day of Judgement."' (38:71–8) Sufis quote prophetic sayings to explain how Satan's arrogance prevented him from prostrating to the Light of Muhammad 襟; a part of which was placed in the forehead of Adam. The poet Ashiq Pasha (d. 1133 AD) writes:

> *Adam was still dust and clay*
> *Ahmad was a prophet then*
> *He had been selected by God*
> *Utter blessings over him.*[10]

As stated earlier, the testimony of Islamic faith, *La Illaha ill Allah Muhammad ur Rasul Allah* translates as, 'There is no God but Allah Muhammad is the Messenger of Allah.' However, English translations often use an 'and' in between Allah and Muhammad 襟 although the Arabic has no separating word. Sufis explain that Allah establishes His *Tawhid*, Oneness, by enjoining the name of His beloved Prophet who is not *ghair*, separate from Him.

Surah Ikhlas, the Chapter of Sincerity, establishes the Oneness of the Almighty in the Quran. 'Say: He is Allah, the One and Only; Allah, the Eternal, Absolute; He begetteth not, nor is He begotten, And there is none like unto Him.' (112:1–4) This verse is addressed to Prophet Muhammad 襟 telling him to inform people of His Oneness. Sufis argue that since God communicates directly only with prophets, it is impossible for us to commune with Him directly. Sufis teach that we know that God exists because the Prophet informed us of His existence. Muslims trusted Muhammad 襟 when he said that the Message of the Quran came from Allah. Therefore the sole way of connecting to God is through him.

The Quran speaks of Muhammad 襟 as the guiding Light, 'Those who follow the apostle, the unlettered Prophet, whom they find mentioned in their own (scriptures), in the law and the Gospel; for he commands them what is just and forbids them what is evil; he allows them as lawful what is good (and pure) and prohibits them from what is bad (and impure); He releases them from their heavy burdens and from the yokes that are upon them. So it is those who believe in him, honour him, help him, and follow the light which is sent down with him, it is they who will prosper.' (7:157)

This *Nur*, Light, enables the Sufi to travel towards *Al Haqeeqa Al Muhmmadiya*, the Reality of Muhammad 🪶 and arrive at the Reality of God. Fariduddin Attar writes:

> *The origin of the soul is the absolute Light, nothing else*
> *That means it was the light of Muhammad 🪶, nothing else.*[11]

THE PRIMIDORIAL LIGHT

The opening lines of *Mantiq ut Tair* (Conference of the Birds) written by the Persian Sufi poet Fariduddin Attar (1157–1220 AD) illustrate the Sufi doctrine, the Light of Muhammad 🪶 enjoying God's company at a time when nothing except Him existed.

> *What first appeared from out the Unseen's depth*
> *Was his pure light—no question no doubt!*
> *This lofty light unfolded signs—The throne,*
> *The footstool, Pen and tablet appeared.*
> *One part of his pure light became the world,*
> *And one part Adam and the seed of man*
> *When this grand light shone up, it fell*
> *Before the Lord, prostrate in reverence.*
> *For ages it remained in prostration*
> *And eras long in genuflection too*
> *And year by year it stood in prayer straight,*
> *A lifetime of profession of the faith*
> *Tis prayer of the secret Sea of Light*
> *Gave the community the prayer rite!*

Ibn al Arabi (1165–1240 AD), one of the greatest Sufi Masters shares the same conviction:

> *The creation began with nur Muhammad 🪶*
> *The lord brought the nur from his own heart.*

Muslim poets throughout the world have written extensively on similar themes. Prophet Joseph is generally exalted as a paragon of beauty. Dazzled with his exceptional handsomeness, Zulekha and her female companions had cut their fingers. Daagh (d. 1905 AD), the Delhi poet, writes:

> *Your light was in Joseph's beauty, O light of God*
> *It healed Jacob's blind eye so that it became well.* [12]

In the Quran, God addresses Muhammad 🕊 lovingly with different names. Muzzammil, 'O thou folded in garments!' (73:1) Muddatthir, 'O thou wrapped up (in the mantle)!' (74:1) Previous apostles are all addressed by name, 'O Moses', 'O Jesus', 'O Abraham', but Muhammad 🕊 is never called 'O Muhammad' 🕊. According to the Quran, the earlier prophets delivered messages meant exclusively for their people, whereas Muhammad 🕊 was sent with the final message for all of humanity and for all times to come. He is declared *rahmatal il alameen*, a Mercy for all living creatures. 'We sent thee not, but as a Mercy for all creatures.' (21:107)

Muslims accept Muhammad 🕊 as *shahid*, the witness for mankind who will testify on the Day of Judgement. 'O Prophet! Truly We have sent thee as a Witness, a Bearer of Glad Tidings, and Warner' (33:45). Sufi scholars assert the Prophet's role of witnessing human actions as proof of his omnipresent spirit, for only one who is able to witness everything in the universe can testify. According to the Quran, Allah knows even our innermost thoughts. 'We Who created man, and We know what dark suggestions his soul makes to him: for We are nearer to him than his jugular vein.' (50:16) Yet, argue the Sufis that on the day when humanity is resurrected, God chooses to delegate the authority of discerning souls to Muhammad 🕊. All believing Muslims accept that Prophet Muhammad 🕊 will intercede for his people on the Day of Judgement.

Rumi writes:

Hence his intercession is sought,
for he is Muhammad ﷺ
A falcon knows all the land that lies beneath him;
thus the Prophet discerns souls.[13]

My Sufi Master would refer to the Day of Judgement as a mere spectacle choreographed by Allah merely to showcase placing the crown of *shafa'a*, intercession, on his beloved Prophet. Poetic images of Sufi poetry paint Allah as the *aashiq*, lover, and Muhammad ﷺ as the *mashooq*, beloved.

Shah Abdul Latif (d. 1752 AD) of Sindh writes a long poem on Muhammad ﷺ turning God's fury into Benevolence on the Day of Judgement:

My prince will protect me—therefore I trust in God
The beloved will prostrate, will lament and cry—
Therefore I trust in God.
Muhammad ﷺ *the pure and innocent,*
will intercede there for his people...
When the trumpet sounds, the eyes will be opened...
The pious will gather, and Muhammad ﷺ, *full of glory...*
Will proceed for every soul to the gate of the Benefactor...
And the Lord will honour him, and forgive us all our sins—
Therefore I trust in God.[14]

The Delhi poet Mir Taqi Mir (d. 1810 AD) writes:

Why do you worry, O Mir, at the thought of your black book
The person of the Seal of Prophets is a surety of your
salvation.[15]

The modern Urdu poet Kaifi Azmi (d. 2002 AD) echoes:

My protector, he whom I praise,
is the intercessor for the people of the world
O Kaifi, why should I be afraid of the Day of Reckoning.[16]

Ibn Khaldun (1332–1406 AD) the North African historian-philosopher pleads:

> *Grant me your intercession, for which I hope*
> *A beautiful page instead of my ugly sins.*[17]

MUHAMMAD 3 IN THE QURAN

In the Quran, God Himself prescribes the norms of etiquette required while engaging with Muhammad 3. He admonishes the companions of the Prophet for calling out loudly to him warning them to speak softly or their acts of worship would be deemed worthless. 'O ye who believe! Raise not your voices above the voice of the Prophet, nor speak aloud to him in talk, as ye may speak aloud to one another, lest your deeds become vain. Those that lower their voices in the presence of Allah's Messenger, their hearts has Allah tested for piety: for them is Forgiveness and a great Reward' (49:2–3).

The companions are ordered to knock at the door before entering the Prophet's house and not to stay longer than necessary for he may wish to retire but politeness prevents him from asking them to leave. 'O ye who believe! Enter not the Prophet's houses—until leave is given you—for a meal, (and then) not (so early as) to wait for its preparation: but when ye are invited, enter; and when ye have taken your meal, disperse, without seeking familiar talk. Such (behaviour) annoys the Prophet: he is ashamed to dismiss you, but Allah is not ashamed (to tell you) the truth'. (33:53)

Sufi Masters stress on remembering that the *sahaaba*, companions of Prophet Muhammad, 3 rank the highest in faith. If the mere act of talking aloud could strip them off virtuous deeds, the extent of God's wrath would be unimaginable towards those disrespectful of the Messenger. When some of my orthodox Muslim friends run down the importance of connecting to Allah through the Prophet, I remind them to be careful of the words they use lest they ignite God's wrath. Sufi Masters teach that God is *Rahim*, Merciful, and forgives everything, except disregard for his beloved Muhammad ﷺ. My Sufi Master often said, 'The sins of one whose heart is filled with love for Prophet Muhammad ﷺ might be forgiven by God while the pious whose hearts are devoid of this love could be in serious trouble. May God have mercy on them, enlighten their souls and show them the path of Love that leads to Him.'

Abu Lahab, a prominent figure of Quraysh (the Prophet's tribe), and his wife tortured and made life miserable for the Messenger and his followers in Makkah. Muhammad ﷺ advised Muslims not to retaliate with violence but endure their trials in the way of Truth. Allah's fury peaks in the Quran where He condemns Abu Lahab for challenging Muhammad's ﷺ prophecy and truthfulness. 'Perish the hands of the Father of Flame! Perish he! No profit to him from all his wealth, and all his gains! Burnt soon will he be in a Fire of Blazing Flame! His wife shall carry the (crackling) wood —As fuel!' (111:1–4)

Mevlana Rumi writes that Abu Lahab was the sole person in the world never to be touched by the flame of Divine love.

'I have not seen lacking Thy flame, anyone but Abu Lahab' [18]

The Quran says, 'You have indeed in the Messenger of Allah a beautiful pattern (of conduct) for any one whose hope is in Allah and the Final Day, and who engages much in the Praise of Allah.' (33:21) 'And thou standst on an exalted standard of character.' (68:4) The Quran commands Muslims to follow Muhammad ﷺ, 'If you do love Allah, Follow me: Allah will love you and forgive you your sins: For Allah is Oft-Forgiving, Most Merciful'. (3:31) Another verse narrates that God would have been merciful had the sinners sought the apostle's intercession. 'We sent not an apostle, but to be obeyed, in accordance with the will of God. If they had only, when they were unjust to themselves, come unto thee and asked God's forgiveness, and the Apostle had asked forgiveness for them, they would have found God indeed Oft-returning, Most Merciful.' (4:64)

The Quran: Chapter Children of Israel (17:1)
Glory to (Allah) Who did take his servant for a journey by night
from the Sacred Mosque to the farthest Mosque, whose precincts
we did bless, in order that we might show him some of Our Signs,
for He is the All Hearing, the All Seeing.

The Sufi's goal of perfecting his *imaan*, faith, is achieved through loving Prophet Muhammad 卿 who said: 'None of you believes until he loves me more than he loves his children, his parents, himself and all people.'[19] When Muslims read the *durood o salaam*, blessings and salutations to the Prophet, they believe it to be the sole action that they share with God and the celestial beings. 'Allah and His angels send blessings on the Prophet: O ye that believe! Send ye blessings on him, and salute him with all respect.' (33:56) Countless *durood* exist in different languages that are recited by Muslim communities the world over.

THE NIGHT JOURNEY OF LOVE

The Prophet's Ascension to the Heavens illustrates the tale of love between Muhammad 卿 and Allah. The celebrated event, *Shab e Miraj*, took place on the twenty-seventh night of Rajab, the seventh month of the Islamic calendar. The Ascension is spirituality at its highest for it carries clues on the secrets of the Heavens. It gives us the remarkable news that the gulf between the finite and Infinite can be bridged.[20] Details of the event are found in countless transmissions of Prophetic sayings. This Night Journey forms the very foundation of the ultimate Sufi experience.

In Makkah the Prophet often visited the Kaaba enclosure at night. Tired, one evening he went to sleep near the House of God. The Archangel Gabriel shook him gently, awakening him from a deep slumber. He escorted Muhammad to *Al Buraq*, the wonderous winged steed standing by to carry him to the Temple of Solomon in Jerusalem. Here, Muhammad 卿 led all previous prophets in prayer with the title of *Imam e Ambiya*, Leader of the Prophets. Makkah is the city of Ishmael whereas Jerusalem is the city of Isaac and this visit to Jerusalem closed the gap between the two great branches of Abraham's family. *Masjid Al Aqsa*, The Dome of the Rock in Jerusalem, Islam's holiest site after Makkah and Madinah, marks the place from where the Ascension took place. At the time of this nocturnal flight the *qibla*, direction of Muslim prayer, was Jerusalem. It changed later during Muhammad's 卵 life when he was instructed by God to face the city of Makkah.

Throughout Islamic history, Muslim scholars have reflected whether the Ascension was of a physical or spiritual nature, with most agreeing that it was both. The narratives of the Ascension are considered the most dramatic words spoken by the Prophet. 'The Buraq was bought to me, and this was an animal larger than a donkey and smaller than a mule, which would place its hoof at every horizon. I mounted it and came to Jerusalem. I then tethered it to the ring used by the prophets. I entered the mosques where I prayed two *ra'kas*. Gabriel then bought me a vessel of wine and a vessel of milk. I chose the milk, and Gabriel said, "You have chosen the *fitra*, the natural way." '

The narrative further describes the gate of the lower heavens opening with the Prophet and Gabriel rising higher. In the successive heavens they encounter Isa (Jesus), Yahya (John the Baptist), Idris (Enoch), Haroon (Aaron), Musa (Moses), and Ibrahim (Abraham). Each one greets Prophet Muhammad 卵 before he reaches the climax of this journey.

'I was then brought to the Lotus tree of the Utmost Boundary (*sidrat al muntaha*) whose leaves were like the ears of an elephant and whose fruit at first seemed small. But then God spread his command over them and they were so transformed that no one in creation could describe their beauty. Then God revealed what he revealed to me.'[21]

The Quran testifies that Muhammad 卵 finally arrived at the highest part of the horizon, at the *maqaam*, the station of 'Two Bows Length' with God—understood as the fine juncture where the two halves of an archer's bow are glued together, forming an almost invisible line of separation. It speaks of Muhammad's 卵 impeccable conduct, his eyes not swerving.

The mystic journey finds another mention in the Quran: 'Glory to Allah Who did take His servant for a Journey by night from the

Sacred Mosque to the farthest Mosque, whose precincts We did bless —in order that We might show him some of Our Signs: for He is the One Who heareth and seeth all things.' (17:1)

Prophet Muhammad ﷺ returns to the world but not worldly, claiming: 'Poverty is my pride.' He returns with the assurance that God is pure Mercy and Goodness. Through this mystic voyage he demonstrates that union with God is possible.

Shams Tabriz (d. 1248 AD) the Master of Mevlana Rumi, taught, 'To follow Muhammad ﷺ is that he went to the *miraj* and you go behind him.'[22]

The daily five prayers that Muslims are required to offer were Allah's gifts to the Prophet during the night journey. Initially the number of prayers was meant to be 50 but Muhammad is believed to have met Moses on the return journey, who told him that people would not be able to fulfil such a burden. The Prophet then returned to Allah several times till the number of daily prayers were reduced to five. These prayers are called *miraj ul muminin*, the ascension of the believer. The salutations offered to the Prophet by the angels 'Peace be upon you, O Prophet, and the mercy and the grace of God', are an integral part of these five mandatory prayers, reminding Muslims of the most glorious moment of his life.

Mevlana Rumi reveals the secret of prayer: 'Formal prayer has an end, but the prayer of the soul is unlimited. It is the drowning and the unconscious of the soul so that all these forms remain without. At that time there is no room for even Gabriel who is pure spirit.'[23]

Muslims believe that Time came to a standstill during the Ascension, for Muhammad ﷺ returned to find his bed warm and the pitcher, which had tumbled over, had not emptied out completely.[24] The Night of Ascension is celebrated in many countries with streets, mosques, houses and *dargahs* illuminated beautifully. The heavenly journey remains the subject of popular poetry and art throughout the Muslim world. Sarmad (d. 1661 AD) the martyred Sufi poet wrote:

> *The Mullah says that Ahmad ﷺ went to heaven*
> *Sarmad says that heaven descended into Ahmad ﷺ.*[25]

Attar's *Illahinama* contains a long poem describing the Night Journey:

> *At night Gabriel came, and filled with joy*
> *He called: Wake up, you leader of the world!*
> *Get up, leave this dark place and travel now*
> *To the eternal kingdom of the Lord!*[26]

Attar describes how Muhammad ﷺ alone was granted full knowledge of the Almighty. The poem ends with the imagined words of God:

> *You are my goal and purpose in creation*
> *And what you wish, request it, seeing eye!*
> *Muhammad ﷺ said: Omniscient without how,*
> *You inward secret, outward mystery*
> *You know my innermost and dearest wish:*
> *I ask you for my community!*
> *Sinful is my community, but sure,*
> *They are aware of you, Your boundless grace*
> *They know the ocean of Your love and grace*
> *How would it be if you forgave them all?*
> *Once more he was addressed by God most High*
> *'I have forgiven altogether, friend*
> *You need not worry for your people, for*
> *My boundless grace is greater than their sins!'*
> *Thou should worship God as if Thou saw Him.*

ISLAM, *IMAAN* AND *IHSAN*

Numerous books of Hadith, including those of Imam Bukhari and Imam Muslim, narrate that Islam engages its followers in three categories of behaviour. The first is *Islam*, submission to Allah through following the five pillars prescribed in the Quran. The second is *Imaan*, the testimony that there is no god but Allah and

Muhammad is His Messenger; while the third is *Ihsan,* a behaviour that commands virtue and sincerity. Archangel Gabriel spoke to Prophet Muhammad 🕊 both in the angelic form and human form. Muhammad's 🕊 companion Umar bin Khattab reported the following tradition:

> One day when we were with the Messenger of God there came to us a man whose clothes were of exceeding whiteness and whose hair was of exceeding blackness, nor were there any signs of travel upon him, although none of us had seen him before. He sat down knee upon knee opposite the Prophet, upon whose thighs he placed the palms of his hands, saying, 'O Muhammad 🕊, tell me what Islam is'. The Prophet answered: 'Islam is that thou should perform the prayer, bestow the alms, fast in Ramadan and make, if thou can, the pilgrimage of the Holy House.' He said 'Thou hast spoken truly.'
>
> We were amazed that having questioned him he should corroborate him. Then he said: 'Tell me what *Imaan* (faith) is.' 'It is that thou should believe in his God and His angels and His book and His apostles and the last day, and thou should believe that no good or evil come but by His Providence.'
>
> 'Thou hast spoken truly,' he said, and then, 'Tell me what is *Ihsan*' (Excellence). The Prophet answered: 'It is that Thou should worship God in a state as if Thou saw Him, for if thou see Him not, verily He see thee.'
>
> Then the stranger went away and I stayed there long after he had gone, until the Prophet said to me: 'O Umar, does thou know the questioner, who he was?' I said: 'God, and his Prophet know best, but I know not at all.' 'It was Gabriel,' said the Prophet. 'He came to teach you your religion.'[27]

Rumi glorfies the Prophetic tradition:

> *Listen to the discourse of the greatest of all masters*
> *Prayer without presence of the heart is imperfect.* [28]

Ali Wali Allah: Ali is the leader of all the friends of Allah.

Islam, the study of outer laws, developed into *Fiqh*, Islamic jurisprudence, represented by various schools such as Hanafi, Hanbali, Maliki, Shafai and Jafari (known by the names of their founding Muslim scholars). 'Difference of opinion among scholars is a blessing,' reassures a widely acknowledged Prophetic saying. Similarly, *Ihsan* grew into the science of mysticism that later organized itself into Sufi orders known by the name of the founders of the disciplines.

GATE TO THE CITY OF KNOWLEDGE

Prophet Muhammad ﷺ entrusted the mystic heritage to his cousin and son-in-law Imam Ali, universally acknowledged as the *Imam*, leader of the *Walis*, friends of Allah. *Man Kunto Maula va Ali un Maula*, 'I am the Master of those of whom Ali is the Master.'[29] These words of the Prophet are known as *Qaul* and inscribed on the walls of numerous *dargahs*. *Sama mehfils*, Sufi musical assemblies, traditionally begin with a rendition of the *Qaul*. Rumi pays a tribute to the Master of all Masters:

> *For this reason did the Prophet*
> *With religious authority*
> *Place upon himself and Ali*
> *The title of Master*
> *Saying, whoever takes me as master and friend*
> *Takes my cousin Ali as a master too.*
> *Who is the master? That one who frees you*
> *Breaking the shackles of slavery from your feet.*[30]

On the Prophetic saying, 'I am the City of Knowledge and Ali is its gate' Rumi continues:

> *You are like the gate of that City of knowledge*
> *You are a ray of that sum of forbearance*
> *O gate, remain open for those who seek you,*

So that those husk-like people reach the kernel through you
Be open forever, O gate of mercy
Upon the court of that one who has no equal.[31]

Sufi Stations: A Drop that Merges with the Sea

Sufi Masters teach inner purification of the soul. Allah says, 'Truly he succeeds that purifies it.' (91:9) Sufism constitutes a path *Tareeqa*, literally meaning ' the way'. The classification of spiritual progression is known as *Maqaam*, mystic stations. When the Sufi reaches a level of excellence, he achieves *fana*, the highest *maqaam*, station, where the self ceases to exist. Similar to the drop that merges with the sea, the mystic's soul merges with the Divine, returning to where it came from. Sufis hope to become the perfect servants of Allah, so He may make them His *khalifas*, 'vicegerents' on the earth. They gain awareness of God by discovering Divine attributes within their own spirit. *Ishq e haqiqi*, love for Allah, is eternal, whereas *ishq e majazi*, love for all else, is illusionary.

Prophet Muhammad ﷺ said, 'Die before you die,' stressing upon the importance of self-realization. He further clarified, 'One who knows himself knows God.' Sufis understand that the removal of the *nafs*, ego, is the way to attain a state of *wasl*, union with God, for even though they continue to live, in a sense they do not exist any more. *Nafs* is explained as the passions of the lower self that relate to sexual impulses and other human tendencies of greed. Sufis experience dreams, visions and *kashf*, extraordinary forms of revelation, directly in the heart.

Spiritualists understand *Tawhid*, the Oneness of God, as there is no god but God and no reality but Reality. This concept of *Tawhid* finds beautiful expression in the lyrical *Mantiq ut Tair*. Attar narrates the consequence of thousands of birds led by the magnificent Hoopoe in their quest for their king, the Simurgh. The birds believe that their King lives beyond the mountain of Kaf that surrounds the world. They cross endless deserts, the Seven Valleys of Understanding, encountering slaves, princesses, hermits and creatures on the way. They confront their fears and eventually just 30 birds reach the end of the journey. To the astonishment of the birds, the king is none other than themselves. The birds are transformed into Simurgh, the great unknown bird, resolving the enigma of I and Thou forever:

> *There in the Simurgh's radiant face they saw*
> *Themselves, the Simurgh of the World—with awe*
> *They gazed, and dared at last to comprehend*
> *They were the Simurgh and the journey's end*
> *They see the Simurgh—at themselves they stare*
> *And see a second Simurgh standing there*
> *They look at both and see the two are one....*

Following the stage of *fana*, the Sufi arrives at the station of *baqa*, a continuous existence in God. Mystic communication and the concepts of *fana* and *baqa* are wonderfully expressed by Mevlana Rumi. His *Mathnawi* tells the story of a merchant and his parrot. The parrot symbolizes the soul of the merchant engaged in conventional life. When the merchant decides to go to India, he asks the parrot if she wants a gift. 'I only request that when you see other parrots in India, tell them a parrot who longs for you is in prison by the destiny of Heaven,' replies the bird.

On reaching India the merchant gives the message to the parrots, one of whom trembles and falls dead upon hearing the news. The sympathetic merchant senses that the bird is somehow related to his bird at home. On returning he tells his parrot the story who also falls down in a corner of her cage. After lamenting the loss of his parrot, the merchant throws her out of the cage. But the bird immediately flies to a bough and the surprised merchant wants to know what sort of communication has taken place between the two birds. The parrot replies, 'The other parrot by her act said, "Die yourself and stop singing so that you may be released to gain freedom".'

THE TRANCE OF LOVE

Drunk on love, Sufis experience *hal*, a state of spiritual ecstasy that can last from moments to days. Sufis believe that the trance is not dependent on the mystic's effort but on Divine graces. In *Diwan e Shams*, Rumi expresses the dynamics of Love:

> *Through Love thorns become roses,*
> *Through love vinegar becomes sweet wine*
> *Through love the stake becomes a throne*
> *Through love the reverse of fortune seems good fortune,*
> *Through love a prison seems a rose bower*
> *Through love a grate full of ashes seems a garden*
> *Through love a burning fire is a pleasing light*
> *Through love the Devil becomes a Houri*
> *Through love the hard stone becomes soft as butter*
> *Through love grief is joy*
> *Through love ghouls turn into angels*
> *Through love stings are as honey*
> *Through love lions are harmless as mice*
> *Through love sickness is health*
> *Through love wrath is mercy.*

The great Sufi Master Ibn al Arabi writes:

> *My heart has opened up in every form:*
> *It is a pasture for gazelles a cloister for Christian monks,*
> *A temple for idols, the Kaaba of the pilgrim,*
> *The tables of the Torah and the book of the Quran.*
> *I practice the religion of Love:*
> *In whatsoever direction its caravan advances,*
> *The religion of Love shall be my religion and my Faith.*[32]

Prophet Muhammad ﷺ spoke of the heart as a repository of knowledge and a vessel sensitive to the needs of the body saying,

'Truly, Allah does not look at your outward forms and wealth, but rather at your hearts and your works.' Many verses of the Quran talk about the importance of the heart. Describing events on the Day of Judgement it says, 'The Day whereon neither wealth nor sons will avail, But only he (will prosper) that brings to Allah a sound heart.' (26: 88–89) Throughout Islamic history, Sufis have devoted their lives to unravelling the hidden mysteries of the universe in order to understand Islam in totality.

In the name of Allah, Most Gracious, Most Merciful.

3

THE EARLY SUFIS

Allah possesses a drink which is reserved for his intimate friends: when they drink they become intoxicated, when they become intoxicated they become joyful, when they become joyful they become sweet, when they become sweet they begin to melt, when they begin to melt they become free, when they become free they seek, when they seek they find, when they find they arrive, when they arrive they join, and when they join there is no difference between them and their Beloved.

Imam Ali Ibn Talib

I will share one of my favourite stories that occurred in the life of a Sufi I know. As a young trainee, he was accompanying a senior Sufi in the jungles for ascetic practice. They came upon two mystics lying on the ground, oblivious to the world and in a deep spiritual state. Suddenly a forest fire began to spread and the clothes of the mystics were set ablaze. The Sufi and his student saw that the fire died out on one of the mystics, while the body of the other began to burn. The Master asked his student which of the two he thought was of superior spiritual rank. The disciple replied that it would surely be the mystic who controlled the fire with his eyes closed and body completely still. But his Master explained that the higher rank belonged to the other mystic, for all his spiritual energies were focused on God's love and he was resigned to God's will, allowing the fire to do what was its natural attribute.

Although miracles form the historical landscape of all major religions, unlike the cannonization of Chrisitan saints, they are not prerequisites for Sufis. Stories of the early Sufis have fascinated me ever since my initiation on the path. I have heard them in discourses and from my mother, who punctuates her conversations with Sufi tales to demonstrate the need for excellence in our quest for God.

Recent Islamic discourse has witnessed a sharp increase in the emphasis on Islam's scientific nature. Although many Islamic traditions may have been scientifically proven to be beneficial, I feel that the stress on rationale is misplaced. I often argue that had God been an academic trophy, the ability to know Him would be restricted to those with powers of the intellect. Stringent modern attitudes, requiring a scientific basis for everything, tend to overlook the importance of the heart and sincere emotions. I believe that the purest form of unconditional love is often irrational and does not look for practical justifications.

The Quran affirms that the devout are those who believe in the existence of what the human eye cannot see. 'A.L.M. This is the Book; In it is guidance sure, without doubt, To those who fear God; Who believe in the Unseen, Are steadfast in prayer, And spend out of what We have provided for them'. (2:1–3) The lives of Mevlana Rumi and Imam Ghazali demonstrate to some extent how Islamic scholars experienced spiritual enlightenment after renouncing the academic world.

The Mystical Path in Early Islam

Islam uses the word *muajzat* for miracles performed by prophets, and *karamat* for those attributed to Sufis. The Quran mentions the opening and purifying of Prophet Muhammad's ﷺ breast preparing it for Divine Revelation. 'Have We not expanded thee thy breast?' (94:1) Traditions place the miraculous event in the early childhood of Muhammad ﷺ. A group of angels descended from heaven and opened his breast washing it with the waters of the Zam Zam, the well near the Kaaba. The holy waters had gushed forth from the desert sands to quench the thirst of Hajra's (Hagar) infant son, Ismael (Ishmael) after Ibrahim left them alone in the desert entrusting them to God. The splitting of the moon by Muhammad ﷺ to prove his truthfulness also finds mention in the Quran. 'The Hour (of Judgement) is nigh, and the moon is cleft asunder'. (54:1) Details of both these miracles are recorded in numerous prophetic sayings.

Islamic traditions tell us that animals lowered their heads before Muhammad ﷺ and a cloud wandered above him, ensuring that shadows did not form. The sighing trunk of the palm tree remains a favourite tale in mystic verse. Muhammad ﷺ would place his arm on a palm while preaching and after the construction of the pulpit, the tree wept pining for his touch.[1] Rumi questions: 'Should we then be lower than the sighing palm trunk?' The Prophet proclaimed: 'Before me every Prophet was given a miracle and they practiced it in their lifetime. Isa cured the sick and revived the dead. Musa was given the cane and I have been given the permanent miracle of the Quran which will remain till the Hour is established.'

Muhammad ﷺ is referred to as an *Ummi*, unlettered, for he did not know how to read or write. Muslim mystics view this attribute as the mystery of the Prophet's proximity with Allah. Muhammad ﷺ was not simply the cup-bearer of Allah's wisdom and guidance, but the cup itself. Rumi describes the Prophet as, 'the vessel with which this wine was offered to mankind'.[2] The mystic poet adds:

A hundred thousand books of poetry
Became ashamed before the Ummi's word.[3]

Muhammad ﷺ exemplified the mysteries Allah shares with His friends. The Messenger revealed mystic secrets to some among his trusted companions. 'One who is revived by knowledge never dies.' Sufis understand this as the knowledge of Divine love.

THE POLITICS OF EARLY ISLAM

In the early days of Islam, Sufism was the personal expression of religion rather than an organized community discipline. Sufis embraced a life of contemplation rebelling against the formalization of religion by the authorities. Thankfully, their endeavours succeeded in ensuring that Islam did not remain confined to a legalistic and ritualistic moral code.

The Omayyad dynasty came to power in 661 AD, after the assassination of Imam Ali, the fourth caliph of the Muslim Caliphate. Contemplative Islam suffered a setback as the new rulers focused their energies on expanding the Muslim empire. Schimmel observes: 'The resistance of the pious circles to the government grew stronger and was expressed in theological debates about the right ruler of the faithful and the conditions for the leadership of the community.'[4] During this period the mystics began to agitate against the stipulation of laws that stifled the freedom of personal spiritual quest.

When the Abbasids came to power in 750 AD, theological issues began to be freely discussed, resulting in the four schools of Islamic jurisprudence. These were formed by Imam Abu Hanifa (d. 767 AD), Imam ibn Malik Anas (d. 795 AD), Imam Shafai (d. 820 AD) and Imam Ahmad ibn Hanbal (d. 855 AD). Their teachings differ from one another but are all based on the Quran and prophetic traditions. These debates on Islam created the space for mystics to explore and promote their philosophies.

Madinah, the city to which Muhammad ﷺ migrated, became the first centre of Islamic mysticism. The early Muslim mystics included Bilal, Salman Farsi, Ammar bin Yassir, Masud al Hudhali and other companions of the Prophet. Commenting on their piety, asceticism and mortification the Prophet said, 'Rejoice, for whoever preserves the state in which you are shall be among my comrades in paradise.'

The early mystics usually lived in solitude outside the city in small hermitages, often accompanied by their circle of followers. Absorbed in meditation and prayer, they were devoid of worldly desires often using beds of straw with bricks for pillows. Their attire was simple, and although strict about ritual purity, they remained unconcerned with outward appearances.

Sufism blossomed in Iraq, Syria, Egypt, Persia and Central Asia. Fariduddin Attar's treatise *Tazkiratul Auliya* contains an authoritative account of 142 Sufis. It provides detailed accounts of the ninth and tenth century Sufis, including Rabia Basri, Hasan of Basra, Junayd of Baghdad and Dhun Nun of Egypt, among many others. Later, Sufi scholars such as Imam Ghazali, Abu Said Ibn Khair, Ibn al Arabi and Mevlana Rumi added scholarly and literary dimensions to Sufism. Rumi's *Mathnawi* and Attar's lyrical *Mantiq ut Tair* are classic masterpieces detailing the Sufi way. Sufis celebrate the spirit of Islam beyond the compulsory ritual prayer. Anecdotes from their lives illustrate the hardships and joys that they experience while drowning in the mystic ocean.

الله

IMAM ALI (D. 661 AD)

Prophet Muhammad ﷺ proclaimed: 'I am the city of knowledge and Ali is its gate.' Imam Ali defined spirituality as 'Knowing Allah through the Light of Allah.'

Ali, the son of Abu Talib ibn Abd al Muttalib, was the cousin and son-in-law of the Prophet. Ali's mother was going around the Kaaba, the House of Allah in Makkah, when she felt the pangs of childbirth and delivered the baby inside its precincts. Prophet Muhammad ﷺ,

the first person to embrace the child, named him Ali meaning 'the exalted one'.

Prophet Muhammad ﷺ transmitted his esoteric knowledge to Ali making him the vital link in the spiritual chains connecting Sufis to the Prophet, and eventually to Allah. Spiritual benevolence continues to flow through Ali, the acknowledged Imam of the *Walis*, friends of Allah for all times to come.

Imam Ali was martyred, while leading the morning prayers, by a poison-coated sword on the 21st of Ramadan in the city of Kufa. He was survived by his sons Imam Hasan and Imam Hussain. After the death of the Prophet, Ali became the fourth and last of the rightly guided caliphs known as *Khulafa e Rashideen* of the Muslim Caliphate. Acclaimed for his eloquence, good governance, and spirituality, Imam Ali became the principal authority on the Quran and Islamic jurisprudence.

الله

UWAIS QARNI (D. 657 AD)

Upon hearing that Prophet Muhammad ﷺ had lost two of his teeth in the Battle of Uhud, Uwais of Qaran broke all his teeth, for he did not know which of the Prophet's teeth had been martyred. The Messenger called him the best of the *Taabeen*, successors of the Prophet's Companions, and advised his followers, 'Get Uwais Qarni to pray for your forgiveness.'

Uwais's duty to his blind and ailing mother prevented him from visiting Muhammad ﷺ in Madinah. Allah spoke through the Prophet: 'Allah, Exalted and Mighty is He, loves of His creation the God-fearing, the pure in the heart, those who are hidden, and those who are innocent, whose face is dusty, whose hair is unkempt, whose stomach is empty, and who, if he asks permission to enter to the rulers, is not granted it, and if he were to ask for a gentle lady in marriage, he would be refused, and when he leaves the world it does not miss him, and if he goes out, his going out is not noticed, and if he falls sick, he is not attended to, and if he dies, he is not accompanied to his grave.'[5]

When the companions enquired where someone like that could be found, Muhammad ﷺ replied, 'Uwais al Qarni is such a one.' Once the Prophet said, '*nafas ar rahman*, the breath of the Merciful, comes to me from Yemen. There is a man at Qaran who at Resurrection will intercede for a multitude of my people, as many as the sheep of Rabia and Mudhar.' Shortly before he died, Muhammad ﷺ described Uwais and instructed Umar and Ali to find the man from Qaran and present his cloak to him. After the Prophet passed away, his companions found Uwais engaged in prayer in a desert. Uwais accompanied Imam Ali to Kufa and was martyed while fighting along with him against the forces of Muawiyah at the battle of Siffin.

Uwais Qarni's story continues to be a favourite in Sufi circles for it represents a spiritual connection with Muhammad ﷺ. Uwais wrote to the Prophet of his longing to meet him and cited the reasons preventing the journey. The Messenger wrote back saying that Uwais' duty to his mother was more important than an audience with him. Uwais was guided solely by Divine grace without the mediation of a living Master. Since then, Sufis who achieve mystic illumination outside the regulated discipline of Sufi orders are known as Uwaisis.

الله

SALMAN FARSI (D. 657 AD)

Salman became the first translator of the Quran into a foreign language, Persian. The seeker was one among the poor who made the Prophet's mosque their home. Known as *Ahle Suffa*, People of the Bench, these people had renounced the world and were looked after by the Prophet's family. Most Sufi orders invoke Salman Farsi's name following that of Imam Ali and Uwais Qarni, linking their spiritual chains to Prophet Muhammad 咖.

The story of Salman the Persian illustrates the search of a true mystic in the search of truth. Salman was born near the city of Isfahan to a Zoroastrian family. Drawn towards Christianity, the young lad often visited the monks. His apprehensive father kept the boy virtually a prisoner in the house. Salman ran away from home and reached Syria where he met many religious preachers, eventually becoming the disciple of a Christian monk. An old, ailing priest infomed Salman that Christian scriptures had prophesied the coming of the last and final prophet of God. He described the characteristics as foretold in holy scriptures, adding that the prophet would be of Arab origin.

When news travelled that a Messenger of God had arrived in the Arabian Peninsula, Salman decided to travel to Makkah. Along the way, the Persian was deceived by a group of Bedouin who promised to help him reach his destination. The Bedouin sold Salman to a Jew who took him to Madinah and put the slave to work on his date plantations. After some months, Salman heard that a man proclaiming himself to be the Messenger of God had migrated from the city of Makkah to Madinah. He recalled his last religious teacher telling him that the true Prophet would be driven out from his motherland and would take refuge in a land filled with date trees. Other signs of prophecy were that the Messenger would not eat anything given out of charity but only edibles presented as gifts. Finally, a distinctive seal of prophecy would be concealed between his shoulders.

When Salman met Muhammad 咖 in Madinah, he offered the Messenger some food clarifying that it was procured with money intended for charity. Muhammad 咖 did not eat it and distributed the food to the hungry. Another time, Salman offered food as a gift to the Prophet who himself ate and shared the food with his companions. On another occasion, realizing that Salman was tryng to steal a glance at him, Muhammad 咖 let his cloak drop a little.

On noticing the seal between the Prophet's shoulder blades, Salman accepted Islam.

Muhammad ﷺ later helped buy Salman's freedom from the Jew by agreeing to plant a certain number of trees in the date plantations. This garden where the Messenger along with his companions planted trees to complete the agreement, remains a revered site in Madinah. Salman became one of the Prophet's most devout followers, honoured for his wisdom, piety and erudition.

ﷲ

HASAN AL BASRI (D. 728 AD)

Aware of the dangers in a society based on worldly pursuits, Hasan of Basra continuously reminded people of the life Hereafter. 'O son of Adam you will die alone and enter the tomb alone, and it is with you alone that the reckoning will be made. Why care so much for this perishable world? Be with this world as if you had never been there and with the Otherworld as if you would never leave it.'[6]

Hasan al Basri, was an outstanding scholar and the son of a freed slave who became a jewel merchant. Born nine years after the death of Prophet Muhammad ﷺ, Hasan grew up in Madinah where Imam Ali is believed to have initiated him into the mystic path. His condemnation of outward pleasures earned him the reputation as the first Master of the Sufi doctrine. During Hasan's life, Arab conquests had crossed the Straits of Gibraltar and made inroads into the Indus Valley. Hasan spoke out against this expansionist attitude of the rulers.[7]

Hasan would say, 'Sheep are more aware than human beings for they respond to the warning of the shepherd, but ignorant men disobey the commands of the Lord.' He met many of Prophet Muhammad's ﷺ companions, including 70 of those who fought at the battle of Badr. Hasan remains an important link in the transmission of many prophetic traditions and Sufi linkages. He spent the greater part of his life in Basra where he died.

الله

HABIB AJMI (D. 738 AD)

One day Habib Ajmi, the moneylender of Basra, visited a woman's house asking her to repay the money she owed him. The woman said that her husband was not at home and they had no money to repay their loans. The neck of the sheep that they ate the previous night was all that was left in the house. Habib then asked her to cook the leftover meat for him but was told that there was no wood for fuel. Habib got the wood from the market, telling the woman it would be added to the debt. While the food was cooking on the stove, a beggar came to the house whom Habib sent away commenting, 'If we give you what we have got, you will not become rich but we will become poor.'[8] The hungry beggar left unfed and when the woman looked at the saucepan she saw that the food had turned to black blood. She shrieked out loud blaming Habib for his cursed practice of usury which had caused the evil omen. The incident had a deep impact on Habib who repented by giving away all his possessions and turning to mysticism.

The eloquent sermons of Hasan of Basra brought about Habib's conversion to an ascetic lifestyle. He became one of Hasan's most gifted disciples and built a hermitage on the banks of the Euphrates. Habib's Persian descent hampered his efforts to speak Arabic fluently. Once, unaware of his master's presence, Habib was leading the ritual prayer. Hasan thought of joining in but finding fault with Habib's pronunciation, refrained from praying with his disciple. That night Hasan dreamt of God saying to him: 'Hasan, you found My pleasure but did not understand its value. I cherish the purity of heart more than mere pronunciation.'

الله

IBRAHIM IBN ADHAM (D. 790 AD)

One night Ibrahim ibn Adham, the Prince of Balkh lay asleep on a luxurious bed in his palace. He heard some noises that seemed to come from the roof. On enquiring about the commotion, Ibrahim heard a voice saying, 'I am looking for a camel.' The prince replied that looking for a camel on the palace rooftop was foolish. The voice retorted, 'O ignorant one, it is just as foolish to seek God in the palace wearing silken clothes and sleeping on a golden couch.' Mystic fire alighted in the prince's heart and he headed for the jungles, leaving his wealth and family.

The prince's life often finds comparison with Gautam Buddha, for both renounced their kingdoms to pursue inner enlightenment. Ibrahim had an entire state under his command where 40 gold maces were carried before and after him. Numerous stories describe his awakening and spiritual achievements. One tale recounts how Gabriel was instructed to inscribe Ibrahim's name on top of the scroll containing the names of Allah's friends.

Once Ibrahim sat by the Tigris river stitching his robe. Someone came up to him and asked what he had achieved by giving up a kingdom. Ibrahim threw his needle into the water and then asked the river for the needle. A thousand fishes popped up in the river each carrying a needle of gold in their mouths. Ibrahim admonished them saying, 'I want my own needle.' A feeble little fish ducked into the water and gave the mystic back his needle. Ibrahim explained the miracle as a small demonstration of Allah's grace on him.[9]

The first Sufi to classify the stages of *zuhd*, piety, Ibrahim held that a man could achieve the ranks of righteousness by following the journey of six steps. He must close the door of bounty and open the door of hardships; close the door of dignity and open the door of humility; close the door of repose and open the door of striving;

Allah Baqi: One whose existence is endless.

close the door of sleep and open the door of vigilance; close the door of wealth and open the door of poverty; and finally close the door of worldly expectations and open the door of preparation for the next world. Ibrahim is the proverbial example of true poverty, abstinence and trust in God.

الله

RABIA AL ADAWIYAH OF BASRA (D. 801 AD)

Rabia's celebrated prayer best demonstrates the Sufi approach, 'Oh God, if I worship thee in the fear of Hell, burn me in Hell; and if I worship thee in the hope of Paradise; exclude me from Paradise; but if I worship Thee for Thine own sake, withhold not Thine Everlasting beauty.' One tale recounts Rabia running while carrying a torch in one hand and a pail of water in the other. When asked the meaning of her actions, Rabia replied, 'I am going to burn paradise with the fire and dampen the fires of hell with this water so that people love God for the sake of God and not for want of paradise or the fear of hell.'

Islam's most celebrated woman mystic, Rabia introduced the concept of Divine love in Sufi philosophy. She remained a celibate since her overwhelming love for God left no room for any worldly relationship. Rabia's remarkable spiritual achievements are illustrated in countless anecdotes. Her name meant 'the fourth' as her father already had three daughters.

Born in the poorest of homes, many miraculous events took place at the time of Rabia's birth. There was no oil in the house to light the lamp or clothes to wrap the newborn. That night, the distressed father dreamt that Prophet Muhammad ﷺ said, 'Do not be sorrowful, for this daughter is a blessed one whose intercession will be desired by seventy thousand of my community.' Muhammad ﷺ then asked him to go to the Amir of Basra and remind him that he had forgotten to send the 100 Prophetic salutations and blessings on Friday. The ruler was thus to pay 400 *dinars* as penance.[10] On learning that the Prophet had remembered him, the delighted Amir made an offering of 2,000 *dinars* to Rabia's father.

The untimely death of her parents left Rabia and her little sisters orphaned in childhood. The family's misfortunes continued and the sisters were separated in a storm. Rabia was then kidnapped and sold as a slave. During the day she attended to her master, while she spent the nights in prayer. One day while she was praying, her master saw a light over her head that illuminated the whole house. On realizing that she was consumed by the love of God, he freed her. Rabia began to live in the wilderness amongst the deer, mountain goats and asses. A broken pitcher, reed mat and a brick pillow were her only belongings.

Rabia's biographers have recorded the interesting conversation between her and Ibrahim Adham. Ibrahim took 14 years to travel from Balkh to Makkah for he stopped at every crossing to offer prayers. Finally, on reaching the Kaaba, he saw the structure missing, and he heard a voice saying, 'The Kaaba has gone to welcome a woman who is approaching the place.' A distraught Ibrahim questioned Rabia on her arrival, 'O Rabia, what is this disturbance and burden you have brought in the world?' Rabia asked the former prince why he had taken so many years to arrive at the House of God. Ibrahim explained that he had been busy with prayer. Rabia retorted back that she came to the House of God with pure love, while he engaged in ritual. After completing the pilgrimage, Rabia returned to Basra and immersed herself in the love of God.

Once Rabia met Hasan al Basri near a lake. Hasan flung his prayer rug on the waters and asked Rabia to join him in prayer. Rabia replied, 'When you show off your spiritual wares in the world, display things that are beyond most humans.' Rabia then threw her prayer mat in the air. Sitting upon the mat in mid-air, she challenged Hasan to join her in prayer. The display was beyond Hasan's spirituality and Rabia sought to console him. 'Hasan, what you can do, fishes can do and what I did any fly can do. The real work is outside these tricks so let us engage in true devotion.'[11]

Islam does not prevent a woman from reaching the highest rank in the mystic hierarchy. When men taunted Rabia about women not achieving prophetic ranks, she retorted: 'There were no eunuchs among women either.' Rabia explained self-worship as an essentially male characteristic. Her poetry throws light on her unique relationship with God:

> *O my Joy and my Desire and my Refuge*
> *My Friend and my Sustainer and My goal,*
> *Thou art my Intimate, and longing for thee sustains me.*
> *Were it not for Thee, O my Life and my Friend.*
> *How should I have been distraught over the spaces of this*
>   *earth.*
> *How many favours have been bestowed,*
> *and how much hast Thou given me*
> *Of gifts and grace and assistance*
> *Thy Love is now my desire and My bliss*
> *And has been revealed to the eye of my heart that was athirst*
> *I have none beside Thee,*
> *Who dost Thou make the desert blossom*
> *Thou art my Joy, firmly established within me*
> *If thou are satisfied with me, then*
> *O Desire of my heart, My happiness has appeared.*[12]

الله

MARUF KHARKI (D. 815 AD)

Maruf authored the definition of Divine love, explaining it as a gift from God and not an acquisition. He preached that there were three signs of true generosity: to keep faith without resistance, to praise without being incited, and to give without being asked. These attributes belonged to God and men had borrowed them from Him. 'It is God who, keeps faith with those who love him, gives without being asked and does not banish those with evil actions.'[13]

Born to Christian parents in Khorasan, numerous stories describe Maruf's conversion to Islam. He embraced Islam under the tutelage of Imam Ali ibn Musa al Reza. Later, a disciple of Dawud Tai, Maruf became the leading Sufi Master of Baghdad. He led an austere life and his steadfastness in prayer was legendary. People from far and near sought Maruf's blessings for his prayers were believed to be granted. One of Maruf's disciples recounts that once when they were in Baghdad, he saw a scar on the mystic's face and insisted on knowing what caused it. Maruf explained, 'Last night I was praying and desired to circumambulate the Kaaba. I approached the nearby well of Zam Zam where my foot slipped and my face struck the well resulting in this scar.'[14] The well and the Kaaba are in Makkah, thus Maruf had referred to visiting the House of God in a spiritual state.

On Maruf's death, his pupil Sari Saqti dreamt of the Master seated at the foot of the Divine throne. God asked His angels, 'Who is this?' They answered that God knew best. Then God told them, 'This is Maruf, who was intoxicated with the love of Me and will not regain his senses except by meeting Me face to face.'

الله

SAYYIDA NAFISA (D. 824 AD)

The people of Egypt were in great distress for they feared a famine would come about. It led them to seek Sayyida Nafisa's intercession with God for mercy. The pious woman gave them her veil and asked the people to cast it in the flowing waters of the Nile. The Egyptians acted on her advice and soon the waters rose to the desired heights.

Born in Makkah, Sayyida Nafisa's great-grandfather was Imam Hasan, the revered grandson of Prophet Muhammad 🕊. Her father held the position of the governor of Madinah. Nafisa memorized the Quran and studied Islamic jurisprudence in great detail. She married Isaq, the son of Imam Jafar al Siddiq, who founded the Jafari School of Islamic jurisprudence and migrated with him to Egypt.

Nafisa offered the mandatory prayers behind her father in the Prophet's mosque, often going inside the sacred chamber containing Muhammad's 🕊 tomb. Once her father addressed the Prophet, '*Ya Rasul Allah*, O Beloved Prophet of Allah! I am pleased with my daughter Nafisa.' One day the Prophet appeared to Nafisa's father in a dream saying, '*Ya* Hasan! I am pleased with your daughter and because you are pleased, Allah is pleased with her.'

Nafisa gained a reputation for her piety and scholarly knowledge of Islam. Many religious scholars including Imam Shafai, who founded one of the four major schools of Islamic jurisprudence, attended Nafisa's discourses and discussed matters of religious law with her. Before Imam Shafai died in 820 AD, he had requested that Nafisa perform the funeral prayers for him. His body was taken to her house, for her constant fasting had rendered her too weak to travel.

Nafisa prepared her own grave in her house by reciting the Quran 6,000 times inside it. On her deathbed, she was as usual fasting and those around her tried to compel her to break the fast. Nafisa refused since throughout her life she had desired to meet God in a state of fasting. She recited verses from the Quran that assure an abode of peace for those blessed by Him. Nafisa's husband wished to take her body for burial to Madinah but the people of Egypt pleaded that she be buried in Cairo. Eventually, she was buried in the grave she had prepared in her home. The numerous titles bestowed on Nafisa include *Nafisat al'ilmi wal Marifa*, Woman of Knowledge, *Nafisat al Tahira*,Woman of Purity and *Nafisat al Darayn*, Woman of Both the Worlds.

ﷲ

FATIMA OF NISHAPUR (D 838 AD)

The Egyptian Sufi Master Dhun Nun was once asked which mystic he ranked the highest, and he replied, 'A lady in Makkah called Fatima Nishapuri. She is one of the friends of God who is my teacher.' Fatima counselled Dhun Nun to watch over his actions never giving in to passions of the self and to remain devoted to God. A towering figure in the history of women mystics, she spent most of her life in Makkah. Another legendary Sufi, Bayazid Bistami said, 'There was no spiritual station, of which I told Fatima, that she had not undergone.'

ﷲ

DHUN NUN MISRI (D. 859 AD)

Dhun Nun could read the mysteries of hermetic wisdom concealed in the ancient Egyptian hieroglyphs. The people of Egypt accused him of heresy, due to his mystic ways, resulting in his imprisonment at Baghdad. According to legend, when his chains were untied, Dhun Nun fell and blood poured from a gash on his head. Not a drop touched his forehead, hair or clothes and it spilt directly on the floor and disappeared immediately. This was interpreted as Divine intervention. Presented before the Caliph, Dhun Nun answered the charges against him. Moved by his eloquence, the Caliph became his disciple and allowed the mystic to return to Cairo.

The Sufi who came from the ancient kingdom of Nubia, travelled extensively in Arabia and Syria studying under different teachers. Dhun Nun shaped the Sufi doctrine of *wahdat ul wujood,* the Oneness of Being, that became central to the worldwide Sufi movement. He defined the attributes of a Sufi as one who is devoid of duplicity, whose speech accords with his behaviour, and whose silence indicates his state. 'Sufis are those whom God had invested with the radiance of His Love, upon whose heads He sets the crown of His joy.'

Enjoying a command over the Arabic language, Dhun Nun developed the Sufi philosophy. He separated *marifa*, knowledge of God, from *ilm*, intellect—connecting it with *mohabba*, the love of God. Dhun Nun is the most famous Sufi of the Malamati Order—the hidden spiritualists who trod the path of affliction and blame. These Sufis behave in inappropriate ways to make sure that people abuse and shun them.

When Dhun Nun died, the following words were written in green on his forehead: 'This is a friend of God. He died in the love of God. This is the slain of God by the sword of God.' While the bier was being carried for burial on a hot afternoon, the birds of the air gathered above, weaving their wings together so as to shadow the body throughout the journey to the graveyard.[15] That night 70 people dreamt of Prophet Muhammad ﷺ saying to them, 'I have come to welcome Dhun Nun, the friend of God.'

The Egyptian reminded his companions of Moses' conversation with God. Moses had asked, 'Oh God, where shall I seek thee.' And God had replied, 'Among those whose hearts are broken.' Moses then said, 'Oh Lord, No heart is more broken and despairing than mine.' And God proclaimed, 'Then I am where thou art.' Dhun Nun wrote:

> *I die, and yet not dies in me*
> *The ardour of my love for thee*
> *Nor hath Thy love, my only goal,*
> *Assuaged the fever of my soul*
>
> *To Thee alone my spirit cries*
> *In Thee my whole ambition lies*
> *And still Thy wealth is far above*
> *The poverty of my small love*
> *I turn to Thee in my final request*
> *To Thee my loud lament is bought.*[16]

الله

Haris Al Muhasibi (d 857 ad)

Whenever Haris al Muhasibi stretched out his hand for food of dubious lawfulness, a nerve in the back of his finger became taut and the finger did not obey the command to move.[17] Providence prevented Haris from eating food brought with the money acquired through usury, gambling, or other means not permissible by Islam. Born in 781 AD in Basra, Muhasibi spent his life in Baghdad where he studied under the leading Sufi teachers of the time. His title comes from the Arabic word *Muhasaba,* meaning self-examination.

Junayd of Baghdad was one of Muhasibi's famous students whose enquiries were turned into books by the teacher. Muhasibi's countless writings include the *Kitab al Re'aya*, containing the principles of Sufism.[18] Imam Ghazali, the Master of moderate medieval Sufism, depended largely on the works of Muhasibi. He authored *Fasl fi Mohabba*, another famed manual on the love of God. Muhasibi wrote that the clearest sign of Divine love is that one should completely surrender to God with continuous meditation and prayer. However, the extent of this love depends on Divine grace bestowed on the devotee. He preached the relentless fight against man's lower nature—not just the outward struggle of the ascetic against the flesh, but also a subtle psychological analysis of every thought along with uninterrupted spiritual training.

الله

Abul Hasan Sari Saqti (d. 867 ad)

One day the bazaars of Baghdad caught fire and Sari Saqti was informed that his shop had burnt down. Relieved, he exclaimed, 'Then I am free from the care of it.' It was later discovered that although all the other nearby shops had been gutted in the fire, Saqti's shop had remained in tact. But having decided to quit, Saqti gave away everything to the poor and embraced the Sufi path.[19] The trader became a disciple of Maruf Kharki, the eminent Baghdad Sufi.

One day, Kharki left an orphan with Saqti, asking him to clothe and feed the child. The Master prayed that his disciple lose interest in worldly matters. Saqti looked after the child and soon distributed all his possessions. His discourses overwhelmed listeners and changed their lives. The king's companion, Ahmad, once sat among the audience. He was dressed in silk finery and accompanied by slaves. Saqti's words touched Ahmad's soul who wept till he fainted. The next day he informed the Master that he wished to seek God.

Saqti asked, 'Which path do you wish to follow? The mystic path or the way of the law. That of the elect or that of the multitude?' He elaborated that while the way of the multitude required following Islamic laws, the way of the elect was to forget the world completely. On hearing the Master, Ahmad set out in the wilderness. Some days later Ahmad's mother came wailing to Saqti requesting him that her son be traced. Saqti grieved at the mother's sadness and assured her of Ahmad's return. Ahmad reappeared the next day and looking at his impoverished state, his family began to wail pleading that he return home and not leave his son orphaned. Ahmad refused to do so and berated his Master for having informed his family of his whereabouts. When Ahmad's mother insisted that his child should accompany him, he stripped the boy of his fine clothing and flung a strip of goat wool over him. He gave the child some money and asked him to go on his own. Ahmad's mother then took the child back, while her son left for the wilderness.

Many years later a man came to Saqti with the message that Ahmad was remembering him. Saqti found Ahmad lying on the ground breathing his last. As Saqti made arrangements for Ahmad's funeral, countless people walked towards the burial site. Surprised,

Saqti asked what brought them to the graveyard. They replied that the previous night a voice from Heaven was heard saying, 'Whoever desires to pray over a friend of God, go to the cemetery of Shuniziya.'[20]

Saqti elaborated on *maqaam*, spiritual stations—preaching that true wisdom was non-attachment to the self and devotion to the truth. Junayd of Baghdad and Abu Bakr al Kharraz were both Saqti's disciples who achieved recognition for their mystic philosophies.[21]

الله

BAYAZID BISTAMI (D. 874 AD)

Bayazid expressed unity with God in an unusual way: 'For 30 years God most High was my mirror and that which I was, am no more, for "I" and "God" are a denial of the Unity of God. Since I am no more, God most High is His own mirror. Now I say that God is the mirror of myself, for with my tongue He speaks and I have passed away.'

The son of a Zoroastrian, Bayazid made a lasting impact on Sufism in Persia. One of the most famous Persian Sufis, he became a theologian, a philosopher and poet. He wrote:

> *If you aspire communion with God*
> *Be kind, magnanimous, just to your fellow beings*
> *If you desire effulgence like the dawn*
> *Be generous to all like the Sun.*

The revered Imam Jafar was among the teachers of Bayazid. The mystics look upon the intoxicated Sufi as one through whom God spoke. Junayd of Baghdad said 'Bayazid holds the ranks amongst us as Gabriel amongst the angels.'[22] When asked his age, Bayazid put it at four years explaining, 'I have been veiled for 70 years, but I have seen Him for four years, the period when God is not seen does not belong to one's life.' One day looking for the mystic someone knocked at his door, and Bayazid replied, 'I too am seeking Bayazid for the last 30 years but have not found him.'

Once on a pilgrimage to Makkah, Bayazid encountered a poor man who asked how much money the traveller had on him. Bayazid admitted to possessing 200 dirhams. The man requested Bayazid to give him the money to save his children from dying of hunger. He suggested that Bayazid circumambulate around him seven times instead of the Kaaba. Bayazid acted accordingly and went into a state of ecstasy proclaiming: 'Subhaani: Glory be to me. How great is My Majesty.' Accusations of heresy were hurled at him and he was turned out of Bistam.

Bayazid's disciples attacked him for a similar utterance, 'Under my garment there is nothing but God.' When they tried to kill him, their knives turned around and wounded them instead. Bayazid demonstrated the perfect mystic state where love, the lover, and the beloved became one. His famed prayer is, 'O lord! Remove the veil of mine and Thine that exists between Thee and me, that I have no existence separate from Thy essence. O Lord, poverty and fasting have brought me close to Thee. I recognize Thee only through Thy grace.'

الله

SAHL IBN ABDULLAH TUSTARI (D. 896 AD)

People said that Sahl ibn Abdullah walked on water without getting his feet wet. Numerous miracles are attributed to Sahl who kept them a secret. Lions and other wild beasts were seen visiting him and he tended to them. The mystic's house in Tustar, where he was born, came to be referred to as 'The house of the wild beasts.' During mystical auditions, Sahl would go into ecstatic raptures that would last for days during which he never ate a morsel. In winter such mystic moments would leave his clothes drenched with sweat.[23]

Sahl came to be known as *Shaykh al Arifin,* Master of the Knowers. In 874 AD, he was forced to seek refuge in Basra where he died. After going on a pilgrimage to Makkah at the age of 16, Sahl trained in mystical discipline for some time under Dhun Nun Misri, while Mansur al Hallaj, the martyred mystic of Iraq studied under him.[24]

By the age of seven Sahl had memorized the Quran and begun to fast, his only food being barley bread. He practised perpetual fasting only broke the fast with an ounce of barley bread without any relish or salt. In this way a single dirham worth of flour would last him a full year. He resolved to break his fast every three days, and later every five days, till he reached the point of breaking it once every 25 days.[25] Sahl believed that supererogatory fasts could bring the gift of miracles and said, 'Hunger is Allah's secret on earth and He does not confide it to one who divulges it.'

When the ruler of Tustar was sick, he ordered the mystic to be produced in court to seek his prayers. Sahl told the king that prayers were effective only for those who were penitent, and he insisted that all the wrongfully detained prisoners be released from the jails. The king acted accordingly and soon regained his health through the mystic's prayers. He offered generous amounts of money as reward, which Sahl refused to accept.

Sahl defined a Sufi as, 'Someone who is pure and filled with reflection and has renounced the human for the Divine; someone for whom gold and mud have the same value, that is to say, someone who doesn't desire or wish anything but his Lord and Master.'

He wrote, 'Allah is the *qibla* (direction of Muslim prayer) of intention, intention is the *qibla* of the heart, the heart is the *qibla* of the body, the body is the *qibla* of the limbs and the limbs are the *qibla* of the world.' Sahl authored the earliest mystic commentary of the Quran explaining the hidden secrets of each verse. As he explains:

The heart of the Knowers have eyes
That see what onlookers cannot see.

When Sahl's body was being carried for burial, accompanied by hundreds of his disciples, a Jew came out on the street to enquire about the commotion. He shrieked saying that he could see angels descending from heaven stroking the bier with their wings.[26]

الله

ABUL HASAN NURI (D. 907 AD)

When Nuri spoke, a light radiated from his mouth illuminating his surroundings. The name Nuri comes from the Arabic word *nur,* meaning light. Abul Hasan Nuri of Baghdad taught the philosophy of *mohabba,* love of God. He preached that passionate fervour must accompany the practice of worship and spoke of being an *ashiq,* lover of God.

The Syrian Ahmad Hawaari was Nuri's Master and both made several pilgrimages to Makkah during the period of tutelage. Nuri succeeded Abu Hamza (d. 881 AD) as the leader of the Hululs, the extreme faction of the Baghdad Sufis. Nuri defined a Sufi as, 'One who belongs to no one and nothing belongs to him. The Sufi gains knowledge through God and every action of his is through Him.'

During the orthodox rule, some mystic friends of Nuri's, including Shibli, were victimized for preaching the Sufi doctrine of pure love. In a gesture of rare friendship, Nuri volunteered to suffer the hardships in place of the accused. Caliph Ghulam Khalil had ordered the Hululs to be hanged. Moved by Nuri's gesture, the state judge acquitted them. After returning to Baghdad, Nuri had the audacity to smash the wine jars that were being carried to the palace and was exiled to the city of Basra. Later, he returned to Baghdad where he died after six years.[27]

In the name of Allah, Most Gracious, Most Merciful.

Nuri's death occurred in a peculiar way. One day a blind man was crying 'God. God!' Nuri went up to him saying, 'What do you know of Him? If you know, you still live?'

Having said that Nuri lost his senses and overpowered with mystic yearning, walked into the freshly harvested reed beds. The reeds pierced Nuri's feet and with every drop of blood that fell, the word Allah appeared. Unconscious of the pain, Nuri bled to death.[28] Nuri's verses describe his passionate love for God:

So passionate my love is, I do yearn
To keep his memory constantly in mind:
But O, the ecstasy with which I burn
Sears out my thoughts, and strikes my memory blind.

And, marvel upon marvel, ecstasy
Itself is swept away; now far now near
My Lover stands, and all the faculty
Of memory is swept up in hope and fear.

On *wahdat ul wujood*, the Oneness of God, Nuri sang:

I had supposed that, having passed away
From self in concentration, I should blaze
A path to Thee, but ah! No creature may
Draw nigh, Thee, save on Thy appointed ways.
I cannot longer live, Lord, without Thee:
Thy hand is everywhere: I may not flee.

Some have denied through hope to come to Thee,
And Thou hast wrought in them their high design:
Lo! I have severed every thought from me,
And died to selfhood, that I might be Thine,
How long, my heart's Beloved? I am spent:
I can no more endure this banishment.[29]

الله

JUNAYD OF BAGHDAD (D. 910 AD)

Once on seeing a thief executed in Baghdad, Junayd went and kissed his feet. When onlookers asked for an explanation, the Sufi scholar replied, 'A thousand compassions be upon him for he proved to be a man true to his trade. He did his work so perfectly that he died for it.'

Abul Qasim al Junayd is considered the greatest exponent of the sober school of Sufism. A glass merchant like his father, Junayd gave up the family business to devote his life to Islamic studies. Sari Saqti, the brother of Junayd's mother was the leading Sufi of the time. As a child Junayd accompanied him on pilgrimages and participated in Sufi assemblies.

Saqti predicted that Junayd's special gift from God would be the power of his speech. When asked if the rank of a disciple could ever be higher than that of a Master, Saqti replied, 'There is manifest proof of this. The rank of Junayd is higher than mine.' As a mark of respect, Junayd was reluctant to discourse on religion until his teacher was alive. Then one night Junayd dreamt of Prophet Muhammad ﷺ saying, 'O Junayd, speak to the people, for God has made thy words the means of saving a multitude of mankind.' That day, Saqti sent for the disciple asking him to obey the Prophetic command. Junayd wondered how the Master learnt of the dream and Saqti answered, 'I dreamt of God who told me that He sent the Apostle to bid you to preach.'[30]

Junayd studied Islamic law and became the Qazi, chief judge of Baghdad, at a time when the clergy were extremely hostile to the Sufis. He held that mystic knowledge was for the select few and should not to be divulged to everyone.[31] He based the Sufi path on eight different attributes including submission, sincerity, liberality, patience, separation, woolen dress, wandering, and poverty as in the lives of the prophets. 'A Sufi must have the heart of Abraham which found salvation in this world by fulfilling God's commandments, the sorrow of David, the poverty of Jesus, the longing for communication with God like Moses, and the sincerity of Prophet Muhammad ﷺ.'[32]

Junayd developed the Sufi doctrine of *fana* and *baqa* that later determined the whole philosophy of orthodox Sufism. '*Fana* is the assimilation of the individual will in the will of God and is experienced by the grace of God. *Fana* is that He should cause thee to die from thyself and exist in Him. *Baqa* is the persistence of the real self in God and the departure of the lower self implies the appearance of the True self.'

Junayd further explained, 'The qualities of the Beloved should eventually replace that of the Lover.' He expresses the dual sense of union and separation:

> *Now that I have known, O Lord,*
> *What lies within my heart:*
> *In secret, from the world apart,*
> *My tongue hath talked with my Adored*
>
> *So in a manner we*
> *United are, and One;*
> *Yet otherwise disunion*
> *In our estate eternally*
>
> *Though from my grace profound*
> *Deep awe hath hid Thy face,*
> *In wondrous and ecstatic Grace*
> *I feel Thee touch my inmost ground.*[33]

Upon the insistence of the Caliph, Junayd was among those who signed the death warrant of Mansur Hallaj. He wrote, 'We judge according to the external law, as for the inward truth, God alone knows.' Junayd had counselled his student to act with restraint or his goblet would be stained with blood. Hallaj responded by predicting that when that happened, Junayd would wear the gown of a scholar. As foretold by the martyr, Junayd took off his Sufi robe and signed Hallaj's death warrant wearing the gown and turban of a scholar.[34]

Junayd's theory of *Tawhid*, Divine Unity, finds root in the pre-eternal covenant sworn by man with God as mentioned in the Quran. He believed that God separates men from Himself granting them individuality and making them absent when in union with Him.[35]

الله

MANSUR AL HALLAJ (D. 922 AD)

Hallaj was beheaded for proclaiming, '*Ana 'l Haqq*', 'I am the Truth' or 'I am God'. The martyr's words are among the most well-known utterances in Sufi history—one among the 99 names of Allah is, '*Al Haqq*'. The words are the mark of Hallaj's spiritual vocation, the cause of his condemnation, and the glory of his martyrdom.[36]

Hussain ibn Mansur al Hallaj, the most controversial figure of Sufism was condemned to death following a political trial in Baghdad, then an important city on the world stage. His heroic story stands for one madly in love with the Divine. Hallaj remains a powerful image in Arabic, Persian, Turkish, Punjabi, Sindhi and Urdu prose and poetry—as one who danced to the gallows and was martyred for upholding the truth. After years of imprisonment, Hallaj was put to death by the establishment. In mystic drunkenness he spoke of the unspoken mystery, lived and died for it.

Born in south Iran, Hallaj grew up in Wasit and Tustar where cotton was cultivated and *Hallaj*, cotton workers, like his father lived. After facing criticism for his beliefs, Hallaj travelled to the holy cities of Makkah and Madinah accompanied by nearly 400 disciples. Later, he took a boat to India and reached Sindh through Gujarat, calling people to the path of God. Hallaj's quest to study philosophy took him from Sindh to China and Central Asia. Eventually he returned to Baghdad and became a disciple of Junayd.

In prison, Mansur was questioned, 'What is love?' He answered: 'You will see it today and tomorrow and the day after tomorrow.' That day Hallaj's hands and feet were cut off, the next day he was beheaded and on the third day his ashes were strewn in the wind. The execution gave rise to many legends. Hallaj went dancing in his fetters to the gallows reciting a quatrain on his love for God. Most onlookers threw stones at him except for his Sufi friend Shibli, who threw a rose. Hallaj remarked, 'They do not know what they do but you should know.' The throwing of the rose gave birth to proverbs in various languages—how a rose thrown by a friend hurts more than a stone thrown by one's enemies. Hallaj often urged the people of Baghdad to kill him so that he could be united with God. 'Kill me O trustworthy friends for in my being killed, is my life.'

Thirteen heavy chains were tied around Hallaj's body while he went to the gallows. When asked why he strutted in such a proud manner, he replied, 'Because I am going to the slaughterhouse.' With a mantle thrown around his shoulders and a loincloth around his middle, Hallaj kissed the wood, climbed the gibbet and turned towards Makkah to offer his final prayer ending with the words:

> And these thy servants gathered to slay me, in zeal for Thy religion and in desire to win Thy favour, forgive them, O lord and have mercy on them; for verily if Thou hast revealed to them that which Thou hadst revealed to me, they would not have done what they have done; and if Thou hast hidden from me that which Thou hast hidden from them, I should not have suffered this tribulation. Glory unto Thee in whatsoever Thou doest, and glory unto Thee in whatsoever willest.[37]

When Hallaj's limbs were cut off, the amputated parts resounded with the sound of *Ana 'l Haqq*. On the third day his body parts were burnt but continued to echo the same words. Finally, when the ashes were thrown into the Dajla river, they formed the words *Ana 'l Haqq*.

The water began to swell to dangerous heights till a disciple threw the martyr's garment on the river. He had been instructed by Hallaj to do so in order to appease the wrath of the river. The level of the waters subsided and some ashes collected from its banks were entombed. The mystics believe that on the Day of Judgement, Hallaj will be brought in fetters lest his ecstasy turns the world upside down.[38]

Hallaj left a considerable number of books containing prose and poetry describing his mystic passions. He gave Persian and Urdu poetry the everlasting imagery of the candle and the self-destructing moth, conveying the fate of true lovers. Other recurring images to convey mystic love are the wine cup, crescent, goblet of intoxication, and birds. The idea of union with the Beloved dominated Hallaj's writings:[39]

> *I am He who I love, and He who I love is I*
> *We are two spirits dwelling in one body*
> *If thou see me, thou see us both*
> *And if thou see Him, thou see us both*
>
> *In that glory is no 'I' or 'We' or 'Thou'*
> *'I', 'We', 'Thou', and 'He' are all one thing.*[40]

الله

ABU BAKR SHIBLI (D. 946 AD)

In states of ecstasy, the eccentric Shibli often uttered sentences considered blasphemous: 'The fire of Hell will not touch me and I can easily extinguish it.' A fellow disciple of Junayd, Shibli is a legendary figure in the history of Mansur Hallaj's execution. He remained the martyr's friend, delivering secret lectures attesting to his affection for Hallaj.

Born in Samara to a family of high public officials, Shibli became the governor of Demavend. A dispatch arrived and he set out with the governor of Rayy with a retinue of soldiers and slaves to present himself before the Caliph who honoured them with robes. On the way back to Demavend, the governor sneezed and wiped his face with the robe. Some soldiers saw this as an insult and reported it to the Caliph who handcuffed the governor dismissing him from the post.

Shibli addressed the Caliph, 'Prince, you are a human being and do not approve that your robe should be treated disrespectfully. The King of the World has given me honour and knowledge of Himself. How would He react if He knew I was using His robe as a handkerchief in the service of a mere mortal?'[41] Shibli left the court and went straight to the assembly of the Sufi Khayr al Nassaj who sent him to seek spiritual guidance from Junayd of Baghdad.

Junayd made the former governor beg in the streets of Baghdad. Each day Shibli gave the collected money to his Master for distribution amongst the poor. After a whole year of begging, Junayd told Shibli, 'You still have some pride and pomp left in you. Go and beg for another four years.' He continued to go from house to house till the day he told Junayd, 'I consider myself to be the least of all God's creatures.' Satisfied with Shibli's progress, Junayd informed the disciple that his faith had been perfected.

Once Shibli accosted someone crying for his dead beloved and said, 'O fool, why love someone who can die?' Legends grew around the mystic's obsessive passion for God. Overwhelmed with ecstasy, Shibli once threw himself into the Tigris river which surged and threw him back on the banks. Another time, he threw himself into fire and the flames did not affect him. He then found some hungry lions but the beasts did not devour him and fled away. Shibli cried, 'I am cursed for neither water nor fire will accept me.' Then an unseen voice said, 'He who is accepted by God will not be accepted by any other.' Declared insane, Shibli ended up being committed to an asylum. Hours before his death, he recited the verse:[42]

> *Whatever house Thou takest for Thine,*
> *No lamp is needed there to shine,*

Upon the day that men shall bring
Their proofs before the Judge and King
Our proof shall be, in that dreaded place
The longed for beauty of Thy face.

When the eighty-six-year-old Shibli lay dying, a group of people sat around to offer his funeral prayers. They asked him to recite the *shahadah*, declaration of Islam affirming that there is no god but Allah. Shibli said, 'If there is no God other than He, how can I utter a negative?' One of them tried to prompt the mystic to repeat the words of attestation. Amused, Shibli remarked, 'Look how a dead man is trying to awaken the living.' Shibli welcomed death whispering; 'I have joined the Beloved.'

الله

ABU AL HASAN KHARQANI (D. 1033 AD)

Legends recount Bayazid Bistami receiving the scent of Abul Hasan from Kharqan long before the mystic was born. During his prayers, Abul Hasan would be spiritually transported to Bistam where he received transmissions from Bayazid who had died in 874 AD.

Kharqani burned with intense love for God and declared he would not surrender his soul to the angel of death. He had received it from God and would return it only to Him. He once dreamt of God declaring that his longing of 60 years was not of any consequence for 'He had loved him in the pre-eternity of eternities.' Abul Hasan knew of his resurrection among the martyrs, 'I have been killed by the sword of longing for Thee.'[43]

Abu al Hasan Kharqani belonged to the town of Kharqan in Iran. He received guidance from the Master Abul al Abbas Ahmad Amuli. Commenting on Sufism, Kharqani said, 'It is an ocean that derives from three springs: the first, abstinence; the second, generosity; and the third, being independent of people. A true mystic is like a bird that has flown from its nest seeking food but has not found any. It then tries to make its way back to the nest, loses its way, and becomes bewildered, wishing but unable to go home.'

الله

ABU SAID IBN ABI KHAIR (D. 1049 AD)

Abu Said ibn Abi Khair reached perfection by ridding himself of any individuality. He once visited a place where people had collected for mourning. The arrival of the visitors was announced with their respective titles of honour. When the hosts enquired of Abu Said's title, the mystic replied, 'Go and tell them to make way for Nobody, the son of Nobody.'

The Sufi poet came from the Persian town of Mayhana and studied under Abu Ali Zihir and Husain al Sulami. He confessed that efforts to achieve spirituality with intellectual proof had failed. Abu Said spent seven years alone in the mountainous deserts of Mayhana. Later, he established a Sufi centre for those who wished to walk the mystic path. He preached, 'Sufism is the subsistence of the heart without any meditation.'[44]

He invented the poetic form of *Rubai*, quatrain to illustrate spiritual ideas, and composed the verses inscribed on his tomb in Mayhana:

> *Love flowed like blood beneath the skin, through veins*
> *Emptied me of myself filled me with the Beloved*
> *Till every limb every organ was seized and occupied*
> *Till only my name remains, the rest is It.*
>
> *I beg, nay charge Thee: Write on my gravestone*
> *'This was love's bondsman,' that's when I am gone*
> *Some wretch well versed in passion's ways may sigh*
> *And give me greetings, as he passes by.*

الله

ABU HAMID MUHAMMAD IBN MUHAMMAD AL GHAZALI (D. 1111 AD)

Imam Ghazali earned the title of *Hujjat ul Islam,* the Proof of Islam. Born in the Persian province of Tus, Ghazali arrived in Baghdad at the age of 33. He achieved recognition and wealth as the professor of Islamic theology at the prestigious Al Nizamiya University.

After some years of teaching, Ghazali felt the need to understand spirituality and resigned from the university. In his search for solitude, the celebrated philosopher distributed his wealth and left for Damascus. Ghazali took two mules loaded with books along with him. On the journey he encountered a robber who stole all the books despite his pleas to spare them. In Makkah Ghazali dreamt of Khidr, the immortal guide. Khidr explained that had the books not been stolen; Ghazali would have remained enslaved to them and never realized the knowledge of the heart.

After years of wandering, Ghazali resumed teaching. He integrated the outer law of the *Sharia* with the inner knowledge of the *Tareeqa.* Ghazali authored numerous books on Islam including the famous *Ihya Ulum al Din* (Revival of Religious Sciences). The book was burned in public but was later accepted as the greatest authority on Islam. It contributed immensely to the development of Islamic theology and influenced Western ideas and Christian philosophers of the Middle Ages.[45]

Ghazali felt enlightened by mystical experiences and his refutation of scholasticism, philosophy and poetry occupies a dozen pages in his *Munqidh.* In autobiographical passages he concludes with the admission:

> I turned my way to the Sufis. I knew it could not be traversed without
> doctrine and practice, that their doctrine lies in overcoming the
> appetites of the flesh and getting rid of its evil dispositions, so that

the heart may be cleared of all but God. The means of cleansing the heart is *dhikr*, the concentration of every thought upon Him. So I began by learning their doctrine from their books and saying of their Shaykhs, until I acquired much of their way as it is possible to acquire by learning and hearing, and saw plainly that what is most peculiar to them cannot be learned but can only be reached by immediate experience, ecstasy and inward transformation. How great is the difference between knowing the definition, causes and conditions of drunkenness and actually being drunk.

I became convinced that Sufis are men of feelings and not words. I had now acquired all the knowledge of Sufism that could be possible by means of study but there was no means of coming to it but by leading the mystical life. From my examination of the religious and intellectual sciences I had gained a sure faith in God, in prophecy and in the last judgement. It also became clear that my hope of happiness in the next world depended in mortifying the flesh and detaching myself from worldly ties. I looked at myself and saw that worldly interests encompassed me on all sides. Even my work as a teacher seemed unimportant and useless in the life hereafter. When I considered the intention of my teaching, I perceived that instead of doing it for God's sake alone I had no motive but the desire for glory and reputation. I realized that I stood on the edge of a precipice and would fall into hellfire unless set about to mend my ways.[46]

Ghazali stated, 'Scientific knowledge is above faith but the mystic experience is above knowledge.' On his inward transformation he wrote:

> Once I had been a slave, Lust was my Master
> Lust then became my servant, I was free
> Leaving the haunts of Men, I sought Thy Presence
> Lonely, I found Thee in my company.

Ghazali returned to his hometown of Tus where he taught till he died. During his last illness the scholar wrote a poem that was found under his pillow after his death. Some of those lines are:

Say to my brethren when they see me dead,
And weep for me, lamenting me in sadness:
Think ye I am this corpse ye are to bury?
I swear by God, this dead one is not I.
When I had formal shape, then this my body,
Served as my garment, I wore it for a while...
A bird I am: this body was my cage
But I have flown leaving it as a token.[47]

ﷲ

IBN AL ARABI (D. 1240 AD)

The nineteen-year-old Ibn al Arabi met the renowned philosopher Ibn Rushd (d. 1198 AD) whom the West knows as Averroes. The philosopher asked the young mystic, 'Do the fruits of mystic illumination agree with philosophical speculation?' Ibn al Arabi replied, 'Yes and no. Between the yes and no, the spirits take their flight beyond the matter.' Impressed with the answer Ibn Rushd exclaimed, 'Glory to Allah. I have lived at a time when there exists a master of this experience, one of those who opens the locks of His doors.' Fourteen years later when Ibn Rushd died, Ibn al Arabi attended the funeral and referred to him as a great leader.[48]

Ibn al Arabi, one of the most influential Sufi authors of later Islamic history is known as Shaykh al Akbar, the Greatest Master. Born in the town of Muricia in Spain, Ibn al Arabi moved to Seville where he studied religious sciences. Since his father was a devotee of the renowned Sufi scholar Abdul Qadir Jilani of Baghdad, Ibn al Arabi grew up in Sufi circles. Arabi was educated by two women, one being Fatima of Cordova, and later travelled to many Islamic countries studying alchemy, astrology, the Hermetic tradition and neo-platonic philosophy.

The mystic spent many years in Andalusia and North Africa. While in Morocco, he dreamt that he should travel to Fez where he would meet a certain Muhammad al Hasar with whom he should travel east. The two men met and travelled together to Tunis, Alexandria and Cairo where Hasar died. Ibn al Arabi then travelled alone to Makkah where he joined a group of Sufis. Here he met Nizam, a beautiful woman who created a lasting impression on the mystic. She was the inspiration behind the book of poetry *Tarjuman al Ashwaq* (The Interpreter of Desires). Accusations were hurled at him for writing erotic verse, so Arabi wrote a commentary on the book proving that the imagery was not in conflict with Islamic teachings.

Ibn al Arabi finally settled in Damascus where he taught and wrote till his death. A prolific writer, he authored numerous books on Sufi philosophy asserting that perfect knowledge of God needed both the eye of reason and the eye of imagination. He coined the term *insaan il kaamil*, the Perfect Man, that became the central theme of Sufism. His theories brought out the nature of human perfection and the means to achieve it.

Ibn al Arabi's philosophy and articulation of *wahdat ul wujood*, remains the most celebrated and controversial idea throughout the Muslim world influencing Sufi ideologies forever. Among the Sufi Master's best-known works are *Fusus al Hakim* (Bezels of Wisdom) and *Futuhat al Makiya* (Meccan Revelations). Ibn al Arabi believed that the ultimate goal of love is to recognize it as God's essence.

> *Were it not for*
> *the excess of your talking*
> *and the turmoil in your hearts,*
> *you would see what I see*
> *and hear what I hear!*
>
> *When my beloved appears,*
> *With what eye do I see him?*

With His eye, not with mine,
For none sees Him except myself.[49]

ﷲ

ALI IBN UTHMAN HUJWIRI DATTA GANJ BAKHSH (D. 1071 AD)

Uthman Hujwiri was born in Ghazna, a town in present-day
Afghanistan, and later settled in Lahore around 1035 AD. He studied
Sufism under several masters and travelled to Turkestan, Transoxania,
Iraq, Iran and Syria. Hujwiri's Master, Shaykh Abul Fazl Muhammad
bin al Hasan Khattali of Syria ordered him to go to Lahore. Even
after moving there, Hujwiri kept in touch with the Sufis of other
lands. When his Master died, Hujwiri was with him in Syria. Some
years later, he returned to Lahore.

Hujwiri wrote many books on Sufism, including the manual *Kashf
al Mahjub* (Uncovering of the Veils) that remains an important study
of the early Sufis and their philosophies. It is the first comprehensive
book on Sufism in the Persian language. According to Hujwiri, 'The
knowledge of God is the science of gnosis, the knowledge from
God is the science of the sacred law, and knowledge with God is
the science of Sufism. Knowledge is a divine attribute and action a
human attribute and the two are not separate from one another.' He
writes that the heart is the seat of knowledge and more venerable
than the Kaaba. 'Men look at the Kaaba but God is ever looking at
the heart. Whoever bowed his head in humility would be exalted by
God in both the worlds. When man is satisfied with God's decree, it
is a sign that God is satisfied with him.'

The *Kashf al Mahjub* describes the perfect state of the intoxicated
Sufi as one of sobriety. It explains *safa*, purity, as the destination of a
Sufi, a station where there is no room for complaint. Hujwiri defined
a Sufi as one who overcomes the passions of the self and annihilates
himself in the path of *Haqq*, Truth. The mystic preached that those

with *Marifa*, Divine knowledge, are the chosen ones to whom God reveals the Divine secrets. According to the treatise, Imam Ali explained *Marifa* as knowing God with His help and seeing His Light in every atom in the universe.

Hujwiri's tomb at Lahore, called that of *Datta Ganj Bakhsh*, Giver of Treasures, remains a popular place of pilgrimage. Khwaja Moinuddin Chishti spent 40 days meditating there before settling in Ajmer, and referred to him as a perfect Sufi.

Bird carrying a letter for Shaykh Abdul Qadir Jilani.

4

THE FORMATION OF SUFI ORDERS

One day We shall call together all human beings with their (respective) Imams: those who are given their record in their right hand will read it (with pleasure), and they will not be dealt with unjustly in the least.

The Quran: Chapter Children of Israel (17:71)

Although born a Muslim, I embraced true faith at the hands of my *murshid*, Sufi Master Shah Muhammad Farooq Rahmani (d. 1983 AD). He belonged to Delhi but migrated to Karachi during the partitioning of India. In 1978, I took the *ba'ya*, oath of allegiance, at the insistence of my mother whose search for the perfect Master took over two decades. Repeating the *shijra,* spiritual lineage, of the Rahmani Chishti Order while the Master held one end of a long scarf and I the other, was an overwhelming experience. I had taken the first step in making a lifelong commitment to spiritual Islam. The tree of spiritual genealogy remains the basic element in the Sufi representation, for spiritual qualities are attached to the reciting of the names of previous Masters.

I attended many discourses at the Shaykh's home in Karachi where a large area served as a *khanqah* for assemblies. Shaykh

Farooq, a *kamil pir*, perfect Master, was a true *ashiq e rasul,* lover of Prophet Muhammad ﷺ. He had internalized prophetic qualities of compassion, generosity, gentleness and the yearning for Allah. The Prophet was alive in his heart and found expression in his conduct. He warned of the dangers in the growing tendency of distancing the teachings of the Prophet from the importance of loving him and the *Ahl e Bait,* People of the House of Muhammad ﷺ. He prophesized that such misguided beliefs would result in a confrontational approach lacking spiritual quest.

Sufi orders are like spiritual families who follow the teachings of the founding Master. According to the Quran, all of humanity shall be raised for the Final Judgement with their respective Imams. A Sufi Master is obligated to protect the disciple in this world and in the Hereafter. I find tremendous solace in the belief that when God's decrees are pronounced, one shall be under the banner and protection of Khwaja Moinuddin Chishti of Ajmer.

The Prophet said, 'Al mumin mirat al muminin', the faithful are a mirror to the faithful. When a devout Muslim recognizes a fault in the behaviour of his brethren, he must correct the fault in his own behaviour so that his life becomes a mirror for the faithful.[1] In order to nurture the spiritual development of Muslims, numerous Sufi retreats were set up where wandering Sufi aspirants sought guidance from accomplished Masters of the Path.

The crystallization of Sufi *silsilas* took place in the eleventh century and the different spiritual lineages can be traced through them. Through a series of transmissions, these *silsilas* eventually link disciples to Prophet Muhammad ﷺ, who they believe connects them to Allah. Even though the early mystics were generally viewed with resentment by orthodox establishments, Sufism turned into a mass movement in the Muslim world. The philosophies of Sufi scholars impacted the devotional expression of the Muslims forever.

Rest houses and hostels were constructed on the outskirts of cities to serve wandering mystics. These spiritual retreats were called *ribat* in Arabia, *tekke* in Turkey, and *khanqah* in Central Asia. Here, arrangements were made to accommodate mystics and their disciples. Sometimes a *hujra*, small cell, was allotted to facilitate meditation. *Khanqahs* have old traditions of hospitality that include serving food to travellers and the poor. In the subcontinent, the complex around the tomb of a venerated Sufi is called *dargah*, door of the court. A visit to the mausoleum of a revered Sufi is commonly called *ziyara* or *hazri*.

Khanqahs are run by donations and *futuh*, unsolicited gifts, while some establishments enjoy state patronage. The Chishti Order had strict rules of not accepting anything from the establishment either in terms of public positions or monetary benefits. Usually the leader of an order lives within the *khanqah* compound making himself available for visitors. *Khanqah* festivities include celebrating events in the Prophet's life, and the death anniversaries of venerated Sufis known as *Urs*. These functions are not exclusive to the inmates of the *khanqahs* and are attended by common people in large numbers.

Many *khanqahs* served women exclusively and during the twelfth century there were seven such establishments in Aleppo alone. In Cairo the Ribat al Baghdadiya was built by the daughter of Malik az Zahir Baibars (d. 1285 AD) for the woman Master, Shaykha Zainab al Barakat. There were others in Baghdad, Egypt and Central Asia.[2]

Sufi orders came to be known by the name of their revered Masters. After completing training at the *khanqah,* disciples travelled to other countries to spread the teachings of their order. Some Sufis formed independent schools that came to be known by their individual names. They developed distinctive disciplinary methods adapting to local devotional traditions. The fusion of Sufi ethics combined with popular regional cultures and contributed enormously to the richness of Islamic heritage.

Among early Sufi orders were the Muhasibis who were followers of Abdulah Haris bin Asad al Muhasibi, the Qassaris of Umar al Qassar, Junaydis of Junayd Baghdadi, Nuris of Abul Hasan Nuri,

Sahlis of Sahl Abdullah Tustari, Hakimis of Ali al Hakim al Tirmidhi, Kharrazis of Abu Said Kharraz, Sayyaris of Abu al Abbas Sayyari of Merv, and Tayfuris of Abu Yazid Tayfur Bistami. The Hululis got their name from the doctrine of *hulul*, incarnation, while followers of Mansur Hallaj were called Hallajis.[3]

The first major Sufi order was the Qadri Order established by Shaykh Abdul Qadir Jilani (1077–1166 AD) of Baghdad. The Shaykh is universally acclaimed the Master of all Masters, and is called *Pir Dastgir* and *Ghaus ul Azam* for his ecstatic utterance, 'My foot is on the neck of every Sufi.'

After studying theology in Baghdad, the Shaykh from Jilan spent 25 years as a wandering dervish, the last 12 in seclusion. At the age of 50, he began to preach in Baghdad where his fame reached incredible heights. The Shaykh taught that *jihad* fought against the self is more important than *jihad* fought against oppression with the sword. The compilation of his discourses include *Futuh al Ghaib* (Revelation of the Unseen), *Futuh al Rabbani* (The Sublime Revelation) and *Jala al Khatir* (The Removal of Care). They remain important Sufi manuals emphasizing that Sufism consists of generosity, cheerfulness, submission, patience, prayers, solitude, poverty, humility, sincerity and truthfulness.

Countless miracles attributed to Shaykh Abdul Qadir Jilani include the crushing of mountains, drying of oceans and raising the dead to life. The twelfth century was a period of strife between the exponents of *Sharia* and *Tareeqa*. The Master struck a balance between them and thousands attended his sermons. He died at the age of 91 and is buried in his *madarsa* at Baghdad, which continues to attract devotees from the world over. The Qadri Order spread to Syria, Turkey, Damascus, Africa, Mauritius, Chechnya and Asia. Muhammad Ghaus (d. 1517 AD), claiming descent from the founder, introduced the Qadri Order in the subcontinent. The teachers of Dara Shikoh, the Mughal prince, Mullah Shah Badakshi and Miyan Mir of Lahore are among the famed Qadri Sufis.

The Syrian Shaykh Abu Ishaq Shami (d. 940 AD) of Chisht e Sharif, a small village 125 km west of Herat in Afghanistan founded the Chishti Sufi Order. The order gained popularity through the teachings of Khwaja Moinuddin Chishti of Ajmer who is an outstanding figure in the history of Islamic mysticism. Born in Sejistan in 1142 AD, the Khwaja was drawn to mystics from early childhood. The quest for knowledge took him to centres of learning in Samaqand and Bukhara. While travelling to Iraq, the Khwaja met Shaykh Uthman of Harwan and joined his circle of disciples.

For two months Khwaja Moinuddin stayed with Shaykh Abdul Qadir Jilani in Baghdad where he met another eminent Sufi, Shaykh Shihabuddin Suharwardi. After travelling to many lands, the Khwaja finally settled at Ajmer laying the founding principles for the Chishti Order: 'Develop ocean-like generosity, sun-like bounty and earth-like hospitality.'

The Chishti Order produced great Sufi Masters including Baba Farid of Punjab, Qutubuddin Bakhtiar Kaki, Hazrat Nizamuddin Auliya, Naseeruddin Chiragh Dilli, and Alauddin Sabir of Kaliyar. The Nizami and Sabri Orders are among the numerous branches of the Chishti *silsila*.

The Suharwardi Order revolves around the teachings of Abu Najib Suharwardi (d. 1168 AD) who was a disciple of Ahmad Ghazali, the younger brother of the famed philosopher Imam Ghazali. The Shaykh authored many books including *Hikmat al Ishraq* (The Philosophy of Illumination) and *Adab al Muridin* (The Etiquette of Sufi Disciples) that have been translated into many languages.

The son of Abu Najib's brother, Shaykh Shihabuddin Abu Hafs Umar Suharwardi (d. 1234 AD), wrote *Awarif ul Marif* (Knowledge of the Knowers). The writings of the influential scholar went a long way in promoting the Suharwardi Order. He wrote that although the formation of *khanqahs* and the periodic retreat to them by Sufis was an innovation in Islam, they were of great significance for the purpose of self-examination and meditation. Abu Hafs became the official Sufi of Baghdad under the Abbasid Caliph Nasir who tried to unite Muslims against Mongol oppression. Shaykh Abu Hafs served as an ambassador to the Ayyubid rulers of Egypt and Syria, and the Seljukids of Rum.[4] As opposed to the Chishti teachings, the Suharwardi Sufis participated in state politics, believing that guiding the state remained a religious duty.

Shaykh Bahauddin Zakariya of Multan promoted the Suharwardi Order in the subcontinent. It became popular in Punjab and Sindh. A branch of the order, the Shattaris, spread in Bengal through the teachings of Muhammad Ala Qazan Shattari and was promoted by Muhammad Ghaus of Gwalior.

The Yasavi Order gets its name from Khwaja Ahmad Yasavi (d. 1166 AD) who came from Yasi in Kazakhstan. It had a major role in bringing the Turkish nomadic tribes to the fold of Islam. The Yasavi traditions contributed to the creative ideas of Yunus Emre the mystic poet of Turkey.

Isma'il Ata who came from a village near Tashkent, became another important Yasavi Master. He taught, 'Accept this advice from me: Imagine that the world is a green dome in which there is nothing but God and you, and remember God until the *al tajalli al qahri*, overwhelming theophany overcomes you and frees you from yourself, and nothing remains but God.' The Yasavi Order spread to various parts in Central Asia, later gaining many followers in Kashmir.

The Kubrawiya Sufi Order was established by Shaykh Najmuddin Kubra (d. 1220 AD) of Central Asia. He earned the title of *Shaykh e Vali Tarash* (The Master who sculpts Sufis) for a number of his disciples became renowned Sufis. The Shaykh came from Khiva, a district in western Uzbekistan but later migrated to the city of Khwarazm. A prolific writer, his *Fawaih al Jamaal wa fawatih al Jalaal* is an interpretation of mystical psychology explaining ecstatic experiences and remains an important treatise.[5] The Kubrawiya Order developed an elaborate symbolism of colours to interpret the revelation of lights seen during meditation. Other books authored by Shaykh Najmuddin are *Al Usul ul Ashra* in Arabic and the Sufi manual of conduct, *Sifat ul Adab* in Persian. The Shaykh was killed while defending his homeland from the invading Mongols. He ordered his disciples to flee leaving him to die a martyr in the catastrophe. A volley of arrows ripped through the Shaykh's body causing his death.

Majdad Din of Baghdad, the Master of the Persian Sufi poet Fariduddin Attar was a disciple of Shaykh Najmuddin.[6] Najmuddin Daya Razi, another disciple authored *Mirsad ul Ibad* that became an essential reading for later Sufis.

The Nuriya in Baghdad, Rukaniya in Central Asia, and the Nurbakshiya in Iran are orders that arose from within the Kubrawiya Order. The Firdawsiya and Hamdaniya Orders found in Kashmir are offshoots of the Kubrawiya Order. The venerated Syed Ali Hamdhani migrated to Kashmir in the fourteenth century with hundreds of followers.

The Rifai Order was founded by Shaykh Ahmad Rifai (d. 1182 AD) of Basra in Iraq. A cousin of Shaykh Abdul Qadir Jilani, he was a close associate of the Great Master. The Rifais were known for extravagant practices and strange miracles. Ibn Batuta wrote of his visit to a Rifai centre near Wasit where *dhikr* sessions were held amidst the beating of kettledrums and dancing. Some followers rolled in the fire while some extinguished it in their mouths.[7] The Rifai Order spread to Egypt, Syria, Turkey and Eastern Europe, and more recently in North America. The Rifais are called the howling dervishes due to their loud meditation practices.

The Shadhili Order was founded by Shaykh Abul Hasan Ali Shadhili of Morocco (d. 1258 AD), a disciple of Abu Abdallah Harazim who was a follower of the famous African Sufi Abu Madyan (d. 1198 AD). The Shaykh often retreated to a cave in the Shadhila village to meditate. However, he did not encourage a life of seclusion and his disciples were expected to realize their spirit amidst social duties. The Master travelled from Morocco to Spain, eventually settling down in the city of Alexandria. The Shadhili Order became the most important order from Morocco to Egypt with a large number of followers in Syria and Arabia. Shaykh Abul Hasan died on the way to Makkah and his tomb is at Humaythra on the coast of the Red Sea in Egypt.

Shaykh Abul Hasan composed the venerated prayer *Hizb al Bahr*, recited by Muslim communities worldwide. Ibn Sulaiman al Jazuli (d. 1465 AD), author of the celebrated Sufi prayer manual *Dalial ul Khairat,* also happened to be a Shadhili mystic. The Shadhili Order has branches throughout North Africa, Sri Lanka, Europe and the Arab world.

The Mevlavi Order crystallized in Turkey around Mevlana Jalaluddin Rumi (d. 1273 AD). Universally recognized as one of the greatest spiritual figures of all times, the Mevlana was born in the Afghan province of Balkh where his father, Bahauddin Walad, was a renowned Islamic scholar. The Mongol oppression of Central Asia led the family to migrate to Konya, which was then governed by the Seljuks of Rum. The mystic poet learnt Islamic theology from his father who headed a seminary in Konya. After his father's death, the Mevlana took over as the head of the religious seminary.

At the age of 37, Rumi met his spiritual Master, Shams Tabriz, who transported the scholar from the sober religious path to larger spiritual horizons. Rumi's collection of *ghazals, Diwan e Kabir* and *Mathnawi,* are acknowledged masterpieces on Sufi philosophy. Rumi dwells on the theme of love explaining that realization of the self is a reflection of the Lord. Reputed for their devotion to music and whirling movements during meditation, followers of the order are called 'the whirling dervishes'.

Khwaja Bahauddin Naqshband of Bukhara (d. 1390 AD) reorganized the *Silsila e Khwajgan* in Central Asia, which came to be called the Naqshbandi Order. The patron Sufi of Bukhara, the Shaykh's activities were initially limited to the city where he and his followers controlled the court.

A sober order, Naqshbandis do not believe in dance or musical assemblies as a means of achieving spiritual states. It is the sole Sufi discipline that traces its lineage of spiritual transmission to Imam Abu Bakr Siddiq, the first *Khalifa* of the Islamic Caliphate and revered companion of Prophet Muhammad ﷺ. Most Sufi disciplines trace their lineage to Imam Ali, cousin and son-in-law of the Prophet. Traditions relate that Prophet Muhammad ﷺ taught Imam Abu Bakr *dhikr e khafi*, silent ways of meditating, when both hid in a cave to escape attackers on the way to Madinah. Silent meditation became the distinct theme of the Naqshbandi *silsila*. It spread to many parts of the world through a network of retreats in Central Asia. The order is found in Indonesia, north- and south-west China, Turkey, Europe and North America. Jami, the famous Persian Sufi poet had followed the Naqshbandi way. In India, Shaykh Baaqi Billa from Central Asia, settled in Delhi and promoted the order.

Shaykh Nuruddin Muhammad Nimatullah (d. 1431 AD) founded the Nimatullahi Order. Born in Syria to Iranian parents, he studied in Islamic cities and became a prolific writer of prose and poetry. His books included several commentaries on Ibn Arabi's acclaimed *Fusus al Hakim*. Expelled by Timur while travelling through Central Asia, he eventually settled at Mahan in Iran. The order gained popularity in Iran and more recently, many branches have grown in the Western world.

The Tijani Order, established by Shaykh Abbas Ahmad ibn at Tijani (d. 1815 AD) in Algeria, has recently spread to South Africa and North America. The order is influenced by the teachings of the Shadhili Sufi Masters.

There exist hundreds of newer orders but most of them originate from those mentioned above. The Qalandars and Malamati mystics do not belong to organized orders and wander from one place to another. Shaykh Shihabuddin Suharwardi wrote that there is a difference between these two types of wandering dervishes. The Qalandars are seized by the intoxication arising from the love of God to such a degree that they reject social pleasantries. They perform mandatory prayers but not the extra vigils. On the other hand, the

In the name of Allah, Most Gracious, Most Merciful.

Malamatis try concealing their spiritual achievements by behaving in an offensive manner so that they may be left alone.

The Qalandars emerged as a separate movement with a distinctive style of dress and behaviour. Shaykh Jamaluddin and Hasan al Jawaliqi of Iran rank among the famed Qalandars. Bu Ali Shah Qalandar of Panipat in India migrated from Iraq. Lal Shahbaz Qalandar of Sindh is another popular Qalandar of the subcontinent.

In the Indian subcontinent Sufi orders embraced local traditions from ascetics belonging to other religions. Interfaith dialogues were held at *khanqahs* where Sufis appealed for peace and tolerance. In the region, conversion to Islam came about primarily due to the teachings of Sufi Masters.

All major Sufi orders were represented in Makkah till the nineteenth century. The holy cities of Makkah and Madinah were important Sufi centres. It was in these cities that the mystics sought to be blessed with vision and direction. Pilgrims visiting the holy cities would usually join one order or another. Some would stay on and train until given permission to return home and initiate other disciples. In countries like Indonesia, Sufi ways were introduced to the people through such pilgrims. Sufi orders from Asia were brought to the Arab world through visiting pilgrims.

The rulers of Saudi Arabia who came to power in the early twentieth century, are the present custodians of the holy cities. They adhere to the stringent Salafi ideology that condemns mystic philosophies. During their early rule, Sufis were accused of heresy, tortured to death, and the tombs of venerated Masters razed to the ground. However, Sufi orders continue to flourish in most parts of the Islamic world representing the spiritual aspirations of Muslim communities.

Allah Al Jalal Hu:
May His glory be exalted. The first letter Alif is the source
of all and the last letter Hu is the most perfect attribute,
free from all associations.

5

THE WAY OF THE SUFI

Come, come whoever you are
Wanderer, worshipper, lover of leaving
It doesn't matter.
Ours is not a caravan of despair.
Come, even if you have broken your vow a thousand times.
Come, Come yet again. Come.

Mevlana Jalaluddin Rumi

At many stages in my life I came close to giving up on the idea of God altogether. Growing up in the 1970s one inherited a mixed bag of values. Progressive writers professed agnosticism and friends jeered at the idea of hell or heaven. Churches, temples, mosques and monasteries were simply not fashionable in the age of rebellion.

Studying in an Irish convent-cum-boarding school, I regularly went to church, sang Christmas carols, baked Easter eggs and imbibed Christian values. During annual holidays a *maulana*, religious teacher, came home to teach all the children the Quran. He instilled the fear of God in us, with the result that fear remained the only emotion that the heart felt for the Creator. Somehow, this overwhelming fear kept me connected to Allah, despite my often wanting to break away completely. Traversing the Sufi path changed my attitude, for it teaches that ritualistic prayer are worth little if unaccompanied by love and sincerity.

On behalf of God, Prophet Muhammad ﷺ declared: 'Heaven and earth cannot contain Me but the heart of My faithful servant contains Me.'[1] Fariduddin Attar illustrates the state of the lovers:

When you seek God, seek him in your heart
He is not in Jerusalem, nor in Makkah nor in Hajj.[2]

The Quran establishes *iman*, faith, as a state of the heart that is separate from *islam*, which is a testimony of faith. When the Bedouin declared Islam their faith, God said: 'The desert Arabs say, "We believe." Say, "Ye have no faith; but ye (only) say, 'We have submitted our wills to Allah.' For not yet has Faith entered your hearts. But if ye obey Allah and His Messenger, He will not belittle aught of your deeds: for Allah is Oft-Forgiving, Most Merciful.' (49:14)

HAL, *KAIFIYAT* AND *MAQAAM*

Islam contains a threefold structure consisting of *Sharia*, the outer law; *Tareeqa* the inward path; and *Haqeeqa*, the arrival at the reality of Allah. The different stages of the Sufi path are called *hal*, state, and *maqaam*, station.

Kaifiyat is an emotional state that can be experienced by ordinary people. We often see people getting emotional and tearful while listening to a heartfelt spiritual discourse or the recitation of Divine scriptures. 'And when they listen to the revelation received by the Apostle, thou wilt see their eyes overflowing with tears, for they recognize the truth: they pray: "Our Lord! we believe; write us down among the witnesses."' (5:83)

Hal can be described as a series of enlightened mystic moments. Sufis believe that *hal* is not self-induced but is caused by *tajalli*, Divine graces that flow from the heavens. In Sufi imagery this flow of blessings is called *sharaab e marifa*, the wine of gnosis, and *sharaab e mohabba*, the wine of love. Most mystics remain sober despite intoxication from this wine, whereas some are unable to contain the drink. Mansur Hallaj and Bayazid of Bistam are among the most famous drunken Sufi who revealed God's mysteries, those that were meant to be veiled. Bayazid sings:

> *I have planted love in my heart*
> *And shall not be distracted until judgement day*
> *You have wounded my heart when you came near me*
> *My desire grows, my love is bursting.*
> *He has poured me a sip to drink.*
> *He has quickened my heart with the cup of love*
> *Which he has filled at the ocean of friendship.*

Sufis of some orders use music to induce *hal,* a state of spiritual ecstasy. *Hal* is *kaifiyat* in a prolonged state and *maqaam* in its permanent state. *Maqaam* is something that descends from God into a man's heart, without his being able to repel it when it comes, or to attract it when it goes, by his own effort.[3] On the perfect mystic states, Rumi writes:

> *The* hal *is like the unveiling of the beauteous bride*
> *While the* maqaam *is the king's being alone with the bride.*[4]

In the last few years of his life, Prophet Muhammad 彛 spent a lot of time with his companions teaching them ways of achieving exalted ranks with God. One day Hanzalah al Usaydi, a companion, confessed to Abu Bakr that he felt divided between contradictory feelings. While in the Prophet's presence he had the ability to see paradise and hell, but away from the Messenger he felt overpowered by worldly affairs. Hanzalah felt he might be counted among the hypocrites of Islam. Abu Bakr confided to having similar thoughts and both decided to seek answers from the Prophet on their spiritual states. Hearing their doubts, Muhammad 彛 replied, 'By He who holds my soul in His hands, if you were able to remain in the state in which you were in my company, and remember God permanently, the angels would shake your hands in the bed and along the path you walk. Hanzalah, there is a time for this and there is a time for that.'[5] Sufis describe Hanzalah's state as *hal* and *maqaam*, the spiritual state where God commands the angels to greet His friends.

THE MASTER AND THE DISCIPLE

Tareeqa, literally means 'the path' in Arabic and one who embarks on it becomes a *salik*, the wayfarer. The Sufi aspirant travels through different stations of spiritual progress that indicate mystic ranks. *Qutub*, axis or pole, is the highest spiritual authority upon whom the well being of the world depends for he exists in perfect tranquility with God. Rumi writes, 'He who does not know the true *Qutub* of his time is an infidel.' Veiled from the people, Sufis are believed to know each other through spiritual bonds. In a Hadith Qudsi, Prophet Muhammad ﷺ affirms Allah's words, 'Verily My friends are under My domes and only I know them.'

In another tradition, the Prophet says, 'When someone has no Shaykh, Satan becomes his Shaykh.' A Sufi Master is called *shaykh, murshid* or *pir* and the disciple *murid*. Once the oath of allegiance to the Shaykh is taken, the aspirant becomes his spiritual child. He nurtures the disciple's progress by monitoring meditations, interpreting dreams, and keeping track of the disciple's conscious and unconscious movements. A close association between master and disciple is an integral part of the mystic discipline. The disciple must learn to surrender his will to the Master.

Mevlana Rumi's life presents a compelling tale of submission. Once Shamsuddin Tabriz asked Mevlana to procure a woman for him. When Mevlana offered his wife, Shams proclaimed her to be a sister. The Master then demanded a youthful boy and Mevlana offered his son. Shams commented that he thought of the boy as a son. Shams then spoke of a desire for wine; Mevlana hurriedly fetched a glassful, but Shams threw it away, revealing that he was simply testing his disciple's obedience.

Rumi had been a religious scholar rooted in the laws of the *Sharia*. Meeting Shams made him realize the limitations of intellect and led him to acquire knowledge of the heart. Rumi writes, 'Companionship with the holy makes you one of them. Though you are rock or marble, you will become a jewel when you associate with the man of the heart.' In the *Mathnawi* Rumi says:

> *Whoever travels without a guide*
> *Needs two hundred days for a two day's journey.*[6]

Fariduddin Attar expresses similar thoughts:

> *The Pir is the red sulphur,*
> *and his breast the green ocean*
> *Who does not make collyrium for his eyes*
> *from the dust of the Pir,*
> *may die pure or impure.*[7]

The Sufis who are not formally initiated with a living Master are called Uwaisis after Uwais of Qaran. The mystic from Yemen lived in the time of Prophet Muhammad ﷺ but could not meet him. Yet, he shared a strong spiritual connection with the Messenger, becoming the prototype of the inspired Sufi.

The spirit of a Sufi is believed to live on, creating the possibility of initiation from a Master no longer in this world. Abul Hasan Kharqani of the eleventh century proclaimed that he received an initiation from the spirit of the ninth-century mystic Bayazid Bistami. Although formally initiated, the Persian Sufi poet Attar claimed mystic inspiration from the spirit of the martyred Persian Mansur Hallaj. The thirteenth-century mystic poet and philosopher Ibn al Arabi received initiation from Khidr, the immortal friend of God mentioned in the Quran. Sufis often spend years wandering in search of the perfect Master and believe that Master-disciple relationships are predestined.

The *murid* undergoes initiation from the *murshid* in a simple ceremony of *ba'ya*. Usually an oath of allegiance is taken while holding the *Pir's* hand and repeating some prayers along with the reciting of the *shijra,* spiritual lineage of the order. The Sufi scholar Abu Hafs al Suharwardi (d. 1234 AD) wrote, 'When the sincere disciple enters on the obedience of the master, keeping his company and learning his manners, a spirituality flows from within the Master to within the disciple, like one lamp lighting another.'

The *murshid* appoints the most deserving disciple as his *khalifa,* successor. The Master and other important witnesses formally sign the *khilafatnama,* a written document. It functions as a licensing authority permitting the disciple to initiate *murids* independently. The presentation of the *khilafat* becomes a festive occasion where gifts like a *khirqa,* cloak, are presented to the *khalifa.* He is often entrusted with the belongings of previous Masters that are traditionally handed down for blessings and safe-keeping. The Master bequeaths his *sajjada,* prayer carpet, to the *khalifa* who becomes the *sajjadanashin,* one who sits on the carpet. If the Master dies without nominating an heir, the elders and members of the order elect a *khalifa.* The inhabitants of a *khanqah* usually consist of three groups of people— *ahl e khidmat,* those who serve the mystics; *ahl e suhbat,* companions learning the ethics of Sufism; and *ahl e khilwat,* those devoted to prayer and meditation.

The discourses of Hazrat Nizamuddin Auliya (d. 1325 AD), the patron Sufi of Delhi are laden with anecdotes narrating the devotion of renowned Sufis to their *Pirs.* His Master Baba Farid once headed from Ajodhan to Makkah with a desire of performing the Hajj pilgrimage. On reaching Uch it occurred to the mystic that his Master, Khwaja Qutubuddin Bakhtiyar Kaki had not performed the Hajj. So instead of travelling to Makkah, Baba Farid presented himself at the tomb of his spiritual mentor in Delhi.

A Pir ensures that disciples perform their religious and spiritual duties. The battle with the *nafs,* passions of the lower self, is the central theme of Sufi discipline. The Master suggests methods to free the disciple's spirit from worldly desires. He interprets their dreams and visions, encouraging them to reach higher spiritual states. Sufi aspirants are recommended to observe 40-day retreats called *chilla* in Urdu and Persian, *arabain* in Arabic. A legacy of prophets, Sufis believe that fountains of wisdom flow from meditative seclusion. Hafez of Shiraz (d. 1389 AD) writes:

> At dawn, a traveller in a distant land
> Recited this riddle to a companion,
> O Sufi, wine will only become pure
> When for forty days it remains in the bottle.[8]

Prophet Muhammad ﷺ once said, 'A Shaykh in his group is like a prophet amongst his people'. *Tasawwur e shaykh* is an important meditation method of concentrating on the image of the Shaykh. The *murid* first annihilates himself in the mentor, a state that is called *fana fi shaykh*. The next stage *fana fi rasul*, is self-annihilation in the love of Prophet Muhammad ﷺ. The final stage *fana fi Allah*, annihilation in the love of God leads to the state of *baqa*, where the Sufi ceases to exist and his soul finds eternal continuance in Allah.

THE SUFI PATH

The Sufi path consists of different spiritual stations including *tawba*, repentance; *zuhd*, piety; *tawakkul*, trust in God; *faqr*, poverty; *dhikr*, remembrance of God; *sabr*, patience; *shukr*, thankfulness; *rida*, contentment; *mohabba*, love; and *marifa*, divine knowledge. These stages are travelled through *mujahida*, self-mortification.

Tawba, repentance is the first station in the Sufi path signifying an awakening of the soul. It involves turning away from sin with the intention of remaining steadfast on the right path. Compassion and mercy are among the foremost attributes of Allah who accepts forgiveness from those who truly seek it. The Sufis believe that loving Allah's friends effectively cleanses one's sins. Bayazid of Bistam said,

'Love those beloved of Allah and make yourself lovable to them so that they love you, because Allah looks into the hearts of those he loves 70 times a day. Perhaps he will find your name in the heart of the one He loves. He will love you too and forgive your wrongdoings. This is the shortest way to reach Him.'

Sufis accord a high rank to those who forgive while in a position to retaliate. The poet Abu Said Abi Khair writes:

> He who is not my friend—may God be his friend
> And he who bears ill will against me, may his joys increase
> He who puts thorns in my way on account of enmity
> May every flower that blossoms in the garden of his life be
> without thorns.

Sufi Masters remind followers that the door of repentance remains open till doomsday. Rumi's mausoleum in Konya has his famous verse inscribed on it, 'Come back, come back, even if you have broken your repentance a thousand times.'

Zuhd, piety, involves renouncing worldly pursuits and being extremely cautious with one's actions. A person practising abstinence of a high degree is known as *zahid*. Prophet Muhammad ﷺ called this inward battle *jihad e akbar*, the higher struggle. The lower instinct is recognized as *nafs al ammara bis su*, in the Quran. 'Nor do I absolve my own self (of blame): the (human) soul is certainly prone to evil, unless my Lord do bestow His Mercy: but surely my Lord is Oft-Forgiving, Most Merciful.' (12:53) The Sufi purifies the *nafs* through virtuous deeds till it becomes *nafs e mutmainna*. 'To the righteous soul will be said: O thou soul, in complete rest and satisfaction! Come back thou to thy Lord, well pleased and well pleasing unto Him! Enter thou, then, among My devotees! Yea. Enter thou My Heaven!' (Surah 89:27–30)

As Schimmel explains, Prophet Muhammad's ﷺ saying 'Die before you die' inspired Sufis to discover the spiritual implications of slaying the lower self and seeking spiritual resurrection in this life.[9] The struggle against the *nafs* has dominated Sufi philosophy through the centuries. The *nafs* has often been compared to a snake that can be turned into a useful rod, similar to the rod of Moses, which became a serpent that destroyed other dangerous serpents. Rumi writes:

> *The nafs has a rosary and a Quran in its right hand,*
> *and a scimitar and a dagger in the sleeve.*[10]

Sufis have a treasure of stories relating to methods used in replacing unworthy attributes by praiseworthy qualities. An often told story is about Imam Ali, son-in-law of Prophet Muhammad ﷺ. Once while engaged in battle, the invincible warrior overpowered his enemy. When Ali pointed his dagger at the opponent's throat, he spat in Ali's face, who said, 'Go away, taking your life is now unlawful for me.' The bewildered enemy enquired why he was being released. Ali said, 'When you spat in my face, my ego was hurt and I would be killing you for myself and not for the sake of fighting oppression for the Truth. Taking your life now will make me a murderer.' Moved by Ali's integrity, the enemy warrior embraced Islam.[11]

Perpetual fasting and spending nights in prayer are common ways to control the lower instincts. Sufi Masters stress that hunger brings about illumination of the soul, for Allah provides spiritual sustenance to those who keep hungry for His sake. Rumi writes, 'Hunger is God's food for which he quickens the bodies of the upright.'[12] Shaqiq Balkhi (d. 809 AD) taught that 40 days of constant hunger could transform the darkness of the heart into light. Sahl Tustari (d. 896 AD) fasted perpetually and earned the title of *Shaykh ul Arifin*, Master of the Knowers. He said, 'Hunger is God's secret on the earth.' Abu Madyan, the African mystic, writes, 'One who is hungry becomes humble, one who becomes humble begs and the one who begs attains God. So hold fast to your hunger, my brother, and practise it constantly for it means that you will attain what you desire and will arrive at what you hope.'

Sufis inculcate *tawakkul*, trust in God, to reach the mystic goal, not relying on anything or anyone except Him. Sahl Tustari writes, 'One who is concerned about his sustenance after the guarantee has been given to him by Allah, has no value for Allah.' *Razzaq* is one among Allah's ninety-nine names, the Provider of sustenance for all in the animal and human world. The Quran says, 'Then let man look at his food, (and how We provide it): For that We pour forth water in abundance, And We split the earth in fragments, And produce therein corn, And Grapes and nutritious plants, And Olives and Dates, And enclosed Gardens, dense with lofty trees, And fruits and fodder, For use and convenience to you and your cattle.' (80:24–32) Prophet Abraham exemplified complete trust in God by refusing the help of Archangel Gabriel when Nimrod cast him in the blazing fire. His trust in Allah was rewarded and the inferno turned into a rose garden.

Faqr, poverty, forms another vital pillar of the Sufi doctrine. Poverty was exalted for Prophet Muhammad ﷺ declared, 'Poverty is my pride.' Numerous anecdotes from the Messenger's life draw a picture of the poverty of his immediate family members. Their home was simple and the Messenger slept on the floor upon a bed of stuffed palm fibers. Muhammad ﷺ prayed, 'O God, make me live lowly and die lowly and rise amongst the lowly.' He added, 'On the Day of Resurrection God will say, "Bring ye My loved ones nigh unto Me;" then the angels will say, "Who are Thy loved Ones?" and God will answer them saying, "The poor and the destitute."'

Uthman Hujwiri, the eleventh-century author of the Sufi manual *Kashf al Mahjub* wrote, 'Know that Poverty has a high rank in the way of the Truth and the poor are held in great esteem by God.' He explained that Sufism was a metaphorical poverty where the mystic is free from bonds of acquisition. However, the idea does not mean that Sufis should not earn their living. On the contrary, Sufi aspirants are encouraged to pursue livelihoods until they reach a definite state of trust with God and are clearly ordered to withdraw from worldly work.

Dhikr (pronounced *zikr* in the subcontinent), the remembrance of God, is central to the Sufi discipline. It is a process where all the faculties of the body including the innermost conscience are involved. Prophet Muhammad ﷺ described *salat*, prayer, as a way of communicating with God. Apart from the five mandatory prayers, mystics attach immense value to additional voluntary prayers, especially *tahajjud*, the night vigil. The Quran emphasizes the vigil: 'Stand (to prayer) by night, but not all night.' (73:2)

Abu Madyan explains, 'They call for darkness during the day, just as a shepherd calls his flock, and they yearn for sunset just as a bird yearns for its nest at sunset. When night falls, when darkness overcomes the light, when the bedspreads are laid out, when the family is at rest, when every lover is left alone with his beloved—then they arise, pointing their feet towards Me, turning their faces to Me, speak intimate words and adorn Me by the virtue of My grace.'

Ritual and free prayer are both regarded as essential to spiritual progress. *Dhikr* requires proper clothing, strict adherence to the Islamic dietary laws and *wudu*, purification of the body, before prayer. While engaged in the remembrance of God, Sufis prefer to sit in a clean place perfumed with extracts of rose oil to welcome both angels and jinns. Devout Muslims believe that celestial bodies visit and bless places where God and the Prophet are honoured. Many Sufis have interpreted the prostration posture of ritual prayer as forming the word Muhammad ﷺ in Arabic.

Reciting the Quran remains the primary duty of the mystic. In a Hadith Qudsi Allah declares, 'I am with My slave as long as his lips are moving with Me.' The Quran is replete with injunctions to remember Allah. 'Keep in remembrance the name of thy Lord and devote thyself to Him wholeheartedly'. (73:8) and 'Then do ye remember Me; I will remember you.' (2:152)

Group sessions of *dhikr* are called *halqa*, the silent *dhikr* is called *dhikr e khafi*, and a vocalized rhythmic chant is *dhikr e jahri*. These methods usually consist of repetitions of one or all the 99 names of Allah, or of a phrase dedicated to His glory. Sometimes specific patterns for breathing are prescribed for the effectiveness of *dhikr*. Certain kinds of *dhikr* are prohibited without initiation and guidance from a Sufi Master.

Sabr, patience, is another important milestone on the Sufi path. The Quran repeatedly informs us that Allah is with those who remain patient during tribulations. The tale of Prophet Job swallowed by the whale and that of Prophet Joseph being reunited with his father after years illustrate ideals of patience. Rumi enlightens us:

> *Patience O Father, is an iron shield*
> *On which God has written 'victory has come'.*[13]

Shukr, gratitude, is a station achieved by God's grace. The enlightened Sufis remain grateful to Allah through the worst afflictions. Bayazid of Bistam told followers, 'If you have a friend whose relationship with you is at its worst, the relationship will improve if you act according to the right code of behaviour. If something is given to you, be thankful to Allah, because He alone turns hearts in your favour. If you suffer calamity, take refuge in repentance and patience, because your being will gather strength.' *Rida*, contentment, like *shukr* is loving acceptance of God's will. The Egytian Master Dhun Nun defines *rida* thus: 'It is the joy of the heart in the bitterness of the Divine decree.'

Mohabba, love, is the highest station reached by a Sufi when the heart has been emptied of all else but love of Allah. No longer troubled by fear of hell or tempted at the thought of heaven, the heart loves Allah for the sake of love. Rabia Basri, the woman mystic, best exemplifies this selfless love. Rabia spoke of her desire to set fire to heaven and dampen the flames of hell so that people stop worshipping God due to fear of hell or desire of heaven. She sings:

> *Thy love is now my desire and my bliss*
> *And has been revealed to the eye of my heart that was athirst*

I have none besides Thee, who dost make the desert blossom
Thou art my joy, firmly established within me,
If Thou art satisfied with me, then
O desire of my heart, my happiness has appeared.

Sufis have interpreted Divine love according to varying personal experiences termed *qurb*, proximity, *shauq*, longing, or *uns*, intimacy. Junayd of Baghdad explains, 'Love is the annihilation of the lover in His attributes and the confirmation of the Beloved in His essence.'[14] Rumi writes, 'This love is a flame that burns everything except the beloved.'[15] Fariduddin Attar sings:

Joy! Joy! I triumph! No more I know
Myself as simply me. I burn with love
Unto myself and bury me in love
The centre is within me and its wonder
Lies as a circle everywhere around me.[16]

Through the vehicle of love, Sufis endure endless trials and tribulations. Imam Ghazali says, 'There is nothing good in love without death.' He relates the story of Abraham, who was called by the angel of death and refused to follow him, since he could not believe that God could take the life of someone who loved him so much. Soon he was addressed, 'Have you ever seen a lover who refuses to go to his beloved?' Upon hearing this, he gladly submitted his soul to the angel.[17]

Sufis believe that death liberates the body enabling the union of the soul with God. The *Urs*, death anniversaries of Sufis are important spiritual and festive occasions. The Quran affirms, 'Say not of those who are slain in the way of God. "They are dead." Nay, they are living, though you perceive (it) not.' (2:154) Another verse reiterates, 'Think not of those who are slain in Allah's way as dead. Nay, they live, finding their sustenance in the presence of their Lord.' (3:169)

There is no power other than Allah.

Marifa, the final Sufi station, signifies the complete annihilation of the conscious self where the lover ceases to exist and merges with Allah's Light. The word *marifa* is derived from the Arabic word *arif,* one who attains knowledge. Rumi explains the mystic state:

> *Like the flame of the candle in front of the sun*
> *he is non-existent, though he is existent in formal form.*[18]

Sufi *khanqahs* represent the vibrancy of Islam and continue to be the popular face of Muslim faith. Devotees offer prayers at the tombs of honoured Sufis with the belief that they have the ranks to intercede with God. *Baraka*, spiritual blessings, are believed to be strongest at the Sufi's tomb. He does not die in the ordinary sense of the word, but is 'hidden' from the world and his spiritual status increases with the passage of time. The underlying feeling of those who seek blessings at *dargahs* is that man is too sinful and therefore cannot approach God directly. *Ziyara,* a visit to the *dargah*, remains a thriving aspect of both Muslim and non-Muslim communities.

Muhammad is the Messenger of Allah,
May peace be upon him.

6

DISHARMONY WITHIN ISLAM

Beware of extremism for it was extremism that destroyed the people before you.

Prophet Muhammad 鑫

In recent years, I have often travelled to Makkah to perform an *Umra*, the smaller pilgrimage. The *Hajj* pilgrimage, one of the five fundamental pillars of Islam, takes place on specified dates of the Islamic calendar. *Hajj* becomes mandatory for devout Muslims who can afford the voyage. An *Umra* involves certain religious aspects similar to that of *Hajj*, but can be undertaken at any time of the year.

Two years ago, when journeying for an *Umra*, I happened to be working on this manuscript and carried some books on Sufism in Urdu and English along with me. I covered them with brown paper, hoping they would not be discovered. At Saudi Airport holy scriptures of other religions and Sufi texts can be confiscated and often thrown away with disregard. My bags were X-rayed and luckily the books escaped a detailed scrutiny.

While in Saudi Arabia, most Muslims travel to the city of Madinah to offer prayers inside Prophet Muhammad's 鑫 mosque housing his tomb. My most cherished moments are reciting the *durood e taj*, my favourite formula of salutation and blessings to the Prophet while facing his chamber. The Saudi policewoman constantly harassed me explaining that one should only read the *durood e ibrahim*, blessings on the Prophet that form an essential part of the mandatory prayers. According to the Saudi authorities, all other kinds of *durood* are wrong. Along with other women, I ignored her protests and continued reciting the popular prayer. Interestingly, neither of these *durood* are from the text of the Quran. Many accepted forms of such salutations exist in the Muslim world and are composed by Sufi scholars. When devotees lift their hands in prayer towards the golden gates of the Prophet's sacred chamber, the police guarding it almost forcibly turn their bodies in the opposite direction, ensuring that they face the direction of Makkah. For the vast number of devotees, turning one's back on the Prophet tantamounts to disrespect.

Till some years ago, my family published the Urdu monthly journal *Shama,* reputed for its literary and film content. We exported a large number of copies to the Middle East catering to the Urdu-speaking residents. Occasionally the magazine would contain a *naat,* poem in praise of the Prophet. This page would be systematically torn from all the copies that were exported to the Middle Eastern countries including Saudi Arabia.

Such a conflict in devotional expression stems from different religious ideologies within the Muslim community. Although historically Sufism has been accepted as an important aspect of Islam, some Muslim societies continue opposing the Sufi doctrine using different interpretations of Islamic scriptures, including the Quran.

Makkah and Madinah were the first centres of contemplative ascetic life inhabited by Sufis from all over the world. Now, the constant patrolling by *mutawwa*, the religious police, ensures that pilgrims do not sit in gatherings of *dhikr,* or caress the exteriors of the Prophet's chamber. Women are allowed in the compound but are subjected to severe restrictions of time and space. Prior to entering the inner area of the Prophet's tomb, women pilgrims are made to sit in groups according to their nationalities and subjected to lectures on the religious ideology of Saudi Arabia. They are warned of the grave sins in praying to the Prophet and seeking his intercession with Allah. Singing praises of the Messenger can lead to harassment or even imprisonment by the religious police. However, inside the precincts of the Prophet's mausoleum their warnings are ignored. In hushed whispers devotees recite 'formulas' for blessings that have gained acceptance through the centuries. The most popular universal greeting is:

> Ya Nabi salaam Alayka   (O Prophet Peace be upon You).
> Ya Rasul salaam Alayka   (O Apostle Peace be upon You).
> Ya Habib salaam Alayka   (O Beloved Peace be upon You).
> Salawatuthu Allah Alayka (The Prayers of God upon You).

Muslim theologians differ on whether it is lawful to address Prophet Muhammad ﷺ as *Ya Rasul Allah* or similar personal addresses that imply his being *hazir o nazir,* present. The Sufi way acknowledges the continued presence of the Prophet.

The Muslims who seek to justify Prophet Muhammad's ﷺ ordinariness usually quote the Quran: 'Say thou: "I am but a man like you,"' forgetting the following line in the same verse explaining the Prophet's exalted position as one in communion with God. 'It is revealed to me by Inspiration, that your Allah is one Allah. So stand true to Him, and ask for His Forgiveness.' (41:6) This Makkah verse, revealed before the migration to Madinah addressed those who ridiculed Muhammad ﷺ for the lack of miracles as proof of his prophecy. The Prophet quoted this verse to Utbah ibn Rabiah, one of the Makkah leaders who offered power and money to him in lieu of abandoning the Message of Islam. In contrast, Muhammad ﷺ shared mystic secrets with his close companions: 'He who has seen me has seen God.'[1]

The Sufis believe God returns the souls of His prophets, martyrs and His friends nourishing them with sustenance, 'Think not of those who are slain in Allah's way as dead. Nay, they live, finding their sustenance in the presence of their Lord.' (3:169)

Singing praises of Prophet Muhammad 鷺, a tradition during his lifetime, has now been decreed unlawful in some Muslim groups. Interestingly, there were 35 poets among the Prophet's companions who composed verses glorifying both Allah and him. Schimmel highlights the work of such poets: 'These included Kab ibn Malik, Abdullah ibn Rawaha and Hassan ibn Thabit, who served the Prophet as his poets denigrating his enemies and extolling the brave deeds of the Muslims. Thabit's poetry remains an important source for the early history of Islam.'[2] His eulogies of the Prophet extol his spiritual virtues with repeated mention of the Light that radiated from him and his role as the intercessor with God. Thabit's poetry contains allusions to wine and love that were commonplace in pre-Islamic poetry. Hassan writes:

> I witness with God's permission that Muhammad 鷺
> Is the Messenger who is higher than heaven.[3]

In another verse he praises the Light of Muhammad 鷺:

> There came to you from God a light and a clear book.[4]

Early biographers of the Prophet tell the story of the poet Kab ibn Zuhayr who used his talent to mock the Message of God. Seeking forgiveness, he arrived one morning at the Madinah mosque. The Messenger forgave the poet and Kab expressed his gratitude through a poetic rendition of love and respect for him. Kab's long poem, a classical masterpiece of Qasidah poetry became the model for later eulogies to the Prophet. Moved by Kab's verses, the Messenger praised his poetic skills and cast his cloak on the poet's shoulders as a sign of forgiveness and acceptance.

The Prophet's biographers write that when he reached Madinah, the residents of the city came out on the streets to celebrate the occasion with singing and dancing. The Prophet informed that

Allah would bless them and that he loved them.[5] Visiting Madinah remains a cherished dream with most Muslims, as expressed by poets through the centuries. Yunus Emre writes:

> *If my lord would grant it,*
> *I would go there weeping, weeping,*
> *And Muhammad ﷺ in Madinah*
> *I would see there weeping, weeping...*[6]

Jami the Persian writes:

> *It is we who, like the tulip in the desert of Madinah,*
> *Bear in our hearts the longing for Madinah,*
> *Passionate longing for paradise may disappear from the wise*
> *   man's head*
> *It is not possible that passionate longing for Madinah should*
> *   leave him.*[7]

SALAFISM: A THREAT TO CLASSICAL ISLAM

The strongest opposition to Sufism comes from the heretical view of it by Wahabi-inspired ideologies. The origins of nearly all twentieth-century extremist movements lie in this new Islamic theology that developed during the eighteenth and nineteenth centuries in the tribal areas of the eastern Arabian Peninsula. The Wahabis view Sufi practices as medieval superstition based upon idolatry. This trend began with certain groups setting out to 'purify' Islam of what they saw as *bida*, innovation. I have used as many quotes and references as I could to tell the Wahabi story.

Wahabi groups have largely been motivated by political upheavals and the rejection of traditional Islamic scholars. Their leaders have dictatorial attitudes decreeing that it is sinful to commemorate Prophet Muhammad's ﷺ birth anniversary (*mawlid* in Arabic, *milad* in Urdu), sit in collective gatherings of *dhikr*, remembrance of God, hold *sama mehfils*, assemblies of music, sing or write verses in praise of the Prophet or of venerated Sufis, and to wear the Sufi-style cloak and *dastar*, turban. Says Ed Hussain, 'Such Muslims are a deeply literalist sect where metaphors, allegories and transcendence mean little. They are exceptionally harsh towards Muslims expressing love and dedication to Prophet Muhammad ﷺ for they believe it borders on worship and therefore idolatrous.'[8]

This literalist Wahabi mindset emerged from the wastelands of Najd in Saudia Arabia among the followers of Abdul Wahab (d. 1786 AD). He adopted the discarded teachings of Imam ibn Taimiyya (d. 1328 AD), a Damascus scholar whose views created intense controversy both during his life and after his death. Taimiyya was barred from teaching and jailed several times for issuing heretic *fatwas*, decrees. He denounced a number of Sufi scholars including Ibn al Arabi and Imam Ghazali. Taimiyya decreed that visiting the *rauda*, chamber containing the Prophet's tomb in Madinah, was *haram*, sinful. Taimiyya debated Prophet Muhammad's ﷺ saying, 'Whoever visits my grave, my intercession is guaranteed for him.' Many among his contemporaries such as Shaykh ul Islam Taqi al din Subki refuted the verdict.[9] Taimiyya faced execution on charges of heresy and although his life was spared on account of repenting publicly, he remained in jail for the rest of his life.

Karen Armstrong observes:

> Taimiyya wished to update the *Sharia* so it could meet the needs of the Muslim community, but his program took an essentially conservative form. He lived during and after the Mongol invasions, when the Muslims were trying to rebuild their society. He argued that the Mongol rulers who had converted to Islam were apostates as they ruled by their own laws instead of the *Sharia*. He believed that to survive the crisis, Muslims must return to the Quran and the Sunnah of the Prophet. This meant overturning much of the medieval jurisprudence and philosophy, which had come to be sacred, in a desire to return to the Muslim archetype.[10]

But as Carl Ernst points out, 'Ironically, Taimiyya, the main source for anti-Sufi polemics writing many treatises against Sufi metaphysics, was initiated in the Qadri Sufi order.'[11] Taimiyya often contradicts himself, for some of his writings are in acceptance of the Sufi way. He is known to have said, 'As for the Sufis, they affirm the love of Allah, and this is more evident among them than all other issues. The basis of their way is simply will and love. The affirmation of the love of Allah is well known in speech of their early and recent Masters just as it is affirmed in the Book, the Sunnah and in agreement with the Salaf.'[12] Commenting on the ecstatic utterances of the mystics Mansur Hallaj and Bayazid Bistami, Taimiyya wrote, '...these are made by those drunk on the love of God which is a pleasure and which they cannot control.'

Although Taimiyya endorsed the celebration of the Prophet's birth anniversary, the Wahabis strongly oppose any gathering to mark the occasion. Taimiyya writes, 'Similar to what some people innovate by analogy with the Christians who celebrate the birth of Jesus, or out of love for the Prophet and to exalt him, and may Allah reward them for this love and effort and to take it as an honoured season, because their intention is honouring the Prophet.'[13] Throughout history, reputed Islamic scholars including Taqi al Din Subki , Imam Hajar Isqalani, Ibn Kathir, Imam Suyuti, Imam Abu Shama and Imam Shawkani regard the practice of *mawlid*, that began during the ninth century, as *bida't ul hasana,* a praiseworthy innovation that draws people nearer to God.

On the growth of the Wahabi movement, Ed Hussain writes:

> In 1774–5 Ibn Wahab negotiated a deal with the then nomadic tribe of Saud, forebears of the current royal family in exchange for support in their quest for political domination. Under the patronage of the Saud tribe, Wahabism went from strength to strength destroying Muslim shrines and deliberately seeking to annihilate those who had a bloodline that went back to Prophet Muhammad 饒, known as the *sayyids* or the *ashraf.*[14]

Observes Armstrong: 'Ibn Wahab declared the Ottoman sultans to be apostates, unworthy of obedience and deserving of death as their *Sharia* was unauthentic. He wanted to return to the Quran and the Sunnah rejecting medieval jurisprudence, mysticism and philosophy. It was an aggressive movement, which imposed itself on the people by force.'[15]

In his Pulitzer prize-winning book that traces the ideology that formed the Al Qaeda, Lawrence Wright says:

> Most Saudis reject the name Wahabi; they call themselves Muwahuddin–Unitarians since the essence of their belief is the Oneness of God, or Salafis, which refers to *salaf*, their predecessors who were the venerated companions of the Prophet. Muhammad Ibn Abdul Wahab, believed that Muslims had drifted away from true religion as it had been expressed during the Golden Age of the Prophet and his immediate successors. He banned holidays, even the Prophet's birthday, and his followers destroyed many sacred sites he considered idols. He attacked the arts for being frivolous and dangerous. He gave a warrant to his followers that they could rape, murder or plunder those who refused to follow his injunctions. Other Muslims in Arabia considered Abdul Wahab a dangerous heretic. In 1774 he was driven out of the Najd, the central part of the peninsula and sought protection from Muhammad ibn Saud, the first founder of the Saudi state. Abdul Wahab's extreme views would always be part of the fabric of Saudi rule. In this blinkered view of the Wahabis, there was only one interpretation of Islam—Salafism—all other schools of thought were heretical.[16]

Ed Hussain's *The Islamist* is a candid personal story of an ex-member of a radical Islamic organization who rejected the stringent Wahabi teachings and undertook to understand traditional Islam. Among those who deeply influenced his changeover was Shaykh Hamza Yusuf, a scholar of classical Islam. Hussain has travelled widely and worked for the British Council in Syria and Saudi Arabia. The book is a must-read for those who wish to understand the ideology of extremism as represented in political Islamic groups. Hussain observes: 'On theological grounds, the Wahabis may disagree with the older more established traditions of Muslim thought; the difficulty arose when they started killing the Sufis, the Shias and other Muslims. By killing those they disagreed with and later by having oil wealth, Wahabis ensured their dominance of modern Muslim thought, in tandem with Islamism and the commitment to an Islamic political state.[17]

Ibn Wahab declared it sinful to build domes over graves and announced that if possible, he would have demolished the structure atop the Prophet's grave. He burnt copies of the Muslim prayer manual *Dalail ul Khairaat* penned by the fifteenth-century Moroccan Sufi Imam Jazuli, because along with poetic salutations and blessings to the Prophet, its narrative included an eloquent portrait of the Prophet's final resting place. Some verses from the venerated prayer that are still recited by millions of Muslims all over the world say:

> *The man of the stalwart staff*
> *The man who wore sandals*
> *The man of argument*
> *The man of reason*
> *The man of power*
> *The wearer of the turban*
> *The hero of the Night Ascent*
> *The devoted follower*
> *The brilliant lamp*
> *He who was pure and yet purified*
> *The light of lights*
> *The spreading dawn*
> *The brilliant star*
> *The trusty handle*
> *The monitor of people over the earth.*

I quote from *The Islamist* again:

> Ibn Wahab's followers plundered and desecrated the mausoleum of Imam Hussain, the Prophet's grandson in Iraq. He discouraged guidance from acknowledged scholars advising followers to interpret the Quran themselves. The House of Saud began their

rule in 1924 taking over as the custodians of the Holy cities. Since then the Saudis have systematically promoted the Wahabi ideology throughout the Muslim world. The government of Saudi Arabia remains committed to training clerics in the Wahabi mould, sending tens of thousands of them to propagate this simple desert form of Islam.[18]

The House of Saud destroyed all historical traces of Sufis and their tombs from the holy cities. In the year 1925, all mausoleums at Jannat ul Maali and Jannat ul Baqi, the graveyards of Makkah and Madinah, including those of the Prophet's family were demolished. Once an incredible compound, reflecting the historical and religious heritage of the Muslims, now looks like a typical Wahabi burial ground with long rows of featureless unmarked graves.

Until 60 years ago, a dome had marked what once used to be Prophet Muhammad's ﷺ house in Makkah. It was destroyed and the same ground turned into a cattle market. Muslim outrage across the world led to the Saudi government building a public library over the area. The house of the Prophet's first wife Khadija has also been demolished and now forms part of the mosque compound. This was where the Prophet had received some of the early revelations and the house where his children were born. The grave of Amina, the Prophet's mother was razed to the ground in 1988, despite thousands of petitions to the Saudi government from throughout the Islamic world. At the site of *Jabal al Khandaq*, the Battle of the Trench, only two out of the seven mosques remain.

ABUL ALA MAWDUDI

In the subcontinent, Salafi and Wahabi movements, were propagated by Abul Ala Mawdudi (1903–79) who in 1941 founded the political party Jamaat e Islami in Pakistan. He gained prominence through his writings and commentary of the Quran, *Tahfeem al Quran*. Mawdudi's work has been denounced of late by most Muslim seminaries, as many passages from his commentary of the Quran were found to be objectionable. In the commentary, Mawdudi alludes to Moses as being a hasty conqueror; Prophet Dawood (David of the Psalms), as one who misused authority and Prophet Nuh (Noah), as one overcome by human deficiency and falling prey to ignorance. Yusuf's (Joseph) request to be appointed in charge of the state treasury is perceived as dictatorial and Prophet Yunus (Jonah), is seen as lacking patience.

Observes Ed Hussain: 'Mawdudi, a journalist translated the Quran outside of the paradigms of classical Muslim scholarship. He rejected Islam as a personal faith and branded it an ideology actively pursued by the political party launched by him saying: 'Islam is a revolutionary doctrine and system that overthrows governments. It seeks to overturn the whole universal order.'[19]

Mawdudi addressed non-Muslims as *kafirs*, infidels, and grouped Muslims into 'partial' and 'true' Muslims. He believed that the objectives of Islam could be realized only when power was in the hands of the righteous. In his book, *Let us Be Muslims*, he asserts that there is only one way of pleasing God, 'Allah's law must be established in Allah's land.'

Observes Karen Armstrong:

> Like any ideologue, Mawdudi was not developing an abstruse scholarly theory but issuing a call to arms. *Jihad* had never before figured as the centrality of Islamic discourse. Mawdudi demanded a universal *jihad*, which he declared as the central tenet of Islam. No major Muslim thinker had ever made this claim before. It was an innovation required, in Mawdudi's eyes by the current emergency. He argues that *jihad* was not a holy war to convert the infidels nor was it purely for self-defence and defined it as a revolutionary struggle to seize power for the good of humanity.[20]

Mawdudi wrote that Muslims must use all means to resist the *jahilya*, ignorance of the West. This form of *jihad* could include writing articles and making speeches; but eventually people should be prepared for an armed struggle.

MUSLIM BROTHERHOOD IN EGYPT

On developments in Egypt Armstrong observes:

> While Mawdudi influenced the subcontinent, Hasan al Banna formed the Muslim Brotherhood in Egypt, which propagated a similar brand of political Islam as the solution to social and political unrest. Banna formulated a six-point program based on the Salafiya reform movements. It included the interpretation of the Quran in the spirit of the age, the unity of Islamic nations, raising the standard of living and achievement of social justice and order, struggle against literacy and poverty, the emancipation of Muslim lands from foreign dominance and the promotion of Islamic peace and fraternity throughout the world. When Banna died in 1949, there were two thousand branches of the society throughout Egypt with each branch representing between three hundred thousand to six hundred thousand Brothers and Sisters.[21]

Banna raised the slogan:

> *Allah is our Lord*
> *Muhammad ﷺ is our Leader*
> *The Quran is our Constitution*
> *Jihad is our way*
> *Martyrdom is our Desire.*

In her book, *Batttle for God* Armstrong elaborates further:

> The leaders of the Muslim Brotherhood were intolerant of dissension in the ranks and Banna insisted on complete obedience. As a result after his death no one could take his place and the society was virtually destroyed by infighting. The most dangerous fallout of this reform movement was the clandestine militant group Al Jihaz al Sirri (The Secret Apparatus). Most of the society's members abhorred the terrorism of the Apparatus. Nevertheless, once a movement has started killing in the name of God, it has embarked on a nihilistic course that denies the most fundamental religious values.[22]

In 1951, Mawdudi's writings were translated and published in Egypt greatly influencing Syed Qutub (1906–66), Islamic ideologue and member of the Muslim Brotherhood. Also a novelist and literary critic, Qutub wrote the controversial book, *The Milestones*. It describes *Jahiliya*, the Age of Ignorance, a term traditionally used to describe the pre-Islamic era as 'a condition that is repeated every time society veers from the Islamic way, whether in the past, the present or the future.'[23] Qutub argued that Marxism and communism had failed the world signifying the arrival of the Islam era. He proclaimed 'I have written *Milestones* for this vanguard (Islamists) which I consider to be a waiting reality about to be materialized.' Qutub believed the ignorance in Egypt and the West to be worse than the *jahiliya* of the Prophet's time. He made *jihad* central to the Islamic vision and further radicalized Mawdudi's ideas. Whereas Mawdudi questioned the beliefs of the Muslim rulers, Qutub declared them to be infidels. While Mawdudi advocated a gradual takeover of the parliament, army and other arms of the state machinery, Qutub declared an all-out war against the *jahiliya*.

Despite pleas of clemency from King Faisal of Saudi Arabia, Qutub was executed in 1966 on charges of attempting to assassinate Gamal Abdel Nasser, the Egyptian head of state, and for advocating violence against many governments. Although banned in many countries, Qutub's books continue to spread radical ideologies of a pan-Islamic vision. His followers divide the world into *Dar al Harb* and *Dar al Islam*, the world of the believers and the world of the infidels, with their slogan *Al Islam al huwa al hall*, Islam is the Solution.

CLASSICAL ISLAM

Religious discourse can go horribly wrong unless accompanied by classical scholarship and guidance from the Masters of the faith. Sufism teaches that companionship of the holy makes you one of them. The Quran says, 'All who obey God and the apostle are in the company of those on whom is the Grace of God, of the prophets (who teach), the sincere (lovers of Truth), the witnesses (who testify), and the Righteous (who do good): Ah! what a beautiful fellowship!' (4:69) 'As to those who turn (for friendship) to God, His Apostle, and the (fellowship of) believers, it is the fellowship of God that must certainly triumph.' (5:56) The Sufi philosophy asserts that one without a Master is easily led astray. Rumi says:

> *Whoever set out on the way without a master*
> *Was misled by ghouls and fell in a well*
> *O meddler, if the shade of the Master is not above you,*
> *The cries of the ghoul will bewilder and dazzle you.*[24]

Prophet Muhammad ﷺ warned of extremism, a recognized discourse even during his time. He taught, 'Moderation. Moderation! For only with moderation will you succeed.'[25] The Quran says 'Thus, have We made of you a People justly balanced.' (2:143) The words 'justly balanced' have also been translated as 'moderation'.

In his book, *The Messenger*, Tariq Ramadan says:

Prophet Muhammad ﷺ himself retained strong ties with the members of different clans and his kin who had not accepted Islam. He demonstrated trust in non-Muslims by sending of many Muslims including members of his family to seek refuge in Christian Abyssynia. His followers continued social and financial interactions with polytheists based on mutual respect and trust. The Prophet remained sympathetic to those who had left Islam due to persecution from their families and no sanctions were issued against them. Some of them like Ayyash and Hisham expressed remorse and came back to Islam. Ubaydullah ibn Jash who had migrated to Abyssynia with the first batch of immigrants converted to Christianity and abandoned his wife Um Habibah bint abi Sufiyan. None of the Muslims in Abyssynia took any action against him and he died upholding the Christian faith. When the Prophet settled in Madinah, he made it clear that he wanted relations with the new society to be egalitarian.[26]

Rues the California-based scholar Shaykh Hamza Yusuf, 'The crisis in rejecting Sufism as one-third of Islam has had devastating results in much of the modern Islamic phenomenon.'[27]

In the rejection of classical scholarship and jurisprudence, radical modern ideologues have turned spiritual Islam into pragmatic political activism. Such stringent behaviour has created confrontational attitudes towards both non-Muslim and Muslim communities. Contrary to popular perception, the majority of Muslims worldwide practise a version of Islam which is moderate, deeply personal and spiritual. Sufi orders, veneration of Prophet Muhammad ﷺ and seeking Sufi intercession are major themes from Muslim pockets ranging from China to Morocco, representing over 80 per cent of the Muslim population in the world.

ISLAM AND *JIHAD*

Terror crimes commited in the name of *jihad* have wounded the general perception of Islam and its followers. It has become imperative to understand the roots of intolerance that are hijacking Islamic traditions of *jihad* as an ethical struggle in the way of God, to a form of militant *jihad*.

Islam classifies *jihad*—which literally means 'to strive'—into *jihad e asghar*, the less important outwardly battle fought against injustices, and *jihad e akbar*, the larger battle against the *nafs* or ego. While returning from the battlefield of Badr (the first of the holy wars), Prophet Muhammad ﷺ defined the two faces of *jihad* thus, 'We are returning from the lesser holy war to the greater holy war against ourselves.'[28]

In her book *Partisans of Allah* Ayesha Jalal writes on the subject of *jihad* in South Asia: 'If submission, faith and good conduct is constitutive of Islam, its moving principle is the notion of *jihad* as a spiritual, intellectual and moral struggle. To isolate *jihad* from faith and virtuous conduct is to lose sight of the high ethical standards that distinguish mere mortals from human beings, and to reduce the sacred to the profane and the transcendent to the purely worldly.'[29]

Unfortunately in present times, the word *jihad* creates images of gun-wielding militants called *jihadis*, a term coined by corporate global media. Grammatically the word does not exist either in Urdu, Persian, Arabic or any other language. The Arabic noun describes one who engages in *jihad* as a *mujahid*. Radicals from other religions —Hindus, Christians and Jews—have often demanded that Muslims expunge verses dealing with *jihad* in the Quran. They quote these verses to prove that militancy is inherent in Islam. Some years ago, the US government allegedly suggested something similar to their close political allies in the Muslim countries whose borders are guarded by American soldiers. Some editions of the American version of the Quran were apparently printed and later martyred in the waters of the Arabian Sea.

Observes Armstrong: 'Verses dealing with violence exist in most religious texts including the Bible and the Torah. In the Jewish holy book, the Israelis are asked to drive the Canannites from their Promised Land, to destroy their religious symbols and not to make any treaties with them. Some Jewish fundamentalists still use these verses to justify the violence against the Palestinians and continue to oppose the Middle East peace processes.'[30]

In the Christian gospels, Jesus sometimes behaves in an aggressive manner commenting that he came to bring the sword and not peace. These passages do not represent Judaism or Christianity just as those relating to *jihad* are not representative of Islamic essence.

Shaykh Hamza Yusuf continues:

> Wars are permitted in Islam but only under certain conditions between armies on battlefields. Muhammad ﷺ stressed that as an armed struggle, *jihad* could not be pursued for economic gain, personal honour or the propagation of narrow nationalism. He laid down the rules of battle, 'Do not kill women or children or non-combatants and do not kill old people or religious people.' The Prophet specifically mentioned priests, nuns and rabbis who serve God in seclusion. He forbade the mutilating of bodies, the cutting

down of trees and the poisoning of the wells of the enemies. He prohibited the burning of houses and cornfields, and the killing of livestock—except when compelled to eat them. The Prophet established an exemplary code of conduct for the prisoners of war. The perpetrators of terror are people who hate too much. The Quran urges not to let the hatred of a people prevent you from being just. Prophet Muhammad 🕊 said, 'Mercy is not taken out of anyone but the damned.'[31]

Imam Feisal Rauf, the author of *Whats Right with Islam* observes:

Two kinds of Islam existed in the first Islamic century where extremism was a recognized discourse. The first was the kind taught by Prophet Muhammad 🕊 and the other Islam was as practised by the Khwarijis, a group that developed *takfiri*, a political philosophy that identified anyone who disagreed with their understanding of Islam as unbelievers. This extremist ideology resulted in the dissident group justifying the killing of innocent people including women and children. In order to protect true Islam, the fourth Caliph Imam Ali militarily fought the *Khwarijis* and was assassinated in the process. The current battle within the Muslim community is between the Islam of Prophet Muhammad 🕊 and the modern *Khwarijis* who are waging a war of terror using Islamic terminology under the banner of the Muslim faith. In linking political activities in Islamic contexts, militant groups have nurtured wrong perceptions of Islam.[32]

Traditional Islam accepts the Quran as a source of spiritual nourishment and not a political document. Creating the space for non-Muslims, the Quran asks the Muslims to say, 'And I will not worship that which ye have been wont to worship, Nor will ye worship that which I worship. To you be your Way, and to me mine.' (109:4–6) The verse is often quoted during interfaith dialogues for it clearly establishes the principle of peaceful coexistence. Another verse on the concept of pluralism is, 'O mankind! We created you from a single (pair) of a male and a female, and made you into nations and tribes, that ye may know each other (not that ye may despise (each other).' (49:13) This verse was revealed when the Prophet returned to Makkah after establishing the victory of Islam. He granted forgiveness to all in Makkah who came to him, or a companion, teaching that former opponents be treated with kindness. He reminded them of Prophet Joseph's story and how his brothers who intended to kill him had sought forgiveness, He said: 'This day let no reproach be (cast) on you: Allah will forgive you, and He is the Most Merciful of those who show mercy!'(12:92)

Abu Jahl had tortured Muslims for years and made the Prophet's life miserable in Makkah. After conquering Makkah, Muhammad ﷺ told his companions to be kind to Abu Jahl's son, Ikrimah, who would come to them as a believer. He asked them to stop condemning Ikrimah's dead father for it would hurt his sentiments. 'By Him in whose hand is my soul, none of you shall enter paradise until you believe, and none of you shall believe until you love one another.'[33]

Thirteen assassination attempts were made on the Prophet's life and not once did he seek revenge. He told the Muslims not to respond to persecution with aggression, assuring them that Allah rewards those who remain patient, quoting the verse, 'What is the life of this world but amusement and play? But verily the Home in the Hereafter—that is life indeed, if they but knew.' (29:64)

It was after 13 years of passive resistance that the verse sanctioning an armed struggle in order to establish peace was revealed,

To those against whom war is made, permission is given (to fight), because they are wronged; and verily, Allah is most powerful for their aid; (they are) those who have been expelled from their homes in defiance of right, (for no cause) except that they say, "Our Lord is Allah" Did not Allah check one set of people by means of another, there would surely have been pulled down monasteries, churches, synagogues, and mosques, in which the name of Allah is commemorated in abundant measure. Allah will certainly aid those who aid his (cause); for verily Allah is full of Strength, Exalted in Might, (able to enforce His Will). (22:39–40)

Jihad is a theological issue and therefore scholastic bodies exist in Islam to explain its relevance. Most traditional scholars agree that *jihad* as battle can only be declared by an Islamic state and not by individuals. I admit becoming rather apprehensive when Muslims talk of reinterpretation of the Quran. Whenever Muslims have tried to do so, it has resulted in radical movements. The Sufi philosophy accepts that there is only one interpretation—that explained by Prophet Muhammad ﷺ and carried forward through classical scholarship.

The early Muslim scholars and jurists incorporated diverse legal opinion but agreed on a core set of beliefs, developing an incredibly sophisticated corpus of Islamic thought, theology and jurisprudence. This heritage assures us of the transmission of Islamic values at the highest level. Leaving aside opinions on newer issues such as bio-ethics, most basic questions regarding day-to-day life have been addressed by the traditional scholars. As a commentator on Muslim issues, I have often been asked the question, 'Does Islam need reform?' I respond that it is not Islam but Muslims who need to reform. We need to reclaim our intellectual heritage with its spiritual traditions.

However, the votaries of 'reformist Islam' including the Jamaat e Islami, Ahle Hadith and Salafis continue denouncing Sufism, permitting no other vision of religious truth. This new face of Islam has nothing to do with Sufis, music, poetry, miracles, or the countless local devotional customs that give a distinctive flavour to a host of Muslim cultures around the world. Sufism is not an innovation, but the continuity of a thought process that links us to our religious predeccesors all the way to Prophet Muhammad ﷺ. Sufism is the preserved path of spirituality that forms the heart of Islam.

There is no god other than He.

BOOK II

Masha'a Allah: What God wants.
It is used in the sense of 'What God does, is done well'.

7

THE MYSTIC DIALOGUE

My body is flooded
With the flame of Love.
My soul lives in
A furnace of bliss.
Love's fragrance
Fills my mouth,
And fans through all things
With each out breath.

Kabir

Most Muslims in the subcontinent, including my family members, converted to Islam due to the influence of the Sufis. Their emphasis on peace, equality and tolerance drew commoners to the fold. The Arab traders first introduced Islam in the subcontinent from the Malabar Coast to Ceylon. The Western Provinces became part of the Muslim Empire in 711 AD, with the Arabs having conquered Sindh and the adjacent provinces northward up to Multan. The second wave of Muslim conquests in India brought scholars like Al Biruni (d. 1048 AD), as well as other historians and Sufis. However, it was during the twelfth and thirteenth centuries that Sufism became a mass movement. The Islamization of the country was achieved largely by the preaching of the dervishes and not by the sword.[1]

Shaykh Saifuddin Kaziruni from Iran became the first Sufi to settle in the subcontinent. He was the nephew and spiritual successor of Shaykh Abu Ishaq Kaziruni (d. 1035 AD) who ordered his disciple to mount a camel and follow whatever direction the animal went, finally settling wherever it rested. The camel halted in the middle of a desert where Shaykh Saifuddin founded the town of Uch.[2] The historian Ibn Batuta wrote that the Sufi was highly venerated by the people of China and India. They recognized him as the protector of travellers. Both traders and rulers made huge gifts to his *khanqah*. Voyagers on the Sea of China made vows of offerings to the Shaykh to return safely from the turbulent waters. The tradition continued with large offerings of money being made even by the later rulers of the Delhi Sultanate.

The annexation of Punjab prompted many Sufis to settle in the region. Shaykh Ali ibn Uthman Hujwiri of Ghazna (d. 1071 AD) became the first great Sufi scholar to settle in Lahore, the capital of the Ghaznawids in India. He had met all the leading Sufi Masters of his time including Qushayri, the author of *Ar risala fi ilm tasawwuf*.[3] Shaykh Hujwiri wrote many books on Sufism including the famed *Kashf al Mahjub*[4] (Uncovering of the Veils) that remains an important Sufi manual.

Sufism began to impact the subcontinent after the consolidation of Sufi orders in the Islamic world during the twelfth and thirteenth centuries. Sufism blossomed when the books of scholars like Imam Ghazali, Junayd Baghdadi, Abu Said ibn Abi Khair, Ibn al Arabi, Ali ibn Uthman Hujwiri, Shihabuddin Suharwardi and Mevlana Rumi reached Indian shores, becoming hugely popular with the local believers. Abul Fazl's *Ain e Akbari* mentions 14 Sufi *silsilas* active in India during the sixteenth century, many of which continue to flourish. Muslims of the Indian subcontinent mostly follow the

Chisti, Naqshbandi, Qadri and Suharwardi Orders. Headquartered at Ajmer, the Chishti Order, with its inclusive traditions, remains the most popular.

Interestingly, the Vedanta and Sufi philosophies had begun to interact before Sufism emerged on the Indian scene. In the eleventh century, the Natha yogis travelled to Central Asia and Iran from their centre in Peshawar. The Sufis learnt breathing techniques from them to facilitate their meditations. Other wandering yogis and Sanskrit scholars impacted Sufi orders in Turkey, Syria, Egypt and Central Asia. The Chinese traveller Hieun Tsang writes of Buddhist monasteries and Hindu temples at Khorasan in Central Asia. Hindu scholars taught Indian sciences at the famed universities of Baghdad where interfaith dialogues were held with Muslim mystics. The *Upanishads* containing the early expositions of pantheistic philosophy inspired Sufi thought in many ways.

Ibn al Arabi of the thirteenth century, who was known as Shaykh ul Akbar or the Greatest Master, articulated the theory of *wahdat ul wujood*, Oneness of God, that became the most powerful thought to dominate later Sufi philosophies. According to A. J. Arberry, 'He advocated an extraordinarily complex theory of self-realization that the *insaan e kamil*, Perfect Man, is a miniature of Reality; he is the microcosm, in whom are reflected all the perfect attributes of the macrocosm, only the Perfect Man knows God, loves God and is loved by God who made the world for man alone.'[5] The Sufi Master believed that Paradise was little else but the Divine form hidden in the mystic's heart. The Advaita philosophy was reflected in the Muslim understanding of this concept.

In India, Vedanta and Sufism came to share a common discipline in their spiritual pursuits. The interaction between Hindu and Muslim mystics became frequent and meaningful, reflected in every area of social life. The topics discussed in the *jamaatkhana*, assembly hall, of Baba Farid at Ajodhan, fuelled the interests of yogis whose beliefs were founded on Hatha Yoga. The Sufis freely borrowed principles of breath control, meditation and concentration from Hindu spiritualists.

Baba Farid composed meditation prayers in Punjabi for his disciples, many of which are still recited by devotees from the Chishti discipline. His verses had a deep impact on Guru Nanak and 134 of the Sufi poet's hymns are included in Sikh holy scriptures. It is believed that Guru Nanak composed the famed *Asa ki var*, a morning hymn sung by Sikhs, at the *khanqah* of the Baba upon a request by one of his successors Shaykh Ibrahim who was known as Farid the Second.

The Sufis preach *al khalq o ayalullah*, all humanity forms the family of God. They draw inspiration from Prophet Muhammad ﷺ who proclaimed, 'All creatures are His family, and he is the most beloved of God who does good to His creatures.' The mystic belief in the Oneness of God defined their humanitarian approach to life. When asked about the highest form of devotion, Khwaja Gharib Nawaz declared it was, 'To redress the misery of those in distress, to fulfil the needs of the helpless and to feed the hungry.' Sufi Masters offered food and shelter to people of every faith at their *khanqahs* and furthered this concept of devotion. Sufis established such hospices throughout the subcontinent, spending their lives cementing ties between people of varying classes and faiths.

Hazrat Nizamuddin Auliya would often say that there was no better way of reaching God than bringing happiness to the human heart. His inclusive outlook often upset the orthodoxy but the masses adorned him with the title *Mehboob e Elahi*, the Beloved of God. His tomb in Delhi remains a place of pilgrimage for people belonging to different faiths. Amir Khusrau, his poet disciple, took great pride in the local culture and language.

Hamiduddin Nagauri, a disciple of Khwaja Gharib Nawaz, adopted the life of a Rajasthani peasant. His wife used to weave cloth and he tilled the land, refusing grants from the Sultans of Delhi.

The Chishti Sufi adopted vegetarianism and spoke the local *Hindavi* dialect. Ignoring the orthodox clergy, he went to the extent of calling a Hindu, *wali*, a friend of God. Even today, no non-vegetarian food is distributed at his *dargah* in Nagaur.

The Sufis of Kashmir preferred to call themselves Rishis and their order adopted local customs, integrating Islamic and Hindu mystic traditions. They remained dedicated servants of the people irrespective of class and religious distinctions. The Rishis generally remained celibate and chose to be vegetarians. Shaykh Nuruddin, popularly called Nund Sanz, was the founder of the Rishi *silsila*. While Nund Sanz acknowledged the famed Kashmiri Shaivite woman mystic Lalla as his spiritual mentor, modern historians write of her being influenced by Islam. Together they became the precursor of the religious fusion between the ancient Vedic heritage and Sufi traditions that define the language and culture of the Kashmiri people. The *Lalla Vakyani*, the Wise Sayings of Lal Ded or Lalla, continues to influence the Kashmiris.

The Indian Sufis contributed to the development of local languages including Hindavi, Bengali, Dakkani and Gujarati. Sayyid Muhammad Gesu Daraz, the spiritual successor of Hazrat Naseeruddin Chiragh Dilli was once asked why Sufis took a greater interest in Hindi. The Chishti Sufi replied that Hindi had a vibrant vocabulary that lent itself well to the articulation of Sufi thought processes. Sufi poets who wrote in Avadhi included Mullah Dawood, Qutbun, Malik Muhammad Jayasi and Manjhan.

The Bhakti Movement that challenged the prevalent religious orthodoxy and crusaded against social divisions, remains the best representative of this composite confluence. The coming together of Hindu and Muslim mystics in the thirteenth century resulted in a dynamic reformist force impacting Indian life, culture and history forever. The mystics rose from various regions to challenge the prevailing social evils: Guru Nanak in Punjab, Ramanand and Kabir in Uttar Pradesh, Chaitanya in Bengal, Tukaram, Namdev,

Tirlochan and Parmanand in Maharashtra, Mira Bai and Dadu in Rajasthan, Vallabha Swami in Telengana, and Sadhna in Sindh.

The spirit of religious ferment was all over the country; people who knew nothing or little of each other felt the pull of the zeitgeist and were voicing the same concepts in their own languages in distant parts of India. By the end of the fifteenth century, the influence of the Bhakta orders was far greater than that of Brahmanical Hinduism. More importantly, many of the Bhaktas had taken positive steps towards a rapprochement with Islam.[6]

Ramanuja (1016–1137 AD) advocated the path of bhakti and travelled extensively to Hindu centres of pilgrimage in the southern and northern part of India. The ideas of Ramananda (1360–1470 AD) helped establish the *Vishisht Advaita* as a significant force in Indian classical philosophy. He preached that the individual human soul is not identical with the Supreme but is a fragment of the Divine force. Ramananda furthered the traditions established by Ramanuja and preached devotion to the incarnation of Vishnu in the form of Rama and Sita. His philosophy greatly influenced the mystics of the Bhakti Movement.

Namdev came from a low-caste family of tailors in Pandharpur. He believed the hidden God to be the only Reality—one that spoke to every heart. He wrote Hindi and Marathi hymns that are marked by his deep Vaishnavite beliefs. There are 60 hymns of Namdev in the Sikh holy book, Adi Granth. Namdev writes:

> *Pure and Splendour He came*
> *As a waft of fragrance,*
> *No one saw Him come,*
> *No one saw Him go.*
> *How claim to know the nature*
> *Of Him who has no lineage?*
> *The flight of birds in the sky,*
> *The way of fish in the water,*
> *Leave no trace for the eye,*

The heat from the heavens creates a mirage
A vision of water for the thirsty deer.
These are illusions
As is knowledge of the Lord of Namdev.[7]

The devotional renaissance swept through medieval India and produced great writers and poets like Mira, Tulsidas, Surdas, Jayasi, Dawood and Qutbun. All of them used the language of the masses to further their message of inclusion. The synthesis was navigated by hundreds of yogis and Sufi poets who worked towards understanding and respecting one another. This people's movement articulated a powerful vision of amity and coexistence.

Kabir (1440–1518 AD), a Muslim weaver, emerged to become the timeless mystic poet whose verses are deeply ingrained in the culture of north India, and even included in the holy scriptures of the Sikhs. A disciple of Ramananda, he became the chief protagonist of Hindus and Muslims criticizing religious orthodoxy. Kabir Panthis (followers of Kabir) provided a link between people of different faiths, and his verses called *sakhis* and *dohas,* doctrinal poems, continue to be sung across the subcontinent. On his death, Kabir left people wondering if he was a Hindu or a Muslim. People from both the communities wished to claim his body. According to legends, only a bunch of flowers was found under his shroud when they opened the room where his body lay. Kabir's internalization of spiritual tenets and Indian lore makes him a complete Hindustani, beyond the barriers of religion, creed and identity politics. Describing himself as a child of Rama and Allah, Kabir is perhaps the simplest of voices from the Bhakti era that speaks of Divine love and universal brotherhood. He writes:

Those stars in the sky
Who has designed them and put them there?
O learned Pandit, know you what hold the heavens?
Only the fortunate ones know the secret.

He has given light to the Sun and Moon
In everything, shines the spirit of the Creator.
Says Kabir, only he will know
Who has God in his heart and His name on his lips.[8]

Khuswant Singh observes:

The Sikh faith was founded by Nanak—the first Guru of the Sikhs— who elevated Reality to the One Supreme God. He spent his time meditating and seeking the company of wandering hermits. A Muslim musician, Mardana, became his first disciple. Nanak composed hymns, while Mardana set them to music, and the two began to organize sessions of community singing. At the age of 30 Nanak had a mystic experience in which he found himself in the presence of God. He went missing for three days and nights. When he came back, the first thing he said was, 'There is no Hindu and no Musalman.' Nanak then took on the life of a preacher. Accompanied by Mardana, he travelled to distant places within India and abroad. He visited many holy cities of the Hindus and Muslims, pointing out the folly of meaningless rituals, and emphasizing the common aspects of both faiths. Nanak died in 1539 AD, acclaimed by both Hindus and Muslims as the king of holy men. It was from the teachings of the Muslim Sufis, notably Shaykh Farid, and the Bhaktas, primarily Kabir, that Nanak drew inspiration.[9]

To further the mystic message Guru Nanak used traditional terms familiar to both Hindus and Muslims such as Allah, Khuda, Sahib, Ram and Hari. In Guru Nanak's hymns *Rida,* the Sufi interpretation of Divine will and *Hukam,* God's command, are used as interchangeable terms. Similar to the Sufi emphasis on *dhikr,* the Sikh form of prayer is usually the repitition of God's name and the chanting of hymns in His praise. Most of the hymns are composed by Shaykh Farid, Kabir, Namdev and the Sikh gurus themselves.

When asked, 'What is superior, Islam or Hindusim?', the Guru replied, 'Devoid of good deeds, both will not find a place in God's court.' Nanak rejected ascetic ways and encouraged a normal life of righteousness. He sang:

> *There is one God,*
> *He is the Supreme Truth*
> *He, the Creator,*
> *Is without fear and without hate,*
> *He, the Omnipresent,*
> *Prevades the universe,*
> *He is not born,*
> *Nor does He die to be born again.*[10]

Sufi poetry in Hindi and other regional dialects added a fresh dimension to Indian literature, presenting a novel way of reaching spiritual states of ecstasy. Indian music and verse, combined with Persian imagery, created a wonderful new genre of Sufi thought. Among the prominent Sufi poets who wrote in Avadhi are Mullah Dawood, Qutbun, Malik Muhammad Jayasi and Manjhan. The earliest known *Mathnawi*, epic poem, written in Hindi is Maulana Dawood's *Chandayan* in the fourteenth century. Popularly called Mullah Dawood, the poet came from a district in Uttar Pradesh near Rae Bareilly and was a Sufi of the Chishti Order. He was among the *khalifas* of Shaykh Zainuddin, a nephew and disciple of Hazrat Naseeruddin Chiragh Dilli. *Chandayan* is a heart-rending love story about Lorak and Chanda, based on a folk tale of Dalmau.

Touched by *Chandayan*, Shaykh Abdul Qudoos of Gangoh translated some of its verses into Persian and often gave discourses on them with the same intensity as he would on the works of Ibn al Arabi. Another preacher of the time, Maulana Shaykh Taqiuddin recited the verses of *Chandayan* from the pulpit of the mosque, which had an ecstatic effect on listeners. He declared Dawood's *Mathnawi* to be Divine truth and Divine love, compatible with the interpretation of some verses of the Quran.

Qutbun composed *Mrigavati*, Manjhan wrote *Madhumati*, and

Malik Muhammad Jayasi wrote the classic *Padmavat* based on the bardic songs of Rajasthan. His other works in Hindi are *Kanhavat, Kahranama, Pustinama* and *Holinama*. Jayasi earned the title of *Muhaqqiq e Hind*, Researcher of Indian Truth. Shaykh Qutbun used Hindu terminology describing the Essence as Light and calling God Niranjan, Kartar, Vidhata, Paramesh, Ekonkar and Alakh.

In Bengal, the Hindus and Muslims came to share a common language and culture. Chaitanya, the Bengali devotee of Krishna had a Muslim disciple, Thakur Haridas. Chaitanya was a Vaishnavite who believed that virtue, knowledge and meditation should be subordinated to one's devotion of Lord Krishna and Radha. He introduced the concept of Krishna Bhakti—and group singing accompanied by drums, cymbals and *ektara,* a single-string instrument, was his favourite form of worship.

The close association of this movement with Sufism gave rise to Baul singers. The Hindu Bauls believe that their first guru Bhirbhadra, a son of Nityananda (d. 1544 AD) received the Baul faith from a Muslim woman called Madhava Bibi. The Hindu Bauls sing in the tradition of Chaitanya, celebrating the union of Radha and Krishna, while the Muslim Bauls sing Sufi verses.

A leading Sufi of Chittagong, Syed Sultan (d. 1648 AD) wrote mystic verse in an attempt to reconcile Hatha Yoga with Sufism. Abul Hakim of the seventeenth century authored a long poem called *Chari Maqamer Bhed*, identifying the *chakras,* energy wheels or centres within the human body as defined by ancient Hindu traditions, with *maqaam*, spiritual stations of the Sufi path.

In Maharashtra, Namdev, Eknath, Tukaram and Ramdas strived to preach the Oneness of God, rejected idol worship, and worked towards reconciling Hindu–Muslim differences. Vedic philosophy is found in the teachings of the Gujarati Sufis Shaykh Ganjul Alim (d. 1391 AD) and Syed Burhanuddin (d. 1411 AD).

The Sufi contribution in the field of music is immense. Among the Chishti Sufis, the commitment and passion for poetry and music is overwhelming. *Sama*, musical assemblies, were regularly held at their *khanqahs*. Khwaja Qutubuddin Bakhtiar Kaki of Delhi died after a long spell of spiritual ecstasy resulting from the recitation of a couplet. Hazrat Nizamuddin Auliya expressed a desire to die during *sama* in a similar spiritual state. In accordance with his wishes, *sama* singers accompanied his funeral procession. His disciple Amir Khusrau contributed greatly to Indian classical music.

The later Sufis persistently walked on the road to amity. Miyan Mir (d. 1535 AD) of Lahore laid the foundation of the Golden Temple at Amritsar. Shah Kaleemullah (d. 1729 AD) of Delhi directed his *khalifas* to instruct disciples in local languages. Shah Abdul Aziz Dehlvi (d. 1824 AD) often told his disciples that Allah and Parmeshwar were one and the same. Mirza Mazhar Jan e Janan of Delhi, a Naqshbandi Sufi of the late eighteenth century, looked upon the Vedas as a revealed book. He commented that the worship of idols was similar to the *dhikr*, the contemplative ritual of the Muslim mystics.

Shaykh Abdul Qudoos Gangohi (d. 1537 AD), the sixteenth-century Sufi scholar, finds the teachings of Gorakhnath identical to the Sufi doctrine of Oneness of Being. His Hindi verse supporting the Nath doctrine is found in the Shaykh's treatise, *Rushdnama*. Shaykh Abdul Qudoos finds the ascetic exercises of the Nath Yogis identical to the Chishti discipline and uses the pen name Alakh for his remarkable Nath poetry.[11] There are many references in the *Rushdnama* to Gorakhnath, Shri Gorakh, and Nath. It also uses the term *Siddha* for the Perfect Man. During a period of political upheaval, the Sufi scholar wrote to Sikander Lodhi exhorting him that an hour in the pursuit of justice was worth more than 60 hours of prayers. The Shaykh advised the ruler to protect the weak in order to avoid anarchy. Once the Sufi admonished his disciple in a letter:

> *Why this meaningless talk about the believer,*
> *The kafir, the obedient, the sinner,*

The righteous, the guided, the misdirected, the Muslim,
The pious, the infidel, the fire worshipper,
All are like beads in a rosary.

Shaykh Rukunuddin, the son and successor of Shaykh Abdul Qudoos of Gangoh compiled a commentary on the *Rushdnama.* When questioned how the poetry of the yogis could embody the teachings of Islam, the Sufi explained how the Quran affirms that more than a hundred thousand prophets have been sent to guide different communities in various parts of the world. The Shaykh argues that it was not possible that Allah did not send a prophet to India. He reinforced that although possibly corrupted, the essence of Indian religions was founded on the concept of *Tawhid*, the Oneness of God.

Prince Dara Shikoh, son of Emperor Shahjehan and disciple of Mullah Shah wrote to Shah Muhibullah, a reputed Sufi of Allahabad, enquiring whether discrimination between Hindu and Muslim subjects is permissible in state matters. The Chishti Sufi replied in the negative, explaining that God sent Prophet Muhammad ﷺ as *Rahmat al Alameen*, Mercy for all of creation and not for Muslims alone. Dara Shikoh translated the *Upanishads* into Persian with the help of learned Hindu scholars.

The *Urs*, death anniversary celebrations and other festive occasions celebrated at *dargahs*, developed into significant cultural institutions. The Sufis have contributed immensely to India's composite culture that we recognize today. For the votaries of Sufism, love and service to mankind irrespective of caste, creed or religion remain the essentials of all spiritual paths. In the words of Mevlana Jalaluddin Rumi:

By loving wisdom does the soul know Life
What has it got to do with senseless strife?
Of the Hindu, Muslim, Christian Turk?

Sufi history in the subcontinent is the story of various challenges and responses. Some of the Sufis presented in the following chapters of the book are among the most well known and venerated ones.

In the name of Allah, the Merciful, the Benificient.

8

THE CHISHTIS

KHWAJA MOINUDDIN CHISHTI (D. 633 HIJRI/1236 AD)

Numerous miracles are attributed to Khwaja Moinuddun Gharib
Nawaz, Patron of the Poor, regarding his arrival at Ajmer during the
rule of the Rajput king Prithvi Raj Chauhan. According to popular
belief, the Queen Mother's knowledge of astronomy and occult
predicted Khwaja's arrival 12 years earlier. Images of him were drawn
and distributed to officers instructing them to ban the Sufi's entry
into the kingdom. At Samana (the old state of Patiala) some Rajput
officials recognized Khwaja and requested him to stay in the palace.
Khwaja then had a vision of Prophet Muhammad ﷺ warning him
of his impending betrayal, he continued his journey to Ajmer with
a group of 40 followers. When the party wanted to rest under some
trees, the local camel keepers did not permit it, insisting that the
spot was exclusively marked for the king's camels. The group led by
Khwaja eventually found shelter near the Anasagar Lake. The next
day, the camels that had rested under those trees refused to move. The
perturbed king ordered the camel keepers to seek Khwaja's pardon,
after which they found that the animals were back on their feet.

Another legend recounts that the Brahmins once prevented
Khwaja and his followers from using the waters of the Anasagar

Lake for their ablutions. Khwaja asked a devotee to collect some water from the lake in a small bowl. While the bowl continued to fill up, the waters of the lake dried up completely. Only when the officials and local people pleaded for forgiveness did water return to the lake.

However, it is not for miracles, but his teachings of humanity for which Khwaja Moinuddin Chishti is honoured. He laid down the principles of the Chishti Order preaching that the way to God lay in developing 'ocean-like generosity, sun-like bounty and earth-like humility'.

Born in Sistan, Khwaja grew up in Khurasan where his parents had migrated. His father, Khwaja Ghiyasuddin Hasan, died when Moinuddin was barely 15 years old. The young lad earned his living from an orchard and watermill that he had inherited from his father. One day while he was tending to the fruit trees, Ibrahim Qunduzi the dervish happened to pass by. Khwaja kissed his hand and requested that he sit under the shade of a tree in his garden. After eating some grapes, the dervish took some seeds out of his mouth and placed them in Khwaja's mouth. It created an illuminating spiritual experience for Khwaja who sold all his possessions and embraced the mystic path.

Khwaja travelled to Samaqand and Bukhara in pursuit of knowledge. After spending a few years in the cities of learning, he sought the guidance of Shaykh Uthman of Harwan, practising religious austerities for two-and-a-half years under the renowned mystic. The Shaykh appointed Khwaja as his principal *khalifa* saying, 'My Moinuddin is the beloved of Allah. I am proud of his being my *murid* and of his *murids*. This is my complete glory.'

Khwaja then travelled to Makkah and Madinah with Shaykh Uthman who prayed for his disciple's success and salvation. Once while the two stood under the canopy of the Kaaba, a heavenly voice proclaimed, 'O Moinuddin, I am pleased with you and have accepted you. Ask for whatever you desire and I shall give it to you.Moinuddin replied, 'O Allah, accept those *murids* who will follow me and those who descend from me.' The order came, 'O Moinuddin, you, all your *murids* and all the *murids* who will be descended from you until the Day of Judgement, I accept them all.' After that Khwaja would often say, ' Whoever is my *murid*, and whoever is the *murid* of my *murids* and whoever is descended from me until the Day of Judgement, Moinuddin will not step into paradise without them.'[1]

Khwaja was bestowed with the title of Gharib Nawaz in Madinah. When he offered greetings to Prophet Muhammad 鷺, 'As salaam o alayka ya Rasul Allah', he heard the reply, 'Va alaikum as salaam ya Gharib Nawaz.' While at the holy city, Khwaja received a spiritual inspiration to settle in the Indian town of Ajmer.

After leaving the Arabian Peninsula, Khwaja set out for Baghdad. In Sanjan he spent some time with Shaykh Najmuddin of the Kubrawi Order. In Baghdad, Khwaja met with leading Sufis of the time, including Shaykh Shihabuddin Suharwardi and Shaykh Abdul Qadir Jilani. He then travelled to Hamdhan where he met Shaykh Yusuf Hamdhani. Khwaja visited the tombs of Shaykh Abu Said ibn Abi Khair in Mayhana and Shaykh Abu Hasan Kharqani in Kharqan. When Khwaja travelled to Herat his fame began to attract large crowds. In search of solitude, he left for Ghazna from where he reached Lahore and spent 40 days meditating at the *dargah* of Hazrat Uthman Ali ibn Hujwiri. From Lahore, Khwaja came to Delhi and after spending a while in the capital city he finally reached Ajmer.

Gharib Nawaz stressed on the renunciation of wealth encouraging self-discipline and prayer. He preached tolerance, advocating respect for all religions. Khwaja did not differentiate between love, the lover, and the beloved. He believed that while the *Hajjis*, pilgrims, walked around the Kaaba—those with Divine knowledge circled the heart, for God resides in the hearts of those who love Him. Khwaja's inclusive message of peace and brotherhood brought hundreds of thousands to the fold of Islam. He had a great fondness for music, and *sama mehfils* held at his *khanqah* attracted both mystics and commoners.

Khwaja died on 6 Rajab 633 Hijri/March 1236 AD and his mortal remains were buried in Ajmer. That night various people dreamt of Prophet Muhammad ﷺ saying, 'I have come to receive Moinuddin al Hasan, the friend of Allah.' and it is said that these words appeared on Khwaja's forehead: 'The Lover of Allah died in the love of Allah.'

Through the centuries Khwaja's devotees have beautified his simple grave. The Ajmer *dargah*, considered the most sacred in South Asia, attracts thousands of pilgrims from different religious and economic backgrounds in the quest of the Sufi Master's blessings. It has enjoyed the constant patronage of ruling families and other individuals. The first recorded ruler to visit the *dargah* was Muhammad bin Tughlaq in 1332 AD. Later in the fifteenth century, the Khiljis of Malwa and Mandu were devotees of Khwaja. On capturing the fort of Ajmer, Mahmud Khilji paid his respects to Khwaja by distributing offerings in his name. Ghiyasuddin Khilji funded the construction of the *Buland Durwaza*, the main entrance of the *dargah* complex.

Emperor Akbar remained an ardent devotee of Khwaja Moinuddin, considering himself blessed by the Master. The *Akbarnama* records Akbar making the pilgrimage to Ajmer 14 times, several of them on foot. It also narrates how the emperor's interest came to be kindled.

One night his majesty went off to Fatehpur to hunt and passed near Madnadhakar which is a village on the way to Agra …. A number of Indian minstrels were singing enchanting ditties about the glories and virtues of the great Khwaja … may his grave be hallowed—who sleeps in Ajmer. Often had his perfections and miracles been in the theme of discourse in the holy assemblies. His Majesty, who was a seeker of the truth, and who, in his zealous quest sought for union with travellers on the road of holiness, and showed a desire for enlightenment, conceived a strong inclination to visit the Khwaja's shrine. The attraction of a pilgrimage thither seized his collar.

Akbar visited Ajmer in 1568 AD after the Chittor conquest, and after the Bihar and Bengal conquests in 1574. He presented the *khanqah* with a huge cauldron, which is still used for cooking during the *Urs* celebrations. The emperor solicited Shaykh Salim Chishti's prayers and intercession to Khwaja for the birth of the crown prince Salim (Jehangir). The *Akbarnama* records Akbar walking from Agra to Ajmer for a thanksgiving pilgrimage.

Jehangir credited Khwaja with his birth and the dignity of the Mughal clan. He lived in Ajmer for nearly three years and visited the *dargah* nine times. The emperor presented another smaller cauldron in 1614 AD, in which food was cooked and distributed to 5,000 people. The two cauldrons are probably the largest and oldest cooking utensils in the world that have been in constant use for centuries. Emperor Shahjehan visited the *dargah* five times, and always on foot. He constructed the striking white marble mosque in the *dargah* compound. His daughter Jehanara, although initiated in the Qadri order remained a lover of Khwaja Gharib Nawaz. The princess authored a well-known book on his life and teachings, recounting her personal spiritual experiences at Ajmer. She had a pillared marble porch constructed in front of Khwaja's tomb. Although Aurangzeb was not inclined towards mystics, he offered tributes at Khwaja's *dargah* after defeating his elder brother Dara Shikoh.

The Scindias who took over Ajmer in 1791 AD were devoted to the *dargah,* repairing its many dilapidated buildings. Nawab Haidar Ali Khan of the Deccan presented the crown-like pinnacle of the mausoleum in 1896 AD. On 23 December 1911, the Queen of Britain visited Ajmer and had the water tank roofed. More recently many Indian and visiting heads of state have made the Ajmer pilgrimage.

Khwaja's teachings transmitted through the Chishti Masters led to the popularity of the Chishti Sufi Order. The legend of Khwaja Moinuddin presents an exemplary life demonstrating Islam as understood by the Sufis.

QUTUBUDDIN BAKHTIAR KAKI (D. 635 HIJRI/1237 AD)

There are different legends on how Khwaja Qutub got the title of Bakhtiar Kaki. The most accepted one narrates that his wife used to take provisions on credit from a nearby grocer to feed her starving family. One day, the grocer taunted her by saying that the family would have starved to death had it not been for his kindness. Khwaja Qutub learnt of the remark and forbade the taking of provisions on credit. Pointing to a niche in the wall, he told his wife to recite '*Bismillah*' and take bread from it. The *kak,* bread, continued appearing miraculously till his wife revealed the secret to others.

Khwaja Qutub, the foremost *khalifa* of Khwaja Moinuddin, earned the title of *Qutub ul Aqtaab*, the central pole. He established the first Sufi centre in Delhi. His family drew its lineage from Imam Hussain, the grandson of Prophet Muhammad. The young Khwaja travelled to Baghdad where he became a disciple of Khwaja Moinuddin, and then followed him to India. Khwaja Qutub was instructed by his mentor to stay in Delhi where Sultan Iltutmish welcomed him. The sultan remained an ardent devotee visiting the Khwaja's *khanqah* twice a week.

The local clerics resented the Khwaja's popularity and used his love for musical assemblies to stir up controversies. On learning of his disciple's troubles, Khwaja Moinuddin came to Delhi and asked Khwaja Qutub to accompany him to Ajmer. When the two mystics began their journey, the citizens of Delhi came out on the streets and followed them for miles. Led by Sultan Iltutmish, the people wept and picked up the dust the Sufis walked on as a holy relic. Touched by the display of affection, Khwaja Moinuddin ordered his disciple to continue residing in Delhi. In gratitude, Sultan Iltutmish kissed the feet of Khwaja Moinuddin and escorted Khwaja Qutub back to his capital city.

Despite his intimacy with the Sultan, Khwaja Qutub led an ascetic life steeped in poverty. He read the entire Quran twice each night and taught his disciples to help the needy without the hope of any reward.

He believed, 'The seekers on the path of God are a community who are overwhelmed in the ocean of Love from head to the nail of the foot'. He taught austerity purifies the soul bringing it close to God.

Khwaja Qutub held that *sama*, musical assemblies, kindled the fire of love, and died in a state of ecstasy listening to mystic verse. He passed away on 14 Rabbi ul awwal 635 Hijri/1237 AD. The funeral prayers were led by Sultan Iltutmush and the Khwaja was buried at Mehrauli, in the land he had purchased for his grave. On account of Khwaja Qutub's exalted rank, Khwaja Moinuddin Chishti decreed that those coming to seek his blessings must first pay homage to Khwaja Qutub. The tradition is still followed and pilgrims travelling to Ajmer Sharif first visit the *dargah* of Khwaja Qutub at Mehrauli.

All the rulers of Delhi venerated Khwaja Qutub, seeking his blessings. Qutubuddin Aibak, the founder of the Slave Dynasty named the Qutub Minar after the Sufi.

SUFI HAMIDUDDIN NAGAURI (D. 673 HIJRI/1274 AD)

Sufi Hamiduddin lived in Suwali, a village near Nagaur, Rajasthan, where he had bought a small piece of land. Refusing offerings of money from the Sultan, he lived off the earnings made from tilling his field. His wife would spin yarn for their simple clothing. Respecting the sentiments of the majority Hindu community, the Chishti Sufi advocated vegetarianism and ate no meat. He requested his followers that even after his death, no meat should be cooked and distributed for the peace of his soul, a sentiment still respected at his *dargah*.

Sufi Hamiduddin was a *khalifa* of Khwaja Moinuddin Chishti. Born in 1192 AD at Lahore, the family migrated to Delhi where he studied under the famed religious scholars Maulana Shamsuddin Halwai and Muhammad Juwayini. He became fluent in Arabic, Persian and the Hindawi dialect spoken in Rajasthan.

At a young age the Sufi became a disciple of Khwaja Moinuddin, and began leading an ascetic life. He accompanied the Master on his first trip to Delhi, amazing audiences with his knowledge of mysticism. On one occasion, Khwaja asked his companions to request anything of God, assuring them it would be granted. Shaykh Hamiduddin replied that having surrendered to God's will, he desired nothing. Pleased with the disciple's annihilation of self-desire, Khwaja bestowed him with the title *Sultan Tariqin,* Master of the Sufi Way.

In contrast to the Chishtis, the Suharwardi Sufis enjoyed and accepted state patronage. Disturbed by the worldly possessions of Bahauddin Zakariya of Multan—the head of the Suharwardi Order, the Chishti mystic wrote him a number of letters but remained dissatisfied with the replies. The two mystics then met in Delhi where they engaged in a discussion on wealth. Sufi Hamiduddin compared money to a dangerous serpent, asserting that storing it was akin to rearing a snake. He reminded the Suharwardi Sufi Master of Prophet Muhammad's ﷺ proclamation, 'Poverty is my pride.'[2]

Equipped with a vast knowledge of Islamic law, Sufi Hamiduddin taught that *Sharia* and *Tareeqa* were similar to body and soul. 'The seekers of God have no will of their own and *futuwwa*, the qualities of the chivalrous were like a tree growing in a garden of friendship, the fruits are taken or given away without any feeling of honour.' He believed that ignorance remained the biggest curse and said, 'Human beings without knowledge were no better than fossils.' The Sufi died on 29 Rabi ath thani 673 Hijri/1274 AD and lies buried in Nagaur, the place where he spent most of his life. In the year 1330 AD, Sultan Muhammad bin Tughlaq constructed a mausoleum over the Sufi's grave.

BABA FARID GANJ E SHAKAR (D. 644 HIJRI/ 1265 AD)

It is said that overpowered by hunger after three days of incessant fasting, Baba Farid put some pebbles in his mouth, which turned into *shakar*, sugar. Another popular anecdote explaining the Sufi's title *Ganj e Shakar*, treasury of sugar, emanates from an event in his childhood. To encourage the habit of offering mandatory prayers, his mother routinely rewarded her son by placing some sugar under his prayer carpet. One day at the early morning prayer, although she forgot to place the sugar, the child found it under the carpet. Sufi piety attributes the miracle to Divine intervention.

Baba Farid, the first Sufi poet of Punjab, inherited the spiritual mantle from Khwaja Qutubuddin Bakhtiar Kaki. He settled on the banks of the Sutlej, and his village Ajodhan came to be called Pakpattan, 'the ferry of the pure.' Details of Baba Farid's life are found in Siyar ul Auliya and Fawaid ul Faa'd, the books containing the discourses of Hazrat Nizamuddin Auliya that were written during his lifetime.

Mongol invasions forced Baba Farid's father Qazi Shuaib of Kabul to leave for Lahore with his three sons. He moved to the district of Qasur where the family was received with respect by the ruling Ghaznavid Sultan. Although the Qazi was reluctant to accept any official positions, the Sultan made him the Qazi of Kathwal. Fariduddin Masud, the second of three sons, was born to Qazi Shuaib and Qarsum Bibi sometime around 1175 AD.

After completing his education in Kathwal, the young mystic joined the *madarsa* of Maulana Tirmidhi where he committed the Quran to memory, reciting it once every 24 hours. Baba Farid met Khwaja Qutub at the mosque of Shaykh Bahauddin Zakariya and recited the verse:

> *He who is approved by you, is approved eternally*
> *And none is disappointed of your blessing*
> *Your mere attention to any particle, even for a while*
> *Makes it better than a thousand splendid suns.*

Baba Farid accompanied Khwaja Qutub to Delhi, who assigned a *hujra*, meditation cell, to the disciple at his *khanqah* in Mehrauli.

Once while Khwaja Moinuddin visited Delhi and saw the young mystic, he remarked, 'Farid is a falcon who will not make his nest anywhere except on a tree in heaven. He is a lamp that will illuminate the order of the Sufis'. Khwaja Moinuddin asked his disciple to bless the young mystic but Khwaja Qutub did not think it proper to do so in front of the Master. Khwaja Moinuddin then blessed Baba Farid, making him the sole Chishti Master to have been blessed by both his Master and the Master of his Master.[3]

Baba Farid traversed the spiritual path under the inspired guidance of Khwaja Qutub. He performed *chilla e makus*, the difficult 40-day ascetic exercise by tying himself with a rope and hanging upside down in a well for 40 days and nights. He undertook this retreat in the secluded forest of Uch with the help of his follower Khwaja Minai of Hansi who pulled the mystic up from the well at prayer times. Baba undertook another 40-day meditation at Ajmer in a cave adjacent to the tomb of Khwaja Moinuddin Chishti.

Khwaja Qutub sent Baba Farid to Hansi, knowing that the disciple was not destined to be present at the time of his death. The Master entrusted Farid with his prayer carpet and staff, informing him that he would leave his *khirqa*, cloak, *dastar*, turban, and sandals with Qazi Hamiduddin Nagauri. He instructed Baba Farid to collect these on the fifth day after his death. A few days later Baba Farid heard of Khwaja Qutub's demise and arrived back in Delhi on the fourth day. As prophesized by Khwaja Qutub, his disciple received the Master's belongings on the fifth day from Qazi Hamiduddin.

Baba Farid lived a life of contemplation and poverty advising all: 'If you desire greatness, associate with the downtrodden.' He had a large family that suffered as a consequence of the severe restrictions he imposed on himself. Baba Farid lived near the Jami mosque in a small mud house with a thatched roof, forbidding the use of burnt bricks as it went against his ascetic principles. He remained absorbed in the worship of God to such a degree that once when he was informed that his child could die of starvation, he commented, 'If fate has so decreed and he dies, tie a rope around his feet and throw him out.' Even at times of affliction, Baba Farid remained devoted to God reciting:

I love thee: I love thee
Is all that I can say,
It is my vision in the night,
My dreaming in the day:
The blessings when I pray,
I love thee:I love thee:
Is all that I can say.

Baba Farid's *khanqah* relied on *futuh*, unsolicited gifts, and did not own any land. Refusing to deal with governments and rejecting offerings of land, Baba Farid often said: 'Do not turn your attention to worldly people. Do not accept grants of villages or gifts from kings. You will not go to the doors of kings and seek rewards from them. If travellers come to you and you have nothing to offer, think of it as a blessing from God.'

The *Siyar ul Auliya* records that Baba Farid's possessions consisted of a small rug, which he used to sit on during the daytime and cover himself at night. Khwaja Qutub's *asa*, staff, rested behind his head and he caressed it respectfully. Baba Farid fasted through the day without having *sehri*, the predawn meal. A glass of sherbet and dried grapes were brought to him at the time of *iftar*, breaking of the fast. His evening meal consisted of a piece of millet bread. In the early days of Ajodhan, a *zanbil*, begging bowl, would be carried to the town twice a day and everyone shared the collected offerings. Provisions at the *khanqah* were not stored for more than a day and were distributed to the needy.

The ascetic discipline and brotherhood of Baba Farid's *khanqah* remains an outstanding example of the life of the early Chishti Sufis. The dervishes lived and worked in one large room. Visitors were welcome and the door remained open till midnight, with the table always spread for unexpected guests. The *khanqah* residents served the Master and the community, occupying themselves with prayer and studies. Baba Farid encouraged a sound education and showed a keen interest in poetry and music. He disseminated Sufi teachings through popular songs, influencing the population, particularly women who took to singing mystic verses while doing their daily work.[4] Baba Farid wrote poetry in Persian, Arabic and the local Hindawi dialect. The Granth Sahib, the holy scriptures of the Sikh faith, contains 135 hymns written by him.

Baba Farid's assemblies attracted scholars, merchants, government servants, artisans and mystics from all sections of society. Some stayed forever, some for a short while, and others simply came to seek his blessings. A broad range of discussions were held and visitors included countless yogis who shared their philosophies and breathing techniques with the *khanqah* inmates.

Despite his fame, Baba Farid spent his last years in extreme poverty. Since there was no money in the house to purchase his shroud, Sufi Amir Khurd's grandmother provided the white sheet to wrap his mortal remains. Baba died on 5 Muharram 644 Hijri/1265 AD and lies buried in Pakpattan, a few hours drive from Lahore.

Baba Farid taught that knowledge of the religious laws should bring humility and one should act upon it rather than harass people with it. He preached that a true mystic aroused love and affection in people's hearts. From among his numerous disciples, Baba Farid appointed seven *khalifa's*, the most outstanding one being Hazrat Nizamuddin Auliya of Delhi.

MAI SAHIBA BIBI ZULEKHA (D. 658 HIJRI/ 1260 AD)

Bibi Zulekha, the mother of Hazrat Nizamuddin, is popularly called Mai Sahiba. Whenever there was no food to eat in the house, she told her children, 'Today we are the guests of God.' She explained to them that God sent spiritual nourishment for them, which differed from worldly food. Mai Sahiba reminded her children of their lineage to Prophet Muhammad 彘. She said that they were among those who fed the hungry and clothed the naked. Weakened by fasts and hunger, Bibi Zulekha inculcated a sense of resignation and contentment in the little ones. She often looked at her son's feet remarking, 'Nizamuddin! I see signs of a bright future for you. You will be a man of destiny some day.' When her son asked her when that would happen, Mai Sahiba would say, 'When I am gone.'

During the Mongol invasions of Bukhara, Khwaja Ali and Khwaja Arab, the maternal and paternal grandfathers of Hazrat Nizamuddin migrated to India. Initially they travelled to Lahore, later settling in Badayun along with many other refugee families. Bibi Zulekha's husband, Khwaja Syed Ahmad, died when their children were a few years old. She brought up her son and daughter, Bibi Jannat, amidst great hardship, earning a living by weaving cloth. Devoted to her son's education, she provided for the best teachers in Badayun. To enable him to pursue further education, the family migrated to Delhi.

Hazrat Nizamuddin recounted that when his mother prayed, she appeared to be in direct communication with God and her prayers were always granted. Each new moon the Shaykh placed his head on her feet seeking blessings. On the night of a new moon, Mai Sahiba said, 'Nizam! At whose feet shall you put your head next month.' The tearful son asked, 'At whose care shall you entrust me.' Mai Sahiba replied, 'I will tell you tomorrow.' She then directed him to sleep in the neighbouring house belonging to Shaykh Najeebuddin Mutawakkil, Baba Farid's brother. In the early hours of the morning the female attendant rushed to Hazrat Nizamuddin, asking him to return home immediately. Mai Sahiba held her son's right hand, whispering her last words, 'O Allah. I entrust him to Thee.'

Mai Sahiba died on 30 Jumada al ula 658 Hijri/1260 AD and lies buried in the village of Adhchini, at the house where she lived. Her *dargah* in Delhi draws hundreds of devotees, especially women. It is believed that Mai Sahiba cannot bear the sorrow of women and their prayers are heeded to immediately. In times of acute distress, Hazrat Nizamuddin prayed at his mother's tomb and said his prayers were always granted.

❀ ❀

HAZRAT NIZAMUDDIN AULIYA (D. 725 HIJRI/1325 AD)

One of the greatest Sufi Masters of the fourteenth century, the masses lovingly addressed Hazrat Nizamuddin Auliya as *Mehboob e Elahi*, the Beloved of God. Emperor Firoz Shah Tughlaq referred to him as *Sultan al Mashaikh*, Emperor of the Mystics. Ziyauddin Barani, a historian of the times, gives the following account of the Sufi's popularity:

> Shaykh Nizamuddin admitted all sorts of people as his disciple, nobles and plebians, rich and poor, learned and the illiterate, citizens and villagers, soldiers and warriors, free men and slaves. These people refrained from many improper activities and the general public showed an inclination to religion and prayer. Out of respect for the Shaykh's discipleship, all talk of sinful acts had disappeared from the people. There was no quarter in the city in which gatherings of the pious was not held every month with mystic songs that moved them to tears. Out of regard for one another, Muslims refrained from open usury and hoarding while the shopkeepers gave up lies and using false weights and deceiving the ignorant.

The Sufi Master maintained that although there were many ways leading to God, none was more effective than bringing happiness to the human heart. He taught that looking after the destitute had far greater value than formal religious practices.

Hazrat Nizamuddin's family migrated from Bukhara to India following the invasion of Central Asia by the Mongols. His grandfather settled in Badayun where the Shaykh was born in 1238

AD. He was brought up by his mother, for his father died when he was five years old. On reaching 16 years of age, the young mystic arrived in Delhi to complete his studies.

Bibi Zulekha faced trying conditions of poverty and often her son and daughter lived without food for days. In Delhi the family found shelter at an inn near the thatched home of Shaykh Najeebuddin Mutawakkil, who lived in the village of Adhchini. Hazrat Nizamuddin qualified for the post of a *Qazi*, religious cleric and requested Shaykh Najeebuddin to pray that he might get the post. The Sufi observed that he should make his life more purposeful, and advised the young Nizamuddin to visit his brother at Ajodhan. On reaching there it seemed to Nizamuddin that Baba Farid awaited his arrival, as he welcomed him with the couplet:

> *Ae Aatish e furaqat dil ha kabab kardah*
> *Selaab e ishtiqat khanaha kharab karda*

> *(The fire of your separation has burnt many hearts*
> *The storm of desire to meet you has ravaged our lives.)*

The dervish from Delhi formally became a disciple of Baba Farid, who encouraged him to go back to the city and complete his education. On the second visit, Baba Farid appointed the 27-year-old mystic as his chief successor, conferring him with the *khilafatnama* in 664 Hijri/1265 AD. He asked the disciple to have it signed by Maulana Jamaluddin in Hansi and Qazi Muntajabuddin in Delhi. When Shaykh Nizamuddin seemed nervous about accepting the responsibility, Baba Farid comforted him with the words, 'Nizam, take it from me, though I do not know if I will be honoured before the Almighty or not, I promise not to enter Heaven without your disciples.'

Shaykh Nizamuddin wondered why Baba Farid had not asked for the *khilafatnama* to be signed by his elder brother, Najeebuddin Mutawakil; on arriving at Delhi, he learnt of Shaykh Najeebuddin's death. He then travelled to Hansi where Maulana Jamaluddin signed the *khilafatnama* with the words: *Gauhar sapurda ba gauhar shanaas,*the pearl has been entrusted to one who knows its value.

During Baba Farid's lifetime, Shaykh Nizamuddin visited Ajodhan thrice. On the last visit the mentor predicted, 'Nizamuddin, you will be a tree under whose shadow people will find rest...strengthen your spirits by devotion...you will receive some of my personal belongings for at the time of my death you will not be present.' After Baba Farid's death, his prayer carpet, cloak and staff were entrusted to his spiritual successor.

At Ajodhan, a friend from Delhi expressed shock at seeing Shaykh Nizamuddin in a miserable condition, wearing tattered clothes. He remarked that had the mystic become a teacher at Delhi he would have been affluent. The Shaykh reported the incident to Baba Farid, who instructed him to carry a tray of food on his head to the friend's house and recite:

> *You're not my fellow traveller*
> *Seek your own path*
> *May you be prosperous and I downtrodden.*

Moved, the friend removed the tray from Shaykh Nizamuddin's head and expressed a desire to meet Baba Farid. He ordered the servant to take the empty tray back to the *khanqah* but Shyakh Nizamuddin insisted on carrying it back on his head.

Aware of his disciple's poor living conditions, Baba Farid gave him a gold coin on his return to Delhi. On learning that it was the last coin in the Master's house, the Shaykh placed the coin back at Baba Farid's feet, who then remarked, 'I have prayed to the Almighty to give you a portion of earthly goods.' Shaykh Nizamuddin became anxious that worldly comfort would destroy his spirituality but Baba Farid assured him that the bounty would not be troublesome.

Since Shaykh Nizamuddin did not have proper accommodation in Delhi, Imad ul Mulk, the maternal grandfather of Hazrat Amir Khusrau, welcomed him to his home. His house was enormous and his sons lived out of town. But two years later the sons returned without any intimation and evicted the guest. Tired of changing many houses, the Shaykh thought of migrating from Delhi, but destiny had other plans. One day while meditating near the garden at Hauz e Rani, the Shaykh heard an inner voice directing him to Ghiyaspur. He had never heard of the name before but found the small village and decided to live there. Today the *dargah* stands in the same place as the Shaykh's *khanqah* and the area is now known as Nizamuddin.

The Shaykh's fame spread and thousands of people became his followers. His *khanqah* stood by the side of the Jamuna River, where he lived in a small room spending time in meditation, fasting and prayer. The Master and the *khanqah* inmates spent their days in starvation. Often a collection bowl for food would be placed at the door. When the time came to break the fast, the contents of the bowl were emptied on the dinner cloth. The Shaykh ate sparingly, tearfully confessing of the trouble he had swallowing food while countless people starved in the city.

Once the Master and his disciples had starved for three days in succession. When a woman from the neighbourhood sent some flour to the *khanqah*, a disciple added water and placed it on the stove to cook. Shortly, a dervish appeared asking for something to eat. On being informed that the food was not ready, he began to display signs of impatience. Shaykh Nizamuddin placed the boiling cooking pot in front of the dervish. To everyone's surprise, the visitor smashed the utensil on the ground uttering, 'Shaykh Farid has bestowed his spiritual blessings on Nizamuddin. I break the vessel of his material poverty.' Soon enormous *futuh* began to flow into the *khanqah* and the kitchen grew to become a huge establishment, distributing food to thousands of people each day. The tiny unknown village of Ghiyaspur turned into a prosperous suburb visited by the rich, poor, learned, and illiterate, townsfolk, villagers, soldiers, warriors and slaves.

Sama mehfils were held regularly and remained a source of spiritual nourishment for the Sufi Master. Amir Khurd writes, 'Any verse or tune which affected the Shaykh during these musical assemblies would become popular among the people for a long time. The young and the old, the nobles and the commons, at their meetings and in the quarters and lanes of the city would enjoy them through the blessings of the Shaykh.'

The area of the *jamaatkhana* served as a welfare centre, attending to the needs of the locality. Once when some houses in the neighbourhood caught fire, the barefooted Shaykh rushed to the spot. He stood there till the flames were completely extinguished, personally counted the burnt houses, and appointed his deputy to help the affected families with silver coins, food and water. There are countless recorded instances where the Shaykh personally looked into the needs of the destitute. Despite a busy routine, he kept his door open and met visitors in the evening.

Thirteen rulers ascended the throne during the Shaykh's lifetime but he never visited their courts. Even though Sultan Alauddin Khilji and his family had great faith in the Sufi, Shaykh Nizamuddin kept away from the royal family. Once, Alauddin Khilji sent a letter to the Shaykh requesting him for guidance. He left the letter unopened remarking, 'We dervishes have nothing to do with the state. I have settled in a corner of the city and spend my time in prayer. If the Sultan does not like this, I will go and settle some place else. God's earth is vast enough.'

On learning of the starving conditions at Shaykh Nizamuddin's *khanqah*, Sultan Jalaluddin made an offer of some villages. A few disciples urged the Shaykh to accept the official grant but he rejected it. The ruler sought an interview with the Shaykh but was politely refused. The Sultan then thought of making a surprise visit to the *khanqah*, but the Shaykh learnt of the plans and sent the message, 'If the Sultan enters by one door, I will make an exit through the other door.'

Political intrigues towards the end of Alauddin Khilji's life, deprived his sons from succeeding to the throne. Princes Khizr Khan and Shadi

Khan were both initiated by Shaykh Nizamuddin before being captured by their political rivals. Before they were blinded and executed, they were asked how their faith benefited them. The princes replied that they had been saved from shedding blood and hoped to be raised under Shaykh Nizamuddin's banner on the Day of Judgement.

Mubarak Khan, the new ruler, hatched conspiracies against Shaykh Nizamuddin, forbidding his noblemen from visiting Ghiyaspur. He built the Masjid e Misri mosque where all the clerics and Sufis of the city were ordered to offer prayers. Shaykh Nizamuddin refused to comply saying, 'The mosque in my nieghbourhood has a bigger claim on me.'

On the first day of the new moon, the nobles and dervishes were expected to gather at the court and pray for the Sultan's well-being. Shaykh Nizamuddin did not go but sent his attendant Iqbal to represent him. Sultan Mubarak took serious offence and threatened the Sufi with dire consequences if he failed to pay homage in person. In a twist of fate, Mubarak Khan was assassinated on the night of the new moon by his favourite protégée Khusrau Khan Barwar.

On becoming the ruler of Delhi, Khusrau Khan gave large sums of money to the dervishes to pray for his success. The Shaykh accepted the gift of 500,000 *tankas,* distributing the money among the needy. Shortly after, Ghiyasuddin Tughlaq ascended the throne of the Delhi Sultanate and ordered that the money be returned to the state treasury. Shaykh Nizamuddin asserted that the money had been distributed to the poor. The Sultan could not take action against the Sufi, but the incident sparked off a conflict between them. Envious of the Shaykh's popularity, some local *ulemas* incited the Sultan further. They alleged that the Sufi Master encouraged musical assemblies that were prohibited by the *Sharia* laws. It led to a major debate on the subject that remained largely inconclusive.

During the rule of Ghiyasuddin Tughlaq the Sufi Master had a *baoli,* water tank, constructed adjacent to his *khanqah.* The vindictive Sultan issued orders from Bengal banning state workers from helping in its construction. Many of the labourers were devotees and they worked in the darkness of the night. On hearing this, the ruler banned the sale of oil to ensure that lamps could not be lit. When the work came to a halt, Shaykh Nizamuddin asked his helpers to collect water from the tank. He then ordered Shaykh Naseeruddin to light the lamps with water. The lamps glowed with light and the construction resumed. Shaykh Nizamuddin awarded his disciple the title *Roshan Chiragh Dilli*, Bright Lamp of Delhi. The water tank was completed in a record number of seven days. It remains part of the *dargah* complex even today, reminding us of the Shaykh's spiritual powers.

An offended Ghiyasuddin Tughlaq sent word that Shaykh Nizamuddin should leave Delhi before he returned from his Bengal compaign. The Shaykh calmed his worried followers saying, '*Hunooz Dilli door ast*', 'Delhi is still far away'. Prince Juna Khan, the future Muhammad bin Tughlaq, made arrangements to welcome the victorious Sultan. The elaborate wooden pavilion at Tughlaqabad collapsed causing the death of Ghiyasuddin Tughlaq and his son Mahmud, who were buried under the debris.

People considered Shaykh Nizamuddin the most favourably endowed man alive but the mystic felt otherwise, 'No one in the world is as sad and unhappy as I am. Thousands of people come to me with their troubles and it afflicts my heart and soul. Strange is the heart that listens to sorrow and is not touched by it. The dervishes who retire in the mountains and jungles are lucky.' Shaykh Nizamuddin was generous, compassionate, forgiving, and praised the religious devotion of women: 'In matters of prayer the intercession of pious women is sought before pious men.' On the subject of women and spirituality, the Shaykh remarked, 'When a lion comes out of a den no one ever asks if it is male or female.'

His teachings added a new dimension to the understanding of Islamic ideals. He believed revenge to be the law of the jungle, 'If a man puts a thorn in your way and you also put thorns in his way, there will be thorns everywhere.'

He often quoted Prophet Muhammad 🕮: 'All God's creatures are His family and he is most loved by God who does good to His creatures.' Prior to death, the Sufi Master told his followers that he dreamt of the Prophet calling out, 'Nizam we are anxiously waiting for you.' An *aashiq e rasul*, lover of the Messenger, he wrote:

> *O breeze! turn towards Madinah*
> *and from this well-wisher recite the Salaam.*
> *Turn round the king of the prophets*
> *and with the utmost humility recite the Salaam.*
> *Sometimes pass the gate of mercy*
> *and with the gate of Gabriel rule the forehead.*
> *Salaam to the prophet of God*
> *and sometimes recite Salaam at the gate of peace.*
> *Put with all respect the head of faith on the dust there.*
> *Be one with the sweet melody of David*
> *and be acquainted with the cry of anguish.*
> *In the assembly of the prophets*
> *recite verses from the humble being 'Nizam'.*

At the age of 82, Shaykh Nizamuddin Auliya died on 18th Rabi ath thani 725 Hijri/1325 AD. Sultan Muhammad bin Tughlaq had just ascended the throne of Delhi. In accordance with the Sufi's wishes, *Sama* singers accompanied the funeral procession in which thousands took part. The Sultan carried the funeral bier and Shaykh Rukunuddin Suharwardi Multani led the funeral prayers. Baba Farid's cloak was spread over the Shaykh's body and his prayer carpet placed upon the disciple's head.

Shaykh Nizamuddin had expressed a desire to be buried under the open sky but Muhammad bin Tughlaq built a dome over the grave. Later kings and nobles made additions to the *dargah* complex. Firoz Shah Tughlaq constructed the latticed screens around the mausoleum. Alauddin Khilji built the *Jamaatkhana* mosque, architecturally the first to be adorned with five huge domes.

Shaykh Nizamuddin appointed many *khalifas*, the chief among them being Naseeruddin Roshan Chiragh Dilli to whom the Shaykh's belongings were entrusted. With the death of Hazrat Nizamuddin Auliya, a historic phase of the Sufi movement in Delhi came to an end.

All the Mughal rulers from Akbar to Bahadur Shah Zafar made pilgrimages to the *dargah* of Hazrat Nizamuddin. On reaching Delhi, Babur sought blessings at the *dargah*. Emperor Akbar selected a place for his father Humayun's mausoleum near the Sufi's tomb. When Akbar escaped an attempt on his life, he attributed it to the blessings of the Sufi. Jehangir prayed at the *dargah* when faced with rebellion from his son Shahjehan. Muhammad Shah, the later Mughal emperor, lies buried at the feet of Hazrat Nizamuddin. Jahanara Begum, Emperor Shahjehan's favourite daughter remained devoted to the Chishti Sufi and chose the site of her grave opposite his tomb. Many renowned people of Delhi, including the poet Ghalib, chose to be buried in graveyards adjacent to the *dargah* complex. Some of Hazrat Nizamuddin's *khalifas* lie buried in the nearby compound called *Chabootra e Yaaran*. People of different faiths continue paying homage to the memory of a life dedicated to the service of humanity.

۞ ۞

HAZRAT NASEERUDDIN ROSHAN CHIRAGH DILLI (D. 757 HIJRI/1356 AD)

Hazrat Naseeruddin, the celebrated *khalifa* of Hazrat Nizamuddin Auliya, came to be called, *Roshan Chiragh Dilli*, Lamp of Delhi. His Master bestowed the title for he lit lamps with water instead of oil, to facilitate the construction of a water tank after the hostile sultan banned the sale of oil.

Naseeruddin Mahmud was born around 1276 AD at Ayodhya in Awadh, the town where his grandfather migrated from Khorasan. The family traces its lineage to Imam Hussain, the grandson of Prophet Muhammad ﷺ. The mystic's father died when he was nine years old, and he was brought up solely by his mother. Drawn to asceticism, the young boy spent his time engaged in prayer and incessant fasting. At the age of 25, he abandoned the world, embracing the Sufi way. The search for a spiritual mentor brought him to Delhi where he became a disciple of Hazrat Nizamuddin.

Used to an ascetic life in the jungles of Awadh, Shaykh Naseeruddin expressed the desire to return to a life of seclusion. Hazrat Nizamuddin ordered the disciple to remain in Delhi, suffering the hardships and indignities that people inflicted on him. A few months before his death, Hazrat Nizamuddin awarded a *khilfatnama* to Shaykh Naseeruddin.

Shaykh Naseeruddin lived in Delhi for 32 years in the area now known as Chiragh Dilli. His early years were steeped in poverty and many nights were spent without a flicker of light. Often, in front of visitors the mystic would cover his tattered garments with Hazrat Nizamuddin's cloak.

Shaykh Naseeruddin fiercely fought Muhammad bin Tughlaq's theory of the state and religion being inseparable. The Chishti Masters traditionally isolated themselves from the court, believing that engaging in government matters hindered spiritual achievements. Tughlaq made it extremely difficult for the Sufi to continue living in Delhi. The ruler had forced the population of the capital city to move to his new capital in the Deccan. The exodus caused a large void in the social, cultural and religious life of Delhi. It took the Shaykh tremendous effort to rebuild the former life around the *khanqah* that had been dismantled due to the Sultan's eccentric decision.

The Sultan resented the popularity of Sufis over the orthodox clergy, whom he utilized to influence public opinion. Shaykh Naseeruddin witnessed bitter doctrinal differences between the mystics and the jurists in the Islamic world. Ibn Taimiyya, the controversial scholar of Damascus, had launched an attack on the practices and institutions of medieval mysticism. The Delhi mystic silenced the orthodox opposition and attracted some outstanding scholars to the mystic fold.[5]

Between the years 1348–50 AD, Muhammad bin Tughlaq was preoccupied suppressing the rebellion in Gujarat headed by Taghi. In 1349 AD the Sultan's rule had been restored in Gujarat and he left in pursuit of Taghi who had escaped to Thata. Passing through Kathiawar, the Sultan summoned a few nobles and clergy from Delhi. These included the Sultan's cousin Firoz Tughlaq and Shaykh Naseeruddin who were implicated in instigating the rebellion. However, the Sultan died before the two reached Thata. Meanwhile an army from Transoxania arrived in Delhi to aid the Sultan against the rebels. On learning of the Sultan's death, they began to attack the Delhi army. In an effort to save Delhi from Mongol rule, the leaders and Sufis supported the ascension of the 46-year-old Firoz Shah Tughlaq to the throne. Shaykh Naseeruddin attended the coronation ceremony, offering prayers for the ruler and the people of the country.

Shaykh Naseeruddin never visited the court again, retreating to the quiet life of the *khanqah*. Although Firoz Shah Tughlaq showered the Sufis with gifts, the Shaykh's *khanqah* remained committed to traditions of poverty. When the Sultan came to meet the Shaykh, the ruler was treated like any other ordinary visitor and often kept waiting. The Shaykh fasted regularly and ate very little at permissible times. He took an interest in *sama* but never allowed the use of musical instruments. Following in his Master's footsteps, Shaykh Naseeruddin chose to remain unmarried.

One day after offering the afternoon prayers Naseeruddin retired to his room. A *qalandar* by the name of Turab entered the room and stabbed him with a knife inflicting 11 wounds on his body. Seeing blood gushing out of the drain near the *jamaatkhana,* some disciples rushed inside and stopped Turab from further attacking the Shaykh. They wanted to retaliate but the Shaykh forbade them, showing concern for the assailant. He then asked Turab for forgiveness, lest the knife had hurt the assailant's hand, and made the disciples promise that they would not harm Turab in any way. When news of the assault spread, people came out crying and wailing on the streets. The Sultan requested that Turab be handed over to the state for punishment. The Shaykh gave Turab 25 silver *tankas,* asking people to forgive him just as he had. Under the protection of the Shaykh, the assailant left Delhi unharmed.

The Shaykh believed it was necessary to associate with people and at the same time withdraw from worldly affairs. He stressed upon the importance of earning a livelihood by honest means and warned that black marketing led to the ruin of a society. He believed that when dervishes slept hungry and meditated in the early morning, they experienced Divine light in their souls. He emphasized the importance of breath control during meditation, defining a perfect Sufi as one with articulated breath.

Shaykh Naseeruddin survived three years after the assault on his life, dying on 18 Ramadan 757 Hijri/1356 AD. He was buried at his own house, in a place he selected for his grave many years earlier. The Shaykh did not consider any among his disciples as worthy of receiving the treasured relics entrusted to him by Shaykh Nizamuddin. In accordance with his wishes, the cloak of his Master was placed over his body, the staff laid beside him, the prayer beads wound upon his finger, the wooden bowl placed over his head, and the Master's sandals rested upon his breast. Shaykh Naseeruddin's foremost disciple Sayyid Muhammad Gesu Daraz bathed his body.[6]

Delhi has been traditionally known as *Baees khwaja ki chaukhat,* the threshold of 22 Sufi Masters. There is a belief that Prophet Muhammad ﷺ gifted some of his personal possessions, including a cloak and prayer carpet, to the elders of the Chishti Order. The Chishti Sufis draw their spiritual lineage from Hasan of Basra who was initiated by the Prophet's son-in-law Imam Ali. These sacred relics came to the subcontinent with Khwaja Gharib Nawaz of Ajmer, and were then entrusted to his successor Khwaja Qutub Bakhtiar Kaki, who passed them on to Baba Farid. They arrived in Delhi with

Baba Farid's disciple Shaykh Nizamuddin Auliya who handed them to Shaykh Naseeruddin. The latter willed that the relics be entombed with him. The spiritual chain from Hazrat Naseeruddin to Prophet Muhammad ﷺ remains an unbroken *silsila* of 22 *Khwajas*, and Delhi became their threshold.

Firoz Shah Tughlaq built Shaykh Naseeruddin Mahmud's mausoleum in 1373 AD. Baba Farid's granddaughter, the Shaykh's nephew and *khalifa* Shaykh Makhdoom Zainuddin, and other mystics lie buried in the graveyard of the *dargah* complex at Chiragh Dilli in New Delhi.

۞ ۞

HAZRAT AMIR KHUSRAU (D. 725 HIJRI/1325 AD)

Hazrat Nizamuddin would often tell Khusrau, 'Pray for my life, for you will not be able to survive me long.' While in Bengal with the army of Sultan Muhammad bin Tughlaq, a sudden sadness overcame Khusrau's heart. The poet took permission from the Sultan to return to Delhi. On his arrival, he heard of the demise of his beloved Master. He immediately rushed to the Shaykh's tomb and began shrieking, 'The sun has gone underground and Khusrau is alive.' The poet blackened his face, tore his garments and laid face down on the tomb of the Master, reciting his last verse:

> *Gori sove sej par, mukh par daare kes*
> *Chal khusrau ghar aapne, rain bahi chahun des.*

> *(The fair one lies on the couch*
> *black tresses scattered over her face*
> *O Khusrau, go home now,*
> *for night has fallen over the world.)*

With his playful riddles, songs, melodies and poems, Amir Khusrau remains a household name throughout the subcontinent. *Tooti e*

Hind, the Nightingale of India, wrote *ghazals, qasidahs, mathnawis,* and *rubais* along with prose in Arabic, Persian and Hindawi. He played a pivotal role in the evolution of Indian classical music, both vocal and instrumental. The invention of the sitar and tabla, several musical compositions set in *qawaali, khayal, tarana,* and *naqsh,* as well as several *ragas* are attributed to Khusrau. These melodies celebrate the fusion of Indian and Persian music and were created by Khusrau them to produce novelty in the *sama mehfils* enjoyed by Shaykh Nizamuddin.

The mystic, philosopher, musician and litterateur enjoyed the patronage of seven successive Sultans of Delhi. Along with Sadi, Nizami and Firdausi, Khusrau is one of the four great pillars of fourteenth-century Persian literature. The historian Ziauddin Barani records in *Tarikh e Firuz Shahi,* 'The incomparable Amir Khusrau stands unequalled for the volumes of his writings and the originality of his ideas, and in addition to his wit, talent and learning, he was an advanced mystic.'

Born in 1253 AD at Patiali, Khusrau lost his father at the age of eight years. He completed his education at Delhi and as a child lived with his maternal grandfather Imad ul Mulk, whom he accompanied to literary assemblies held in the city.

Khusrau's first appointment was by Sultan Balban's nephew Alauddin Kishli Khan, who welcomed him to the royal court. Later he joined the court of Bughra Khan, the governor of Samana in Punjab. Khusrau then moved to the court of Bughra Khan's elder brother, Muhammad Khan, the governor of Multan. He stayed there for five years along with Amir Hasan Sijzi, poet and fellow disciple of Hazrat Nizamuddin.

The event of Muhammad Khan's death while battling the Mongols saddened Khusrau, who wrote a moving elegy for him. Khusrau and Amir Hasan were both captured by the Mongols but managed to escape to Delhi. By this time, Khusrau had compiled two collections, *Tuhfatus Sighar,* Gifts of Childhood, and *Wastul Hayat,* Verses of Midlife.

Khusrau continued as the court poet during the tumultuous period of the Delhi Sultanate. His literary works include *Mathnawi Miftah ul Futuh, Ghurrat ul Kamal, Khaza in ul Futuh, Ashiqa, Baqiya Naqiya,* and *Khamsa.* The works *Nuh Siphir* and *Nihayat ul Kamal* were compiled just before his death. *Tughlaqnama,* an account of the victory of Ghiyasuddin Tughlaq over Naseeruddin Khusrau, remains another important historical treatise.

In 1319 AD Khusrau compiled the voluminous *Ijaz e Khusrawi* that features articles, treatises, and copies of official and non-official documents. The four volumes include the description of urban trades, the skills of blacksmiths, embroiderers, bow masters, arrow manufacturers, artists, cobblers, tanners, tailors, rope makers and other craftspeople. These accounts recreate urban life in Delhi during the medieval period. Khusrau had a passion for the living language of the people as spoken in towns and villages. He created a number of poetic works in *Khari Boli* dialect and compiled a Hindi–Persian dictionary in verse. One of the most prolific genres composed by Khusrau are the *pahelis,* riddles that children of the subcontinent grow up enjoying.

Deeply influenced by the spiritual philosophy of Hazrat Nizamuddin, Khusrau believed in tolerance and affection between people of separate faiths. Khusrau loved Hindustan, India, with all its fragrant flowers, fruits, vegetables, trees and animals and likened it to Paradise:

> *The heavens said that of all the countries which have come out of the earth,*
> *Among them it is Hindustan that has achieved the height of excellence.*

Once Hazrat Nizamuddin and Khusrau came upon a group of Brahmins engaged in prayer. The Shaykh remarked:

> *Har qaum raast rahay deeney va qibla gaahey.*
>
> *(Each people have their own path and direction in prayer.)*

Khusrau spontaneously completed the verse:

Man qabla raast, ber terfe kajkulahey

*(I have straightened my direction of prayer towards the
slanting cap.)*

Alluding to Hazrat Nizamuddin who wore his cap with a slant,
Khusrau continues:

Har aashiqe yaad agar dar qibla gard butkada
Aashaqaane dost raba kafoor imaan kar neest

*(Lovers of the beloved take us to Kaba and to the temple
of idols*
Lovers of the Friend do not bother with infidelity and faith.)

Amir Khusrau had been devoted to Hazrat Nizamuddin from an
early age, since the time he was introduced to the Shaykh by his
father. On his first visit, the eight-year-old Khusrau stood outside
the *khanqah* refusing to enter the premises. The child composed a
quatrain and sent it to the Shaykh. It read:

Thou art such a King that when a pigeon perches up
On top of thy palace it becomes a falcon
A poor and distressed person stands on thy threshold
Is he permitted to go in or should he return?

Shaykh Nizamuddin composed a reply, dispatching it to the child
peering from outside.

The seeker of truth should enter
To share our secrets for a while
But if he is ignorant and a fool
He should return.

Khusrau would present his verses to the Master for correction,
acknowledging that he was a disciple in both spirituality and
literature. The Shaykh would pray for the disciple's success. Often,

the poet brought some sugar and placed it under the Master's cot. Later, the Shaykh would sprinkle some over Khusrau's head and ask the disciple to eat from it. Almost all of Khusrau's *diwans* begin with sincere tributes to the Master:

Whereever his breath has reached
Thousands of the mountains of grief have melted away.

Hazrat Nizamuddin loved his disciple, addressing him as, 'My Turk'. He would say, 'Khusrau is the keeper of my secrets. And I shall not set foot in paradise without him. If permissible by Islamic law, I would have willed that Khusrau be buried in the same grave as I.'

Once Shaykh Nizamuddin refused to grant an audience with Sultan Jalaluddin Khilji. The ruler began to plan a surprise visit to the Sufi's *khanqah*. Amir Khusrau learnt of the Sultan's intent and informed his Master, who left Delhi and travelled to Baba Farid's *dargah* at Ajodhan. The Sultan took Khusrau to task for divulging royal secrets, and the disciple pleaded: 'In disobeying the Sultan I stand in danger of losing my life but in being untrue to my Master, I stand in danger of losing my faith.' Impressed with the poet's eloquence and devotion, the Sultan let the incident pass without trial for treason.

Aware of the Shaykh's affection for Khusrau, other disciples sought his intercession with the Master. Once when the Master showed displeasure with Burhanuddin Gharib, Khusrau secured his pardon. Another time Shaykh Nizamuddin professed, 'When God questions the offering I have brought from this world, I will present the sorrow in the heart of Khusrau the Turk.'

After the Shaykh's death, Khusrau distributed his wealth to the poor, spending the rest of his days beside the Master's tomb. His health deteriorated for he lost the desire to live, and he died exactly six months later on 18 Shawwal 725 Hijri/1325 AD. Khusrau lies buried in the *dargah* complex of Hazrat Nizamudin Auliya in Delhi. Whenever Khusrau travelled out of town, Shaykh Nizamuddin wrote him affectionate letters addressing him as *Turkullah*, God's

Turk. As willed by Khusrau, these letters were placed in his shroud and entombed with him.

Devotees who seek the blessings of Hazrat Nizamuddin Auliya, begin with offering homage to Amir Khusrau. His poetry continues to be sung in all the *dargahs* of the subcontinent, enthralling devotees through the centuries.

🕉 🕉

BIBI FATIMA SAM (D. 644 HIJRI/1246 AD)

Referring to Bibi Fatima's spiritual rank, Hazrat Nizamuddin commented: 'When a lion emerges out of the forest, nobody asks if it is male or female; the children of Adam must obey and show respect to all human beings, whether male or female. I have met her and she was a great woman. Bibi Fatima was the adopted sister of my Shaykh Farid and his brother Shaykh Najeebuddin Mutawakkil. She recited verses on every subject. I have heard her verses.' He quoted these two lines from her:

> *Hum ishq talab kuni va hum jan khwahi*
> *Har do talabi valey mayasar na shavad.*
>
> *(You may seek love, and you may seek soul.*
> *Seek them both, but it won't be easy.)*

Bibi Fatima Sam, a disciple of Baba Farid lived in Delhi. The Sufi Master treated her like a sister. Hazrat Nizamuddin often visited her tomb for prayers and meditation. He remembered Bibi Fatima saying, 'The saints will cast away both worldly and religious blessings to give a piece of bread or a drink of water to someone in need. This state is something one cannot obtain by one hundred thousand fasts and prayers.'

Once the virtues of Bibi Fatima were being discussed in the *khanqah* of Naseeruddin Chiragh Dilli. He said:

After her death, Bibi Fatima Sam appeared in a friend's dream and said, 'One day by appointment I went to the revered Lord. I passed by the round of angels', and suddenly an angel said, 'Who are you? Why should you be proceeding so carelessly?' I replied, 'I have sworn an oath; I am just sitting here until the Most High Lord of Power summons me; I will go no further.' After an hour went by Bibi Khadija and Bibi Fatima Zahra, the wife and the daughter of Prophet Muhammad ﷺ came and I fell at their feet. They said to me, 'Fatima Sam, who is there like you today? For God Most High has sent us in search of you.' I said, 'I am your slave; what honour could be higher than for you to come in search of me? But I have sworn an oath.' Then the decree came from God: 'Fatima Sam speaks rightly. You both must depart from here and leave her alone.' Then I heard God call, 'Come to Me, to Me.' I moved from that place. To God I said, 'Lord, in Your presence there are such mannerless ones that Your visitors will not recognize You.' She spoke these words, sighing from the midst of her tomb.

Bibi Fatima Sam died on 17 Shaban 644 Hijri/ 1246 AD. She is called the Rabia of Delhi, after the famed Rabia of Basra. Her *dargah* is not far from that of Hazrat Nizamuddin.

۞ ۞

MAKHDOOM ALAUDDIN SABIR KALIYARI (D. 690 HIJRI/1291 AD)

After being widowed, Jamila Khatun had entrusted her son Alauddin to her younger brother's care. Baba Farid made his nephew in charge of the community kitchen at his *khanqah* in Ajodhan. After some years Alauddin's mother returned to find him very weak and enquired about his poor physical condition. Baba Farid thought this could not be for the lack of food since the boy's duty was in the kitchen. The young mystic provided the explanation, 'True, I was in charge of distributing the food but I was not told that I could eat from it.' On hearing this, Baba Farid awarded him the title of *Sabir*, the Patient One.

Barring some legends and anecdotes, little is recorded of the life of Shaykh Alauddin, a prominent Chishti mystic. Baba Farid sent him to Kaliyar in the year 1253 AD where he spent all his time in meditation, gaining a reputation for piety and asceticism. Large numbers of devotees began to seek his prayers and feeling threatened, the local clerics began to indulge in conspiracies against him.

One Friday, Shaykh Alauddin went to offer prayers at the mosque but conspirators ensured that he did not get a place inside. It is believed that the Shaykh's wrath led to the destruction of the mosque, which collapsed, wiping out everything around it except a *guler*, berry tree. Subsequently, a plague gripped Kaliyar, taking a heavy toll of life, and the city become deserted. On learning of the devastation, the Sultan of Delhi, Naseeruddin Mahmud Shah pleaded with Baba Farid for protection. Shaykh Alauddin's Master advised the emperor to stay miles away from Kaliyar.

Shaykh Sabir meditated in standing position under the *guler* tree, for 12 years. No one had the courage to approach him. Baba Farid was worried about his disciple, and enquired if anyone could induce the Shaykh to sit down. Shamsuddin Turk, a mystic from Panipat, volunteered for the service and proceeded to Kaliyar. Fearing the Shaykh's wrath, Shamsuddin Turk stood at a distance and began to recite the Quran. Moved by the recital, Alauddin signalled him to sit down, but Shamsuddin replied, 'How can I sit while an esteemed Shaykh stands?' Shaykh Alauddin let go of the tree's bough and finally sat down. The tree still stands at the spot, with devotees lighting candles around it and eating the fruit to invoke the Sufi's blessings.

It is believed that the veiled person who offered Shaykh Alauddin funeral prayers, was none other than the Shaykh himself in a spiritual form. The exact place of his grave remained unknown for over a hundred years. It was said that the mystic's *jalal,* wrath, burnt those who ventured near it. Eventually, the Chishti Sufi Abdul Qudoos Gangohi discovered the site of the tomb in the fifteenth century. While he swept the grave of his grandfather in the adjoining graveyard, he heard Shaykh Alauddin's voice asking for his grave to be swept too. The mystic from Gangoh meditated and prayed at the site of Shaykh Alauddin's grave for 40 days. He pleaded with the Sufi to shower benevolence on people. Shaykh Alauddin finally shunned his wrath and devotees in large numbers began to flock to Kaliyar.

The Chishti Sabri Order was spread through Shamsuddin Turk of Panipat, the sole *khalifa* of Shaykh Alauddin Sabir. The Delhi Sultan, Ibrahim Lodhi, built a mausoleum over the grave of the exalted mystic. Kaliyar is in the present-day district of Hardwar and the *Urs* celebrations are held each year on 13 Rabi ul awwal.

❀ ❀

Khwaja Bandanawaz Gesudaraz (d. 825 Hijri/1422 ad)

Khwaja Gesudaraz was once carrying the palanquin of his Master, Shaykh Naseeruddin Chiragh Dilli, on his shoulders. His long locks of hair got entangled in the wheel but he chose not to wince, continuing the journey. On learning of the incident, the Shaykh recited a couplet conferring upon him the title *Gesudaraz*, one with long locks, and *Bandanawaz*, one who comforts. It was Shaykh Burhanuddin who introduced the Chishti Order in the Deccan. Gesudaraz's efforts turned it into a mass movement.

Khwaja Gesudaraz was born in Delhi in 1321 AD and given the name Syed Muhammad Hussaini. His family had lived in the capital city for 12 generations. When Sultan Muhammad bin Tughlaq shifted his capital to Daulatabad in the Deccan, the family migrated settling in a place called Roza Khuldabad. After the death of his father, the fourteen-year-old returned to live in Delhi. Having heard of Shaykh Naseeruddin's piety, he became his disciple and served him with devotion. Pleased with his disciple's achievements, within six months Shaykh Naseeruddin declared him to be his leading *khalifa* and spiritual successor. In Delhi, Khwaja Gesudaraz continued his education in religious sciences for 23 years.

The erudite and prolific Khwaja Gesudaraz wrote in Arabic, Persian, Hindawi and Dakhani, often dictating four or five books at a time. No other Sufi of the Chishti Order has authored as many books. The subjects of his countless books include a commentary on the Quran, biographies, prophetic traditions, jurisprudence, poetry, letters and discourses. Notable among these are *Asmar ul Asrar* (Nocturnal Secrets), *Khatima, Hadaiq ul Uns* and *Hazair ul Quds*. In the *Asmar ul Asrar* he wrote: 'Everyone who traverses the path to God is bestowed with a particular aptitude. God has bestowed upon me the gift of explaining His secrets.' His commentaries on classical works of Sufism—*Awarif ul Maarif, Fusus al Hakim, Risalah e Qushayrriyah* and *Kitab Adab al Muridin*—remain important mystic manuals.

Khwaja Gesudaraz disputed Ibn al Arabi's theory *wahdat ul wujood*, the Oneness of Being, that had begun to influence Indian Sufis. The Shaykh favoured the theory of *wahdat ul shuhud*, everything flows from Him, which was being advocated by the Kubrawi Sufi Alauddawla Simnani (d.1336 AD).

The Khwaja remained at the head of the Chishti Order in Delhi for more than four decades. However, in November 1398 AD, the mystic left Delhi with his family and disciples with the intention of migrating to Daulatabad. During the journey, they halted at many places including Gwalior, Chanderi, Baroda and Cambay. The Khwaja's discourses along the 10-month journey to the Deccan were recorded by his eldest son and disciple, Akbar Hussaini, in the famous *Jawami al Kalim*.

In the year 1400 AD, Khwaja Gesudaraz visited his father's tomb in Khuldabad and considered residing there. Meanwhile Firoz Shah, Sultan of the Bahmani Kingdom (r. 1397–1442 AD) invited the mystic to make his home in the capital city of Ahsanabad, now called Gulbarga. The Khwaja accepted the invitation and the Sultan built a *khanqah* for him near the fort. Some 20 years later, Khwaja moved to another place nearby, where his *dargah* stands today. Ahmad Shah Bahmani built a beautiful mausoleum over his grave. The hundred-year-old Khwaja died on 16 Dhul Qada 825 Hijri/November 1442 AD.[7]

💮 💮

SHAYKH BURHANUDDIN GHARIB (D. 737 HIJRI/1337 AD)

About 1,400 eminent Sufis were sent to Daulatabad in the Deccan by a decree of Muhammad bin Tughlaq. Prominent among them were members of the Chishti Order led by Khwaja Burhanuddin Gharib, a disciple of Hazrat Nizamuddin Auliya. They settled in Khuldabad and their cluster of *dargahs* is one of the most remarkable centres of Sufi pilgrimage in South Asia. These whitewashed tombs, 25 kilometres from Aurangabad, still draw pilgrims to the beautiful valley.[8]

Shaykh Burhanuddin supervised the preparation of food at Hazrat Nizamuddin's *khanqah* in Delhi. He once fell out of favour with the Master who was informed that the 70-year-old disciple sat on a folded carpet, contrary to the Chishti traditions of humility. The Shaykh was overcome with grief and was later pardoned through the intervention of Amir Khusrau.

Zaynuddin Shirazi, initially a critic of Sufism, converted under the influence of the Shaykh and became his chief disciple. His diaries record the teachings of Shaykh Burhanuddin that focussed on *dhikr* and *sama*. Extremely fond of musical assemblies, the Shaykh invented a particular form of dancing which came to be known as the Burhani style. His followers were highly educated and familiar with a broad range of subjects including Islamic theology and Sufi philosophies. Although the Chishti doctrine did not allow political indulgence, the Deccan Sufis gave audiences to state figures and provided for their spiritual instruction.

Documents of the early fourteenth century do not give any indication that these Sufis were engaged in deliberate contact with non-Muslims, nor did they show any interest in the conversion of Hindus to Islam. Nevertheless, the open kitchen at their centres and the annual *Urs* festivals must have encouraged the local Hindus to regard the Sufis with reverence.[9]

The *dargah* of Shaykh Burhanuddin enjoyed the patronage of the Bahmani rulers. The Faruqi rulers of Khandesh were also devoted to the Deccan Chishti Sufis. Malik Raja (r. 1382–99 AD) named the Faruqi capital city Burhanpur after Burhanuddin Gharib and the satellite town Zaynabad after his companion Zaynuddin Shirazi. On conquering Khandesh in 1601 AD, the Mughals took over the patronage of these *dargahs* and strengthened their claim over the Deccan through these important pilgrimage centres. Fifteen *farmans*, royal decrees, dating from 1605 to 1832 AD, which have been preserved in Khuldabad, document the extensive patronage of the Mughal rulers, from Akbar onwards, to the time of their successors, the Nizams of Hyderabad. The most famous royal tomb in Khuldabad belongs to Mughal Emperor Aurangzeb who lies buried within the *dargah* complex of Zaynuddin Shirazi in a simple grave.[10]

Khwaja Burhanuddin died on 8 Safar 737 Hijri/1337 AD. Other than the tombs of Shaykh Burhanuddin and Shaykh Zaynuddin Shirazi, there are a number of important *dargahs* in and around Khuldabad, including the Panch Bibiya (the five sisters of Shaikh Burhanuddin), Jalaluddin Ganj e Ravan, Khwaja Hussain, Khwaja Omar and Momin Arif. Although Hazrat Nizamuddin did not confer a formal *khilafatnama* to Maulana Burhanuddin, the senior disciple played a vital role in popularizing the Chishti Order in the Deccan.

۞ ۞

SHAYKH SALIM CHISHTI (D. 979 HIJRI/1572 AD)

Emperor Akbar sought the prayers of Shaykh Salim Chishti in his quest for a male heir. The Sufi reassured the emperor of having at

least three sons. Akbar's wife, the daughter of the Raja of Amber, gave
birth to Salim Mirza in August 1569 AD. Several of the emperor's
children had died in infancy and he credited the birth of the future
king to the mystic's prayers.

In the words of the court historian Abul Fazl, 'In as much as his
(Akbar's) exalted sons had taken birth in Sikri and the God-knowing
spirit of Shaykh Salim Chisti had taken possession thereof, his holy
heart desired to give outward splendour to this spot which possessed
spiritual grandeur.' The historian ranked the Sufi among those 'who
pay less attention to the external world but acquire vast knowledge
and understand the mysteries of the heart.' The Mughal emperor
adopted the Chishti principle of *sulh e kul*, peace with all, as the
official state policy.

Born in Delhi, the young mystic moved to the town of Sikri
with his father Shaykh Bahauddin, who drew their ancestry from
the Chishti Master Baba Farid. Shaykh Salim travelled frequently
outside of India, his first pilgrimage to Makkah being around the
year 1544 AD. After another long journey he settled at Sikri in 1564
AD, the year Akbar made his first pilgrimage to Khwaja Moinuddin's
dargah in Ajmer—a tradition that he continued almost annually.

Shaykh Salim died on 29 Ramadan 979 Hijri/1571 AD, soon after
the order to build a new city at Sikri had been proclaimed. Under his
supervision, the mosque and *khanqah* were built into the complex.
The Shaykh lies buried in the beautiful tomb erected on the site of
his cell near the grand Jama Mosque.

Even though Sikri became an abandoned city, the Mughal
emperors continued to visit the *dargah* of Shaykh Salim. It is the
sole Sufi *dargah* in India to be located in the heart of an imperial
citadel. Each day the *dargah* at Fatehpur Sikri attracts hundreds of
visitors who marvel at the exquisite architecture and seek spiritual
solace.

SHAH MUHAMMAD FARHAD (D. 1135 HIJRI/1723 AD)

Shah Farhad was the son of the governor of Burhanpur. He was born
in Delhi, but spent his childhood in Burhanpur studying under the
supervision of his father. In those days a well-known Sufi, Shaykh
Dost Muhammad, a disciple of the famous Syedna Shah Amir Abul
Ulai Ahrari of Agra, resided in Burhanpur. The young child often
accompanied his father to Shaykh Dost Muhammad's *khanqah*.
Drawn to the mystic, the child began visiting him frequently. His
spiritual inclination disturbed his father who requested the Sufi to
put an end to these visits.

Despite being dissuaded by the Sufi, the child continued to seek
his company. The father appealed to the mystic with folded hands,
'Farhad is my only son, and if such visits continue he will lose
interest in worldly affairs. I am grooming him to be my political
successor.' The Sufi assured the father that he would advise the child
to stay away from him. Nevertheless, the young lad continued the
visits. When his father repeated his fears to the mystic again, Shaykh
Dost Muhammad commented, 'You desire that your son stands with
folded hands in front of kings, but God desires that kings should
stand with folded hands in front of your son.' The father resigned
himself to God's will and entrusted the child to the mystic.

Shaykh Dost Muhammad initiated Shah Farhad in the Abul Ulai
Order, an offshoot of the Chishti Order. Shah Farhad achieved an
enlightened spiritual rank, and was reputed to cleanse the souls he
glanced upon. Continually absorbed in the remembrance of God,
he remained unmindful of outwardly appearance, food or drink.
Often the Sufi Master appeared to be searching for something and
referring to himself would comment, 'I am looking for Farhad who
was here a while ago, do you know where he has gone.' He had
crossed the stage of *fana*, annhilation of self, and reached the state of

baqa, continuance in God. Shaykh Dost Muhammad ordered Shah Farhad to leave Burhanpur and settle in Delhi. Shah Farhad died on 25 Jumada al akhira 1135 Hijri/1723 AD. His *dargah* in Delhi attracts a huge numbers of devotees.

SHAYKH KALEEMULLAH (D. 1142 HIJRI/1729 AD)

Shaykh Kaleemullah embraced the Sufi path in a unique way. In his youth, he fell desperately in love with a Khattari boy. However, the boy remained indifferent to his passions. The Shaykh sought the help of a mystic, after which the boy began to respond. Soon the Shaykh grew tired of the boy and became fascinated with the mystic's spirituality. The mystic advised him to seek proper spiritual training from Shaykh Yahya Madani in Madinah. Tales recount of Shaykh Kaleemullah making the journey right away, without even wishing farewell to his family.

Once in Madinah someone called out Kaleemullah's name at the inn where he stayed. The Delhi mystic did not respond, presuming the call to be for someone else. The man surfaced again the next day calling out, 'Shaykh Kaleemullah from Shahjehanabad.' He turned out to be a messenger sent by Shaykh Madani, the Master who awaited the seeker's presence. Shaykh Yahya Madani, a Gujarati immigrant to Madinah initiated Shah Kaleemullah in the Chisti Order, appointing the Delhi mystic his successor. On returning to Delhi, the Shaykh led a simple life, rejecting offers of official grants. His sole income came from a house which he rented out for two rupees a month. He stayed in a house with a cheaper rent of 50 paise, using the remaining money for his personal needs. The mystic offered Friday prayers at the Jama Masjid along with the emperor of Delhi, who could not talk to him without seeking prior permission.

Following the death of Shaykh Naseeruddin Chiragh Dilli, the Chishti *silsila* suffered a setback in Delhi. Shaykh Kaleemullah revived the order, spearheading the formation of Chishti *khanqahs* in various parts of the subcontinent. The Sufi made his *khanqah* in the famed Khanam Bazaar of Delhi close to the Red Fort. Innumerable Sufis and scholars regularly visited the Shaykh.

Shaykh Kaleemullah was born in the city of Shahjehanabad (Delhi) on 24 June 1650 AD to a family of Turkish descent. His grandfather Shaykh Ahmad e Mimar happened to be a famed mathematician and the chief architect for the magnificent Taj Mahal, the Jama Masjid and the Red Fort of Delhi. Emperor Shahjehan awarded Shaykh Mimar the title of *Nadir e Asr*. All of his three sons were architects and engineers. The Shaykh's father Haji Nurullah, a skilled calligrapher made the drawings for the inscriptions at the Jama Masjid in Delhi. Commenting on the architectural and scholarly skills of the family, Maulana Azad wrote that Shaykh Kaleemullah was an architect of peace, directed by God to construct brotherhood among humanity.

The highly educated Shaykh Kaleemullah wrote commentaries on Bahauddin Amuli's work on astronomy and on Ibne Sina's (Avicenna) treatise on medicine. Among his teachers were Shaykh Burhanuddin, known by the title of Shaykh Bahlol, and his uncle Shaykh Abul Riza.

Shaykh Kaleemullah authored a total of 32 books, including a commentary on the Quran and other masterpieces on Sufi philosophy, such as *Muraqqa* and *Ashra e Kamila*. His treatise *Kashkol* is considered important devotional literature by followers of the Chishti Order. The Shaykh taught that union with God is marked by an unconscious and trance-like state resembling death, except that in death one does not partake in the Divine mystery. He defined a Sufi as one invested with Divine knowledge, asserting that each action of the seeker should be towards annihilation of the self.

The Shaykh believed that the constant remembrance led to the seeker's awareness of God. He elaborated on many forms of *dhikr*, that of the tongue, heart, soul and spirit. He affirmed that the Sufi performing *dhikr* of the spirit would be bathed in Divine colours.

He advocated *habs e nafs*, breath control, acknowledging that Sufis had borrowed the breathing techniques from the yogis. The Shaykh recommended many meditative yogic postures to his disciples.[11]

Always cheerful by nature, Shaykh Kaleemullah was extremely fond of *sama mehfils*. The Mughal emperor, Farrukhsiyar, became his ardent devotee. The Shaykh died in Delhi on 24 Rabi ul awwal 1142 Hijri/1729 AD, and was buried in the house where he lived. Shaykh Nizamuddin of Aurangabad inherited the spiritual mantle, and was in turn succeeded by his son Maulana Fakhruddin to head the Chishti Order in Delhi.

WARIS SHAH (D. 1203 HIJRI/1798 AD)

Waris Shah revisited and immortalized the story of Hir and Ranjha, the celebrated folk story of Punjab in his work, *Hir*. The story is believed to be based on a historical event that took place in the sixteenth century. Ranjha, the son of a landlord in Sargoda district fell in love with Hir, the beautiful daughter of the ruler of Jhang. Their families opposed the romance but the lovers continued to meet secretly in the fields. One day, Hir's uncle spotted the couple and informed her father who placed the young girl under house arrest. A distraught Hir was then forcibly married to a Rajput, but managed to send a letter to her beloved Ranjha. After a series of tribulations, the lovers died and various legends tell how they eventually became united in death.

The love story has been retold through the ages in different languages, but it was given its classical form by Waris Shah. It became a powerful commentary on the social, cultural and religious customs of the times he lived in. The verses of *Hir* are short, and commonly interpreted in a mystical sense. As Mohan Singh Diwana translates: 'Our soul is the tragic Heroine Hir, Our body is the lover Ranjha,

Our spiritual preceptor is the yogi Balmath, the five helpful saints
are our five senses, who support us in our adventures dread. Truth
is our judge.'

Waris Shah came from the village of Jandyala Sher Khan in
Sheikhupura, now in Pakistan. He studied under the famous teacher
Hafiz Ghulam Murtaza. In his youth he fell in love with Bhag Bhari, a
village girl of Pakpattan. The poet's family belonged to the upper class
and were scandalized at the thought of his association with lowly
people. Thus Waris Shah moved to another place, seeking solace
by sublimating his own unrequited love in the poetic expression
of Hir and Ranjha. He wrote the celebrated story of the martyred
lovers in 1766 AD. The opening verses of the tale begins, 'First let us
acknowledge God, who has made love the worth of the world/It was
God that first loved, and Prophet Muhammad ﷺ is His beloved.'

Although best known for *Hir*, the mystic poet wrote other books
among which the *Ibratnama* and *Ushtarnama* are famous. Waris
Shah died on 21 Muharram 1203 Hijri/1798 AD and his *dargah* is at
Jandyala Sher Khan in Punjab, Pakistan.

Allah the Sustainer. The All Knowing. The Loving One. The Powerful.
Glorious and Generous.

9

THE SUHARWARDIS

Qazi Hamiduddin Nagauri (d. 643 Hijri/1245 ad)

The Chishtis confer a special status upon Qazi Hamiduddin Nagauri as the close companion and teacher of Khwaja Qutubuddin Bakhtiar Kaki. The Qazi's father, Ataullah Mahmud, belonged to a royal family from Bukhara who drew their lineage from Hazrat Abu Bakr Siddiq, a companion of Prophet Muhammad ﷺ. Qazi Hamiduddin's wit and knowledge of Islamic law often frustrated the effort of the clerics in curbing the musical gatherings at the *khanqahs* of Delhi. Once the Qazi and Khwaja Qutub were enjoying a *sama mehfil* at the house of a local dervish. Maulana Ruknuddin Samarqandi arrived there, accompanied by a group of followers, with the intention of opposing the gathering. Since it is against Islamic law to enter a house without seeking permission from the owner, the Qazi advised the dervish to leave. On learning of the house owner's absence, the Maulana was bound to go away and the gathering continued without a confrontation.

Shaykh Hamiduddin's family migrated to Delhi during the rule of Muhammad Shahabuddin Ghori in the early thirteenth century. Sultan Iltutmish appointed Shaykh Hamiduddin the Qazi of Nagaur, following the death of his father. Three years later he left Nagaur to pursue his overwhelming interest in Sufism. The Shaykh travelled to Baghdad where he became a disciple and *khalifa* of Shaykh Shihabuddin Suharwardi. While in Baghdad, he met Khwaja Qutubuddin Bakhtiar and they became extremely close friends.

He then left for a pilgrimage to Makkah and Madinah where he spent another three years. Finally he settled down in Delhi, buying a small house where Khwaja Qutub also stayed for a while. They shared a deep passion for *sama* as a source of inducing mystical ecstasy. The local clerics continuously opposed these musical assemblies but were overruled by Sultan Iltutmish, a devotee of Khwaja Qutub.

Qazi Hamiduddin's writings are studied by followers of both the Chishti and Suharwardi Orders. Unfortunately, his *Lawamiah* (Flashes of Light), an important treatise on Sufism, has not survived. Baba Farid would often quote from the manual to his devotees. Among other books written by Qazi Hamiduddin on the Sufi doctrine that have survived are *Tiwali Shumus* and *Rasala min Kalam*.

The Shaykh proclaimed that the 'lover' and the 'beloved' may seem to be different, but are in fact identical. He emphasized that one whose entire self is lost in God's attributes merges with the Almighty, and ultimately the lover and the beloved mirror each other. His *Tiwali Shumus* is a detailed exposition of the names of Allah.

Qazi Hamiduddin wrote of the *Sharia* and *Tareeqa* sharing an intimate connection, '*Sharia*, the law of Islam is required for the moral development of the soul, while *Tareeqa*, the mystic path remains a spiritual discipline.' He believed that God granted spiritual knowledge, some souls being created more perfect than others. He wrote of love being the driving force of the mystic:

> *Love is the source of everything that exists,*
> *fire the burning quality of love,*
> *air the aspect of restlessness in love*
> *and water the movement of love.*

Hazrat Nizamuddin Auliya spoke of Qazi Hamiduddin's divine status as unparalleled. He often visited Mehrauli, praying at the vacant space between the tombs of Qazi Hamiduddin and Khwaja Qutub. The Qazi's letters were unfortunately not compiled in book form, however, those written to Baba Farid have been preserved. Once Baba Farid expressed a desire for a *sama mehfil*, but no musicians were available. He asked a disciple to read Qazi Hamiduddin's letters out aloud, going into ecstasy on hearing a quatrain composed by him:

> *Aan aqal kuja ke dar kamal tu rasad*
> *Vaan ru kuja ke dar jamal e tu rasad*
> *Giram ke tu purdah bar girafti za jama*
> *Aan deeda kuja ke bar Jamaal e tu rasad*

> *(How can I gain that intellect which can perceive*
> *Thy Perfection?*
> *How can I get that spirit which can comprehend*
> *Thy Majesty?*
> *I know that Thou removeth the veil from Thy beauty*
> *Where can I get that eye which can perceive it?)*

Qazi Hamiduddin died on 9 Ramadan 643 Hijri/1245 AD and lies buried in the compound of Khwaja Qutubuddin Bakhtiar Kaki's *dargah* in Delhi.

SHAYKH BAHAUDDIN ZAKARIYA (D. 720 HIJRI/1262 AD)

Once Abdullah, a musician, intended travelling to Multan from Ajodhan. He requested Baba Farid to pray for his safe journey. The Baba told him that the limit of his spiritual influence remained up to a certain water tank, after which the area belonged to Shaykh Bahauddin whose prayers should also be sought. The musician acted on the Sufi's advice and completed his journey safely.[1]

The Suharwardi Order came to be established in the subcontinent through the efforts of Shaykh Jalauddin Tabrizi, a disciple of Shaykh Abu Hafs Umar Suharwardi who migrated to Bengal, where he died in 1244 AD. The order still flourishes in Bengal and has produced a number of important mystics. But it is Shaykh Bahauddin Zakariya Multani, a contemporary of the Chishti Sufi Baba Farid of Punjab, who made a larger impact.

Shaykh Bahauddin's ancestors came to Sindh with the armies of Mohammed bin Qasim. The Shaykh was born at Kot Karor near Sindh, and his father died when he was twelve years old. After completing his studies in Khurasan and Bukhara, he left for a pilgrimage to Makkah. He lived in Madinah for five years studying Hadith from the great scholar Maulana Kamaluddin. The Shaykh then travelled to Baghdad where he met his spiritual mentor, Shihabuddin Suharwardi.

The Shaykh returned to Multan, where he acquired the reputation of a scholar and became an important figure of the city. His *khanqah* attracted huge crowds; however, it was not a meeting place for the common people. Mostly eminent citizens, wealthy merchants and religious scholars were permitted there. Unlike the open table of the Chishtis, the Shaykh had fixed hours for visitors who were invited for meals.

The Suharwardis accepted state grants, and played an active role in advising on state policies. Abu Hafs Umar Suharwardi himself had served under Caliph Nasir. Despite the differences in their outlook, the relationship between the Chishtis and the Suharwardis remained amicable. They seemed to have divided areas of their respective spiritual influence, which helped avoid misunderstandings.

Shaykh Bahauddin sided with Sultan Iltutmish in the matter of annexing Multan and Sindh to the Delhi Sultanate. He even wrote a letter to the Sultan inviting him to conquer Multan. The Qazi of Multan also wrote a similar letter to the Sultan encouraging the annexation. The letters fell into the hands of Qubacha, the ruler of Multan, and the Qazi was executed for treason and Shaykh Bahauddin summoned to the palace. On meeting the ruler he admitted to writing the letter, claiming the action to be divinely prompted. He added that Qubacha could take whatever action he wished. However, the ruler's anger subsided after sharing a meal with the Shaykh who usually never ate outside his *khanqah*.[2]

After the annexation of Multan and Sindh in 1228 AD, the relations between Sultan Iltutmish and Shaykh Bahauddin became close. The Sultan invited him to preside over the *mazhar*, conference, organized to judge the allegations against Shaykh Jalaluddin Tabrizi by the Shaykh ul Islam, Najmuddin Sughra. After the latter's dismissal, the Sultan awarded Shaykh Bahauddin the post of Shaykh ul Islam.[3]

Shaykh Bahauddin stressed on the importance of the Master and discouraged his disciples from seeking guidance from different mystics. He taught that true contemplation required the expulsion of everything from the heart except God. He died after living in Multan for almost half a century and his *dargah* is the most celebrated one in the region.

Shaykh Bahauddin has been immortalized in the poetry of his disciple Fakhruddin Iraqi (d.1289 AD) who attached himself to the Shaykh in Multan. The Master, although not inclined towards poetry and music, acknowledged Iraqi's greatness and true love. Iraqi's poems continue to be sung at the Shaykh's tomb in Multan. Shaykh Bahauddin presented the poet with his own *khirqa* and later gave Iraqi his daughter in marriage.

Iraqi's *Lamaat* inspired by Ibn al Arabi's theories remains an important book in the history of Sufi thought. For Iraqi, the lover, beloved and love are one, with God as the eternal Beloved. Soon after the Master's death, Iraqi left Multan for Konya, where he met Sadruddin Qonawi and perhaps Jalaluddin Rumi. He is buried in Damascus near the tomb of Ibn al Arabi whose thoughts he had expressed poetically.[4]

Shaykh Bahauddin died on 16 Shawwal 720 Hijri/1262 AD. He had many famous disciples including Sayyid Jalaluddin Bukhari. Following the Shaykh's death, his son became his spiritual successor. The leadership of the Suharwardi order in the subcontinent remained largely in the family.

〰

SHAYKH MAKHDOOM SAMIUDDIN SUHARWARDI
(D. 901 HIJRI/1496 AD)

Shaykh Samiuddin migrated to Delhi during the rule of Bahlul Lodhi. After the ruler's death, Prince Nizam ascended the throne with the title of Sultan Sikander. He sought the Sufi's blessing on the occasion of his coronation. The new Sultan held Shaykh Samiuddin in great respect, seeking his advice on political matters. On one occasion the Shaykh told the Sultan, 'Three types of people can never hope for Divine blessings—old men who have sinned, young men who have sinned and are hoping to repent, and unjust kings.'

The Suharwardi Order gained a stronghold in Delhi largely because of the eminent Shaykh and Jamali, his poet disciple. The Shaykh, a *khalifa* of Shaykh Kabiruddin Ismail, had studied under Mir Sayyid Sharif Jurani, a famed scholar at Timur's court.

After receiving a *khilafat* at Multan, the Shaykh travelled through many Indian destinations, including Nagaur, Bayana and Gujarat. He happened to be in Bayana during the reign of Bahlul Lodhi, when the ruler of Delhi was engaged in battle against Sultan Hussain Shah Sharqi. The Afghan governor Sultan Ahmad Jalwani who secretly plotted to support the opponent, approached Shaykh Samiuddin to pray for Sharqi's success. The request angered Samiuddin and the Afghan abandoned his plans.

Shaykh Samiuddin authored the book *Mifatah ul Asrar* (Key

to Divine secrets). He wrote that even if one remained an ascetic for a thousand years, Divine mysteries could not be unravelled. Before the Shaykh died on 17 Jamada al ula 901 Hijri/1496 AD, he recounted a dream to his followers where Khwaja Qutubuddin Bakhtiar Kaki stood near the *Hauz e Shamsi* (water tank) near Mehrauli, pointing to his final resting ground. In accordance with his wishes, Shaykh Samiuddin was buried at the embankment of the tank.

SHAYKH JAMALI (D. 942 HIJRI/1536 AD)

Hamid bin Fazlullah Jamali, the favourite *khalifa* of Shaykh Samiuddin changed his pen name from *Jalali*, wrath, to *Jamali*, glory, on the advice of his spiritual mentor. The poet's father died early, leaving the young boy under the care of Shaykh Samiuddin. Throughout his life, Jamali remained extremely devoted to the Shaykh.

Jamali travelled extensively through western and central Asia, Anatolia and Yemen, meeting a number of prominent Sufis. He is believed to have met the famed Persian Sufi poet Jami in Baghdad. Jamali's travels form a link between the Indian Sufi disciplines and those in the rest of the Muslim world.

Jamali's fame as a poet grew during the Lodhi regime, and he came to be respected by the Sultans of Delhi. He shared a close friendship with Sikander Lodhi, and wrote an elegy on his death. However, Ibrahim Lodhi dealt severely with his father's favourites and this resulted in Jamali falling out with the court. When Babur defeated Ibrahim Lodhi, Jamali wrote a panegyric celebrating the victory. The Sufi poet struck a friendship with both Babur and Humayun, accompanying the young Crown prince on his Gujarat campaign.

Jamali compiled a *mathnawi* called *Merat al Maani*. However, he is best remembered for *Siyar ul Arifeen e Tazkira*, a comprehensive hagiographic account of the Indian Sufis. He also wrote a *mathnavi* in Persian with over 8,000 verses.

Jamali died on 10 Dhul Qada 942 Hijri/May 1536 AD and was buried alongside his spiritual mentor Shaykh Samiuddin near *Hauz e Shamsi*, Mehrauli. His verses are beautifully calligraphed on the walls of his mausoleum.

SHAH ALAM (D. 880 HIJRI/1475 AD)

Sayyid Sirajuddin Muhammad, the son and successor of Burhanuddin Qutub e Alam, came to be called Shah Alam. Burhanuddin was the grandson of the celebrated Sayyid Jalauddin Hussain Bukhari of Uch who arrived in Gujarat during the beginning of the fifteenth century, settling in the outskirts of Ahmedabad. Following the Suharwardi tradition, the family established close contact with the local rulers and played an active role in the social and political life of the city. The Sultans of Gujarat became deeply devoted to Qutub e Alam and Shah Alam, ascribing their victories to their blessings. The Sufis infused the local people with a spirit of religiosity and homogeneity.

Shah Alam assisted his father in playing host to many men of spiritual eminence. He was related to the royal houses of Sindh and Gujarat through marriage to Bibi Marqi, the second daughter of Jam Saheb of Sindh. He taught people to trust in God and spend time in reflecting on His glory.

Many stories recount how the young Shah Alam yearned for his heart to be engulfed with Divine love. He spent six days a week in solitary meditation, remaining inaccessible even to the rulers. He received visitors only on Fridays, when open discussions were held and anyone could seek his guidance. Some of these accounts are compiled but have not survived, and much of Shah Alam's valuable library containing rare manuscripts is lost.[5] The Sufi died on 20 Jumada al akhira 880 Hijri/1475 AD. A large number of devotees continue to visit his *dargah* in Gujarat.

SHAH ABDUL LATIF BHITAI (D. 1165 HIJRI/1752 AD)

Shah Abdul Latif invented a number of new melodies akin to the folk ballads of the Indus Valley. He unmortalized the story of Sohni, the love-stricken damsel whose beloved Mahiwal grazed cattle on an island in the Indus. She slipped away from her husband and swam across the river every night to meet her lover, encountering all sorts of dangers. Sohni's secret was finally discovered by her sister-in-law. One night, she replaced the baked jar that Sohni used for a float, with an unbaked vessel. Tragically, the girl drowned on the way to her beloved.

The poet uses the backdrop of the romantic folktale of *Sasi Punhun* to demonstrate mystical teachings of quest, separation and eternal union with the beloved. In Rumi's style, Shah Latif sings:

> *By dying live that thou mayst feel,*
> *The beauty of the beloved,*
> *thou wilt surely do the righteous thing,*
> *If thou wilt follow this advice,*
> *Die that thou prosper,*
> *Sit down: O woman,*
> *live after death,*
> *thou wilt unto Punhun come,*
> *They who so died before their death,*
> *By death are not in death subdued,*
> *assuredly they live who lived,*

Before their life of living was,
From age to age will live for aye,
They will not die again who died,
Before the dying came to them,
Thou didst not know thy death was there,
In quiet questing for thy live.
Thou didst not hear,
O woman this : Die, why dost thou behead thyself.[6]

Shah Latif's verses are compiled in *Shaha jo Risalo,*[7] that contains 30 chapters named according to their *sur,* musical odes. The first in a long line of Sindhi mystical poets, he is considered the most outstanding master of popular Sufi poetry in Sindh, which has traditionally been the land of the Suharwardi Sufis. He was born into a family of mystics in 1689 AD near Hala.The mystic's father Shah Habib encouraged him to follow the Sufi path.

Although Shah Abdul Latif did not have much of a formal education, he was well versed in the Quran, Hadith, and Mevlana Rumi's *Mathnawi.* The young poet fell in love with the daughter of Mirza Mughal Beg, a proud scion of the Afghan rulers. Although Shah's family were Sayyids, who drew their lineage from the family of the Prophet through Imam Zain ul Abideen, there was a difference in the social status of the families. The ruling family was aristocratic, while the Shah came from a family of mystics and priests. In 1713 AD, some robbers assassinated Mughal Beg and decamped with all his riches. Reduced to poverty, the Mirza's family eventually agreed to give their daughter in marriage to Shah, who had by then gained fame as a poet.

In his early years, Shah wandered through the country with a group of yogis. Gradually, his disciples increased and the mystic migrated to Koti, in search of solitude. He made his *khanqah* at a sand mound called Bhit, a few miles away from Hala. Shah Abdul

Latif died on 14 Safar 1165 Hijri/1752 AD. His *dargah* at Bhit Shah is one of the most beautiful structures among Islamic monuments. On Thursday nights, devotees assemble to hear the musicians sing his lyrics that remain popular all over the subcontinent.

Allah ho Akbar: Allah is the Greatest.

10

THE QADRIS

بسم الله الرحمن الرحيم

SHAYKH SHAHUL HAMID (D. 977 HIJRI/1570 AD)

Many miracles are associated with Shahul Hamid of Nagore in Tamil Nadu. One story recounts how he cured the illness of Achyutappa Nayakar, the king of Thanjavur who apparently was the victim of sorcery. The Shaykh found a pigeon in the palace attic and removed the pins that were stuck on it. The king regained his health and in a show of gratitude presented 80 hectares of land for the Sufi's *khanqah*. Pilgrims to the *dargah* of Shaykh Shahul traditionally release pigeons to invoke his blessings.

Shahul Hamid is said to be a thirteenth-generation descendant of the great Shaykh Abdul Qadir Jilani of Baghdad. He was born in 1491 AD in Mannikapur, a district in the modern state of Uttar Pradesh. He left home when he was 18-years-old and studied mysticism under Shaykh Muhammad Ghaus of Gwalior for ten years. The Shaykh then travelled extensively through west Asia, sailing back across the Indian Ocean and settling at Nagore around the year 1558 AD.

The Nagore Sufi died in 977 Hijri/1570 AD and his death anniversary is celebrated every year from the first day of the Islamic month Jumada al akhira for 14 days. The celebrations are known as the Kandoori festival, attracting devotees from India, Malaysia, Singapore, Sri Lanka and Pakistan. Shaykh Shahul is affectionately called *Nagore Andavar*—the ruler of Nagore, *Qutub*, *Nayakar* or just *Miran Sahab*, meaning leader. The reverence for the mystic emanates from the matrix of language, myth and ritual, drawn from the shared experiences of Tamil-speaking Hindus and Muslims.[1]

﷽

MIAN MIR (D. 1045 HIJRI/1635 AD)

Mian Mir holds a pivotal rank in Sikh history for laying the foundation stone of the Harmandir Sahab at the Golden Temple in Amritsar, upon the request of Guru Ram Das. Muslim mystics and the Sikh Gurus were affectionate and respectful towards one another.

The Qadri Order was established at Uch near Multan by Shaykh Muhammad al Hussaini al Jilani, a direct descendant of Shaykh Abdul Qadir Jilani during the second half of the fifteenth century.

Mian Mir's ancestors, a family of *Qazis* came from Siwistan in Sindh. Although Mian Mir did not undergo a comprehensive religious education, his mother taught him mystic disciplines. At the age of 12 the young mystic went into the jungles to practise self-mortification where he became the disciple of Shaykh Khizr. Later, Mian Mir studied religion under Maulana Sadullah, an outstanding scholar of Lahore.

Mian Mir soon began to initiate disciples and drew huge crowds. Fame became a burden and in pursuing seclusion, he migrated to Sirhind. However, a year later he returned to settle in Lahore. Mian Mir avoided contact with crowds and returned offerings of gifts. He pleaded that people mistook him for a beggar, whereas he was rich with God's company. He often ventured into the forests during the day, retiring in his cell at night. In his biography of Mian Mir, Dara Shikoh records that the mystic never slept at night and for several years used only two breaths from night till sunrise. The Shaykh's life was based upon *tawakkul*, trust in God, epitomized by his once throwing out water on a hot Lahore evening so that none of it remained for the next day.[2]

While on the way to Kashmir from Sirhind in 1620 AD, Emperor Jehangir learnt of this outstanding Sufi. At the emperor's invitation, Mian Mir visited the royal camp and overwhelmed Jehangir with his spiritual discourse. Emperor Shahjehan called twice on Mian Mir at his home at Lahore. Despite attention from the rulers, the mystic remained aloof from worldly authorities.[3] Prince Dara Shikoh was introduced to the Shaykh through his disciple Mullah Shah. The prince despised the religious orthodoxy of the clerics and became deeply influenced by the teachings of Mian Mir. He subsequently became a disciple of Mullah Shah.

Mian Mir taught that *Sharia* was the first step towards *Tareeqa*, the Sufi way. He did not encourage wearing the Sufi cloak, lest it attract attention and gifts. He wore a turban of coarse cloth and a cotton cloak, and washed his own clothes, urging his disciples to remain clean and tidy. Mian Mir remained an ardent follower of the Sufi doctrine *wahdat ul wujood*. He died on 7 Rabi ul awwal 1045 Hijri/1653 AD and was buried in Lahore, He continues to be venerated by Muslims and followers of the Sikh faith.

۝

MULLAH SHAH (D. 1072 HIJRI/1661 AD)

While travelling to Lahore, Mullah Shah heard of Mian Mir and sought a meeting with the famous mystic. He became his disciple, undergoing severe ascetic training under the guidance of the Shaykh. The Master permitted him to spend the summers in Srinagar where he lived at the Hari Parbat, meditating and writing poetry. Although Mian Mir had advised restraint in ecstatic utterances, the mystic did not refrain from writing poetry that bordered on blasphemy. In 1634 AD, the clergy at Shahjehan's court persuaded the emperor to sentence Mullah Shah to death. Prince Dara Shikoh, who later became the Sufi's disciple, advised his father to wait till Mian Mir was consulted on the issue. With the intervention of the Master, the execution did not take place.

Allah is the Greatest

Shah Muhammad, affectionately called Mullah Shah, became the most prominent of Mian Mir's disciples. He belonged to the village of Arkasai, near Rustaq in Badhakshan, where he completed his early education. Mullah Shah then travelled to Balkh for Islamic studies from where he went to Srinagar, staying in the valley for three years.

Mullah Shah lived a hard life of self-mortification and remained a celibate. He never cooked anything in his house and did not even light a lamp at night. He practised meditation with breath control, even during the severest of Kashmir winters and taught these practices to disciples including the crown prince Dara Shikoh. Dara credited his spiritual progression to the blessings of Mullah Shah.

Mystic wisdom is reflected in Mullah Shah's countless *mathnawis, rubais, ghazals* and commentaries. He held that Sufis who concentrated their attention on the Divine essence did not get involved in the differences between believers and infidels, heaven and hell, reward and punishment; whereas the ignorant would probably indulge in such frivolous matters. He believed that Sufis should recognize that their heaven was a dedication to the Divine essence.[4]

Emperor Shahjehan invited Mullah Shah to the palace in 1640 AD, seeking his spiritual guidance. Initially the mystic refused to go, insisting that the kings of this world would not benefit from his teachings. However, later he changed his mind and instructed the emperor in Sufi doctrines. The same year Prince Dara and Princess Jehanara became disciples of Mullah Shah. It took a great deal of persuasion for the Master to agree to initiate the children of the royal family into the Qadri Order.

Shahjehan, Dara and Jehanara continued to meet Mullah Shah regularly, both in Kashmir and Lahore. He renamed the Chashm e Shahi Gardens to Chashm e Sahiba, after Jehanara's title of Begum Sahiba. The emperor invited Mullah Shah to Delhi but he did not go there since his eyesight had begun to fail.

Following Dara Shikoh's defeat, Aurangzeb launched an attack on all those close to the prince. He decreed that Mullah Shah be bought to Delhi, but the mystic could not travel on account of ill health. Jehanara pleaded with Aurangzeb to excuse her spiritual Master. Aurangzeb then issued orders for Mullah Shah to leave the valley and go to Lahore.

In Lahore, Mullah Shah lived in the house assigned to him by Shahjehan. Jehanara arranged for one of her personal servants to look after him. The Shaykh spent the rest of his life meditating in solitude and died on 15 Safar 1072 Hijri/1661 AD. He is buried close to the tomb of Mian Mir in Lahore. Jehanara had a red sandstone mausoleum built over his grave, adding a beautiful garden in the compound.

﷽

ABDUL HAQQ MOHADDITH DEHLVI (D. 1052 HIJRI/1642 AD)

Shaykh Abdul Haqq's ancestors had migrated from Bukhara to Delhi during the reign of Alauddin Khilji. They held senior positions in the royal court, excelling both in military and literary skills. His father Shaykh Saifuddin served among the retinue of nobles, writing poetry under the pen name of Saifi. Drawn towards Sufism, he gave moving lectures on the Oneness of God.

Shaykh Saifuddin personally supervised his son's education, and the young lad was an enthusiastic student. He arrived at school before daybreak, continuing his studies well into the night. In his youth, Abdul Haqq pursued a rigorous schedule of prayer and fasting. After completing his education at the age of 22, he began to teach advanced theological scholars.

Abdul Haqq became a disciple of Shaykh Musa Jilani who lived at the court of Emperor Akbar in Fatehpur Sikri. Although Shaykh Musa was close to the courtiers Abul Fazl and Faizi, Abdul Haqq remained aloof from court politics. He spent most of his time in Delhi, looking after his widowed mother.

In 1588 AD Shaykh Abdul Haqq left for a pilgrimage to Makkah and Madinah. One day he informed his friends of a dream in which the Prophet delivered sermons on Hadith. At Makkah he became a disciple of Shaykh Abdul Wahab Muttaqi, a migrant from India who initiated him into the Chishti, Qadri, Madani and Shazili Orders. He wished to stay in the holy cities longer but his mentor urged him to return to India.

On returning to Delhi, the Shaykh continued to stay away from the royal court. He spent his time teaching and compiling Hadith, earning the title of *Mohaddith*, one who compiles the Hadith, traditions of Prophet Muhammad ﷺ. He became a close friend of Khwaja Baaqi Billa, who established the Naqshbandi Order in Delhi. Following his example and disturbed by Akbar's new religious doctrine *Din e Ilahi*, Abdul Haqq corresponded with members of the Mughal nobility including Murtaza Khan and Abdur Rahim Khan e Khanan.

Shaykh Abdul Haqq's *khanqah* in Delhi, where he taught Hadith, came to be called *Khanqah e Qadriya*. The Shaykh lived through the reign of Emperors Akbar and Jehangir. Although Jehangir often rewarded his scholarship with lavish gifts, Abdul Haqq stood by his decision to disassociate with royalty.

Sometime prior to his death, Jehangir became alienated from the Shaykh and exiled him along with his son Nur ul Haqq, the *Qazi* at Agra, to Kabul. The emperor first ordered Abdul Haqq to come to Kashmir where he had camped. On the way to the valley, the Shaykh stopped at Lahore where he met Mian Mir. The Lahore Sufi predicted that before the Shaykh met the emperor, he would return safely to Delhi. Jehangir died four days later, the prophecy coming true.

According to Dara Shikoh, Jehangir's actions were due to unfair allegations by some people that the Shaykh and Nur ul Haqq had befriended the rebellious Prince Khurram, later known as Shahjehan. After Shahjehan's ascension to the throne, both father and son were allowed to return to Delhi, Nur ul Haqq being reappointed the *Qazi* of Agra.

Shaykh Abdul Haqq translated the famous collection of sermons by the Baghdad Master, Shaykh Abdul Qadir Jilani, *Futuh al Ghayab*, into Persian. The effort went a long way in popularizing the Sufi doctrines of the Qadri Order. He also wrote a biography of Shaykh Ali Muttaqi and his pupil Shaykh Abdul Wahab bin Waliullah Muttaqi, the migrants to Makkah. The work titled *Zad ul Muttaqin fi suluk tariq ul yaqin*, throws light on the religious and intellectual links between India and Arabia. Manuscripts of these works are available at the Raza library in Rampur and the British Museum. Muhammad Sadiq Hamdhani, the author of *Kalimatus Sadiqin*, containing the biographies of 125 Delhi Sufis was a student of Shaykh Abdul Haqq. The book written during the rule of Shahjehan remains an important source of Delhi's Sufi history.

Shaykh Abdul Haqq also wrote a history of Madinah, *Jazb al Qulub ila diyar al Mahbub*, which he began writing at Madinah and completed in 1592 AD at Delhi. Most of the Shaykh's writings attempted to reconcile *Sharia* with *Tareeqa*. Another important contribution is his writing in *Akhbaar ul Akhyaar*, a celebrated manual on Indian Sufis.

Shaykh Abdul Haqq died on 21 Rabi ul awwal 1052 Hijri/1642 AD at the age of 94. His *dargah* is near the *Hauz e Shamsi* at Mehrauli, Delhi. His sons and disciples continued the teachings of the Qadri *silsila* throughout India.

ﷲ

SULTAN BAHU (D. 1102 HIJRI/1691 AD)

Sultan Bahu founded the Sarwari Qadri Order, an offshoot of the Qadri Order. From his original name of Sultan Muhammad, he came to be called Bahu (one who is with Him), for his constant remembrance of *Hu*, He Alone. He wrote, 'With one dot Bahu becomes *Ya Hu*, and Bahu is always steeped in the remembrance of *Ya Hu* (O Allah).'

The imagery of Sultan Bahu's poetry is derived from the daily activities of villagers, like gardening and planting. Developing on the ideas of the earlier Sufis, he presented them to the rural folk in a simple poetic form. Each of his verses ended with the word *Hu*. 'Alif: Allah is like the jasmine plant which the preceptor planted in my heart—*O Hu*: By water and the gardener it remained near the jugular vein—*O Hu*: It spread fragrance inside when it appeared at the time of blossoming—*O Hu*: May the efficient preceptor live long, says Bahu, who planted this plant—*O Hu!*'[5]

More than 40 books on mysticism are attributed to Sultan Bahu, among which are *Nur ul Huda* (Light of Guidance) and *Risaala e Ruh* (Journal for the Soul). However, it is his collection of Punjabi verses, *Abiyaat e Bahu* on the theme of Oneness of God, that have generated popular appeal. In a highly emotive style, he elaborates on the traditional belief in self-manifestation of the Absolute and the importance of a spiritual life dedicated to the pursuit of God. Sultan Bahu's verses are sung in many forms of Sufi music including *kafis* and *qawaalis*. The traditional singing of his *kafis* has established a particular form of melody not used in any other genre of music.

The mystic poet's family belonged to the Hashmi tribe who were descendants of the Prophet's son-in-law Imam Ali. His father Sultan Bayazid was a senior official at Shahjehan's court. The family settled in Sherkot village in the Jhang district, which was awarded to Sultan Bayazid for his services to the government.

Sultan Bahu's religious education began at the feet of his enlightened mother Rasti, who had the greatest influence on him. She directed him to seek guidance from Shaykh Habibullah Qadri, who later sent him to Delhi to pursue further studies under the tutelage of Shaykh Abdul Rahim Qadri. On completing his education, he returned to the familiar surroundings of Punjab.

Sultan Bahu died on 1 Jumada al akhira 1102 Hijri/1691 AD. His *dargah* is in Gargh Maharaja in the Pakistan part of Punjab where the annual *Urs* celebrations are held amidst singing of the Sufi poet's verses.[6]

﴾

JEHANARA (D. 1092 HIJRI/1681 AD)

Jehanara, the Sufi princess wielded tremendous influence during the reign of her father, Emperor Shahjehan. She enjoyed an allowance of six lakh rupees, half in cash and half in land. The princess built the Jama Masjid at Agra and laid out the Chandni Chowk Bazaar in Delhi. She patronized several other architectural projects including some of the Mughal gardens.

Mumtaz Mahal gave birth to her eldest daughter on 23 March 1614 AD. After the death of her mother, Jehanara enjoyed the status of the first lady in the royal household. She remained staunchly devoted to her father and looked after him during his incarceration on being deposed by his younger son Aurangzeb. The princess earned the displeasure of Aurangzeb for being extremely close to Dara Shikoh, the brother with whom she shared her passion for Sufism.

Jehanara authored two Sufi manuals, *Munis al Arwah* (Confidant of Spirits) and an incomplete biography of her spiritual mentor Mullah Shah. According to her own admission, she was the first woman in the House of Timur to walk the Sufi path. Although the princess was a disciple of Mullah Shah of the Qadri Order, she remained devoted to the Chishti Sufis. Her book *Munis al Arwah* contains the life and teachings of Khwaja Moinuddin Chishti. The biography compiled from other works on Sufis, is highly regarded for its literary value. It describes the author's pilgrimage to Khwaja Moinuddin Chisti's *dargah* during the *Urs* at Ajmer Sharif in 1643 AD and conveys her personal engagement with Sufi practices. Jehanara recited verses from the Holy Quran offering them to the inhabitants of the tomb, seeking the blessings of the blessed. The princess wrote of the mosque where she prayed in Ajmer, which had recently been reconstructed by her father.

The Sufi princess uses the word *faqira*—the feminine form of *faqir*—to signify her own spiritual vocation. Jehanara regarded Khwaja Moinuddin Chishti as the supreme Sufi of India and felt a deep spiritual bond with him. In the book, she writes:

> Praise and favour be to God, and a hundred million thanks, for on Thursday, the fourth of the blessed month of Ramadan, I attained the happiness of pilgrimage to the illuminated and perfumed tomb of the revered saving Master (May God be pleased with him). With an hour of daylight remaining, I went to the holy sanctuary and rubbed my pale face on the dust of the threshold. From the doorway to the blessed tomb I went barefoot, kissing the ground. Having entered the dome, I went around the light-filled tomb of my master seven times, sweeping it with my eyelashes, and making the sweet-smelling dust of that place the mascara of my eyes. At that moment, a marvelous spiritual state and mystical experience befell this annihilated one, which cannot rightly be written. From extreme longing I became astonished, and I do not know what I said or did.

Jehanara continues:

> For the several days when I stopped in the above mentioned buildings, from extreme courtesy I did not sleep on a leopard skin that night, I did not extend my feet in the direction of the blessed sanctuary of the revered saving master, and I did not turn my back towards him. I passed the days beneath the trees. If I had the choice, I would always have stayed in the sanctuary of that revered one, which is the marvelous corner of security—and I am a lover of the corner of security. I would also have had the honor and happiness of walking around it continuously.

A true lover of Khwaja Moinuddin she wrote,

> *Our Moinuddin is annihilated in God,*
> *Now he subsists in the Divine essence.*

Princess Jehanara never married and spent the last days of her life devoted to the *dargah* of Hazrat Nizamuddin Auliya. She died in 1092 Hijri/1681 AD and according to her wishes is buried opposite the tomb of Hazrat Nizamuddin. She had the marble mausoleum constructed during her own lifetime. The tomb is devoid of any dome and she lies under the open skies. Jehanara's epitaph is a verse from one of her books:

> *He is the Living, the Sustaining.*
> *Let no one cover my grave except with greenery,*
> *For this very grass suffices as a tomb cover for the poor.*
> *The annihilated faqir Lady Jahanara,*
> *Disciple of the Lords of Chisht,*
> *Daughter of Shahjehan the Warrior*
> *(May God illuminate his proof).*

BULHE SHAH (D. 1181 HIJRI/1768 AD)

Bulhe Shah remains the most popular of all Sufi poets in Punjab. His ancestors came from Bhawalpur where his father, Shaykh Muhammad Darvesh taught Arabic, Persian and the holy scriptures. The family later migrated to Sahiwal and the child went to Qasur for his education under the guidance of Hazrat Ghulam Murtaza. Like other contemporary Sufi poets Mir Dard and Mazhar Jan e Janan, Bulhe Shah witnessed political upheavals after Aurangzeb's death. He took solace in the world of mysticism, writing poetry in Punjabi and Persian.

Bulhe belonged to the Qadri Order founded by Shaykh Abdul Qadir Jilani, called the Master of all Masters. He glorified the Shaykh of Baghdad thus: 'My Master of Masters hailed from Baghdad, but my Master belongs to the throne of Lahore. It is all the same. For he himself is the kite and he himself is the string.'

Shah Inayat, Bulhe's spiritual mentor belonged to the Arain caste that earned their livelihood from agriculture and gardening. He had a profound effect on his disciple's spirituality. Bulhe wrote, 'O Bulhe, My Lord Inayat knows God, He is the Master of my heart, I am iron, he is the philosopher's stone.'

Bulhe's family drew their ancestry from the Prophet's family and thought it was demeaning for him to have become a disciple of someone from a lower caste. However, Bulhe felt spiritually enlightened in the company of Shah Inayat and proclaimed , 'O Bulhe, if you seek the pleasure of a garden in spring, go and become a servant of the Arain.'

Bulhe Shah's *khanqah* at Qasur, near Lahore, gained popularity with Sufis of the region. He initiated disciples into many orders including the Madari, Chishti and Suharwardi Orders. Bulhe invented a new imagery in explaining the Oneness of God, making his verses extremely popular. He died in 1181 Hijri/1768 AD and is buried in Qasur.

Allah

11

THE NAQSHBANDIS

KHWAJA BAQI BILLA (D. 1012 HIJRI/1785 AD)

Sufi literature records Khwaja Baqi Billa's disciples questioning him on the doctrine of *fana*, annihilation of the self, and *baqa*, continuance in Allah. The Khwaja advised them to pose the question to the person who would lead his funeral prayers. He had willed that the man who offered these prayers should never have sinned, not once missed the mandatory prayers or the voluntary night vigil. On the Khwaja's death, while his disciples sat wondering who should lead the funeral prayers, a veiled person joined their assembly. He declared that the Khwaja had asked him to lead the prayers, and after offering them, the stranger readied to leave. The disciples then remembered the Khwaja's instruction and they requested the stranger to explain the concepts of *fana* and *baqa*. The man removed his veil and the disciples saw that he was none other than the Khwaja himself. The Khwaja's title Baqi Billa, literally means 'one who finds continuance in Allah'.

Khwaja Muhammad Baqi Billa established the Naqshbandi Sufi Order in Delhi. He lived during the reign of the Mughal Emperor Akbar and protested over the state policies that he believed to be wrong. The Khwaja's father was the reputed Sufi scholar Qazi

Abdus Salam Khaji of Samarqand. The Khwaja's real name was Syed Raziuddin and at an early age he became a disciple of the prominent Maulana Sadiq Halwai of Samarqand. The Maulana settled in Kabul at the request of Mirza Muhammad Hakim, the brother of Emperor Akbar. The young disciple travelled with his teacher to Transoxania but did not complete the prescribed education, rejecting traditional studies for the pursuit of Sufism.

After collecting the wisdom of the Transoxania Sufis, the Khwaja moved on in search of an inspired spiritual life. He travelled to Lahore with his mother, acquiring knowledge from the mystics of the city. In the pursuit of a spiritual mentor, he travelled to Delhi and Kashmir, and his quest ended in the valley where Baba Wali initiated him into the Naqshbandi fold. Baba Wali, a migrant from Khwarazm, lived at the *khanqah* of Mir Sayyid Ali of Hamdhan. Khwaja Baqi Billa later travelled to Balkh and Badakshan where he met Khwaja Amkinagi who advised him to go back to India.

The Khwaja settled in Delhi around the year 1600 AD, staying at the Firozabad Fort near the Jamuna. He had two wives who bore him one son each, Khwaja Abdullah and Khwaja Obaidullah. The Master stressed on the importance of *fana* in seeking God, and believed that *wahdat ul wujood* was the ultimate truth. A polite and courteous man, he avoided publicity remaining selective about initiating disciples. He refused any financial assistance and lived a life of extreme poverty.

Khwaja Baqi Billa authored many books on Naqshbandi teachings and delighted in writing poetic verse. A compilation of his quatrains, *Silsila al Ahrar*, was later published. The Khwaja's disciple Shaykh Ahmad Sirhindi wrote a commentary on them. The Khwaja died at the age of 40 on 25 Jumada al akhira 1012 Hijri/1603 AD in Delhi. The area around his *dargah* has remained a preferred burial ground for the city's Muslims.

※

SHAYKH AHMAD SIRHINDI (D. 1034 HIJRI/1624 AD)

The Naqshbandi Sufis took an active role in politics, since they thought that educating the ruling classes was a religious duty. Traditionally, the Naqshbandi Sufi Order is a sober one that denounces music assemblies of *sama*.

Shaykh Ahmad Sirhindi, a disciple of Khwaja Baqi Billa, earned the title of *Mujadid Alf e Thani* (Reviver of the Second Islamic Millenium) and played a major role in Indian religious and political life. Widely known for his 534 letters, he wrote 70 of these to Mughal officials. The letters, originally written in Persian, have been translated into many languages including Arabic, Urdu, Turkish and English.

Shaykh Ahmad was born in 1564 AD to the scholar Shaykh Abdul Ahad who initiated his son into the Chishti and Qadri Orders. Despite his father believing in the Sufi doctrine of *wahdat ul wujood*, Oneness of Being, Shaykh Ahmad promoted the superiority of *wahdat ul shuhud*, Oneness of Vision. The Chishtis believed Ibn al Arabi's mystical philosophy of *wahdat ul wujood* to be the greatest development in Sufi thought. But the Naqshbandis reacted sharply against the doctrine, particularly opposing Akbar's syncretism through his ideas of a universal religion of Din e Elahi.

After learning the Quran from his father, Shaykh Ahmad travelled to Sialkot where he studied under Maulana Kamal Kashmiri, who had trained under many leading Central Asian Sufi scholars, including Ibn Hajar Asqalani. After acquiring considerable grounding in the religious sciences, Shaykh Ahmad engaged in philosophical discussions with Akbar's courtiers Abul Fazl and Faizi. Annoyed by the freedom with which religious issues were discussed, Shaykh Ahmad dedicated himself to upholding the dignity of orthodox Islam. He wrote *Isbat un Nabuwah* (Proofs of Prophecy) to vindicate the Sunni viewpoint on prophecy. He remained in Agra where he showed an interest in the Naqshbandi Order under the guidance of Khwaja Ubaid Kabuli, whom Akbar later banished to Thata.[1]

Subsequently, the Shaykh returned to Sirhind where he taught a number of his father's disciples. Hearing about the fame of Khwaja Baqi Billa, he went to meet him in Delhi and became his disciple. The Khwaja held his disciple in great esteem, entrusting his children and wives to him. After Khwaja Baqi Billa's death in Delhi, Shaykh Ahmad succeeded him as the head of the Naqshbandi Order.

The Shaykh asserted that the esoteric knowledge of Sufis remained superior to the knowledge of the *ulema*, scholars, and that they should be given greater respect. He believed that the Naqshbandi Order was superior to other orders, for it inherited the traditions of both Imam Ali and Imam Abu Bakr Siddiq through Imam Jafar, the sixth Imam.

The first volume of Shaykh Ahmad's letters in his works, *Mankubat*, was written to Khwaja Baqi Billa. These letters illustrate his departure from *wahdat ul wujood* to *wahdat ul shuhud* as propagated by the Kubrawi mystic Alauddawla Simnani. This became the turning point in his life. However, the Shaykh wrote commentaries on his Master's poetry based on *wahdat ul wujood*, making it more acceptable to the orthodox believers. Ibn al Arabi's theory had divided the world of Sufis into two groups, one who venerated him and the other who thought him to be misguided. The Shaykh found both groups to have exaggerated views and held a moderate view of Ibn al Arabi's philosophy.

In some of the Shaykh's letters to his Master, he describes how he crossed the mystical stages occupied by the Imams of the House of Prophet Muhammad ﷺ and the mystical stages occupied by the *khalifa e rashidin*, the companions of the Prophet. He perceived that the only stage he had not achieved was that of the Seal of the Prophets.[2]

It is not known whether Khwaja Baqi Billa objected to his disciple's mystical perceptions, but the overwhelming majority of Sufis were upset. Even the orthodox Sufi scholar Shaykh Abdul Haqq accused Shaykh Ahmad of contradiction in his mystic statements. The

Shaykh believed that Prophet Muhammad ﷺ had divinely inspired his *kalam*, scholastic knowledge of theology.

The Shaykh's most astounding theories were on prophetology, where he provided new mystic orientation for the second Islamic millennium. As Schimmel observes:

> He spoke about the two individuations of Prophet Muhammad ﷺ, the two m's in Muhammad's ﷺ name pointing to them. In the first millennium the first *m* disappeared to make room for the letter *alif*, the letter of Divinity, so that the manifestation of Ahmad remains purely spiritual and unconnected with the worldly needs of his community. In a complicated process, the new millennium had to restore the perfections of prophethood. It is no accident that the change of name from Muhammad ﷺ to Ahmad coincides with the very name Ahmad Sirhindi, pointing to his discreet hidden role as the common believer to restore these perfections. He suggested he was the *qayum*, the highest elected representative of God, through whom the world is kept in order. Naqshbandi manuals such as the *Raudat al Qayummiya* record that he claimed that the highest ranks in the hierarchy of beings was held by him and three of his successors, beginning with his son Muhammad Masum. The manual is not a historical work and was written at the time of the breakdown of the Mughal Empire after 1739 AD.[3]

The Shaykh's letters containing new mystical interpretations caused something of a sensation among the Sufis, scholars and the nobles of the Mughal court. Emperor Jehangir summoned the Shaykh to his court, questioning his mystical claims. Unconvinced by his explanations, the emperor imprisoned him. After a year, Jehangir released the Shaykh, presenting him with a robe and money for personal expenses. He was given the choice of remaining in court or retiring in Sirhind. The Shaykh described the prison experience as invaluable, choosing to live in the imperial camp for the next three years. He spent his time delivering sermons, some of which were attended by the emperor. When his health began to deteriorate, the Shaykh went back to Sirhind where he died on 28 Safar 1034 Hijri/1624 AD.

Shaykh Ahmad remains an icon of the conservative reaction to the heterodoxy of Akbar and the syncretic philosophies of the Indian Chishti Sufis. However, the mystic scholar had a role in nurturing the Naqshbandi Order in the Indian subcontinent.

SHAH WALIULLAH (D. 1176 HIJRI/1762 AD)

The modern approach to Islam begins with Shah Waliullah, where scholars were no longer interested in the miracles of the Prophet but rather in his role as a nation builder and model for social conduct. This viewpoint confronts the Muslims with the ideals of the Prophet and the reality of their own political disintegration, thus creating a permanent tension between the elusive ideals and the sad political reality.[4]

Shah Waliullah was born in 1703 AD to a family of Sufi scholars. His father Shah Abdur Rahim (1647–1719 AD) founded the *Madarsa Rahimiya* seminary in Delhi. Waliullah studied under the tutelage of his older brother Shaykh Abdur Riza, the most notable disciple of Khwaja Khwurd, the son of Khwaja Baqi Billa. Although Khwaja Khwurd initially trained with Shaykh Ahmad Sirhindi following the death of his father, he and his elder brother Khwaja Abdullah broke away from the Shaykh's teachings. The two brothers were fond of musical assemblies and supported the controversial theory of *wahdat ul wujood*. They formed their own Naqshbandi centre at Delhi, opposing the orthodox approach of Shaykh Ahmad Sirhindi.

Shah Waliullah's grandfather, Waijuhuddin, served in the military under the Mughals, devoting his later years to contemplation and prayer. His younger son, Abdur Rahim, taught religious texts committed to Arabis' theory of *wahdat ul wujood*. Shaykh Abdur Rahim remarried at the age of 60, believing the decision to be divinely inspired. Qutubuddin Ahmad, born of the second marriage later came to be called Shah Waliullah. Shaykh Abdur Rahim personally supervised his son's education, initiating him in the Naqshbandi Order. In his book *Anfas ul Arifin*, Waliullah praises his father's spiritual achievements. After his father's demise, Shah Waliullah took charge of his seminary in 1719 AD.

In 1731 AD Shah Waliullah travelled to Makkah and Madinah where he met many eminent Islamic scholars. In Madinah he experienced recurring visions of Prophet Muhammad ﷺ and other mystical inspirations, foretelling his role as the restorer of righteousness. Shah Waliullah recorded these spiritual experiences in *Fuyuz al Haramain* (Bounties of Makkah and Madinah). He returned to India inspired with ideas on redirecting the religious, cultural and political life of the Muslim community.

Waliullah's works focussing exclusively on Sufism include *Al Qaul al Jamil, Al Intibah Fi Salail Auliya Allah, Hamat, Altaf al Quds, Sat'at, Al Khair al Kasir* and *Lamhat*. He tried to bridge the gap between *Sharia* and *Tareeqa*, the ways of the Sufis and the jurists. He confirmed that the esoteric and the exoteric were two aspects of Islam, God having assigned the duty of inviting people to the path of righteousness to His friends, the *Auliya*. Shah Waliullah attempted to explain the different schools of Islamic jurisprudence as historical facts with no fundamental differences. He believed that throughout the history of Islam, a group of scholars had waged an incessant struggle to stop the violations of the principles of the faith and that in every century a *mujadid* was born whose duty it was to strengthen the faith.[5]

Shah Waliullah wrote that Sufism began with Prophet Muhammad ﷺ and his companions, the second phase starting with Junayd of Baghdad, the third with Shaykh Said Abi Khair and Shaykh Abul Hasan Kharqani, and the fourth with the great Shaykh Ibn al Arabi. Waliullah reconciled the differences between the mystic doctrines of *wahdat ul wujood* and *wahdat ul shuhud*, and became the first scholar to translate the Quran in Persian. His major book on socio-political thought is *Hujjat Allah Balighah*. Other relevant works on the subject include *Izalat al Khafa an Khilafat al Khulafa* and *Al Badur al Bazigah.*

After the death of Aurangzeb in 1707 AD, the Mughal Empire began to crumble, with internal and external wars signalling the end of its supremacy in India. A group of theologians and mystics from the Naqshbandi Order set forth a new 'Muhammedan' theology intended to give the Muslims a new impetus by leading them back to the Golden Age of the Prophet and his companions. Shah Waliullah, the most famous among them saw himself as called by God and the Prophet as 'his vicegerent in blaming', *mu'ataba*.[6] The reformers emphasized the practical aspects of the Prophet's message aimed at helping the Muslim community cope with resurgent non-Muslim communities such as the Marathas, Sikhs and the British. Shah Waliullah invited the Afghan king Ahmad Shah Durrani Abdali to India in order to defend the Muslims against the Marathas and Sikhs. However, he did not take into account the British who gained their first decisive victory at Plassey during his lifetime.

Convinced of his God-given duty, Shah Waliullah attacked those who studied philosophy instead of concentrating on the words of God and prophetic traditions. He was harsh with those who neglected religious duties. The Arab character of Islam in its pristine purity is clearly contrasted by the scholar with the confusing plethora of the pluralistic Indian religious traditions.

Although Shah Waliullah belonged to the Naqshbandi Order, it is in the role of a reformer theologian and Sunni revivalist that he is most remembered. His ideas inspired the poet philosopher Iqbal (1877–1938 AD) and the educationist Sir Syed Ahmad (1817–98 AD) in their modernist approach to religion. Iqbal praises Shah Waliullah as the first Muslim who felt the need for a new spirit in Islam. The poet developed on the idea that every prophet educated one special people, who could be used as the nucleus for building an all-embracing law.

Shah Waliullah remains the spiritual patron of the seminary Dar ul Uloom in Deoband, founded in the district of Saharanpur in

1879 AD by Maulana Abul Qasim Nanovti. It adopted his theological teachings without the mystical attitudes, defining the religious attitude to imperialism in the subcontinent.

Shah Waliullah is buried in Delhi where he died on 29 Muharram 1176 Hijri/1762 AD. His son Shah Abdul Aziz took charge of the seminary run by his father and grandfather.

〰

MIRZA JAAN E JANAN SHAHEED (D. 1195 HIJRI/1781 AD)

It is said that Mevlana Rumi predicted Mirza Jaan e Janan's birth 500 years before the event in the verse:

Jaan e dar awwal mazhare dargah shud
Jaan e jaan an khud mazhar e allah shud.

His ancestors, who were descendants of Imam Abu Hanifa's family, migrated in the early sixteenth century from Taif near Makkah to Turkey. Some family members accompanied Humayun to India, serving as officials in the Mughal court. Mirza's father travelled with Humayun to the Deccan but later resigned his post and left for Agra. During his travels back north, Mirza was born in Malwa in 1700 AD and given the name Shamsuddin.

Mirza received spiritual training from his father who was devoted to some learned mystics. After completing his education, he became a disciple and *khalifa* of Sayyid Nur Muhammad Badayuni, the Naqshbandi Sufi. The poet successfully bridged the differences between religious orthodoxy and Sufism.

The mystic asserted that Shia–Sunni differences had no relevance to essential Islamic beliefs. However, he criticized the Shia tradition of perpetuating the tragedy of Kerbala on Muharram and its reverence towards replicated tombs of Imam Hussain. Reacting to such statements, an Irani, along with two accomplices, shot the Sufi with a pistol. He survived for three days, refusing to identify the assailant at the emperor's court. The bullet wounds led to his death on 7 Muharram 1195 Hijri/1781 AD.

The poet-mystic compiled a selection of 1,000 poems from his 20,000 Persian verses. His spirit of self-criticism is perhaps why so little of his Urdu poetry exists—much of it lies scattered in various anthologies. Mirza Jaan e Janan is recognized as one of the four pillars of eighteenth century Urdu poetry, alongside Sauda, Mir Taqi Mir and Khwaja Mir Dard. The Sufi poet's tomb is in the old city of Delhi.

〽

KHWAJA MIR DARD (D. 1199 HIJRI/1785 AD)

Contrary to Naqshbandi practices, Khwaja Mir Dard enjoyed music and poetry. He arranged musical assemblies in his house twice a month, which became famous in Delhi. Even the emperor, Shah Alam II, who wrote under the pen name Aftab, often attended these *sama mehfils*. The Khwaja's love for music came under attack by some Sufis. In an effort to remove misunderstandings arising from his mystic verse, the Khwaja authored the book *Hurmat e Ghina*. In it he wrote 'a gnostic without a book is like a man without children' and expressed that he had been granted, 'like the candle, the tongue of clear speech'. The mystic explained that he did not write poetry on commission, his verse being divinely inspired.

Khwaja Mir Dard remains one of the most famous Sufi poets of the Urdu language. He was the son of the mystic poet Muhammad Nasir Andalib (d. 1758 AD) who gave up military service to follow the life of a Sufi. He was a descendant of Shaykh Bahauddin, and belonged to a Sayyid family from the Turkish lands. His spiritual Master was Pir Muhammad Zubair, the fourth and last of the *qayums*, spiritual Masters from the House of Shaykh Ahmad Sirhindi. He composed the *Nala e Andalib* (The Lamentation of the Nightingale) after the death of his mentor, and dedicated the book to his son, who considered it to be the highest expression of mystical wisdom.

A disciple of his father, Khwaja Mir spent his life promoting the *Tareeqa al Muhammadiya*, the path of Prophet Muhammad ﷺ as defined by the Naqshbandi Masters. The Khwaja thought his father to be the perfect guide and carried on his legacy. He stayed on in Delhi despite the tribulations that fell upon the capital, his poetry reflecting the change. He wrote:

> *Delhi which has now been devastated,*
> *tears are flowing now instead of its rivers;*
> *This town has been like the face of the lovely,*
> *and its suburbs like the town of the beloved ones.*[7]

Khwaja prayed for the unhappy population of the city as he saw foreign armies ravage the town and oppress its citizens. He never left Delhi, living in the compound given to him and his father by one of Emperor Aurangzeb's daughters.

A prolific writer in both Urdu and Persian, Khwaja Mir instructed a number of Urdu poets. In his greatest work *Ilm ul Kitab* (Book of Knowledge), the Khwaja details his mystic ideologies and experiences. Some years later he wrote *Chahar Risala*, four beautiful spiritual diaries, where he elaborates on the theories of the Divine as reflected in the different levels of creation. 'Although Adam has not got wings, yet he has reached a place that was not destined for angels.'

Khwaja Mir Dard also wrote Persian poetry, but he is mostly remembered for his Urdu *Diwan* containing 12,000 couplets, which are songs of Divine unity. He writes, 'In the state of collectedness the single beings of the world are one, all the petals of the rose together are one... Pain and happiness have the same shape in the world, You may call the rose an open heart, or a broken heart.' His lyrical verses have outlasted most poets of the eighteenth century. The Khwaja's son was also a poet, writing under the pen name of Alam (pain) and so was his younger brother Akhtar with whom he shared a close bond. Khwaja Mir Dard died on 1 Rabi ul awwal 1199 Hijri/1785 AD and is buried in Delhi.

The Quran: Chapter Read (96:5)
Taught man which he knew not.

12

THE RISHIS

SHAYKH UL ALAM NUND RISHI (D. 842 HIJRI/1439 AD)

For three days after his birth, the infant Nund did not suckle at his mother's breast. The ascetic, Lal Ded, visited his parent's home and said to the child, 'You were not ashamed to be born, then why are you ashamed of sucking at your mother's breast?' Local traditions narrate that the baby subsequently began to drink his mother's milk and the ascetic continued to visit the house. Lal Ded was the famous Shaivite yogini who had rebelled against the oppressive social order perpetuated by the caste-conscious Brahmins.

Shaykh Nuruddin called himself Nund Sanz, the name by which his family addressed him since childhood. His father, Salar Ganai, was a village watchman and among the early converts to Islam in Kashmir. Nund became the true heir of Lal Ded and looked upon her as his spiritual mentor. He wrote:

> *That Lalla of Padampore,*
> *Who had drunk the fill of nectar,*
> *She was an avtaar of ours,*
> *Oh Lord, grant me the same spiritual power.*

The Shaykh's life can be viewed in three stages: his being orphaned early and struggling through abject poverty in his youth, becoming an ascetic and living as a recluse, coming out into the public sphere again in order to spread Sufi ethics.

After their father's death, two of Nuruddin's older brothers turned to theft for survival and once sought his help in a burglary. Upon entering the scene of the crime Nuruddin was so repulsed by the idea that he threw his blanket over the victims and came out empty-handed. On another occasion, the brothers ordered the lad to take care of a cow they had stolen. While grazing the animal, Nuruddin heard a dog bark, 'wow, wow'. The word 'wow' literally means, to sow, in the Kashmiri language. Overcome with remorse, he thought that the dog was reminding him of the universal principle of truth that what one sows in this world is what one reaps in the Hereafter. He articulated the thought in his verse:

> The dog is calling from the courtyard,
> My brothers pay heed to that voice,
> He who sows here shall reap there,
> The dog is urging to sow, oh sow.

Nund's mother sent him to learn weaving in order to earn an honest livelihood. The mystically-inclined boy found a deeper meaning in the movement of the threads and the weaving tools, which reminded him of two doors, birth and death. The shuttle resembled man carrying the thread of destiny, moving between the world and departing when the thread was exhausted. However, Nund soon gave up his apprenticeship, choosing to become an ascetic. Inspired by the Hindu rishis and Buddhist monks, he followed their ways of meditation, praising their penance and quest for spiritual ascent.

Nund Sanz retired to a cave at Kaimuh, the place of his birth. He wrote:

> In the pursuit of mundane affairs, my desires become limitless,
> So I retired to the jungle, early in life,
> May the Lord saturate the Rishi's mind with longing for thee,
> For I remember with gratitude how kind Thou art.'

Many verses written during the period of seclusion have elements of Shaivite philosophy based upon self-realization.

> *He is near me I am near Him,*
> *I found solace in His nearness,*
> *In vain did I seek Him elsewhere,*
> *Lo: I found Him within my heart.*

Later in life, Shaykh Nuruddin travelled throughout the valley spreading the mystic message of devotion, sincerity and brotherhood. In tune with the local sentiment, he remained a vegetarian. Many villages continue to commemorate his visit through an annual celebration of the event. Like Lal Ded, he spoke out against the caste system:

> *Why are you harping on the caste,*
> *His is the only caste,*
> *His essence is beyond the bounds of knowledge,*
> *The doers of noble deeds all have the same caste,*
> *If O brother you surrender to Him,*
> *Then alone will you become pure.*

The Shaykh wrote of the eternal longing of the human heart and in his efforts to spread Islamic values, he often used the local name for God:

> *Nirguna manifest Thyself unto me,*
> *Thy name alone I have been chanting.*
> *Lord, help me to reach the height of my spiritual desires,*
> *I do remember with gratitude how kind You are,*
> *Thou removed all veils between Thyself and the Prophet,*
> *And Thou revealed Quran unto him,*
> *Lord the Prophet is one who remained steadfast in Thy way,*
> *I do remember with gratitude how beneficent You are.*

In other verses he addresses Prophet Muhammad ﷺ as the first Rishi. Shaykh Nuruddin came into contact with the visiting Kubrawi Sufi,

Mir Sayyid Muhammad Hamdhani, son of Mir Sayyidd Ali Hamdhani, both of whom played an important role in the spread of Islam in Kashmir. The mystical ideas of Shaykh Nuruddin and his disciples deeply impacted the Kashmiri language, religion and culture. This unique identity of the Kashmiri people came to be called *kashmiriyat*.

Bamuddin, Zainuddin, Latifuddin and Qiyamuddin were among the Shaykh's leading disciples and are believed to have converted from Hinduism to Islam. The majority of the Kashmiri people were drawn to Islam gradually through the teachings of the Sufis. The patron Sufi of Kashmir, Shaykh Nuruddin died on 26 Ramadan 842 Hijri/1439 AD. His *dargah*, *Charar e Sharif* on the outskirts of Srinagar, continues to attract hundreds of thousands of Kashmiris from across the valley. The poetry of Lal Ded and Shaykh Nuruddin was orally transmitted through the centuries and continues to remain popular among the Kashmiris to this day.

ZAINUDDIN RISHI (D. 853 HIJRI/1448 AD)

As a young child Zia Singh once became critically ill. His anxious mother met Nund Rishi and pledged that her family would embrace Islam if the boy regained his health. The boy recovered but his mother did not keep her promise. One day, Nund Rishi appeared to her in a dream reminding her of the commitment and she left her home in Kishtwar for the valley, to meet the mystic and fulfil the pledge.

Most hagiographic sources describe this story regarding Zia Singh's conversion to Islam. Some, however, maintain that he was looking for a spiritual leader, and accepting Nund Rishi as his Master came to be known as Zainuddin. He became one of the most distinguished disciples of Nund Rishi who commented, 'My Zaina is the fountainhead of nectar. Such is his devotion to God that he surpasses his guide.'

After serving the Master for many years, Shaykh Zainuddin retired in a cave on the peak of a mountain at Aishmaqam. In the Rishi tradition, he lived an ascetic life and remained a celibate. Many miracles, including the emergence of a spring near the cave, are attributed to the Shaykh.

Another tale recounts how the Shaykh earned the displeasure of Zain ul Abideen, the ruler of Kashmir, since he did not care to attend on the sultan when he visited him. The enraged sultan ordered the Rishi to leave the kingdom, and thus he travelled to Tibet where he was given a warm welcome. When the ruler's son died, the people blamed the Rishi, threatening him with death. The Rishi prayed to God and the prince came back to life.

Shaykh Zainuddin popularly called Zain Shah, had willed that his body be kept in a coffin and placed in a corner of the cave. The disciples did as he had advised, discovering later that the body had disappeared from the coffin. One of the disciples then dreamed of their Shaykh asking them to build a grave over the place where the coffin had been kept.

Impacted by the story, Abul Fazl writes in *Ain e Akbari*, 'For 12 years Zainuddin occupied this cell and towards the end he closed its mouth with a huge stone and went forth again, and no one has ever found trace of him.'

The Rishi died in 853 Hijri/1448 AD and his tomb at Aishmaqam, in Pahalgam district, draws devotees from all over Kashmir. The *dargah* of Zain Shah remains particularly venerated by the boatmen of Kashmir who perform the rite of cutting their child's first lock of hair at Aishmaqam since they believe it ensures the well-being of the child. The venerated Baba Shukruddin was among the Rishi's chief disciples.

ﴼ

BAMUDDIN RISHI (D. 823 HIJRI/1420 AD)

Shaykh Bamuddin is said to have been a famous Brahmin from Bamuzu who was credited with miraculous powers. People said he was seen bathing daily at five different places in the valley. Different stories describe his conversion to Islam at the hands of Nund Rishi.

Miracles continued to be attributed to Shaykh Bamuddin even after he became a Rishi. People believed that for 12 years the Rishi lived on a diet of crushed stones and water.

When Sultan Ali Shah (r. 1413–20 AD) sought an appointment, the Rishi Sufi sent word that he would have to appear without his stately robes. Thus the Sultan came to him wearing the clothes of a peasant. Inspite of that, the Shaykh said, 'You have taken off the royal robes but your mind is not free from the thoughts of your kingdom. You do not remove the wool of heedlessness from the ears so what use is my advice to you. The attribute of kings is fire and the counsel of mystics is oxygen, the fire will flare in its presence.' He requested the king not to visit him again, throwing the mat on which the king sat into the river.

Shaykh Bamuddin is believed to have turned wine into milk when asked by the royal courtiers Shaukat Mir and Fakhruddin Mir to play the role of a cup-bearer. Impressed with the mystic, the courtiers gave up their life of luxury and became his disciples.

On his deathbed, Shaykh Bamuddin asked that his disciple Shaykh Zainuddin should wash the corpse. Zainuddin was travelling in Tibet at the time, but is believed to have miraculously appeared to perform the last rites. Shaykh Bamuddin died in 823 Hijri/1420 AD and is buried at Bamuzu near Pahalgam, the place where he spent the larger part of his life.

Baba Rishi (d. 889 Hijri/1575 AD)

One day, while riding a horse, the nobleman Payamuddin came across an army of ants carrying tiny specks of grain to store up for the winter months. The scene impacted the young man who realized that he had not thought enough on life after death. Payamuddin soon gave up his courtly position and sought the company of Baba Shukruddin in Wular. After spending a few years in training, the Rishi Master sent his disciple to Baba Zainuddin at Aishmaqam.

Payamuddin underwent a long period of training in the Sufi path under the discipleship of Baba Zainuddin, after which his master instructed him to travel to the village of Ranbuh, in the Bangal Pargana. This area was believed to have been infested by devils and ghouls who would harass the local people. Payamuddin Rishi apparently drove them all away and spread Islam in the area. After staying there for many years, he shifted to the village of Haji Bal in Tanmarg where he spent the rest of his life in the thick forests and came to be known as Baba Rishi. He died at the age of 77 on 3 Dhul Qada 889 Hijri/1575 AD and his *dargah* in Tanmarg near Gulmarg remains highly venerated.

◀)

BABA HARDE RISHI (D. 986 HIJRI/1577 AD)

Harde Rishi's real name was Haidar and he was born to a poor family of blacksmiths. The boy earned his livelihood by grazing cattle. Tales narrate the first meeting between the Suharwardi Sufi Master Makhdoom Sahab and Harde Rishi. Indicating that his heart was full of love, Harde offered a full cup of milk to Shaykh Makhdoom who placed a rose petal over the milk. Harde understood that despite his spiritual knowledge, he required initiation in the Sufi tradition. He then took the oath of allegiance, becoming a formal disciple of Makhdoom Sahab.

The Rishi Order began to merge with the Suharwardi Order, impacting the mystic discipline. Despite Harde Rishi's aversion to meat, he tasted it once while sharing a non-vegetarian meal that had been cooked to welcome Makhdoom Sahab at his house. However, Harde Baba continued to abstain from eating meat and garlic even though his Master had sanctioned its consumption.

Harde Rishi continued to earn his livelihood through tilling the land, encouraging his followers to do the same. He died in 986 Hijri/1577 AD and lies buried at Anantnag. Until today both Hindus and Muslim who visit his shrine, abstain from eating or distributing meat during the *Urs* festivities of Harde Rishi.

'Allah' in mirror image.

13

OTHER ORDERS

THE SHATTARIS

SHAYKH MUHAMMAD GHAUS (D. 970 HIJRI/1563 AD)

The Shattari *silsila* came to the subcontinent during the fifteenth century. It draws inspiration from the older Bistami Order that traces its lineage from the ninth-century mystic Bayazid Bistami. In Iran and Transoxania the order was called 'Ishqiya', but in India people chose to call it 'Shattari', due to the speed with which followers achieved mystic heights. Shah Abdullah from Bukhara brought the order to India, and gave it its name. It spread in Bengal, Burhanpur and Gujarat from where it travelled to Indonesia, Malay and Madinah. Shah Abdullah is buried in Mandu where he enjoyed the patronage of Sultan Mahmud Khalji I.

Abul Muyyad Muhammad, popularly called Shaykh Muhammad Ghaus, was the disciple of Shaykh Zuhur Hajji Hamid. Shaykh Ghaus undertook rigorous ascetic exercises for 14 years in the caves of Chunar, near the River Ganges, in the district now called Mirzapur. He later made a *khanqah* at Gwalior.

Shaykh Muhammad Ghaus, and his brother Shaykh Phul, became the most influential Shattari Sufis in sixteenth-century India. Mughal Emperor Humayun sat at the feet of Shaykh Phul, learning the ways of mysticism. While in Bengal, Humayun sent Shaykh Phul to persuade his rebel brother Mirza Hindal to join him in a war against the Afghans. Mirza Hindal rejected the proposal and killed Shaykh Phul, declaring himself the emperor.[1]

In 1526 AD Shaykh Ghaus had helped Babur's army seize the Gwalior Fort, winning the confidence of the emperor. After Sher Shah acceded the throne in 1540 AD, he declared the Sufi's book *Risala e Mirajiyya* blasphemous and the Sufi deserving of capital punishment. The Shaykh left for Gujarat where Humayun remained in touch with him through an exchange of letters. The mystic wrote to Humayun that the emperor would experience tribulations associated with God's *jalal*, wrath, since in his case the *jamal*, benevolence, had expired. He explained that in order to make chosen people perfect, God endows them with *jamal* and *jalal*, both attributes of His name.[2]

Shaykh Ghaus faced vigourous attacks from the clergy led by a certain Shaykh Ali Muttaqi. A number of *fatwas* had been passed asking the ruler Sultan Mahmud III to execute him for the violation of the *Sharia*. One day the venerated religious scholar Shaykh Wajihuddin, a disciple of Shaykh Ghaus, went to Muttaqi's house. Tearing up the *fatwas*, he wrote a rejection explaining that Shaykh Ghaus followed the spirit of Islam. The Sultan thus did not take any action against the Shaykh who left Gujarat for Delhi soon after the ascension of Emperor Akbar to the throne.

Shaykh Ghaus arrived at the young Mughal emperor's court where the orthodox clergy was shocked by his veneration of non-Muslims. Bairam Khan, Akbar's guardian, respected the Shaykh, but other opponents argued that the contents of the mystic's book were blasphemous. The Shaykh thus left Delhi and returned to Gujarat. Emperor Akbar visited Shaykh Ghaus at Gwalior in 1599, where the Sufi presented him with a number of prized bullocks and symbolically initiated him into the Shattari Sufi Order.

Shaykh Ghaus died on 17 Ramadan 970 Hijri/1563 AD and is buried in Gwalior. His outstanding works on mysticism are *Jawahar e Khamsa* that includes *Bahrul e Hayat, Kalid e Makhazin, Zamair,*

Basair, *Kanzul Wahdat* and *Risala e Mirajiyya*. The great scholar's writings have left an indelible mark on India's Sufi tradition.

〴

THE KUBRAWIS

SAYYID MIR ALI MUHAMMAD HAMDHANI (D. 786 HIJRI/1385 AD)

Popularly known as Shah e Hamdhan, Sayyid Mir Ali Muhammad came from Hamdhan in western Iraq. His father Ali bin Shihabuddin belonged to the ruling elite of the city, playing an important role under the Seljuks. The family traced their lineage to Prophet Muhammad ﷺ through Imam Ali.

The Kubrawiya centre in Kashmir came to be established towards the end of the fourteenth century. After completing his education, Shah e Hamdhan became a disciple of some well-known Sufis of the Kubrawi Order, which had gained prominence in the central Asian region under Shaykh Alauddawla Simnani. He came to Kashmir in 1384 AD during the reign of Sultan Qutubuddin and remained a royal guest. Prior to the journey, the Sufi had sent his cousins, Sayyid Hussain Simnani and Sayyid Tajuddin to explore the situation in the valley. They became the first Kubrawi Sufis to settle in the valley and were given land grants by the Sultan. Both Sufis made a considerable impact on the local population. Sayyid Hussain Simnani established a *khanqah* in the village of Kulgam that became the nucleus of welfare activities. As Ishaq Khan observes: 'It was his teachings that led Nund Rishi's father Salat Sanz, the village watchman to embrace Islam and is believed to have enrolled Lal Ded as a disciple. The Shaivite wandering mystic is said to have had a spiritual experience with Sayyid Mir Ali Muhammad Hamdhani.'[3]

Shah e Hamdhan is said to have written over 100 books of which 50 short treatises have survived. The most famous of these is the treatise *Zakhirat ul Muluk* that explores the social and political ethics which rulers and the governing classes were expected to follow. His greatest achievement was creating an ambience for the evolution of an Islamic consciousness. The scholar's classification of state subjects as Muslims and non-Muslims, coupled with a missionary zeal, have sometimes been criticized. He supported his arguments by quoting Caliph Umar, the third ruler of the Islamic Caliphate. However, he wrote that a Muslim ruler, being the shadow of God should render equitable justice and beneficence to both believers and non-believers. He was concerned with ensuring the viability of the *Sharia* through reforming the behaviour of the Sultans and the ruling elite. To quote Ishaq Khan again, 'Although Sayyid Ali was deep-rooted in the *Sharia*, his chief mission was not to enforce religious laws through the state machinery. His primary objective was to sensitize the ruler and the small minority of his Muslim subjects in respect of following the *Sharia* in personal matters.'[4]

The more advanced manuals on mysticism written by Shah e Hamdhan support Ibn al Arabi's theory of *wahdat ul wujood*, a departure from the strong criticism expressed against it by Shaykh Alauddawla Simnani and his followers. The Sayyid in fact translated Ibn al Arabi's *Fusus al Hakim* into Persian and wrote many treatises explaining his mystic philosophies. Another important book written by the Sufi scholar is *Risala e Futuwwa*, where he defines the different concepts of chivalry in Sufism. These ideas of brotherhood and chivalry added a mystic flavour to the organization of Anatolian and Iranian dervishes, involved or associated with merchants and artisans.

The Sayyid is credited with the revival of Kashmiri handicrafts, an industry that was then on the decline. Nearly 700 Sayyids (descendants from the family of Prophet Muhammad ﷺ) from central Asia are said to have accompanied him to Kashmir, many of whom were skilled artisans and masters in the art of shawl weaving. Encouraged by the Sultan, they shared their skills with the local craftsmen, giving a boost to the handicraft sectors. The Sufi encouraged people to earn their livelihood through honest and hard-working means.

Even today, shawl-making in Kashmir is often called *kar e amiri*, the work of a king, referring to Shah e Hamdhan, who earned a living by making caps with his own hands. He gifted a cap that he had made to Sultan Qutubuddin, who wore it under his crown. The cap remained a family treasure, worn by several descendants of the sultan. Eventually, the ruler Fath Shah willed that the cap be placed in his shroud and buried with him.

Although Shah e Hamdhan stayed for a year in the valley, his visit is viewed as a major event in the history of Islam in Kashmir. His teachings impacted the religious, social, economic and cultural aspects of Kashmiri society. There are many miracles, including that of circling the world thrice, that are attributed to him. He propounded the virtues of self-knowledge for the creation of a vigilant, virtuous and just society. The Master travelled extensively in Kashmir, leaving behind many Iranian Sufis who established *khanqahs* in different parts of the valley.

After a brief spell in Kashmir, Shah e Hamdhan headed towards Makkah for a pilgrimage. He died on the way at Pakhli on 6 Dhul Qada 786 Hijri/1385 AD. His body was carried to Khuttalan, in present-day Tajikistan where it lies buried. The *Urs* of Shah e Hamdhan is celebrated with great fervour in the valley. Thousands of devotees gather at the *Khanqah e Moulla*, the mosque built on the banks of the Jhelum river by Sultan Sikander in 1400 AD to honour the Sufi.

SACHAL SARMAST (D. 1241 HIJRI/1826 AD)

Traditions recount a young lad visiting Shah Abdul Latif who immediately recognized that the child would one day reveal the mysteries of the Heavens that he had not unveiled. The mystic poet's name Sachal means 'truth', alluding to the word *Haqq*, among the 99 names of Allah. Born in 1739 AD as Abdul Wahab, he also came to be called Sarmast, one intoxicated with Divine love. Sachal Sarmast was initiated in the Shah Darazi Sufi Order, a branch of the Kubrawi Order. He is aptly called the 'Attar of Sind', due to Fariduddin Attar's visible influence on the imagery of his poetry. Sachal wrote:

'Tis not in religion I believe
'Tis love I live in.
When love comes to you.
Say Amen!
'Tis not with the infidel
that love resides
Nor with the faithful.
O friend! this is the only way to learn
the secrets of the path:
Follow not the road of another,
However virtuous he may be.
Rend the veil over thee,
Searcher expose thy being.[5]

The poet led a life of solitude, composing couplets in Sindhi, Persian, Saraiki and Urdu. He wrote whatever came to his heart revealing the mysteries of Divine love. Lamenting on the afflictions of true lovers, he said:

> Welcome, welcome Thou art, to which place wilt, thou bring me? Thou wilt gain cut off a head, Giving a kick to Sarmad Thou killed him; Thou hast bought Mansur to the gallows, Cut off Shiekh Attar's head—Now Thou art asking the way here! Thou hast split Zakariya with a saw, Thrown Joseph into a well, Thou hast made Shams to be killed at the hand of the mullas, Thou usest to afflict the lover. Thou hast made Sanan bind the Brahmin's thread, Thou hast made to be slaughtered Bulle Shah, Jafar to be drowned in the sea, in misfortune hast Thou pressed Bilawal, hast killed, Inayat in the fighting arena, has sentenced Karmal....[6]

Sarmast memorized the Quran and trained in Islamic theology, although he remained completely uninhibited while expressing mystical ecstasy. He died on 14 Ramadan 1241 Hijri/1826 AD and is buried in Sindh. His legacy lives on in his poetry sung by Sufi singers in the subcontinent.

THE FIRDAUSIS

Shaykh Sharfuddin Maneri (d. 783 Hijri/1381 ad)

Shaykh Sharfuddin Maneri, the Sufi of a Hundred Letters, is called the perfect Sufi. A paragon of mercy, generosity and patience, he stayed hungry to feed others and blessed those who cursed him. He taught that one single act of kindness equalled hundreds of prayers and fasts. The Shaykh's letters containing his teachings on mysticism, uphold the superiority of Sufis over the clergy:

> *Those who travel along the Way live by the life of Another,*
> *The birds flying in His air come from the nest of Another,*
> *Do not look at them with your earthly eye since they,*
> *Belong neither to this world nor the next but Another.*[7]

The Firdausi Order is an offshoot of the Suharwardi Order that traces its spiritual descent from Shaykh Saifuddin Barkhazi of Central Asia. Berke, the grandson of Chengiz Khan, embraced Islam at the hands of Shaykh Barkhazi. Khwaja Badruddin Samarqandi migrated to India and founded the Firdausi Order. Since Delhi had become a stronghold of the Chishtis, the Firdausi mystics moved to Bihar.

The outstanding Firdausi Sufi, earlier known as Shaykh Ahmad, was awarded the title of Sharfuddin (Glory of Faith). He was the son of the famed mystic Shaykh Yahya, and completed his primary education in Maner. When Ahmad was 15 years of age, a noted religious scholar Abu Tawwamma of Bukhara stopped at Maner while on the way to Sonargaon in eastern Bengal. Expressing a desire to study under him, the young boy accompanied him to Bengal. He lived with the Master's family, marrying his daughter by whom he had a son. Some years later when his father died, he returned to Maner. Entrusting his son to the care of his mother, the Shaykh began living an ascetic life.

Searching for a Sufi Master, the Shaykh travelled to Delhi, where he met Hazrat Nizamuddin Auliya and Shaykh Bu Ali Shah Qalandar of Panipat. Eventually, he became the disciple of Shaykh Najiduddin Firdausi. After the death of his spiritual mentor, Shaykh Sharfuddin went back to Bihar, living in the jungles of Bihia and Rajgir. After spending many years in solitude, the mystic began going to the mosque for the Friday prayers. Gradually, people began seeking his blessing and he moved closer to the town. The reigning Sultan of Delhi, Muhammad bin Tughlaq, had a *khanqah* built for the Shaykh where he lived for nearly 44 years. Thousands of people flocked to him in search of spiritual guidance.

A gifted scholar, Shaykh Sharfuddin's teachings are primarily known through his letters contained in *Maktubat e Sadi*,[8] (The Hundred Letters). He wrote two letters to Firoz Shah Tughlaq, advising the Delhi Sultan to rule justly. The Shaykh was upset with the Sultan for executing two of his Sufi friends, Shaykh Izz Kakui and Shaykh Ahmad Bihari, for their outspoken ideas on the mystical theory of *wahdat ul wujood*. A *fatwa* condemning them had been issued by the orthodox *ulema*. On learning of the Shaykh's unhappiness, the ruler issued a *farman* to summon the Sufi to court, seeking an explanation for his conduct. Later, the *farman* was cancelled through the intervention of some religious leaders.[9]

The Shaykh died on 5 Shawwal 783 Hijri/1381 AD and lies buried in Maner. He remains the principal Sufi of Bihar, his *dargah* attracting thousands of devotees throughout the year.

۩

THE UWAISIS

MAKHDOOM ALI MAHIMI (D. 834 HIJRI/1431 AD)

The Sufi from Konkan, Makhdoom Ali Mahimi, is acknowledged for his scholarly contribution and humanist ideals. He came from a family of Arab travellers, who in the ninth century settled in the island of Mahim, one of the seven islands that later formed the city of Bombay.

Shaykh Makhdoom's father was a learned religious scholar and his mother Fatima bint e Nakhuda Hussain came from an aristocratic Central Asian family. She became a widow when her son was just nine years old.

Shaykh Makhdoom is called an Uwaisi for he did not have a living spiritual Master, and he acquired mystic knowledge from Khidr, the immortal friend of God mentioned in the Quran. The Shaykh had many names including Ali, Alauddin and Abul Hasan. He later came to be known as Makhdoom Ali Mahimi. Due to a large following of people living on the Konkan coast, he is also referred to as Qutub e Konkan. The Sultan Ahmad Shah of Gujarat had appointed him Qazi for the Muslims of Thana district, for both civil and criminal cases.[10] Thana, Mahim and the neighbouring districts had come under Muslim rule in 1318 AD when the Khiljis of Delhi dominated Gujarat.

Shaykh Makhdoom became one of the first Sufi scholars to write a commentary on the Quran, *Al Tafsir ar Rahmani*, explaining its mystical content. His other literary works include commentaries on Ibn al Arabis's *wahdat ul wujood* and on Shihabuddin Suharwardi's *Awarif ul Marif*. The scholar quoted liberally from other famous Sufi philosophers such as Razi, Qushairi, Sulami and Makki. He died on 13 Shawwal 834/1431 AD and his *dargah* is in Bombay.

〰️

THE QALANDARS

ABU BAKR TUSI MATKA PIR (D. 657 HIJRI/1257 AD)

Hazrat Nizamuddin Auliya narrated that when seized with ecstasy, Abu Bakr Tusi held red-hot iron rods as if they were made of wax and twisted them into necklaces and bangles that he later wore. The historian Ibn Batuta, records the Haidari Qalandars as wearing iron rings through their ears, hands and other parts of their bodies. Qalandars are intoxicated mystics who neglect mandatory rituals of prayer.

Shaykh Abu Bakr Tusi, popularly known as 'Matka Pir' belonged to the Haidari group of Qalandars. These mystics were followers of Haidar, the Turkish Qalandar from Sawa, a province 70 miles south of Nishapur in Iran. When the Mongols invaded Sawa in 1220 AD, some of the Haidaris migrated to India.

Shaykh Abu Bakr settled in Delhi around the middle of the thirteenth century, making his *khanqah* on the banks of the Jamuna river. Hazrat Nizamuddin often participated in the musical assemblies that the Qalandar held.

Shaykh Jamaluddin of Hansi, a senior disciple of Baba Farid, was a close friend of Shaykh Abu Bakr. He had awarded him the title *Baz e Safid,* the white falcon. Whenever Shaykh Jamaluddin visited Delhi, he stayed with the Qalandar. Matka Pir died on 20 Ramadan 655 Hijri/1257 AD and his tomb is in south Delhi. When the prayers of those seeking his intercession are granted, *matkas,* earthen clay pots, are offered at the *dargah.*

BU ALI SHAH QALANDAR (D. 724 HIJRI/1324 AD)

Shaykh Bu Ali Qalandar meditated standing in the waters of Karnal Lake for years, until his flesh got eaten away by fishes. He had a vision of Prophet Muhammad ﷺ endowing him with the *bu*, fragrance, of his cousin Imam Ali.

In the thirteenth century some Qalandars began to adopt a *khanqah* life. Many among them were initiated into the Chishti and Qadri Orders, a trend brought to the subcontinent by Shah Khizr Rumi. Bu Ali Qalandar is believed to be the disciple of Shaykh Khizr or of Sayyid Najmuddin who was connected with Khwaja Qutub from the Chishti Order. He is the sole Indian Sufi who met Mevlana Rumi during his travels.

Bu Ali's name was Sharfuddin, and his ancestors migrated to India from Iraq. Although a Qalandar, he wrote letters that established him as a Sufi poet and scholar. He said that the recognition of beauty led to the understanding of the Beloved, resulting in the lover and the Beloved becoming identical. Heaven was the station for lovers and hell was the station of separation.

The mystic lived in the village of Karnal before moving to the city of Panipat. He died on the 13 Ramadan 724 Hijri/1324 AD and was buried there.

LAL SHAHBAZ QALANDAR (D. 673 HIJRI/1274 AD)

One of the most popular *qawaalis*, *Dam a dam mast qalandar, Ali da pehla number, Ali Shahbaz Qalandar*, invokes the name of the Sindhi Sufi Lal Shahbaz. His verse demonstrating deep love for Imam Ali is inscribed on his grave: 'I am a Haidari, Qalandar and intoxicated, I am a slave of Ali Murtaza, I am a leader of those intoxicated with love, For I am a dog of the lane of "Allah's Lion".' His real name was Sayyid Uthman Shah but he acquired the title of *Lal*, red, due to his habit of wearing red garments, and *Shahbaz*, falcon, for his soaring Divinity.

Born to the mystic Syed Ibrahim Kabiruddin, Lal Shahbaz's family drew their lineage from the House of Imam Ali. They migrated from Iraq and lived in Mashad before migrating to Marwand. He lived during the age of the famous Chishti Sufi Baba Farid of Ajodhan, Shaykh Bahauddin Zakariya of Multan, and Jalauddin Bukhari of Uch. They were all close friends and came to be called 'the four great friends'.

Lal Shahbaz claimed to be the spiritual disciple of Mansur Hallaj, the tenth-century martyred mystic poet of Baghdad. He lived at the site of an old Shiv temple on the west bank of the Indus. A scholar, Lal Shahbaz was fluent in Arabic, Persian, Sanskrit and Sindhi. He died on the 13 Shaban 673 Hijri/ 1274 AD.

In the name of Allah, Most Gracious, Most Merciful.

BOOK III

There is no god other than He.

14

THE WISDOM OF THE SUFIS

IMAM ALI IBN ABI TALIB (D. 661 AD)

There is no greater wealth than knowledge, no greater poverty than ignorance, no greater heritage than culture and no greater friend than consultation.

Faith is of no use without resignation, endurance and patience.

Greed is a form of permanent slavery.

I would not worship a God whom I did not see.

IMAM JAFAR SADIQ (D. 765 AD)

Whoever does not behave towards his brethren as he behaves towards himself is not paying brotherhood its due.

It is a sin to be vain about your worship.

Repentance for sin must precede worship, for Allah prefers repentance to adoration.

HASAN BASRI (D. 728 AD)

The friends of God are those who renounce the world and attain Divine Truth.

A grain of genuine piety is better than a thousand prayers and fasts.

The wise man does not seek anything from this world or the next save His proximity.

Sheep are more aware than men for they respond to the warnings of the shepherd, but men disobey the commands of the Lord.

IBRAHIM IBN ADHAM (D. 790 AD)

A man attains the rank of the righteous after passing through six steps. He must close the door of bounty for hardship, of dignity for humility, of repose for struggle, of sleep for vigil, of wealth for poverty, of worldly expectations for the preparation of the Hereafter.

We consign our parents to the grave and yet behave as though we are immortal.

Hunger and asceticism are one. He who is hungry abstains and he who abstains arrives and he who arrives attains union with the Lord.

RABIA BASRI (D. 801 AD)

Seclusion is the perfect path for the seeker of the Truth.

For those who are resigned to God's will, afflictions delight as much as blessings.

One who seeks to amass material goods is nearest to heresy and farthest from Reality.

SHAQIQ BALKHI (D. 809 AD)

The best way to atone for sin is to help the needy and downtrodden.

Complaining about afflictions is like fighting with God holding a spear in the hand.

HAZRAT MA'RUF KARKHI (D. 815 AD)

A true servant of God is a God-intoxicated saint who sees nothing else but God.

The love of God is a Divine favour and grace.

DHUN NUN MISRI (D. 859 AD)

A sign of God's displeasure is that the servant is fearful of poverty.

The key to worship is reflection.

Spiritual music is an inspiration, which stirs the heart towards the Truth. Whosoever listens to it truthfully will realize the Truth.

ABUL HASAN SARI SAQTI (D. 867 AD)

The genuine mystic dwells in the state of unity.

On the day of resurrection their respective prophets will call all the nations but Allah Himself will call His friends.

We deem all torments more desirable than being veiled from Thee. When Thy beauty is revealed to our hearts, we take no thought of affliction.

BAYAZID BISTAMI (D. 874 AD)

The Sufi sees nothing other than God in his sleep and nothing but God in the hours that he is awake. He looks at nothing but God.

God is the mirror of myself, for with my tongue He speaks and I have ceased to be myself.

'Glory be to Me! How great is my Majesty.'

Salih bin Abdullah Tustari (d. 896 ad)

A Sufi is one who is not concerned with hunger, nakedness, poverty and disgrace.

Allah protects the hearts of those who protect others from indulging in evil deeds.

Allah is the *qibla* of the intention; intention is the *qibla* of the heart; the heart is the *qibla* of the body; the body is the *qibla* of the limbs; and the limbs are the *qibla* of the world.

Abul Hasan Nuri (d. 907 ad)

The Sufi knows God through God and loves through Him.

Rational knowledge can never disclose the secrets of divinity because reason is a veil between the knower and the known.

I looked into the light till I became that light.

Junayd Baghdadi (d. 910 ad)

The Sufi is one whose heart, like the heart of Abraham, has found salvation from the world in fulfilling God's commandments, his resignation is the resignation of Ishmael, his sorrow is the sorrow of David, his poverty is the poverty of Jesus, his longing is the longing of Moses and his sincerity is the sincerity of Prophet Muhammad 卐.

Sincerity is a secret between God and His servant.

Affliction is a lamp for the Sufis, an awakening for the novices and destruction for the heedless.

Mansur Hallaj (d. 922 ad)

Love is the essence of God and lies at the root of all creation; it is the cause of the origin of the world and the heavens.

An al Haqq—I am the Truth. I saw my Lord with the eyes of the heart. I said, 'Who art Thou?' He answered, 'Thou.'

The rose thrown by a friend hurts more than any stone.

Oh men, save me from God, who has robbed me of myself.

ABU BAKR SHIBLI (D. 946 AD)

Sincere recollection of God is that the devotee forgets his recollection because awareness of recollection implies the association of one's own self.

Thankfulness is an awareness of the Giver of blessings, not the blessings.

Love is a blazing cup of fire. It takes root in the senses and when it settles in the heart it annihilates.

ABU TALIB MAKKI (D. 966 AD)

The love of God illuminates the soul of the lover and Divine mysteries are revealed to Him.

O Lord! Increase the light within me and give me light to illuminate me.

Patience is a true means for reaching God.

ABUL AL HASAN KHARQANI (D. 1033 AD)

The Sufi is one who in the daylight doesn't need the sun and in the night doesn't need the moon.

True happiness lies in the secrets Allah shares with the soul.

I am not a hermit, I am not an ascetic, I am not a seeker, I am not a Sufi.

ABU SAID IBN ABI KHAIR (D. 1049 AD)

Were it not for the excess of your talking and the turmoil in your hearts, you would see what I see and hear what I hear!

To bring joy to a single heart is better than to build many

shrines for worship, and to enslave one soul by kindness is worth more than the setting free of a thousand slaves.

When my Beloved appears, with what eye do I see Him? With His eye, not with mine, for none sees Him except Himself.

ALI IBN UTHMAN HUJWIRI (D. 1071 AD)

Knowledge of God is the science of gnosis, knowledge from God is the science of the sacred law, and knowledge with God is the science of the Sufi path.

When a man is satisfied with God's decree, it is a sign that God is satisfied with him.

The heart is the seat of knowledge and is more venerable than the *Kaaba*. Men are forever looking at the *Kaaba* but God looks towards the heart.

ABU HAMID AL GHAZALI (D. 1111 AD)

To be a Sufi means to abide continuously in God and to live at peace with men. Treat others as you would like to be treated, for the faith of God's true servant is not perfect unless he desires for others what he desires for himself.

Scientific knowledge is higher than religion but mysticism is higher than knowledge.

Once I had been a slave: Lust was my master, lust then became my servant, I was free.

Leaving the haunts of men, I sought Thy pressure, lonely; I found Thee in my company.

ABDUL QADIR JILANI (D. 1166 AD)

Try that your left hand must not learn of the alms that your right hand gives.

To talk about seed and cultivation is futile at a time when people are busy harvesting their crops.

The reality of truth is that you speak truthfully when you do not see deliverance without telling a lie.

ABU NAJIB SUHARWARDI (D. 1168 AD)

Silence is praiseworthy because it is a veil for the ignorant and an adornment for the intelligent.

Ecstasy is the secret of the inner qualities and obedience a secret of the external qualities.

The Sufis are distinguished by their lofty sciences, noble state and moral qualities.

ABU MADYAN (D. 1198 AD)

One who knows God learns from Him in wakefulness and sleep.

The heart is pardoned when it is emptied of lust.

Souls are valued trusts and bodies are their protection.

FARIDUDDIN ATTAR (D. 1220 AD)

If you have the power to discern, join the company of the dervishes. Love for the dervishes is the key to the door of Paradise.

The valley of gnosis has neither beginning nor end. No other path is like the mystic path which is hidden, but the traveller of the body is different from the traveller of the spirit.

The road is revealed to each one according to his capacity for the revelation.

If you have not attained the joy of union with the Beloved, lament on the separation from Him. If you have not looked upon the beauty of the Beloved, arouse yourself, do not sit still, but seek those mysteries destined for you.

NAJMUDDIN KUBRA (D. 1220 AD)

Prayer according to the *Sharia* is service, according to *Tareeqa* it is proximity and according to *Haqeeqa* it is union with God.

The traveller must give up resistance to God's decree and refrain from prayer that seeks rewards in the Hereafter.

In the state of elevation, the mystic may be able to read heavenly books in languages previously unknown to him and learn the heavenly names of things and beings including his own name, which is different from his worldly name.

SHAHABUDDIN ABU HAFS SUHARWARDI (D. 1234 AD)

The knowledge of God is a light from the candle of prophecy in the heart of the faithful slave.

The condition of the soul after death depends upon the degree of illumination and purification it has reached during this life.

MOINUDDIN CHISHTI (D. 1236 AD)

Those who are blessed with the love of God have ocean-like generosity, sun-like bounty and earth-like hospitality.

The heart of a lover constantly burns with the fire of love so much that whatever intrudes upon its sanctity is burnt to ashes.

The highly prized gift of a dervish is his association with other dervishes while his greatest loss is to remain away from them.

QUTUBUDDIN BAKHTIAR KAKI (D. 1237 AD)

Austerity in the life of a dervish purifies the soul and brings him close to God.

The seekers on the path of God are a community who are overwhelmed in the ocean of love from head to toe.

The day an affliction does not befall, I conclude that God's blessing has been taken away from me. Divine affliction is necessary for the moral and spiritual progress of the soul.

IBN AL ARABI (D. 1240 AD)

There is no lover and no beloved but God. Lovers grasp this when they succeed in seeing God in everything that exists.

We are ourselves the attributes by which we describe God; our existence is merely objectification of His existence. God is necessary to Him in order that we may exist, while we are necessary to Him in order that He may manifest to Himself.

The real *khalifa*, vicegerent of God, is the spirit of Muhammad ﷺ, which is forever manifesting itself in the form of prophets and saints. All the saints derive gnosis from this spirit. The prophet was given the all comprehensive words and the words of God are never exhausted. The most perfect *qutub*, pole, is the Pole of Muhammad and all poles proceed from this Pole.

SHAMSUDDIN TABRIZ (D. 1248 AD)

There is no difference between joy and sorrow. Joy is like pure clean water; wherever it flows, wondrous blossoms grow. Sorrow is like black flood; wherever it flows it wilts the blossoms.

Until a disciple ceases to exist he is not a disciple.

The dancing of the men of God is elegant. It is like a leaf flowing on the surface of water. On the inside they are like mountains and like straws on the outside.

BAHAUDDIN ZAKARIYA MULTANI (D. 1262 AD)

A mystical person should always try his or her level best to earn a livelihood and at the same time always iterate the name of Allah.

It is inward isolation that must be sought by the true seeker.

FARID GANJ E SHAKAR (D. 1265 AD)

Do not quarrel in a manner that leaves no room for reconciliation.

If you desire greatness, associate with the downtrodden.

Mystic music moves the hearts of the listeners and breathes the fire of love in their hearts.

JALALUDDIN RUMI (D. 1273 AD)

If you want to be with God, be with the Sufis. If you do not consort with them you will be lost and separated from the whole. The Sufis die to themselves and live in God.

The Perfect Man is Prophet Muhammad ﷺ. He is pure Light fashioned by God from the Majesty of His Essence. In him, the eternal world of God was revealed. He is the mirror of God and God is his mirror. He is the direct reflection of God's knowledge.

The tale of the reed flute is the tale of the soul, the tale of the perfect man. It is the tale of my soul's painful severance from God and its passionate longing for Him.

Sama is to hear the sound of the soul's affirming the Lordship of God on the day of the primordial covenant. It is to become unconscious of individual existence and savour everlasting life in absolute self-extinction.

LAL SHAHBAZ QALANDAR (D. 1274 AD)

I know nothing except love, intoxication and ecstasy.

I am burning with the love of the Beloved. At one moment I am writing on the dust and in the other I am dancing on the thorns.

I have come to a raging river where man is in great travail. How strange that there is neither a boat nor a boatman. *Sharia* is the boat, *Tareeqa* is the sail and *Haqeeqa* is the anchor. Reason alone cannot find the way.

SHAYKH SADI (D. 1292 AD)

Grieve not when people injure you because neither grief nor peace come from the people. The contrasts of friend and foe come from God. Although the arrow is not shot from the bow, wise men look at the archer.

The friends of God are those who drink the wine of grief and bear their trials and tribulations silently.

No one is more unfortunate than an oppressor of men for in the days of calamity he has no friend.

MAHMOOD SHABISTARI (D. 1329 AD)

Under the veil of each particle is concealed the soul-refreshing beauty of the face of the beloved.

Contemplation is to go from vanity to Truth and perceive the absolute Whole within the part.

There is no duality in God. In His presence 'I', 'We' and 'You' do not exist. They all become one.

BU ALI SHAH QALANDAR (D. 1324 AD)

Search your heart for within lie the keys to all Divine mysteries and it is in the heart that God has placed the spiritual treasures.

The way of the mystics is difficult, so tread on the path if you have courage and aspiration, otherwise remain outside of it.

When you open your inner eyes you will see the radiant beauty of the Beloved everywhere.

NIZAMUDDIN AULIYA (D. 1325 AD)

A man is his worst enemy when he considers himself good and pious.

Dishonest dealings and corruption lead to the destruction of cities.

Lordship and slavery are unknown to mystic life.

The surest way of attaining closeness to God is by bringing happiness to another's heart.

NASEERUDDIN CHIRAGH DILLI (D. 1356 AD)

A mystic should not behave differently from others and should mix with people of all temperaments as if he is one of them.

One should learn their livelihood through strictly honest means.

The *qibla* of the heart is God and the heart is the ruler of the body. When the heart turns away so does the body. Divine light first descends on the soul and is then transmitted to the body that is subordinate to the heart.

SHARFUDDIN MANERI (D. 1381 AD)

A Sufi is one who continuously enjoys Divine favour in all his activities and is protected by God.

Mystical knowledge is the seed of love.

The people of the mystical path are lost within themselves and gain awareness of their own beings. The knowledge of God is found within oneself.

BAQI BILLA (D. 1603 AD)

May Allah save us from the prison of ego and deliver us from the veil of self-deception.

Stay away from exoteric scholars who have made their learning means to achieve high ranks, dignity and worldly fame. Keep the company of those who aspire to gain gnosis.

A sign of Divine grace is when one becomes immune to celestial boons and is permanently delivered from anxiety.

MIAN MIR (D. 1635 AD)

The first prerequisite of a mystic way is the abdication of both the worlds with one stroke of the toe.

He who is oblivious of God for even a moment is as good as an infidel.

In a state of ecstasy, the Sufi is annihilated from his own being and subsists in the Absolute Being.

MULLAH SHAH BADAKSHI (D. 1661 AD)

Every individual has the ability to acquire intuitive knowledge.

Divine secrets must not be divulged and it is only permissible to speak of it to the confidants.

Aspirations lead to the mystic path and the end of this path. Gnosis has no end and its gate is always open. The traveller must travel through this gate.

Ya Allah.

15

A SELECTION OF SUFI POETRY

In the dead of night, a Sufi began to weep.
He said, 'This world is like a closed coffin, in which
We are shut and in which, through our ignorance,
We spend our lives in folly and desolation.
When Death comes to open the lid of the coffin,
Each one who has wings will fly off to Eternity,
But those without will remain locked in the coffin.'
So, my friends, before the lid of this coffin is taken off,
Do all you can to become a bird of the Way to God;
Do all you can to develop your wings and your feathers.

Fariduddin Attar
Translation: Andrew Harvey and Eryk Hanut

Who is man? The reflection of the Eternal Light.
What is the world? A wave on the Everlasting Sea.
How could the reflection be cut off from the Light?
How could the wave be separate from the Sea?
Know that this reflection and this wave are that very
    Light and Sea.

Jami
Translation: W. C. Chittick

Come, let's scatter roses and pour wine in the glass;
we'll shatter heaven's roof and lay a new foundation.
If sorrow raises armies to shed the blood of lovers,
I'll join with the wine bearer so we can overthrow them.
With a sweet string at hand, play a sweet song, my friend,
so we can clap and sing a song and lose our heads in dancing.

Hafiz Shirazi
Translation: Carl W. Ernst

Whether your destiny is glory or disgrace,
Purify yourself of hatred and love of self.
Polish your mirror; and that sublime beauty
From the regions of mystery
Will flame out in your heart
As it did for the saints and prophets.
Then, with your heart on fire with that Splendour,
The secret of the Beloved will no longer be hidden.

Jami
Translation: Andrew Harvey and Eryk Hanut

Lord, said David, since you do not need us,
why did you create these two worlds?
Reality replied: O prisoner of time,
I was a secret treasure of kindness and generosity
and I wished this treasure to be known,
so I created a mirror: its shining face, the heart;
its darkened back, the world;
The back would please you if you've never seen the face.
Has anyone ever produced a mirror out of mud and straw?
Yet clean away the mud and straw, and a mirror might be
　　revealed.

Until the juice ferments a while in the cask,
it isn't wine. If you wish your heart to be bright,
you must do a little work.
My King addressed the soul of my flesh:
You return just as you left.
Where are the traces of my gifts?
We know that alchemy transforms copper into gold.
This Sun doesn't want a crown or robe from God's grace.
He is a hat to a hundred bald men,
a covering for ten who were naked.
Jesus sat humbly on the back of an ass, my child!
How could a zephyr ride an ass?
Spirit, find your way, in seeking lowness like a stream.
Reason, tread the path of selflessness into eternity.
Remember God so much that you are forgotten.
Let the caller and the called disappear; be lost in the Call.

Mevlana Rumi
Translation: Kabir Helminski

Inside this new love, die.
Your way begins on the other side.
Become the sky.
Take an axe to the prison wall.
Escape.
Walk out like someone suddenly born into colour.
Do it now.
You're covered with a thick cloud.
Slide out the side. Die,
and be quiet. Quietness is the surest sign
that you've died.
Your old life was a frantic running
from silence.

The speechless full moon
comes out now.

Mevlana Rumi
Translation: Coleman Barks

Don't worry about saving these songs!
And if one of our instruments breaks,
it doesn't matter.

We have fallen into the place
where everything is music.

The strumming and the flute notes
rise into the atmosphere,
and even if the whole world's harp
should burn up, there will still be
hidden instruments playing.

So the candle flickers and goes out.
We have a piece of flint, and a spark.

This singing art is sea foam.
The graceful movements come from a pearl
somewhere on the ocean floor.

Poems reach up like spindrift and the edge
of driftwood along the beach, wanting!

They derive
from a slow and powerful root
that we can't see.

Stop the words now.
Open the window in the centre of your chest,
and let the spirits fly in and out.

Mevlana Rumi
Translation: Coleman Barks

Everyone is overridden by thoughts;
that's why they have so much heartache and sorrow.
At times I give myself up to thought purposefully;
but when I choose,
I spring up from those under its sway.
I am like a high-flying bird,
and thought is a gnat:
how should a gnat overpower me?

Mevlana Rumi
Translation: Camille and Kabir Helminski

My heart tells me it is distressed with Him,
but I can only laugh at such pretended injuries.

Be fair, You who are the Glory of the just.
You, Soul, free of 'we' and 'I,'
subtle spirit within each man and woman.

When a man and a woman become one,
that 'one' is You.
And when that one is obliterated, there You are.

Where is this 'we' and this 'I'?
By the side of the Beloved.
You made this 'we' and this 'I'
in order that you might play
this game of courtship with Yourself,
that all 'you's' and 'I's' might become one soul
and finally drown in the Beloved.

All this is true. Come!
You who are the Creative Word: Be
You, so far beyond description.

Is it possible for the bodily eyes to see You?
Can thought comprehend Your laughter or grief?
Tell me now, can it possibly see You at all?
Such a heart has only borrowed things to live with.

The garden of love is green without limit
and yields many fruits other than sorrow or joy.
Love is beyond either condition:
without spring, without autumn, it is always fresh.

Mevlana Rumi
Translation: Kabir Helminski

O pilgrim who visits the Holy Land
I'll show you heaven in a grain of sand

Why traverse deserts, why confront the storm
If within you resides the formless form

Of the Beloved? If he's in your heart
Your pilgrimage has ended where you start.

So, from that garden did you bring a rose?
You saw the House of God, now just suppose

Arriving at a house unoccupied
Will leave the pilgrims' thirst unsatisfied

Remember Haji wherever you roam
His love will have to make your heart his home.

Mevlana Rumi
Translation: Farrukh Dhondy

A host of angels dancing in a storm
Define the dance which never takes a form
Who is that bride brought to her love today?
The moon has fetched its gold piled on a tray

Your destiny will shoot its arrows now
The ship will cut the waters with its prow

From shores of the Divine arrives the drift
Of truths that cause the human heart to lift

So when your soul departs you must not mourn
Your soul has merely gone to be reborn

Now marvel that The Ocean None Contains
Is evident in all our human stains.

Mevlana Rumi
Translation: Farrukh Dhondy

How could I ever thank my Friend?
No thanks could ever begin to be worthy.
Every hair of my body is a gift from Him;
How could I thank Him for each hair?
Praise that lavish Lord forever
Who from nothing conjures all living beings!
Who could ever describe His goodness?
His infinite glory lays all praise waste.
Look, He has graced you a robe of splendour
From childhood's first cries to old age!
He made you pure in His own image; stay pure.
It is horrible to die blackened by sin.
Never let dust settle on your mirror's shining;
Let it once grow dull and it will never polish.
When you work in the world to earn your living

Do not, for one moment, rely on your own strength.
Self-worshiper, don't you understand anything yet?
It is God alone that gives your arms their power.
If, by your striving, you achieve something good,
Don't claim the credit all for yourself;
It is fate that decides who wins and who loses
And all success streams only from the grace of God.
In this world you never stand by your own strength;
It is the Invisible that sustains you every moment.

Mevlana Rumi
Translation: Andrew Harvey

Someone who keeps aloof from suffering is not a lover.
I choose your love above all else.
As for wealth if that comes, or goes, so be it.
Wealth and love inhabit separate worlds.
But as long as you live here inside me,
I cannot say that I am suffering.

Mevlana Rumi
Translation: Coleman Barks

Don't speak of your suffering…He is speaking.
Don't look for Him everywhere…He's looking for you.
An ant's foot touches a leaf, He senses it;
A pebble shifts in a stream bed, He knows it.
If there's a worm hidden deep in a rock,
He'll know its body, tinier than an atom,
The sound of its praise, its secret ecstasy—
All this He knows by divine knowing.
He has given the tiniest worm its food;
He has opened to you the Way of the Holy Ones.

Sanai
Translation: Andrew Harvey and Eryk Hanut

The drink sent down from Truth,
we drank it, glory be to God.
And we sailed over the Ocean of Power,
glory be to God.

Beyond those hills and oak woods,
beyond those vineyards and gardens,
we passed in health and joy, glory be to God.

We were dry, but we moistened.
We grew wings and became birds,
we married one another and flew,
glory be to God.

To whatever lands we came,
in whatever hearts, in all humanity,
we planted the meanings Taptuk taught us,
glory be to God.

Come here, let's make peace,
let's not be strangers to one another.
We have saddled the horse
and trained it, glory be to God.

We became a trickle that grew into a river.
We took flight and drove into the sea,
and then we overflowed, glory be to God.

We became servants at Taptuk's door.
Poor Yunus, raw and tasteless,
finally got cooked, glory be to God.
Translated by Kabir Helminski and Refik Algan
Ask those who know,
what's this soul within the flesh?
Reality's own power.
What blood fills these veins?

Thought is an errand boy,
fear a mine of worries.
These sighs are love's clothing.
Who is the Khan on the throne?

Give thanks for His unity.
He created when nothing existed.
And since we are actually nothing,
what are all of Solomon's riches?

Ask Yunus and Taptuk
what the world means to them.
The world won't last.
What are You? What am I?

Yunus Emre
Translation: Kabir Helminski and Refik Algan

What are 'I' and 'You'?
Just lattices
In the niches of a lamp
Through which the One Light radiates.
'I' and 'You' are the veil
Between heaven and earth;
Lift this veil and you will see
How all sects and religions are one.
Lift this veil and you will ask—
When 'I' and 'You' do not exist
What is mosque?
What is synagogue?
What is fire temple?

Sa'd al-din Mahmud Shabistari
Translation: Andrew Harvey and Eryk Hanut

I have made You the Companion of my heart.
But my body is available to those who desire its company,
And my body is friendly toward its guest,
But the Beloved of my heart is the guest of my soul.

Rabi'a al-'Adawiyya
Translation: Andrew Harvey and Eryk Hanut

Brothers, my peace is in my aloneness.
My Beloved is alone with me there, always.
I have found nothing in all the worlds
That could match His love,
This love that harrows the sands of my desert.
If I come to die of desire
And my Beloved is still not satisfied,
I would live in eternal despair.
To abandon all that He has fashioned
And hold in the palm of my hand
Certain proof that He loves me –
That is the name and the goal of my search.

Rabi'a al-'Adawiyya
Translation: Andrew Harvey and Eryk Hanut

Hadith: Allah is Beautiful and loves beauty.

16

HADITH

بِسْمِ اللهِ الرَّحْمَنِ الرَّحِيمِ

Hadith is a body of literature that comprises the sayings, teachings and actions of Prophet Muhammad ﷺ, which provide for the moral, ethical and spiritual guidance of Muslims.

The Divine Sayings—words spoken by Allah through Prophet Muhammad ﷺ are known as Hadith Qudsi. Although they contain God's words, they do not form part of the Quran. Hadith Qudsi are believed to have been revealed both through Gabriel and through Divine inspiration. Presented here are some Hadith and Hadith Qudsi that are taught and often quoted in Sufi circles.

O My servants, I have forbidden oppression for Myself and have made it forbidden amongst you, so do not oppress one another.

O My servants, all of you are astray except for those I have guided, so seek guidance of Me and I shall guide you.

O My servants, all of you are hungry except for those I have fed, so seek food of Me and I shall feed you.

O My servants, all of you are naked except for those I have clothed, so seek clothing of Me and I shall clothe you.

O My servants, you sin by night and by day, and I forgive all sins, so seek forgiveness of Me and I shall forgive you.

O My servants, you will not attain harming Me so as to harm Me, and will not attain benefiting Me so as to benefit Me.

O My servants, were the first of you and the last of you, the human of you and the jinn of you to be as pious as the most pious heart of any one man of you, that would not increase My kingdom in anything.

O My servants, were the first of you and the last of you, the human of you and the jinn of you to be as wicked as the most wicked heart of any one man of you, that would not decrease My kingdom in anything.

O My servants, were the first of you and the last of you, the human of you and the jinn of you to rise up in one place and make a request of Me, and were I to give everyone what he requested, that would not decrease what I have, any more than a needle decreases the sea if put into it.

O My servants, it is but your deeds that I reckon up for you and then recompense you for, so let him who finds good praise Allah and let him who finds other than that blame no one but himself.

Hadith Qudsi on the authority of Abu Dharr al Ghifari (one of the Bench) and related by Muslim, Tirmidhi and Ibn Majah

The Prophet David said, 'O lord, why did you cause creation to come into being.?' God replied, 'I was a hidden treasure. I wanted to be known so I created all off creation.'

Hadith Qudsi cited in Manaratas Sahirin *compiled by Najmuddin Bakr*

When Allah decreed the Creation He pledged Himself by

writing in His Book which is laid down with Him: My mercy prevails over My wrath.

Hadith Qudsi on the authority of Abu Huraia and related by Muslim and Bukhari

Spend (on charity), O son of Adam, and I shall spend on you.

Hadith Qudsi related by Bukhari and Muslim

Whosoever shows enmity to someone devoted to Me, I shall be at war with him. My servant draws not near to Me with anything more than the religious duties I have enjoined upon him, and My servant continues to draw near to Me with supererogatory works so that I shall love him. When I love him, I become his hearing with which he hears, his seeing with which he sees, his hand with which he strikes and his foot with which he walks. Were he to ask something of Me, I would surely grant him it. I do not hesitate about anything as much as I hesitate about seizing the soul of My faithful servant: he hates death and I hate hurting him.

Hadith Qudsi related by Bukhari

If God has loved a servant He calls Gabriel and says 'I love so-and-so, therefore love him.' Then Gabriel calls out in heaven, saying 'God loves so-and-so, therefore love him.' And the inhabitants of heaven love him. Then acceptance is established for him on earth. And if God has abhorred a servant, He calls Gabriel and says 'I abhor so-and-so, therefore abhor him.' So Gabriel abhors him. Then Gabriel calls out to the inhabitants of heaven 'God abhors so-and-so, therefore abhor him.' So they abhor him, and abhorrence is established for him on earth.

Hadith Qudsi related by Muslim, Bukhari, Malik and Tirmidhi

The gates of paradise will be open on Mondays and Thursdays, and every servant of Allah who associates nothing with Allah will be forgiven, except for the man who has a grudge against his brother. About them it will be said: Delay these two until they are reconciled.

Hadith Qudsi related by Muslim.

O son of Adam, so long as you call upon Me and ask of Me, I shall forgive you for what you have done, and I shall not mind. O son of Adam, were your sins to reach the clouds of the sky and were you then to ask forgiveness of Me, I would forgive you. O son of Adam, were you to come to Me with sins nearly as great as the earth and were you then to face Me, ascribing no partner to Me, I would bring you forgiveness nearly as great as it.

Hadith Qudsi related by Tirmidhi and by Ibn Hanbal

Fasting is Mine and it is I who give reward for it. A man gives up his food, sexual passion and drink for My sake. Fasting is like a shield, and he who fasts has two joys: a joy when he breaks his fast and a joy when he meets his Lord. The change in the breath of the one who fasts is better in Allah's estimation than the smell of musk.

Hadith Qudsi related by Muslim, Tirmidhi and Bukhari

I am as My servant thinks I am. I am with him when he makes mention of Me to himself, I make mention of him to Myself; and if he makes mention of Me in an assembly, I make mention of him in an assembly better than it. And if he draws near to Me a hand's span, I draw near to him an arm's length; and if he draws near to Me an arm's length, I draw near to him a fathom's length. And if he comes to Me walking, I go to him at speed.

Hadith Qudsi related by Muslim, Tirmidhi, Ibn Majah and Bukhari

I have provided for My true slaves that which neither the eye has seen nor the ear heard; nor has it ever descended into the hearts of men.

Hadith Qudsi related by Bukhari and Muslim

Our Lord descends each night to the earth's sky when remains the final third of the night, and He says: Who is saying a prayer to Me that I may answer it? Who is asking something of Me that I may give it to him? Who is asking forgiveness of Me that I may forgive him?

Hadith Qudsi related by Bukhari, Tirmidhi, Abu Dawud and Malik

Whoever has seen me has seen God.

Hadith related by Bukhari and Muslim

I am the City of Knowledge and Ali is the Gate.

Hadith related by Tirmidhi

The Prophet said to Ali: Are you not content that your rank is to mine what Aaron's was to Moses.

Hadith related by Bukhari

Ihsan, excellence, is that you worship God as if you saw Him, for if you do not see Him, He sees you.

Hadith related by Muslim

The *Sharia*, religious law, is my discourse; the *Tareeqa*, spiritual path my deeds; the *Haqeeqa*, reality is my state; Gnosis is my wealth; *aql*, intellect is my religion; *mohabba*, love, the foundation of my work; *shauq*, yearning, my vehicle; *khauf*, fear of God, my companion; *ilm*, knowledge, my weapon; *sabr*, patience, my friend; *tawakkul*, trust in God, my sustenance; *qanaat*, contentment, my treasure; *sidq*, sincerity, my place; *yaqin*, faith, my refuge and *faqr*, poverty, my pride—and I am proud that in this, I surpass all previous prophets.

Hadith related by Mojli ibn Abi Jonhur Ahsai

Verily all deeds are dependent upon intentions.

Hadith related by Muslim

Outwardly I am the last of all, but inwardly I preceded everyone.

Hadith related by Muslim and Bukhari

Moderation is the best course of action.

Hadith related by Muslim and Bukhari

The most odious of men to God is the one who is most quarrelsome.

Hadith related by Bukhari

One who repents of a sin is like one who has no sin.

Hadith related by Ibn Majah

Whoever is not merciful will not be shown mercy.

Hadith related by Bukhari

Whoever goes out in search of knowledge is on the path of God until returning.

Hadith related by Bukhari

If you really trusted in God as God should be trusted, God would sustain you as God sustains the birds—they go out in the morning hungry, and come back to rest in the evening full.

Hadith related by Bukhari

Good companions and bad companions are like sellers of musk and the furnace of the smithy. You lose nothing from the musk seller, whether you buy some or smell or are imbued with its fragrance. The furnace of the smithy, on the other hand, burns your house and your clothes, or you get a noxious odour.

Hadith related by Bukhari

Whoever would be glad to have his livelihood expanded and his life prolonged should maintain family ties.

Hadith related by Bukhari

Cleanliness is half of *iman*, faith, and the words *al-Hamdulillah*, Praise to God fills the scale and the word *Subhanallah wa'l-hamdullilah*, Glory be to God, Praise be to God fill up what is between the heavens and the earth. Prayer is light. Charity is a proof. Endurance is brightness. The Quran is a proof for you or against you. All men go out early in the morning and sell themselves, thereby setting themselves free or destroying themselves.

Hadith reported on the authority of Abu Malik Ash'ari

Whoever pleases his parents has pleased God, and whoever angers them has angered God.

Hadith related by Ibn an Najjar

Whoever has the following four characteristics is a pure *munafiq*, hypocrite. And whoever has one of the following four characteristics will have one of the characteristics of hypocrisy: Whenever he is entrusted, he betrays and whenever he speaks, he lies. Whenever he makes a promise, he breaks it and whenever he argues he behaves very badly.

Hadith related by Bukhari and Muslim

The example of the one who remembers his Lord in comparison with the one who does not remember his Lord is that of the living and the dead.

Hadith related by Bukhari

O Allah, illuminate my heart with light, and my eyes with light and my ears with light and let there be light on my right and light on my left. Let there be light above me and light below me, let there be light in front of me and light behind me. O Allah, make me a light.

Hadith related by Bukhari

To acquire some useful knowledge is of greater merit than to perform a hundred devotional prayers voluntarily.

Hadith related by Sunan ibn Majah.

The search for knowledge is incumbent on every Muslim man and woman.

Hadith related by Sunan ibn Majah

Veiling the faults of the faithful is akin to restoring life to the dead.

Hadith related by Tabrani

Whoever fails to care for our youth, respect our aged, enjoin right, and denounce wrong is not counted among us.

Hadith related by Ahmad

The most virtuous behaviour is to engage those who sever relations, to give to those who withhold from you, and to forgive those who wrong you.

Hadith related by Tabrani.

A good dream is from God. So if any of you have a dream of what you love, do not speak of it except to someone you love. And if any of you has a dream of what you dislike, then seek refuge in God from its evil and from the evil of obsession; and spit thrice and do not tell anyone of it, for in fact it will not harm you.

Hadith related by Bara'a bin Azib

Never is a believer stricken with discomfort, hardship, illness, grief or even with mental worry except that his or her sins are expiated thereby.

Hadith related by Muslim

Do you think that if there was a river at the door of one of you and he bathed in it five times a day, there would remain any dirt upon him? They said: 'No dirt would remain on him.' He said: 'That is how it is with the five daily prayers, through them God washes away the sins.'

Hadith related by Bukhari

If anyone wrongfully kills even a sparrow, let alone anything greater, he will face God's interrogation.

Hadith related in Mishkat al Masabih

A man asked the Prophet, upon him be peace, 'Who are the people most entitled to good companionship from me?' The Prophet said: 'Your mother, then your mother, then your mother, then your father, then your nearest relatives and then the next nearest.

Hadith related in Riyad al Salihin

A strong person is not the person who throws his adversaries to the ground. A strong person is the person who contains himself when he is angry.

Hadith related by Bukhari and Muslim

When a person dies the benefit of his/her deeds ends, except three: a continuous charity, knowledge from which benefit is derived, or a pious child praying to God for him/her.

Hadith related by Muslim and Ahmad

You will not enter Paradise until you have faith, and you will not have faith until you love each other. Shall I direct you to something which if you fulfil you will love one another? Spread the salutation of peace amongst yourselves.

Hadith related by Muslim

A man was walking on a road when he became very thirsty. He found a well and went into it and drank and came out. There was a dog panting and eating earth out of thirst. The man said, 'This dog has become as thirsty as I was.' He went down into the well and filled his shoe and then held it in his mouth until he climbed out and gave the dog water to drink. Allah thanked him for it and forgave him. They said (The Prophet's companions), 'Messenger of Allah, do we have a reward for taking care of beasts?' He said, 'There is a reward for service to every living creature.'

Hadith on the authority of Abu Huraira by Muslim and Bukhari

Free the captives, feed the hungry and pay a visit to the sick.

Hadith narrated by Abu Musa and related by Bukhari

Give in charity and do not give reluctantly lest Allah should give you in a limited amount; and do not withhold your money lest Allah should withhold it from you.

Hadith related by Bukhari

God is Beautiful and loves Beauty.

Hadith related by Muslim

He will not enter Paradise whose neighbour is not secure from his wrongful conduct.

Hadith narrated on the authority of Abu Huraira and related by Muslim

Love for the material world is the source for every affliction for he who loves it forgets the way of Hereafter.

Hadith related by Suyuti

The majority of man's sins emanate from his tongue.

Hadith related by Tabrani

قُلْ هُوَ اللّٰهُ اَحَدٌ
اَللّٰهُ الصَّمَدُ
لَمْ يَلِدْ وَلَمْ يُولَدْ
وَلَمْ يَكُنْ لَّهُ كُفُوًا اَحَدٌ

The Quran: Chapter Purity (112: 1–4)
Say: He is Allah, the One and Only;
Allah, the Eternal, Absolute;
He begetteth not, nor is He begotten;
And there is none like unto Him.

17

QURAN VERSES

بِسْمِ اللَّهِ الرَّحْمَٰنِ الرَّحِيمِ

To Allah belong the east and the west: Whithersoever ye turn, there is the presence of Allah. For Allah is all-Pervading, all-Knowing.

The Heifer (2:115)

When My servants ask thee concerning Me, I am indeed close (to them): I listen to the prayer of every suppliant when he calleth on Me: Let them also, with a will, listen to My call, and believe in Me: That they may walk in the right way.

The Heifer (2:116)

Then do ye remember Me; I will remember you. Be grateful to Me, and reject not Faith.

The Heifer (2:152)

And say not of those who are slain in the way of Allah. 'They are dead.' Nay, they are living, though ye perceive (it) not.

The Heifer (2:154)

Be sure we shall test you with something of fear and hunger, some loss in goods or lives or the fruits (of your toil), but give glad tidings to those who patiently persevere, who say, when afflicted with calamity: 'To Allah we belong, and to Him is our return.'

The Heifer (2:155–6)

He it is Who has sent down to thee the Book: In it are verses basic or fundamental (of established meaning); they are the foundation of the Book: others are allegorical. But those in whose hearts is perversity follow the part thereof that is allegorical, seeking discord, and searching for its hidden meanings, but no one knows its hidden meanings except Allah. And those who are firmly grounded in knowledge say: 'We believe in the Book; the whole of it is from our Lord,' and none will grasp the Message except men of understanding.

The Family of Imran (3:7)

Say: 'If ye do love Allah, follow me: Allah will love you and forgive you your sins: or Allah is Oft-Forgiving, Most Merciful.'

The Family of Imran (3:31)

Behold! in the creation of the heavens and the earth, and the alternation of night and day, there are indeed Signs for men of understanding,

The Family of Imran (3:190)

We sent not an apostle, but to be obeyed, in accordance with the will of God. If they had only, when they were unjust to themselves, come unto thee and asked God's forgiveness, and the apostle had asked forgiveness for them, they would have found God indeed Oft-returning, Most Merciful.

The Women (4:64)

All who obey God and the apostle are in the company of those on whom is the Grace of God, of the prophets (who teach), the sincere (lovers of Truth), the witnesses (who testify), and the righteous (who do good): Ah! what a beautiful fellowship!

The Women (4:69)

O ye who believe! Do your duty to God, seek the means of approach unto Him, and strive with might and main in his cause: that ye may prosper.

The Table Spread (5:35)

O ye who believe! if any from among you turn back from his Faith, soon will God produce a people whom He will love as they will love Him, lowly with the believers, mighty against the rejecters, fighting in the way of God, and never afraid of the reproaches of such as find fault. That is the grace of God, which He will bestow on whom He pleaseth. And God encompasseth all, and He knoweth all things.

The Table Spread (5:54)

Obey God, and obey the apostle, and beware (of evil): if ye do turn back, know ye that it is our apostle's duty to proclaim (the message) in the clearest manner.

The Table Spread (5:92)

As to those who turn (for friendship) to God, His apostle, and the (fellowship of) believers, it is the fellowship of God that must certainly triumph.

The Table Spread (5:56)

What is the life of this world but play and amusement? But best is the home in the Hereafter, for those who are righteous. Will ye not then understand?

The Cattle (6:32)

It is He Who maketh the stars (as beacons) for you, that ye may guide yourselves, with their help, through the dark spaces of land and sea: We detail Our signs for people who know.

The Cattle (6:97)

Those who follow the apostle, the unlettered Prophet, whom they find mentioned in their own (scriptures), in the law and the Gospel; for he commands them what is just and forbids them what is evil; he allows them as lawful what is good (and pure) and prohibits them from what is bad (and impure); He releases them from their heavy burdens and from the yokes that are upon them. So it is those who believe in him, honour him, help him, and follow the light which is sent down with him, it is they who will prosper.

The Heights (7:157)

When thy Lord drew forth from the Children of Adam—from their loins—their descendants, and made them testify concerning themselves, (saying): 'Am I not your Lord (who cherishes and sustains you)?' They said: 'Yea! We do testify!'

(This), lest ye should say on the Day of Judgement: 'Of this we were never mindful.'

The Heights (7:172)

Whom God doth guide, he is on the right path: whom He rejects from His guidance, such are the persons who perish.

The Heights (7:178)

Of those We have created are people who direct (others) with truth. And dispense justice therewith.

The Heights (7:181)

Hold to forgiveness; command what is right; but turn away from the ignorant.

The Heights (7:199)

But Allah doth call to the Home of Peace: He doth guide whom He pleaseth to a way that is straight.

Yunus (10:25)

Behold! verily on the friends of Allah there is no fear, nor shall they grieve.

Yunus (10:62)

But celebrate the praises of thy Lord, and be of those who prostrate themselves in adoration.

The Rocky Tract (15:98)

Invite (all) to the Way of thy Lord with wisdom and beautiful preaching; and argue with them in ways that are best and most gracious: for thy Lord knoweth best, who have strayed from His Path, and who receive guidance.

The Bee (16:125)

One day We shall call together all human beings with their (respective) Imams: those who are given: their record in their right hand will read it (with pleasure), and they will not be dealt with unjustly in the least.

The Children of Israel (17:71)

Establish regular prayers—at the sun's decline till the darkness of the night, and the morning prayer and reading: for the prayer and reading in the morning carry their testimony.

The Children of Israel (17:78)

And say: 'Truth has now arrived, and Falsehood perished: for Falsehood is (by its nature) bound to perish.'

The Children of Israel (17:81)

We send down (stage by stage) in the Quran that which is a healing and a mercy to those who believe: to the unjust it causes nothing but loss after loss.

The Children of Israel (17:82)

And keep thy soul content with those who call on their Lord morning and evening, seeking His Face; and let not thine eyes pass beyond them, seeking the pomp and glitter of this Life; nor obey any whose heart We have permitted to neglect the remembrance of Us, one who follows his own desires, whose case has gone beyond all bounds.

The Cave (18:28)

So they found one of Our servants, on whom We had bestowed
Mercy from Ourselves and whom We had taught knowledge
from Our own Presence.

The Cave (18:65)

On that Day shall no intercession avail except for those for
whom permission has been granted by (Allah) Most Gracious
and whose word is acceptable to Him.

Ta Ha (20:109)

He knows what is before them, and what is behind them, and
they offer no intercession except for those who are acceptable,
and they stand in awe and reverence of His (Glory).

The Prophets (21:28)

Verily, this brotherhood of yours is a single brotherhood, and
I am your Lord and Cherisher: therefore serve Me (and no
other).

The Prophets (21:92)

Do they not travel through the land, so that their hearts (and
minds) may thus learn wisdom and their ears may thus learn
to hear? Truly it is not their eyes that are blind, but their hearts
which are in their breasts.

The Pilgrimage (22:46)

Allah chooses messengers from angels and from men for
Allah is He Who hears and sees (all things).

The Pilgrimage (22:75)

Allah is the Light of the heavens and the earth. The Parable of His Light is as if there were a niche and within it a lamp: the lamp enclosed in glass: the glass as it were a brilliant star: Lit from a blessed tree, an olive, neither of the east nor of the west, whose oil is well-nigh luminous, though fire scarce touched it: Light upon Light! Allah doth guide whom He will to His Light: Allah doth set forth parables for men: and Allah doth know all things.

Light (24:35)

Deem not the summons of the Messenger among yourselves like the summons of one of you to another: Allah doth know those of you who slip away under shelter of some excuse: then let those beware who withstand the Messenger's order, lest some trial befall them, or a grievous penalty be inflicted on them.

Light (24:63)

And those who strive in Our (cause), We will certainly guide them to our Paths: For verily Allah is with those who do right.

The Spider (29:69)

Those who establish regular Prayer, and give regular Charity, and have (in their hearts) the assurance of the Hereafter. These are on (true) guidance from their Lord: and these are the ones who will prosper.

The Wise (31:4–5)

And if all the trees on earth were pens and the ocean (were ink), with seven oceans behind it to add to its (supply), yet would not the words of Allah be exhausted (in the writing): for Allah is Exalted in Power, full of Wisdom.

The Wise (31:27)

Among the Believers are men who have been true to their covenant with Allah. Of them some have completed their vow (to the extreme), and some (still) wait: but they have never changed (their determination) in the least.

The Confederates (33:23)

For Muslim men and women, for believing men and women, for devout men and women, for true men and women, for men and women who are patient and constant, for men and women who humble themselves, for men and women who give in charity, for men and women who fast (and deny themselves), for men and women who guard their chastity, and for men and women who engage much in Allah.s praise, for them has Allah prepared forgiveness and great reward.

The Confederates (33:35)

O ye who believe! Celebrate the praises of Allah, and do this often; glorify Him morning and evening. He it is Who sends blessings on you, as do His angels, that He may bring you out from the depths of Darkness into Light: and He is full of Mercy to the Believers.

The Confederates (33:41–3)

O Prophet! Truly We have sent Thee as a Witness, a Bearer of Glad Tidings, and Warner.

The Confederates (33:45)

Allah and His angels send blessings on the Prophet: O ye that believe! Send ye blessings on him, and salute him with all respect.

The Confederates (33:56)

If any do seek for glory and power, to Allah belong all glory and power. To Him mount up (all) Words of Purity: It is He who exalts each Deed of Righteousness. Those that lay Plots of Evil, for them is a Penalty terrible; and the plotting of such will be void (of result).

Creation or The Angels (35:10)

He said: 'I will go to my Lord! He will surely guide me!'

Those Ranged in Ranks (37:99)

It is Allah I serve, with my sincere (and exclusive) devotion.

The Crowds (39:14)

It is Allah that takes the souls (of men) at death; and those that die not (He takes) during their sleep: those on whom He has passed the decree of death, He keeps back (from returning to life), but the rest He sends (to their bodies) for a term appointed, verily in this are Signs for those who reflect.

The Crowds (39:42)

So hold thou fast to the Revelation sent down to thee; verily thou art on a Straight Way.

Gold Ornaments (43:43)

And know that among you is Allah's Messenger. Were he, in many matters, to follow your (wishes), ye would certainly fall into misfortune: But Allah has endeared the Faith to you, and has made it beautiful in your hearts, and He has made hateful to you unbelief, wickedness, and rebellion: such indeed are those who walk in righteousness.

The Inner Apartments (49:7)

It was We Who created man, and We know what dark suggestions his soul makes to him: for We are nearer to him than his jugular vein.

Qaf (50:16)

On the earth are signs for those of assured Faith. As also in your own selves: Will ye not then see?

The Winds that Scatter (51:20-1)

By the Star when it goes down, Your Companion is neither astray nor being misled. Nor does he say (aught) of (his own) Desire. It is no less than inspiration sent down to him: He was taught by one Mighty in Power, endued with Wisdom: for he appeared (in stately form); While he was in the highest part of the horizon: Then he approached and came closer, And was at a distance of but two bow-lengths or (even) nearer; So did (Allah) convey the inspiration to His Servant—(conveyed) what He (meant) to convey. The (Prophet's) (mind and) heart in no way falsified that which he saw. Will ye then dispute with him concerning what he saw?

The Star (53:1-12)

All that is on earth will perish: But will abide (forever) the
Face of thy Lord, full of Majesty, Bounty and Honour.

The Most Gracious (55:26–7)

He is the First and the Last, the Evident and the Immanent:
and He has full knowledge of all things.

Iron (57:3)

He it is Who created the heavens and the earth in Six Days, and
is moreover firmly established on the Throne (of Authority).
He knows what enters within the earth and what comes forth
out of it, what comes down from heaven and what mounts up
to it. And He is with you wheresoever ye may be. And Allah
sees well all that ye do.

Iron (57:4)

He is the One Who sends to His Servant Manifest Signs, that
He may lead you from the depths of Darkness into the Light
and verily Allah is to you most kind and Merciful.

Iron (57:9)

O ye who believe! When ye are told to make room in the
assemblies, (spread out and) make room: (ample) room will
Allah provide for you. And when ye are told to rise up, rise
up, Allah will rise up, to (suitable) ranks (and degrees), those
of you who believe and who have been granted (mystic)
Knowledge. And Allah is well acquainted with all ye do.

The Woman Who Pleads (58:11)

Stand to prayer by night, but not all night.

Folded In Garments (73:2)

Some faces, that Day, will beam (in brightness and beauty.

The Resurrection (75:22)

There is a Register (fully) inscribed, to which bear witness those Nearest to Allah. Truly the Righteous will be in Bliss: On Thrones (of Dignity) will they command a sight (of all things). Thou wilt recognise in their faces the beaming brightness of Bliss.

Dealing in Fraud (83:20–4)

But those will prosper who purify themselves.

The Most High (87:14)

By the Sun and his (glorious) splendour; By the Moon as she follows him; By the Day as it shows up (the Sun's) glory; By the Night as it conceals it; By the Firmament and its (wonderful) structure; By the Earth and its (wide) expanse: By the Soul, and the proportion and order given to it; And its enlightenment as to its wrong and its right; Truly he succeeds that purifies it. And he fails that corrupts it!

The Sun (91:1–10)

We have indeed created man in the best of moulds.

The Fig (94:4)

Say: He is Allah, the One and Only; Allah, the Eternal, Absolute; He begetteth not, nor is He begotten; And there is none like unto Him.

Purity (112:1–4)

Translations: Abdullah Yusuf Ali

I witness there is no god other than Allah.
Muhammad is His Messenger.
May peace be upon him and his progeny.

BOOK IV

Allah

THE MOST BEAUTIFUL NAMES

The Most Beautiful Names correspond to God's attributes that
Sufis try to realize within themselves. The remembrance of these
Divine names remains a vital part along the Sufi way. Allah describes
Himself in the Quran as the Possessor of the Most Beautiful Names.
An entire mystical theology developed around the *Asma ul Hasna*
or 99 names ascribed to the Lord. The hundredth name, believed to
be the greatest, lies hidden.

Sufi Masters have repeatedly written on the qualities of the Divine
names, some which are connected with His compassion and others
with His wrath. These two categories work together to form the
tapestry of the world, mysteriously connected with human beings.
Different formulae of repeating the names are prescribed by Sufis
for spiritual benefits. The names are repeated using a *Ya* before them
like, *Ya Rahman Ya Rahim* meaning 'O Merciful, O Compassionate'.
Prophet Muhammad ﷺ said, 'Verily, Allah has 99 characteristics and
whoever patterns himself on them shall enter paradise.'

THE QURAN ON THE MOST BEAUTIFUL NAMES

'The most beautiful names belong to God: so call on Him by them;
but shun such men as use profanity in his names: for what they do,
they will soon be requited' (7:180).

'Say: "Call upon Allah, or call upon Rahman": by whatever name ye call upon Him, (it is well): for to Him belong the Most Beautiful Names. Neither speak thy Prayer aloud, nor speak it in a low tone, but seek a middle course between' (17:110).

'Allah is He, than Whom there is no other God—Who knows (all things) both secret and open; He, Most Gracious, Most Merciful. Allah is He, than Whom there is no other god—the Sovereign, the Holy One, the Source of Peace (and Perfection), the Guardian of Faith, the Preserver of Safety, the Exalted in Might, the Irresistible, the Supreme: Glory to Allah. (High is He) above the partners they attribute to Him. He is Allah, the Creator, the Evolver, the Bestower of Forms (or Colours). To Him belong the Most Beautiful Names: whatever is in the heavens and on earth, doth declare His Praises and Glory—and He is the Exalted in Might, the Wise' (59:22–4).

In his *Diwan e Kabir* Mevlana Rumi comments on the Divine Names:

> *Just as a person is in relation to you a father*
> *and in relation to another either son or brother–*
> *So the names of God in their number have relations:*
> *He is from the viewpoint of the infidel the Tyrant* (qaher);
> *from our viewpoint, the Merciful.*[1]

In the *Mathnawi*, Mevlana Rumi writes:

> *With us, the name of everything is its outward appearance;*
> *With the Creator, the name of each thing is its inward reality.*
> *In the eye of Moses, the name of his rod was 'staff';*
> *in the eye of the Creator, its name was 'dragon.'*
> *In brief, that which we are in the end*
> *is our real name with God.*

THE DIVINE NAMES

1.	Ar Rahman	The Compassionate; The Beneficent
2.	Ar Rahim	The All Merciful
3.	Al Malik	The Absolute Ruler; The Sovereign
4.	Al Quddus	The Pure One
5.	As Salaam	The Source of Peace
6.	Al Mumin	The Inspirer of Faith
7.	Al Muhaymin	The Guardian; The Protector
8.	Al Aziz	The Victorious
9.	Al Jabbar	The Compellor; The Restorer
10.	Al Mutakkabir	The Majestic; The Imperious
11.	Al Khaliq	The Creator
12.	Al Bari	The Maker of Order; The Producer
13.	Al Musawwir	The Shaper of Beauty; The Fashioner
14.	Al Ghaffar	The Forgiver
15.	Al Qahar	The Subduer
16.	Al Wahab	The Bestower
17.	Ar Razzaq	The Sustainer; The Provider
18.	Al Fattah	The Opener
19.	Al Alim	The All-knowing
20.	Al Qabid	The Constrictor
21.	Al Basit	The Reliever
22.	Al Khafid	The Abaser
23.	Ar Rafi	The Exalter
24.	Al Mui'zz	The Enhancer
25.	Al Mudhil	The Humilator
26.	As Sami	The Hearer of All
27.	Al Basir	The Seer of All; The All-seeing
28.	Al Hakam	The Judge
29.	Al Adl	The Just
30.	Al Latif	The Subtle One
31.	Al Khabir	The All-aware
32.	Al Halim	The Forbearing

33.	Al Azim	The Magnificent
34.	Al Ghafur	The Forgiver and Hider of Faults
35.	Ash Shakur	The Rewarder of Thankfulness
36.	Al Ali	The Highest
37.	Al Kabir	The Greatest
38.	Al Hafiz	The Protector
39.	Al Muqit	The Nourisher; The Giver of Strength
40.	Al Hasib	The Reckoner; The Accounter
41.	Al Jalil	The Majestic
42.	Al Karim	The Generous
43.	Ar Raqib	The Watchful One
44.	Al Mujeeb	The Responder
45.	Al Wasi	The All-embracing
46.	Al Hakim	The Perfectly Wise
47.	Al Wudud	The Loving One
48.	Al Majid	The Majestic One
49.	Al Ba'ith	The Resurrector
50.	Ash Shahid	The Witness
51.	Al Haqq	The Truth
52.	Al Wakil	The Trustee; The Representative
53.	Al Qawi	The Possessor of All Strength
54.	Al Matin	The Forceful One
55.	Al Wali	The Friend; The Patron
56.	Al Hamid	The Laudable; The Praised One
57.	Al Muhsi	The Appraiser
58.	Al Mubdi	The Originator
59.	Al Mu'id	The Restorer
60.	Al Muhyi	The Giver of Life
61.	Al Mumit	The Destroyer; The Death Giver
62.	Al Hayy	The Ever-living One
63.	Al Qayyum	The Self-existing; The All-sustaining
64.	Al Wajid	The Finder; The Illustrious
65.	Al Majid	The Glorious

66.	Al Wahid	The Only One
67.	Al Ahad	The One
68.	As Samad	The Satisfier of All Needs
69.	Al Qadir	The All-powerful
70.	Al Muqtadir	The Creator of All Power
71.	Al Muqaddim	The Expediter
72.	Al Muakhkir	The Delayer
73.	Al Awwal	The First
74.	Al Akhir	The Last
75.	Az Zahir	The Manifest
76.	Al Batin	The Hidden
77.	Al Waali	The Governor
78.	Al Muta'ali	The Supreme
79.	Al Barr	The Doer of Good; The Benefactor
80.	At Tawaab	The Relenting
81.	Al Muntaqim	The Avenger
82.	Al 'Afu	The Pardoner
83.	Ar Ra'uf	The Clement
84.	Malik ul Mulk	The Owner of All
85.	Dhul Jalali Wal Ikram	The Lord of Majesty and Bounty
86.	Al Muqsit	The Equitable
87.	Al Jami	The Gatherer
88.	Al Ghani	The Rich One
89.	Al Mughni	The Enricher
90.	Al Mani	The Preventer of Harm
91.	Ad Dar	The Creator of the Harmful
92.	An Nafi	The Creator of Good
93.	An Nur	The Light
94.	Al Hadi	The Guide
95.	Al Badi	The Originator
96.	Al Baqi	The Everlasting One
97.	Al Warith	The Inheritor of All
98.	Ar Rashid	The Righteous Teacher
99.	As Sabur	The Patient One

Muhammad ﷺ. May peace be upon him.

THE NOBLE NAMES

بسم الله الرحمن الرحيم

The Sufis attach great significance and spiritual blessings in reciting the 99 names of Prophet Muhammad ﷺ. The twelfth-century mystic, Shaykh Abdul Qadir Jilani of Baghdad preached that whoever recited these names once every morning and evening would be preserved from all kinds of afflictions. Sufi Masters teach that the recitation of these names keeps faith intact and provides for forgiveness of all sins. Most Sufi litanies and prayer books begin with a recitation of Divine Names followed by the recitation of the Noble Names.

The veneration of Prophet Muhammad's ﷺ name began during his lifetime. His poet, the famed Hasan ibn Thabit wrote: 'God derived from him, in order to honour him, part of his name—thus the Lord of the Throne is called Mahmud and this one Muhammad ﷺ.'

Mahmud is the passive principle of the word Muhammad ﷺ, which means 'he who is praised'.[2]

Among the Prophet's names, Ahmad ﷺ holds a special rank, for the Quran states that Allah 'will send a prophet by the name of Ahmad' (61:6). This is the name that is believed to have been foretold in the earlier revealed texts such as the Christian Gospels.

Muhammad and Ahmad are very popular first and middle names for Muslim children. In a prophetic tradition related by Imam Jafar al Sadiq, it is reiterated 'On the day of judgement, everyone who bears the name of Muhammad 🕮 shall rise and enter Paradise.'

Most copies of the Quran enumerate the Divine Names at the beginning and the names of Prophet Muhammad 🕮 on the last two pages. The manner of reciting the Noble Names is that one recites *Sayyidna*, then the name ending with repeating *sallallahu alayhi wa sallam*, May peace be upon him. For example, *sayyidna Muhammad sallallahu alayhi wa sallam, Sayyidna Ahmad sallallahu alayhi wa sallam*.

NAMES OF THE MESSENGER

1.	Muhammad	The Most Praised
2.	Ahmad	The Praised
3.	Hamid	The Praising
4.	Mahmud	The Praised One
5.	Qasim	The Distributor
6.	Aqib	The Following, The Last
7.	Fatih	The Opener, The Conqueror
8.	Shahid	The Witness
9.	Hashir	The Gatherer of People on the Day of Judgement
10.	Rashid	Well Guided
11.	Mushahid	The One Who Witnessed
12.	Bashir	The Bringer of Good Tidings
13.	Nadhir	Warner
14.	Da 'i	Caller
15.	Shafi	Healer
16.	Hadi	He Who Guides Right
17.	Mahdi	He Who Is Well Guided
18.	Mahi	He Who Wipes Out Infidelity
19.	Munji	He Who Delivers
20.	Naji	Safe
21.	Rasul	Messenger

22.	Nabi	Prophet
23.	Ummi	Unlettered
24.	Tihami	From Tihama
25.	Hashmi	From the Family of Hashim
26.	Abtahi	Belonging to al Batha, the region around Makkah
27.	Aziz	Noble, Dear
28.	Haris Alaikum	Full of Concern for You
29.	Rauf	Mild
30.	Rahim	Merciful
31.	Taha	(Surah 20: 1)
32.	Mujtaba	The Elect
33.	Ta Sin	(Surah 27:1)
34.	Murtada	Content
35.	Ha Mim	(Beginning of Surah 40–6)
36.	Mustafa	The Chosen One
37.	Ya Sin	(Surah 36:1)
38.	Aula	Most Worthy
39.	Muzammil	Wrapped
40.	Wali	Friend
41.	Mudaththir	Covered
42.	Matin	Firm
43.	Musaddiq	Who Declares for True
44.	Tayyib	Good
45.	Nasir	Helper
46.	Mansur	Helped by God, Victorious
47.	Misbah	Lamp
48.	Amir	Prince, Commander
49.	Hijazi	From the Hijaz
50.	Tarazi	–
51.	Qurayshi	From the Quraysh Clan
52.	Mudari	From the Mudar Tribe
53.	Nabi ut Tauba	The Prophet of Repentance

54.	Hafiz	The Preserver
55.	Kamil	Perfect
56.	Sadiq	The Sincere One
57.	Amin	The Trustworthy
58.	Abdullah	Allah's Servant
59.	Kaleemullah	To Whom Allah Has Spoken
60.	Habib Allah	Allah's Beloved
61.	Naji Allah	Allah's Intimate Friend
62.	Safi Allah	Allah's Sincere Friend
63.	Khatam al Ambiya	The Seal of the Prophets
64.	Hasib	Respected
65.	Mujib	Complying, Replying
66.	Shakur	Most Grateful
67.	Muqtasid	Adopting a Middle Course
68.	Rasul ar Rahma	The Messenger of Mercy
69.	Qawi	Strong
70.	Hafi	Well Informed
71.	Ma'mun	Trusted
72.	Malum	Well Known
73.	Haqq	Truth
74.	Mubin	Clear, Evident
75.	Muti	Obedient
76.	Awwal	The First
77.	Akhir	The Last
78.	Zahir	Outward, External
79.	Batin	Internal
80.	Yatim	Orphan
81.	Karim	Generous
82.	Hakim	Wise, Judicious
83.	Sayyid	Lord
84.	Siraj	Lamp
85.	Minir	Radiant
86.	Muharram	Forbidden, Immune

87.	Mukarram	Honoured, Venerated
88.	Mubashshir	Bringer of Good News
89.	Mudhakkir	Who Makes Remember, Preacher
90.	Mutahhar	Purified
91.	Qarib	Near
92.	Khalil	Good Friend
93.	Mad'u	Who Is Called
94.	Jawwad	Generous
95.	Khatim	Seal
96.	Adil	Just
97.	Shahir	Well Known
98.	Shahid	Witnessing, Martyr
99.	Rasul al Malahim	The Messenger of the Battle of the Last Days

THE ISLAMIC CALENDAR

بِسْمِ اللَّهِ الرَّحْمَنِ الرَّحِيمِ

They ask thee concerning the New Moons. Say: They are but signs to mark fixed periods of time in (the affairs of) men, and for Pilgrimage (2:189).

The number of months in the sight of Allah is twelve (in a year)—so ordained by Him the day He created the heavens and the earth; of them four are sacred: that is the straight usage (9:36).

The Muslim year is a lunar year consisting of 354–5 days, and 12 months of 29 or 30 days, depending on the sighting of the new moon. The Islamic calendar begins with Prophet Muhammad's ﷺ migration from Makkah to Madinah in 622 AD. The year 2009 corresponds to 1430 of the Hijri calendar.

Muharram	The first month of the Islamic calendar. The tenth of Muharram marks the martyrdom of the Prophet's grandson Imam Hussain.
Safar	The second Islamic month.
Rabi ul awwal	The third Islamic month. Prophet Muhammad ﷺ was born on the twelfth of this month for

which reason it is considered auspicious and is celebrated throughout the Muslim world.

Rabi ath thani	The fourth Islamic month.
Jumada al ula	The fifth Islamic month.
Jumada al akhira	The sixth Islamic month.
Rajab	The seventh Islamic month. The Prophet's ascension to the Heavens known as *Shab e Miraj*, took place on the twenty-seventh of Rajab.
Shaban	The eighth Islamic month. The fifteenth of Shabaan marks the *Shab e Baraat*, the Night of Pardon during which destinies are decided for the coming year.
Ramadan	The ninth Islamic month. It is the month of fasting and piety. The last ten days are particularly auspicious.
Shawwal	The tenth Islamic month which begins with Id ul Fitr, the festival marking the end of Ramadan.
Dhul Qada	The eleventh Islamic month.
Dhul Hijja	The twelfth Islamic month which is the month for the Haj Pilgrimage and the Id ul Adha, the Feast of Sacrifices.

SUFI TERMINOLOGY

'And if all the trees on earth were pens and the ocean (were ink), with seven oceans behind it to add to its (supply), yet would not the words of Allah be exhausted (in the writing) for Allah is Exalted in Power, full of Wisdom' (3127).

Words are the keys needed to unlock Divine mysteries. Every field of study has its own specific terminology. I have attempted to explain some of the words necessary to understand the mystic language of Islam.

Adab	Etiquette
Ahad	One
Ahl e Bait	The People of the House of Prophet Muhammad ﷺ.
Ahl e e kitaab	People of the Book; members of those religious communities who have received Divine scriptures.
Ahl e sunna wa'l jamaat	Followers of the Prophet's traditions, the Sunnis.
Ahl ul Allah	God-fearing people who abide by His laws.
Ahle kamaal	The people of perfection.

Akhirat	The hereafter.
Akhlaq	The morality of character and the correctness of manners.
Alam	The universe.
Alif	The first letter of the Arabic alphabet with the numeric value of one, cipher for Allah.
Alim	One who is learned
Amaal	One's actions.
Ambiya	The prophets, plural for *Nabi*.
Ana	Ego, self, I.
Ana'l Haqq	'I am the Truth'.
Aqeeda	Creed.
Aql e Kul	Universal intellect.
Aql e Salim	A refined intellect.
Arif	One who has knowledge of the Divine.
Arsh e Akbar	The Supreme Heaven.
Ashiq	A lover with a passion for the Beloved.
Ashura	The tenth day of Muharram marks the day of Imam Hussain's martydom at Kerbala.
Asma ul Husna	The most beautiful names of Allah.
Asrar	Mysteries.
Auliya	The friends of Allah.
Awraad	The prayer routine followed by those on the Sufi path, usually prescribed by a Sufi Master. It often consists of some verses of the Quran along with litanies used by the founding Masters of Sufi orders.

Baraka	A blessing to increase life, food, provisions, etc.
Bashar	The human race.
Batin	The hidden.
Baqa	A state of continuance in God after annihilation.
Ba'ya	The rite of initiation into a Sufi order.
Bida	An unacceptable innovation to the *Sharia*.
Buraq	The heavenly steed upon which Prophet Muhammad ﷺ made the Heavenly journey.
Burdah	Cloak.
Chadar	A covering of cloth or flowers offered at darghas.
Chilla	Forty days of seclusion.
Dalail	Proofs.
Dastaar	A turban draped ceremoniously.
Dervish	A Sufi, one who searches for Allah.
Dhikr	Remembrance of Allah.
Diwan	A collection of poetry.
Dua	Free prayer, a supplication.
Fana	Annihilation.
Fana fil Allah	Annihilation in Allah.
Fana fil Shaykh	Annihilation in the Sufi Master.
Fana fil Rasul	Annihilation in Prophet Muhammad ﷺ.
Fatihah	The Opening Chapter of the Quran.
Fatwa	A legal decision.
Faqir	One who is poor. It signifies the spiritual poverty of a Sufi where nothing but God exists.
Faryad	A petition.

Furqaan	The Quran.
Futuh	Unsolicited gifts.
Futuwwa	Virtue.
Ghafla	Heedlessness, negligence.
Ghaus	The title given to the highest member of the Sufi hierarchy.
Ghusal	The annual cleansing ceremony of a Sufi tomb with rose water during the *Urs* ceremony.
Habib	The beloved.
Hadith	The recorded sayings of Prophet Muhammad ﷺ based upon a chain of transmitters.
Hadith Qudsi	Divine Sayings.
Hadiyya	Gift of love.
Hajj	The pilgrimage to Makkah during specified days in the month of Dhul Haj.
Hamd	Praise.
Hazri	A visit to a Sufi tomb with the intention of seeking blessings.
Hal	A mystical state.
Halqa	Circle, a spiritual gathering.
Haqeeqa	The Divine reality.
Haram	Holy and sacred. The word is specifically used for the two cities of Makkah and Madinah.
Haq ul yaqeen	Reality of certitude.
Haya	Bashfulness.
Hazrat	A prefix to a name indicating respect.
Haraam	Strictly impermissible by *Sharia* laws.

Hijra	Muhammad's ﷺ emigration to Madinah, which marks the beginning of the Muslim calendar in 622 AD.
Hikma	Wisdom.
Hilya	Ornamental description of Prophet Muhammad ﷺ in calligraphy.
Hujra	Cells used by Sufis for prayer and meditation.
Husn o ishq	Beauty and love.
Ibadat	Worship.
Ihsan	Excellence in virtue.
Ijtihaad	Individual effort to explore new possibilities in Islamic law.
Ijtima	People collecting together for an assembly.
Ikhlas	Sincerity.
Ilham	Divine inspiration.
Ilm Ladunni	Divine knowledge that descends directly to the heart from God.
Imaan	Faith.
Imam	One who leads the mandatory prayers.
Insaan i Kamil	The perfect man.
Irada	Intention.
Ishq e Haqiqi	True love of Allah.
Ishq e Majazi	Illusionary and worldly love.
Isnaad	The chain of transmitters in Hadith.
Isra	The Ascension of Prophet Muhammad ﷺ to the Heavens.
Istiqamat	Steadfastness.

Jabr	Compulsion or coercion.
Jahalat	Ignorance.
Jamaal	Divine beauty.
Jamaatkhana	An assembly hall.
Jihad e Akbar	The inner struggle against passions of the self.
Jihad e Asghar	The struggle against tyranny and oppression.
Junoon	A lover's obsession with the beloved.
Kalam	Speech or words.
Kayenaat	The universe.
Kalima	The declaration of Muslim faith.
Karamaat	Miracles attributed to Sufis.
Kashf	Unveiling of Divine knowledge in the hearts of the lovers of God.
Khaliq	Creator, one of the names of Allah.
Khatim al Ambiya	The seal of the Prophets.
Khalq	Creation.
Khalifa	The successor of a Sufi Master.
Khanqah	Hospice.
Khilafat	A degree conferred by a Sufi Master to a disciple that allows him to initiate disciples; succession.
Khirqa	A Sufi's cloak or patched garment.
Khwaja	Master.
Kufr	Infidelity.
Kun	'Be'; God's creative word.
La Maqaam	The highest spiritual station reached by the Sufis, one of perfection and divinity.

Laila tul Qadr	The Night of Power during which Allah descended the Quran.
Latif	Subtle or delicate.
Madhab	Legal school; way.
Majlis	An assembly in the remembrance of God or his loved ones.
Malaika	The Angels.
Malakut	The celestial realm inhabited by Angels.
Manqabat	Glory.
Maqaam	Spiritual stations.
Marifa	The knowledge of Divine Mysteries.
Martaba	A spiritual rank or station.
Marsiya	Poems in remembrance of the Kerbala Martyrs.
Mehfil e Sama	A concert of Sufi Music where God and His friends are invoked through musical renditions.
Miraj	A ladder, specially referring to the heavenly ascension of Prophet Muhammad ﷺ.
Misbah	Lamp.
Miskin	A poor person.
Momin	A believer.
Muajzat	The miracles of prophets.
Muflis	One in a state of poverty.
Muharram	The first month of the lunar year devoted to the memory of Kerbala martyrs.
Mujahida	The spiritual struggle in the way of God.
Mukhlis	One who is sincere.
Murad	The object of desire.

Muraqba	A meditative response.
Murid	A disciple.
Murshid	A spiritual guide.
Mutawalli	Custodian.
Naat	A poem in praise of Prophet Muhammad ﷺ.
Nafs	The ego or the self.
Namaz	Formal prayer.
Niya	Intention.
Nur	Radiant rays from the Light of Allah.
Qadam e Rasul	The footprint of Prophet Muhammad ﷺ left on a rock, a holy relic.
Qahr	Divine wrath.
Qalandar	A mystic intoxicated with the love of God leading to neglect of mandatory religious duties.
Qalb	Heart.
Qana	Contentment.
Qaul	Words.
Qibla	The direction of prayer towards the Kaaba in Makkah.
Qirat	The art of reciting the Quran.
Qul	'Say'; the Divine address to the Prophet in the revelations of the Quran.
Qurb	Closeness to Allah, a spiritual station of perfection.
Qurbat	Spiritual intimacy.
Qutub	The pole or axis. The Qutub is the occupant of the highest seat of authority in spiritual hierarchy.

Rahim	Merciful; one of the 99 names of Allah.
Rahmat	Divine blessing and mercy.
Rasul Allah	The Messenger of God.
Rida	Satisfaction.
Risalat	The Message.
Risq	Provisions.
Ruh	The spirit.
Sabir	One who is patient.
Sabr	Patience.
Sahaaba	The pious and trustworthy companions of Prophet Muhammad ﷺ.
Safa	Purity.
Sajda	Prostration.
Sajjada	A carpet on which a Sufi Master sits.
Salat	Prayer.
Salik	A seeker on the path of Truth.
Sayyids	Descendants from the family of Prophet Muhammad ﷺ.
Shafaa	Intercession.
Shafi	Intercessor.
Shahadah	The declaration of Muslim faith.
Shahadat	Martyrdom.
Shaheed	One who has been martyred.
Shahid	Witness.
Shaq ul Qamar	The splitting of the moon by Prophet Muhammad ﷺ.

Shauq	A yearning for God.
Shijra	The spiritual family tree of a Sufi order.
Shirk	Associating others with Allah.
Sidq	Truth.
Sifat	Attributes.
Silsila	A spiritual chain of a Sufi order.
Sirat	Biography, especially of the Prophet.
Suluk	Path.
Sunnah	The customs of Prophet Muhammad ﷺ.
Surah	The 114 Chapters of the Quran.
Tabarruk	Something that has been blessed.
Tajalli	Manifestation of Divine radiance; illumination.
Talab	Quest.
Taqwa	Piety.
Tareeqa	The way or path of the Sufi.
Tasawwuf	The doctrine of Sufism.
Tassawur	Imagination.
Tawba	Repentance.
Tauhid	To declare that Allah is One.
Tawakkul	Complete trust in God.
Umma	Community.
Ummi	Unlettered.
Umra	The lesser pilgrimage to Makkah at any time other than the specified time of the Hajj.
Urs	The death anniversary celebration of the Sufi, that is understood as a union with Allah.

Uruj	Exaltation.
Wahdat ul wujood	The Oneness of Being.
Wajd	Intense religious frenzy.
Wali	A friend of Allah.
Wasila	The means through which man can come closer to God.
Wasl	Union.
Wilayat	The highest Sufi station where one attains Allah's friendship.
Wird	A specific litany.
Wujood	Existence, being.
Yaqin	Faith.
Yatim	Orphan.
Zahid	One who is pious.
Zawal	Fall or Decline.
Ziayara	A visit to a sacred place.
Zuhd	Piety.

NOTES

READ

1. Hadith, Tirmidhi.

THE FOUNDATIONS OF SUFISM

1. Ali bin Uthman Hujwiri, *Kashf Al Mahjub* (the first Persian treatise on Sufism written in the eleventh century by the Sufi scholar, also called Datta Ganj Baksh), ed. Ahmed Ali Shah, Ilahi Baksh, Lahore, 1923.
2. Hadith quoted by Dr. Javad Nurbakhsh, *Traditions of the Prophet* (vol.1), Khaniqahi Nimatullahi Publications, New York, 1981.
3. Nurbakhsh, Javad Dr., *Traditions of the Prophet* (vol.1), Khaniqahi Nimatullahi Publications, New York, 1981.
4. Eastwick, Edward, *The Rose Garden*, Octagon Press, UK, 1997.
5. Schimmel, Annemarie, *And Muhammad Is His Messenger*, University of North Carolina Press, 1985.
6. Nurbakhsh, Javad Dr., *Jesus in the Eyes of the Sufis*, Khaniqahi Nimatullahi Publications, London, 1983.
7. Ibid
8. Hadith, Sahih Bukhari
9. Ali bin Uthman Hujwiri, *Kashf Al Mahjub*, translated by R.A. Nicholson, Adam Publishers, Delhi, 2006.
10. Ibid
11. Nurbakhsh, Javad Dr., *Traditions of the Prophet*; (vol. 2) Khaniqahi Nimatullahi Publications, New York, 1983.

12. Hadith, Sahih Bukhari

13. Nurbakhsh, Javad Dr., *Traditions of the Prophet*; (vol. 1) Khaniqahi Nimatullahi Publications, New York, 1981.

14. Schimmel, Annemarie, *And Muhammad Is His Messenger*, University of North Carolina Press, 1985.

15. Schimmel, Annemarie, *Mystical Dimensions Of Islam*, University of North Carolina Press, 1975.

16. Cleary, Thomas, *The Essential Koran*, HarperSanFrancisco, 1994.

THE ESSENCE OF THE SUFI EXPERIENCE

1. Nurbakhsh, Javad Dr., *Traditions of the Prophet*, (vol. 1) Khaniqahi Nimatullahi Publications, New York, 1981.

2. Schimmel, Annemarie, *And Muhammad Is His Messenger*, University of North Carolina Press, 1985.

3. Hadith, Sahih Bukhari.

4. Nurbakhsh, Javad Dr., *Traditions of the Prophet*, (vol. 1) Khaniqahi Nimatullahi Publications, New York, 1981.

5. Schimmel Annemarie, *And Muhammad Is His Messenger*, The University of North Carolina Press, 1985.

6. Ibid.

7. Hadith, Sahih Bukhari

8. Nurbakhsh, Javad Dr., *Traditions of the Prophet*, (vol. 1) Khaniqahi Nimatullahi Publications, New York, 1981.

9. Schimmel, Annemarie, *And Muhammad Is His Messenger*, University of North Carolina Press, 1985.

10. Ibid.

11. Schimmel, Annemarie, *Mystical Dimensions Of Islam*, University of North Carolina Press, 1975.

12. Schimmel, Annemarie, *And Muhammad Is His Messenger*, University of North Carolina Press, 1985.

13. Murad, Abdal Hakim, *A Tribute to the Prophet Muhammad*, The Light Inc, New Jersey, 2006.

14. Schimmel, Annemarie, *And Muhammad Is His Messenger*, University of North Carolina Press, 1985.

15. Ibid.

16. Ibid.
17. Ibid.
18. Ibid.
19. Hadith, Sahih Bukhari and Sahih Muslim.
20. Murad, Abdal Hakim, *A Tribute to the Prophet Muhammad*, The Light Inc, New Jersey, 2006.
21. Ibid.
22. Schimmel, Annemarie, *And Muhammad Is His Messenger*, University of North Carolina Press, 1985.
23. Arberry, A.J., *Discourses of Rumi*, John Murray, London, 1961.
24. Baihaqi, *Dala'il ul Nabuwwa*, ed. Abdur Rahman Muhammad Uthman, Al Maktaba al Salafiya, Medina, 1969.
25. Schimmel, Annemarie, *And Muhammad Is His Messenger*, University of North Carolina Press, 1985.
26. Ibid.
27. Hadith, Sahih Muslim.
28. Nurbakhsh, Javad Dr., *Traditions of the Prophet*, (vol. 1) Khaniqahi Nimatullahi Publications, New York, 1981.
29. Hadith, Tirmidhi.
30. Nurbakhsh, Javad Dr., *Traditions of the Prophet*, (vol. 1) Khaniqahi Nimatullahi Publications, New York, 1981.
31. Ibid.
32. Translation by R. A. Nicholson.

THE EARLY SUFIS

1. Hadith, Bukhari
2. Schimmel, Annemarie, *And Muhammad Is His Messenger*, University of North Carolina Press, 1985.
3. Ibid.
4. Schimmel, Annemarie, *Mystical Dimensions Of Islam*, University of North Carolina Press, 1975.
5. Hadith Qudsi, recounted by Abu Huraira, a close companion of Prophet Muhammad and one of the Bench.
6. Schimmel, Annemarie, *Mystical Dimensions Of Islam*, University of North Carolina Press, 1975.

7. Ibid.

8. Farid al Din Attar, *Muslim Saints And Mystics*, translated by A.J. Arberry, Routledge & K. Paul, London, 1966.

9. Ibid.

10. Smith, Margaret, *Rabia Basri—The Mystic And Her Fellow Saints In Islam*, Kitab Bhavan, Delhi, 2005.

11. Farid al Din Attar, *Muslim Saints And Mystics*, translated by A.J. Arberry, Routledge & K. Paul, London, 1966.

12. Smith, Margaret, *Rabia Basri—The Mystic And Her Fellow Saints In Islam*, Kitab Bhavan, Delhi, 2005.

13. Ali bin Uthman Hujwiri, *Kashf Al Mahjub*, translated by R.A. Nicholson, Adam Publishers, Delhi, 2006.

14. Farid al Din Attar, *Muslim Saints And Mystics*, translated by A.J. Arberry, Routledge & K. Paul, London, 1966.

15. Ali bin Uthman Hujwiri, *Kashf Al Mahjub*, translated by R.A. Nicholson, Adam Publishers, Delhi, 2006.

16. Translation by A.J. Arberry.

17. Farid al Din Attar, *Muslim Saints And Mystics*, translated by A.J. Arberry, Routledge & K. Paul, London, 1966.

18. *Kitab al Re'aya*, ed. Dr. Margaret Smith, Luzac, London, 1940.

19. Ali bin Uthman Hujwiri, *Kashf Al Mahjub*, translated by R.A. Nicholson, Adam Publishers, Delhi, 2006.

20. Farid al Din Attar, *Muslim Saints And Mystics*, translated by A.J. Arberry, Routledge & K. Paul, London, 1966.

21. Abu Bakr al Kharraz is among the disciples of Sari Saqti who is known in the West through Prof. A. J. Arberry's translation of his book *Kitab as Sidiq* (The Book of Truthfulness).

22. Ali bin Uthman Hujwiri, *Kashf Al Mahjub*, translated by R.A. Nicholson, Adam Publishers, Delhi, 2006.

23. Farid al Din Attar, *Muslim Saints And Mystics*, translated by A.J. Arberry, Routledge & K. Paul, London, 1966.

24. Massignon, Louis, *Hallaj—Mystic and Martyr*, Princeton University Press, New Jersey, 1994. (Massignon devoted his life to the exploration of the spiritual world of Hallaj. His comprehensive biography of the mystic was first published in 1922, a thousand years after Hallaj was executed in Baghdad).

25. Farid al Din Attar, *Muslim Saints And Mystics,* translated by A.J. Arberry, Routledge & K. Paul, London, 1966.

26. Ibid.

27. Massignon, Louis, *Hallaj—Mystic and Martyr*, Princeton University Press, New Jersey, 1994.

28. Farid al Din Attar, *Muslim Saints And Mystics,* translated by A.J. Arberry, Routledge & K. Paul, London, 1966.

29. Arberry, A.J., *An Account of the Mystics of Islam*, Cosmo Publications, New Delhi, 2003.

30. Ali bin Uthman Hujwiri, *Kashf Al Mahjub*, translated by R.A. Nicholson, Adam Publishers, Delhi, 2006.

31. Lings, Martin, *What is Sufism?*, Islamic Texts Society, UK, 1999.

32. Ali bin Uthman Hujwiri, *Kashf Al Mahjub*, translated by R.A. Nicholson, Adam Publishers, Delhi, 2006.

33. Arberry, A.J., *An Account of the Mystics of Islam*, Cosmo Publications, New Delhi, 2003.

34. Farid al Din Attar, *Muslim Saints And Mystics,* translated by A.J. Arberry, Routledge & K. Paul, London, 1966.

35. Schimmel, Annemarie, *Mystical Dimensions Of Islam*, University of North Carolina Press, 1975.

36. Massignon, Louis, *Hallaj—Mystic and Martyr*, Princeton University Press, New Jersey, 1994.

37. Nicolson, R.A., *Legacy of Islam*, Oxford University Press, London, 1931.

38. Farid al Din Attar, *Muslim Saints And Mystics,* translated by A.J. Arberry, Routledge & K. Paul, London, 1966.

39. Nicholson, R.A., *Mystics of Islam*, Routledge & K. Paul, London, 1914.

40. Farid al Din Attar, *Muslim Saints And Mystics,* translated by A.J. Arberry, Routledge & K. Paul, London, 1966.

41. Ibid.

42. Ibid.

43. Schimmel, Annemarie, *Mystical Dimensions Of Islam*, University of North Carolina Press, 1975.

44. Ali bin Uthman Hujwiri, *Kashf Al Mahjub*, translated by R.A. Nicholson, Adam Publishers, Delhi, 2006.

45. Numerous translations of Imam Ghazali's books are available in English since no other thinker of medieval Islam has attracted as much interest from Western scholars.

46. Stoddart, W. & Nicholson, R.A., *Sufism—The Mystical Doctrines and the Idea of Personality*, Adam Publishers, Delhi, 2004.

47. Translation by Martin Lings.

48. Baldock, John, *The Essence of Sufism*, Arcturus Publishing Ltd, UK, 2006.

49. Translation by R.A. Nicholson.

THE FORMATION OF SUFI ORDERS

1. Schimmel, Annemarie, *Mystical Dimensions Of Islam*, University of North Carolina Press, 1975.

2. Trimingham, J. Spencer, *The Sufi Orders in Islam,* Oxford University Press, New York, 1971.

3. Ali bin Uthman Hujwiri, *Kashf Al Mahjub*, translated by R.A. Nicholson, Adam Publishers, Delhi, 2006.

4. Schimmel, Annemarie, *Mystical Dimensions Of Islam*, University of North Carolina Press, 1975.

5. Ibid.

6. Trimingham, J. Spencer, *The Sufi Orders in Islam,* Oxford University Press, New York, 1971.

7. Ibid.

THE WAY OF THE SUFI

1. Hadith Qudsi recorded in Imam Ghazali's *Ihya al Uloom*, (vol. 2).

2. Schimmel, Annemarie, *And Muhammad Is His Messenger*, University of North Carolina Press, 1985.

3. Ali bin Uthman Hujwiri, *Kashf Al Mahjub*, translated by R.A. Nicholson, Adam Publishers, Delhi, 2006.

4. Schimmel, Annemarie, *Mystical Dimensions Of Islam*, University of North Carolina Press, 1975.

5. Hadith, Sahih Bukhari and Sahih Muslim.

6. Schimmel, Annemarie, *Mystical Dimensions Of Islam*, University of North Carolina Press, 1975.

7. Ibid.

8. Nurbakhsh, Javad Dr., *Traditions of the Prophet*; (vol. 2) Khaniqahi Nimatullahi Publications, New York, 1983.

9. Schimmel, Annemarie, *Mystical Dimensions Of Islam*, University of North Carolina Press, 1975.

10. Ibid.

11. Ibn al Husayn al Sulami, *The Way of Sufi Chivalry—An Interpretation*, translated by Tosun Bayrak al Jerrahi, Inner Tradition International, Vermont, 1991.

12. Schimmel, Annemarie, *Mystical Dimensions Of Islam*, University of North Carolina Press, 1975.

13. Ibid.

14. Ali bin Uthman Hujwiri, *Kashf Al Mahjub*, translated by R.A. Nicholson, Adam Publishers, Delhi, 2006.

15. Schimmel, Annemarie, *Mystical Dimensions Of Islam*, University of North Carolina Press, 1975.

16. Ibid.

17. Ibid.

18. Ibid.

DISHARMONY WITHIN ISLAM

1. Hadith, Sahih Muslim.

2. Schimmel, Annemarie, *And Muhammad Is His Messenger*, University of North Carolina Press, 1985.

3. Ibid.

4. Ibid.

5. Hadith, Imam Bukhari, Sahih Muslim.

6. Schimmel, Annemarie, *And Muhammad Is His Messenger*, University of North Carolina Press, 1985.

7. Ibid.

8. Hussain, Ed, *The Islamist*, Penguin Books UK, 2007.

9. Taqi al Din Subki of the fourteenth century wrote the landmark book *Shifa al Siqam fi ziyarati Khayri al Anam* (The Healing of Sickness Concerning Visits to the Prophet's tomb in Medina).

10. Armstrong, Karen, *Battle for God—A History of Fundamentalism*, Random House, New York, 2001.

11. Ernst, W. Carl, *Sufism*, Shambala Books, South Asia Editions, 2001.
12. Ibn Taimiyya, *Al Ihtijaaj bial Qadar*, Al Matba al Salafiya, Cairo, 1974.
13. Ibn Taimiyya, *Majma Fatawa* and *Iqtida al Sirat al Mustaqim*, in section titled 'The innovated festivities of time and place'.
14. Hussain, Ed, *The Islamist*; Penguin Books UK, 2007.
15. Armstrong, Karen, *Battle for God—A History of Fundamentalism*, Random House, New York, 2001.
16. Wright, Lawrence, *The Looming Tower—The Road to Al Qaeda*, Vintage Books, USA, 2007.
17. Hussain, Ed, *The Islamist*, Penguin Books UK, 2007.
18. Ibid.
19. Ibid.
20. Armstrong, Karen, *Battle for God—A History of Fundamentalism*, Random House, New York, 2001.
21. Ibid.
22. Ibid.
23. Ibid.
24. Schimmel, Annemarie, *And Muhammad Is His Messenger*, University of North Carolina Press, 1985.
25. Hadith, Sahih Bukari.
26. Ramadan, Tariq, *The Messenger*, Penguin Books UK, 2007.
27. Shaykh Hamza Yusuf in a talk on 4 May 1997 at Standford University, California.
28. Hadith recorded in Imam Ghazali's *Ihlya ul Uloom*.
29. Jalal, Ayesha, *Partisans of Allah—Jihad in South Asia*, Permanent Black, India, 2008.
30. Armstrong, Karen, *Muhammad, A Biography of the Prophet*, Phoenix, UK, 2002.
31. Hadith, Tirmidhi.
32. Feisal Imam (of Al Farah Mosque New York) on the BBC television series, 'The Doha Debates'. The debate is posted on the internet.
33. Hadith, Sahih Muslim.

The Mystic Dialogue

1. Schimmel, Annemarie, *Mystical Dimensions Of Islam*, University of North Carolina Press, 1975.

2. Gibb, H.A.R., *The Travels of Ibn Batuta*, Cambridge, 1962.
3. Abul Qasin al Qushayri's *Ar Risala al Qurasihya* remains a widely read and translated book on early Sufism.
4. Ali bin Uthman Hujwiri, *Kashf Al Mahjub*, translated by R.A. Nicholson, Adam Publishers, Delhi, 2006.
5. Arberry, A.J., *An Account of the Mystics of Islam*, Cosmo Publications, New Delhi, 2003.
6. Singh, Khushwant, *A History of the Sikhs* (vol. 1), Oxford University Press, New Delhi, 1999.
7. Ibid.
8. Ibid.
9. Singh, Khushwant, *Songs of the Gurus*, Penguin Viking and Ravi Dayal Publisher, India, 2008.
10. Ibid.
11. Rizvi, S.A.A., *A History of Sufism in India* (vol. 1), Munshiram Manoharlal, New Delhi, 2002.

THE CHISHTIS

1. Currie, P.M., *The Shrine and Cult of Muin al Din Chishti of Ajmer*, Oxford University Press, Delhi, 1992.
2. Rizvi, S.A.A., *A History of Sufism in India* (vol. 1), Munshiram Manoharlal, New Delhi, 2002.
3. Nizami K.A, *The Life and Times of Shaikh Fariduddin*, Idara i Adabiyat, Delhi, 1998.
4. Schimmel, Annemarie, *Mystical Dimensions Of Islam*, University of North Carolina Press, 1975.
5. Nizami, K.A, *The Life and Times of Shaikh Naseeruddin Chiragh e Delhi*, Idarah i Adabiyat, Delhi, 1991 (This is the most comprehensive account of the Delhi Sufi and draws largely from *Khair ul Majalis* containing the discourses of Shaykh Naseeruddin).
6. Ibid.
7. Hussaini, Syed Shah Khushro, *Dargahs, Abodes of the Saints*, eds. Mumtaz Currim and George Michell, Marg Publications, Mumbai, 2004.
8. Ernst, W. Carl, *Dargahs, Abodes of the Saints*, eds. Mumtaz Currim and George Michell, Marg Publications, Mumbai, 2004.

9. Ibid.
10. Ibid.
11. Rizvi, S.A.A., *A History of Sufism in India* (vol. 1), Munshiram Manoharlal, New Delhi, 2002.

THE SUHARWADIS

1. Nizami, K.A., *The Life and Times of Shaikh Nizamuddin Auliya*, Idarah i Adabiyat, Delhi, 1991.
2. Ibid.
3. Rizvi, S.A.A., *A History of Sufism in India* (vol. 1), Munshiram Manoharlal, New Delhi, 2002.
4. Schimmel, Annemarie, *Mystical Dimensions Of Islam*, University of North Carolina Press, 1975.
5. *Dargahs, Abodes of the Saints*, eds. Mumtaz Currim and George Michell, Marg Publications, Mumbai, 2004.
6. Schimmel, Annemarie, *Mystical Dimensions Of Islam*, University of North Carolina Press, 1975.
7. *Shah jo Risalo* (The Book of the Shah) was first compiled and published by the German missionary Ernest Trump in 1866.

THE QADRIS

1. Vasudha, Nayaran, *Dargahs, Abodes of the Saints*, eds. Mumtaz Currim and George Michell, Marg Publications, Mumbai, 2004.
2. Rizvi, S.A.A., *A History of Sufism in India* (vol. 1), Munshiram Manoharlal, New Delhi, 2002.
3. Ibid.
4. Ibid.
5. Schimmel, Annemarie, *Mystical Dimensions Of Islam*, University of North Carolina Press, 1975.
6. Ernst, W. Carl, *Teachings of Sufism*, Shambhala, New Delhi, 2004.

THE NAQSHBANDIS

1. Rizvi, S.A.A., *A History of Sufism in India* (vol. 1), Munshiram Manoharlal, New Delhi, 2002.
2. Ibid.

3. Schimmel, Annemarie, *Mystical Dimensions Of Islam*, University of North Carolina Press, 1975.

4. Schimmel, Annemarie, *And Muhammad Is His Messenger*, University of North Carolina Press, 1985.

5. Rizvi, S.A.A., *A History of Sufism in India* (vol. 1), Munshiram Manoharlal, New Delhi, 2002.

6. Schimmel, Annemarie, *And Muhammad Is His Messenger*, University of North Carolina Press, 1985.

7. Ibid.

OTHER ORDERS

1. Rizvi, S.A.A., *A History of Sufism in India* (vol. 1), Munshiram Manoharlal, New Delhi, 2002.

2. Ibid.

3. Khan, Ishaq, *The Valley of Kashmir,* ed. Aparna Rao, Manohar, New Delhi, 2008.

4. Ibid.

5. Schimmel, Annemarie, *Mystical Dimensions Of Islam*, University of North Carolina Press, 1975.

6. Ibid.

7. Jackson Paul, *Letters from Maneri–Sufi Saint of India*, Horizon Books, New Delhi, 1990.

8. Jackson Paul, *Dargahs, Abodes of the Saints*, eds. Mumtaz Currim and George Michell, Marg Publications, Mumbai, 2004.

9. Rizvi, S.A.A., *A History of Sufism in India* (vol. 1), Munshiram Manoharlal, New Delhi, 2002.

10. Abdus Sattar, *Dargahs, Abodes of the Saints*, eds. Mumtaz Currim and George Michell, Marg Publications, Mumbai, 2004.

THE MOST BEAUTIFUL NAMES

1. Translation, Schimmel Annemarie.

2. Ibid.

SELECT BIBLIOGRAPHY

Ad Darqawi, Shaykh, *Letters of a Sufi Master*, translated by Titus Burckhardt, Fons Vitae, USA, 1998.

Arasteh, A. Reza, *Growth to Selfhood*, Routledge & Kegan Paul, London, 1980.

Arberry, A.J., *An Account of the Mystics of Islam*, Cosmo Publications, New Delhi, 2003.

Arberry, A.J., *An Introduction to the History of Sufism*, Longman, London 1943.

Arberry, A.J., *Sufism*, Allen & Unwin, London, 1950.

Armstrong, Karen, *Muhammad—A Biography of the Prophet*, Phoenix Press, London, 1991.

Armstrong, Karen, *The Battle For God*, Ballantine Books, USA, 2001.

Armstrong, Karen, *The History of God*, Mandarin Paperbacks, London, 1984.

Armstrong, Amatullah, *Sufi Terminology*, Ferozsons, Pakistan, 2001.

Attar Fariduddin, *The Conference of the Birds*, translated by Afkham Darbandi and Dick Davis, Penguin Books UK, 1984.

Attar Fariduddin, *Muslim Saints and Mystics*, translated by A.J. Arberry, Arkana, London, 1990.

Baldock, John, *The Essence of Rumi*, Arcturus, London, 2006.

Baldock, John, *The Essence of Sufism*, Arcturus, London, 2006.

Chittick, C. William, *Sufism A Short Introduction*, Oxford-Oneworld, 2000.

Cleary, Thomas, *The Essential Koran*, HarperSanFrancisco.

Cleary, Thomas, *The Wisdom of the Prophet*, Shambhala Classics, South Asia Editions, 2004.

Currie, P.M., *The Shrine and Cult of Mu`in al-Din Chishti of Ajmer*, Oxford University Press, New Delhi, 1989.

Chishti, Shaykh Hakim Moinuddin, *The Book of Sufi Healing*, Inner Traditions International, USA, 1991.

Cornell, J. Vincent, *The Ways of Abu Madyan*, The Islamic Texts Society, Cambridge, 1996.

Ernst, W. Carl, *Sufism*, Shambhala, South Asia Editions, 1997.

Ernst, W. Carl, *Teachings of Sufism*, Shambhala, South Asia Editions, 1999.

Eaton, J. Richard, *Essays on Islam and Indian History*, Oxford University Press, New Delhi, 2000.

Ezzeddin, Ibrahim, *Forty Hadith Qudsi*, Dar al Koran al Karim, Germany, 1980.

Farid al Din Attar, *Muslim Saints And Mystics,* translated by A.J. Arberry, Routledge & K. Paul, London, 1966.

Haeri, Shaykh Fadhlalla, *The Journey of the Self*, Element Books, UK, 1989.

Haeri, Shaykh Fadhlalla, *The Elements of Sufism*, Element Books, UK, 1993.

Helminski, Camille Adams, *Women of Sufism*, Shambhala, Boston, 2003.

Helminski, Kabir and Algan, Refik, *The Drop That Became The Sea*, Threshold Books, UK, 1989.

Hussain, Ed, *The Islamist*, Penguin Books, UK, 2007.

Ibn al Arabi, *Journey to the Lord of Power*, translated by Rabbi Terri Harris, Inner Traditions, New York, 1981.

Ibn al Husayn Sulami, *The Way of Sufi Chivalry,* translated by Tosum Bayrak al Jerrahi, Inner Traditions International, USA, 1983.

Lings, Martin, *What is Sufism*, Islamic Texts Society, Cambridge, 1993.

Lings, Martin, *Muhammad*, Islamic Texts Society and George Allen & Unwin, London, 1983.

Khan, M. Ishaq, *Kashmir's Transition to Islam: The role of Muslim Rishis*, Manohar Books, Delhi, 2002.

Massignon, Louis, *The Passion of Al Hallaj,* translated and edited by Herbert Mason, Princeton University Press, New Jersey, 1994.

Currim, Mumtaz and Mitchell, George, *Dargahs—Abodes of the Saints*, Marg Publications, Mumbai, 2004.

Nicholson, R.A., *The Mystics of Islam*, Arkana, London, 1989.

Nicholson, R.A., *Rumi: Poet and Mystic*, Unwin Paperbacks, London, 1978.

Nicholson, R.A., *Studies in Islamic Mysticism*, Jayed Press, Delhi, 1976.

Nizamuddin Auliya, *Morals of the Heart,* translated by Bruce. B. Lawrence, Paulist Press, New York, 1992.

Nurbakhsh, Dr. Javad, *Jesus in the Eyes of the Sufis,* Khaniqahi Nimatullahi Publications, London, 1983.

Nurbakhsh, Dr. Javad, *Traditions of the Prophet, Volume 1,* Khaniqahi Nimatullahi Publications, USA, 1981.

Nurbakhsh, Dr. Javad, *Traditions of the Prophet, Volume 2,* Khaniqahi Nimatullahi Publications, USA, 1983.

Pickthall, Marmaduke, *The Meaning of the Glorious Koran*, George Allen & Unwin, London, 1930.

Qadri, Muhammad Riaz, *The Sayings and Teachings of the 101 Great Mystics of Islam,* Adam Publishers, New Delhi, 2006.

Ramadan, Tariq, *The Messenger*, Penguin Books, UK, 1997.

Rizvi, Sayyid Athar Abbas, *A History of Sufism in India, Vol 1 & 2,* Munshiram Manoharlal Publishers, New Delhi, 1978.

Schimmel, Annemarie, *Mystical Dimensions of Islam*, University of North Carolina Press, 1975.

Schimmel, Annemarie, *And Muhammad Is His Messenger*, University of North Carolina Press, 1985.

Schimmel, Annemarie, *Rumi's World*, Shambhala, Boston, 2001.

Sharib, Zahurul Hasan, *The Sufi Saints of the Subcontinent*, Munshiram Manoharlal, Delhi, 2006.

Smith, Margaret, *Readings from the Mystics of Islam*, Luzac, London, 1950.

Smith, Margaret, *Rabia Basri—The Mystic And Her Fellow Saints In Islam*, Kitab Bhavan, Delhi, 2005.

Stoddart, William, *Sufism: The Mystical Doctrines of Methods of Islam*, Aquarian Press, UK, 1982.

Subhan, John A., *Sufism—Its Saints and Shrines*, Indigo Books, New Delhi, 2002.

Trimingham, J. Spencer, *The Sufi Orders in Islam*, Oxford University Press, USA, 1971.

WEBSITES

http://sacred-texts.com/isl/quran

http://www.mountainoflight.co.uk

http://www.uga.edu/islam

http://www.uga.edu/islam/Sufism

http://pourjavady.com

http://www.poetry-chaikhana.com

http://www.faithtube.com/video/Isra-wal-Miraaj-by-Sh-Abdal-Hakim

http://www.sufism.org

http://www.sufism.org/society/articles/women.html

http://www.aulia-e-hind.com

http://www.nimatullahi.org/sufism

http://www.sufismjournal.org

http://www.zaytuna.org

http://www.masud.co.uk/nuh

http://www.minhaj.org/en.php

http://www.allaahuakbar.net

http://www.chishtihijazi.com/Intro.htm

http://www.shadhilitariqa.com

http://www.colemanbarks.com

http://www.poetseers.org

http://www.razarumi.com

http://www.usc.edu/dept/MSA/fundamentals/hadithsunnah

http://www.sacred-texts.com/isl/bukhari/index.htm

http://www.40hadith.com

http://www.sunnah.org/events/hamza/hamza.htm

http://hamzayusuf.blogspot.com

http://www.yusufislam.com

http://www.aswatalislam.net

http://www.esnips.com/_t_/tahir-ul-qadri

INDEX